WICKED
Opportunity

SIAN CEINWEN

ISBN: 978-1-922559-15-9 (eBook)
ISBN: 978-1-922559-23-4 (Paperback)

Any references to historical events, real people, or real places are used fictitiously. Names, characters, and places are products of the author's imagination.

Front cover image by Mark Reid at authorpackages.com.
Book design by Lorna Reid at authorpackages.com.

Acknowledgement of Country

I would like to acknowledge the Traditional Owners of Country throughout Australia and recognise their continuing connection to land, waters, and community.

The Whadjuk people of the Noongar Nation are the traditional custodians of the land this book was written on.

I acknowledge that sovereignty throughout these lands was never ceded. I pay my respect to them and their cultures, and to the strength and resilience of Elders both past and present.

Dedication

This book is for you, dear reader, because you deserve cock in the first chapter.

Don't let anyone tell you that reading about three fine men ploughing one woman (and occasionally each other) is dirty or shameful...and, apparently, you should invest in a rechargeable vibrator to save on batteries.

How much sex is too much sex? This book. This book is too much sex because I decided to take out precisely none of the sex scenes when editing. Oh, well. RIP Lexi's pussy, I guess...and her ass...and her mouth.

Chapter One

A One-Man Woman

D ante and I step out of the limousine that's brought us to Tempest tonight. It's one of the hottest clubs in Los Angeles, and we're here to meet our friends. We thank our driver and walk to the entrance.

The people lining up to get in notice us and whisper to themselves as the bouncer smiles and lets us walk straight into the club. Some of them get their phones and take our pictures. I don't mind because I got used to this a long time ago. I'm wearing a tight red dress and silver boots that I know look good on me. My long, auburn hair hangs in loose waves, and I've got my signature red lipstick on.

Dante is looking as good as ever. He's wearing jeans and a tight t-shirt that shows off his muscled torso nicely. He's got short, brown hair and gorgeous chocolate brown eyes and is one of the most fuckable men on the face of the planet. He's also the bass guitarist in one of the world's biggest rock bands, Wicked Stallion.

The rest of the band is probably already in the VIP area waiting for us. I made us late tonight because I took too long getting ready, and I definitely paid the price for that. Dante is a stickler for timing and likes to be on time or early for everything, so he was most displeased that we were late this evening.

We get drinks from the bar before we head into the VIP area. Sure enough, our friends are holding court in prime position on the banquette. There's a small crowd of celebrities and hangers-on listening as Nathaniel Walker is talking.

He has his arm around a brunette woman I've never seen before. Unsurprising. Nate is hot as hell, and he knows it. He has black hair, startlingly blue eyes, an amazing body, and is ridiculously charming, along with being the lead singer for Wicked Stallion. His favorite pastime is groupies, and it seems like he's found one for tonight.

The remaining two members of the band are here, as well. Logan Ballantine is the drummer and has very similar features to Dante. He also has brown hair and eyes, a great body, and is chill and happy most of the time. The band's lead guitarist is Ashton Woodford. He's got blonde hair, bright blue eyes, and we tease him that he could play the role of Thor because he looks like a Norse god.

"Hey, guys," I greet our friends when we get near enough.

Nate looks me up and down. "You're looking hot as shit, as usual."

"Thanks, you like?" I spin in a circle; the skirt of my dress flares slightly, and I can feel the air on my bare legs as I laugh.

"Definitely. That dress leaves very little to the imagination, but I do have a great imagination to work with," he smirks at me.

"Why don't you give Nate a hug to say hello, Angel?" Dante asks me, and I smile at him.

I walk forward to the banquette and place my arms around Nate's neck to hug him. He removes his arm from around the brunette woman and wraps his arms around my waist. The woman he's with glares at me, but I don't bother responding in any way because I'm pretty sure she'll be gone by morning.

I move on to greet Logan and Ash, giving each of them a hug. Ash's girlfriend, Cassandra Foster, is here as well. She's nice, and we've become good friends since they started dating.

"Hey, Cassie," I smile at her, and she smiles back.

"Hi, Lexi. It's so good to see you."

Dante sits down next to Logan, leaving a space between himself and Nate.

"Come sit down next to me, Angel," Dante says.

I move immediately to sit next to him and reply, "Yes, Honey."

So, this is a thing we do. Dante is very quiet and introverted, while I'm loud and outgoing. Except when it comes to sex, that's when Dante takes over. We've had a BDSM relationship for pretty much the entire time we've been together. There's something incredibly hot and sexy as hell about him dominating me in the bedroom the way he does.

We can be out with our friends on a night like tonight, and he will casually instruct me to do something for him, then I'll be wet for the rest of the evening waiting for us to get home so he can fuck me. I can already feel the effect it's having on me from him telling me what to do this evening.

The trick in public is for it to seem like any other kind of request, but we've been doing it so long that I always know. He'll give me a tone, a tone that only I can hear, and he always calls me 'Angel' when he does it. I drop onto the banquette between Dante and Nate, then wait for my next instruction.

"Hey, Lexi, I need a love interest for our next music video. Want to bust out your acting skills?" Nate nudges me to get my attention as he says this.

I look at him and laugh, "Can they not find an actress willing to work with you? Or did you already sleep with the one they chose?"

"The second one"—he grins at me—"besides, you're hotter than she is, anyway."

"Well, thanks for the compliment, but what will the fans think if I'm in a music video grinding away against you when they know I'm Dante's wife?" I raise an eyebrow at him.

"They'll probably just think that Dante's very nice for sharing you with me."

Nate gives me a cheeky grin, and Dante's deep laugh comes from behind me before he says, "I really am nice like that. If you want to be in the music video, Lexi, that would be okay with me. It'll be great to have you on set with us."

So, I know that Nate is in love with me. Everyone in our group knows it, I think, even Dante. We don't talk about it. Nobody does. If we don't talk about it, we can be friends. He makes these jokes about having sex with me, which is probably unhealthy as fuck. I'm not sure why I indulge him, I guess because it's fun.

He treats me like I'm his girlfriend, and I love him like he's my boyfriend...that I don't have sex with. I never would. Because I love him to death, but my heart *belongs* to Dante and always has. By the time I realized Nate was in love with me, we were about a year into dating.

I'm not sure what gave it away, but I distinctly recall when I figured it out. He'd picked up a woman, and we were all out at a club on a night pretty much like this one. Dante was sitting next to me, and Nate was on the other side with the woman next to him. He kept talking to me, asking me questions. There was nothing strange about it, but he just *looked* at me, and I realized.

I don't know when everyone else figured it out because nobody talks about it, but I know they all know. Which is why I'm surprised by Dante's reply to the suggestion of me playing the role of Nate's lover.

I whip my head around to look at Dante. "Really?"

"Sure. I think you should agree to be Nate's love interest in our music video, Angel." He smiles at me, and my eyes widen.

I'm wet, and I don't know what exactly about this whole thing has me turned on, but I know an instruction from Dante when I hear one, so I turn to look at Nate.

"You've got yourself a love interest, I guess." I smile at him.

He allows his gaze to roam over me from head to toe, and I can feel it in a way that I never have, despite the fact he's done it to me a thousand times before.

"No shit, I do," he grins back at me.

"Can we go dance now, Nate?" the brunette woman asks in a slightly whiny voice as she shoots daggers at me.

Nate looks at her, then back at me, then back at her before shrugging. "Sure, why not. See you guys later."

"Bye, Nate," Ash says.

"I can't believe you're going to play his love interest, Lexi," Cassie says after they've left, and when I look at her, she grimaces.

"Why?" I ask her.

"He sleeps with *so* many women," she wrinkles her nose as she looks over at the dance floor where Nate is dancing with the woman in a way that's almost indecent.

I frown at Cassie. "Okay, but what does that have to do with it?"

"I don't know. I'm surprised Dante's okay with it." She looks over at Dante.

Cassie and Ash have only been dating for about six months, so she's new to our friend group. I'm not sure if she's worked the Nate thing out yet, but she has a tendency to be a bit judgmental of people.

We've all known each other since we were teenagers, so there's a lot of history between us that she wasn't a part of, and she doesn't get a lot of our jokes.

Dante smiles at her, "We're all friends, Cassie. It'll be fun to have Lexi on the set for our music video and working with us."

"Wouldn't it make more sense for her to play *your* love interest, though, not Nate's?" Cassie asks.

Dante shrugs at her, "My character doesn't have a love interest in the video, so no."

The conversation moves on, and I relax into Dante's embrace as we sit on the banquette and talk to our friends. Some other celebrities join the conversation occasionally before drifting away, and it's a good evening. Nate and the brunette woman disappear from the dance floor, and I realize this after about an hour has passed.

"Go get me a whiskey, Angel," Dante says in a quiet, husky

voice, and I smile.

"Yes, Honey."

He places his hand on my chin and turns my face up to his before kissing me passionately. Arousal swirls throughout my body, and I can't wait to get somewhere private with him. Once our kiss ends, I head to the bar to get his drink and decide to get myself a rum and Coke while I'm there.

"Hey there, Sexy. Wanna go back to my place tonight?" a voice says in my ear while I'm standing at the bar, waiting for the bartender to notice me so I can order the drinks.

I smile and don't turn to look at Nate because I'd know his voice anywhere, but I raise my left hand and wiggle my ring finger at him, "Sorry, stranger, I'm taken."

"What a shame. Think I could take him in a fight?" he laughs.

"I doubt it. He's bigger and stronger than you and a really mean drunk," I turn to grin at Nate as I say this.

He looks me over from head to toe, and I get butterflies in my stomach when he does. "I think you'd probably be worth trying."

My breathing rate has increased, and I'm confused as hell because none of this is anything out of the ordinary. We've made these jokes a thousand times before, but it's as though from the moment Dante said I should play Nate's lover in the video, some strange door has opened that has made this oddly meaningful.

"Where's your friend?" I ask him, desperate to ignore whatever I'm feeling and find some semblance of normality.

Nate gives me a wickedly amused grin and says, "We had our fun. Now I'm all yours again."

"In the toilets?" I ask him as I wrinkle my nose at him.

"It wouldn't be the first time, but no. There's a nice, quiet corner upstairs that's mostly private. Want me to show it to you?" He raises an eyebrow at me, and my breath catches slightly.

I've got images in my head of Nate doing dirty things to an unknown woman in a quiet, dark booth upstairs. I pretend I don't know her, but she's definitely got auburn hair.

"God, Nate, if you want to show me all the places you've had sex with women in this club, we'll be here all night," I tell him in what I hope is a haughty tone.

"Probably," he concedes, "but there are plenty of other things I'd like to spend all night doing with you instead."

"Playing pool?" I ask him.

"Something like that," he grins.

I'm grateful that the bartender is here to ask for our drink order because Nate is looking at me in a way that is making me feel strange again. While we wait for the bartender to make our drinks, Nate puts his arm around my shoulders and pulls me close to him.

"You know I love you, right, Lexi?" he asks me.

I blink up at him. His eyes are so blue, and he's looking at me intensely. I wonder how many drinks he's had tonight, but I know that I need to shut this shit down. He's said things like this in the past when he's been drunk, but there's a path out of the conversation that we always take, the one that allows us all to remain friends.

"I love you, too, Nate. You're one of my best friends." I smile at him, and he nods at me.

"You're one of my best friends, too. That's why I love you."

I swallow heavily and say, "Thanks, Nate."

I'm not sure whether I'm thanking him for being my friend or giving me the out from this awkward conversation. Finally, the bartender gives us our drinks, and we turn to head back to the VIP area.

"You lead the way, Lexi. I want to enjoy the view," Nate tells me with a grin.

"Why can't *I* enjoy the view, for once?" I ask him with a wicked grin back at him as I take a sip from my drink.

Nate laughs and shrugs, then heads back to the VIP area with me following him. I didn't actually intend to do it, but I can't seem to stop my eyes from drifting to his ass as we walk there. He really does have a great body, but I'm finding this evening strange because I'm wet, and the fact that I'm following an instruction from Dante has all but flown out of my head while I was flirting with Nate.

"Oh, you found our lost sheep," Logan laughs when he sees me walking back with Nate.

"Actually, I found her," Nate announces as he drops onto the banquette, leaving a space between himself and Dante.

"Nate can always be counted on to find Lexi," Dante says with a smirk as he looks up at me.

I hand him his drink and then sit on his lap instead of next to him. He looks at me in surprise and then smiles at me. I kiss him, and I pour as much of my passion and love for him into our kiss as I can, trying to burn away the guilt I feel for indulging in flirting with Nate at the bar.

I'm married to Dante, and I love Dante. Yes, I love Nate, too. It's not the same, though. I love him the way I love Ash and Logan. Dante is my husband and the only man for me.

As soon as we're in the limousine driving home to our apartment, I close the privacy screen between us and the driver and slide onto Dante's lap.

"Something got you worked up, Angel?" he smiles at me.

"Yes, you. I've wanted to fuck you all night," I tell him.

"Just me?" he asks.

I look at him, unsure of how to respond. What he's asking is huge, and I don't know what to say. The unwritten rule that we never talk about Nate's feelings for me seems destined to be broken, and I don't want to be the one to do it.

"Of course, who else?" I say, then I'm on edge while I wait for his reply.

Dante doesn't reply, but instead, he pushes me off himself before unzipping his jeans. He pulls them and his briefs down to his ankles, revealing his semi-hard cock.

"On your knees, Angel."

I drop to my knees in front of him and lower my mouth to begin sucking him. This is probably my favorite sex act, and I love feeling him grow to a full-blown erection in my mouth.

I suck him for a few minutes before he says, "Get on me so that I can fuck you, Angel."

I remove him from my mouth, licking him from base to tip as I do, and slide my underwear off before straddling him on the limo's seat. I lower myself onto his cock, and he fills me so completely. Dante kisses me deeply while we fuck, and I close my eyes in ecstasy while my orgasm builds.

He reaches a hand up and pulls my dress down, so it's sitting underneath my breasts. I didn't wear a bra tonight, and my breasts are exposed for him to play with them. It doesn't take long with him sucking on one breast while thumbing my other nipple for me to come on his cock.

When I do, he keeps one breast in his mouth but places both hands on my waist to bounce me up and down roughly on his cock, pounding me hard until he explodes inside me.

"I love you, Angel," he pants at me when I collapse forward onto him.

"I love you, too, Honey."

Chapter Two
Celebrate Good Times

I smile as I enter the Black Lilac store from the rear entrance. It's one of three clothing stores that I own. I'm so proud of my stores. Dante helped me open the first one, but he's been a silent investor, and I've run them myself. He got his money back in our second year, and I opened the second store in the third year. This is our third store, and it came two years later last year.

"Morning, Vera," I say with a smile at the perky brunette woman who manages this store.

"Hey, Lexi. How are you this morning?"

"I'm good. Anything big happened in the last couple of days?"

I rotate the days that I spend at each of the stores so that I'm across all of them equally.

Vera shakes her head and says, "Nothing big."

"Cool. I'll be in my office, then."

I head to the office I have at the back of the store and dock my laptop. After I turn it on, I go to the break room and make myself a coffee that I take back to my desk.

I'm drinking my coffee and looking through my emails when my phone lights up with a text from Cassie.

Is it the weekend yet?

I laugh as I type out a reply to her.

Not quite. I can't wait to see you and Ash tonight.

Everyone's coming to our place, and we're going to hang out together to celebrate Dante's birthday. As much as I like big parties, Dante definitely doesn't, and I do enjoy spending time with my friends in private rather than going out to clubs. There aren't a thousand eyes on us, and it feels like old times back before the guys got famous.

Me too. You're at the Orange County store today, aren't you? Are we doing lunch?

Cassie and I usually do this when I'm at this store, but some days the store will get busy, or she'll have a meeting at work, and we can't.

Definitely. Sushi place at 12?

Her reply comes through swiftly.

Sounds good. I'll book us in. See you then…if I haven't died of boredom first.

I laugh and turn back to my emails. I have some contracts from my lawyer that I have to print out and sign before I send them back to him. I've landed a new supplier for the stores, and I'm very excited about it. I'm always looking for new clothes to stock, especially ones that present a good business value, and this supplier has access to some awesome designs that I think will really fit my stores perfectly.

I spend the morning working through my emails before I head to lunch with Cassie. I arrive before she does, and the hostess sees me through to our table. I'm drinking a rosé when Cassie approaches.

She's wearing a stunning purple blouse with a built-in tie that looks like it's from Gucci and black wide-leg trousers. I stand to give her a hug when she approaches the table.

"You look gorgeous as usual," I tell her as we take our seats.

"Thanks. I went shopping with Ash's credit card," she tells me with a smile.

"Sounds dangerous. Is my husband going to have to go into the studio sometime soon to help make Ash some more money?" I tease her.

Cassie laughs and nods. "Yup. I think a wardrobe full of Louboutins would suit me really nicely, too, so Ash had better keep those albums coming."

"I guess he'd better. Touring, too," I joke.

"But if he's off on tour, he's not in bed with me. What use is a wardrobe full of sexy clothes and shoes if he's not here to see me wearing them?"

"Good point," I say with a grin as I take a sip of my wine.

A waiter comes to take our food order and, after he's left, Cassie toys with the stem of her wine glass as she looks at me. "When's the music video shoot?"

"Next Friday," I manage to say casually, despite the butterflies that seem to have gathered in my stomach.

I'm so nervous about the shoot. I don't know if it's a good idea for me to pretend to be Nate's lover. It's a little too close to home, and I'm worried that it's going to cause issues, but Dante told me to do it, so I know he's okay with it. I keep reminding myself of that fact whenever the nerves hit me.

"I still can't believe you're going to be in their video with Nate." She shakes her head as she looks at me.

This isn't helping my nerves at all.

"I know, but it should be fun getting to be on set with the guys. I've seen them film stuff before, so it'll be cool to actually get to be a part of it this time."

"But what exactly is your role? What if you have to make out with him or something?"

I inhale sharply as images of Nate come into my mind. I envisage his gorgeous face coming closer to mine before we kiss, and a dart of arousal shoots to my pussy.

I shake my head to try and rid myself of the image. "No. It's not like that on video shoots. You're just playing a role, and Dante will be right there with us. They're not exactly going to say, 'Okay, guys, time for seven minutes in heaven,'" I laugh.

"If you say so. It's just weird. What will people say?" She frowns at me.

"I don't know. I'm freaking out as it is. Can we talk about something else?" I cringe.

"I'm just thinking of your reputation, that's all." She shrugs and says, "I mean, it's Nate. You know what people will think. It's a bad idea."

"Well, it's happening, so I don't know what to say."

"Surely, you don't have to do it. They could find plenty of actresses for the role."

Not unless I safeword.

Cassie doesn't know that, of course. I'm not nervous enough to do that yet, but I do know that I can if I need to.

"I've told them I'll do it, and it's happening next week. I don't want to leave them in the lurch. It'll be fine. Anyway, how's your week been?"

I'm grateful when Cassie accepts my change of topic and tells me about what's been happening in her job in human resources for an accounting firm. By the time her lunch hour is almost up, I pay the bill and give her a hug before we part ways.

"I'll see you at our place tonight," I tell her.

"Maybe. I still can't guarantee I won't die of boredom this afternoon. Who books a meeting to discuss headcount and staffing numbers for three in the afternoon on a Friday?" she moans.

I laugh and say, "Your boss, I'm guessing?"

"Bingo." She grins at me. "I'll see you later."

My conversation with Cassie stays at the back of my mind for the rest of the day. I try not to think too hard about the upcoming music video shoot, but it's hopeless.

Dante and I haven't talked about it, except for logistics about when it's happening and how we're traveling to the set.

It hasn't stopped me from having some pretty intense dreams about Nate that I've felt guilty about. It's made it hard to forget about the way I felt the night Nate asked me. I've been avoiding him this week, but I won't get out of seeing him tonight at Dante's birthday dinner. The butterflies return as I think about seeing Nate.

I'm completely on edge by the time I've reached our apartment after picking up the cake I ordered for Dante's birthday. I find Dante relaxed on the sofa, reading something on his phone.

"Hi, Honey. Have you had a good birthday?" I ask as I sit next to him, and he puts his arm around me.

"Yeah. We had a meeting with Isaac to discuss the music video, and his assistant had even organized a birthday cake for me, which was nice," he says with a grin.

"Aww, that was nice of him," I say, as the butterflies tumble around my stomach. I hesitate for a second, then ask, "Are you really okay with me being in your music video?"

He looks me over and then asks in a low voice, "Why wouldn't I be?"

"I don't know. Cassie was saying at lunch—"

"Don't worry about Cassie. I'm telling you that I'm fine with it. I'm looking forward to having you on set with us and starring in our music video. It'll be amazing." He gives me a tight squeeze. "When do you have to start dinner?"

I glance at the clock on the wall. "Half an hour, maybe."

"Hmm," he says with a wicked grin on his face. "Take your panties off and give them to me, then sit on the coffee table, Angel."

This. He loves to do this. I take my thong off and hand it to him before he slips it into his pocket. I sit on the coffee table in front of him and spread my legs wide. As I do, my skirt slides up my thighs and exposes my pussy to his view.

"Very nice," he murmurs.

He goes back to looking at his phone, and I bite my lip as I watch him. I don't know if he's going to even fuck me before I have to start preparing dinner. We're swiftly running out of time, and my pussy aches as the cool air hits it.

I love being exposed like this, but Dante doesn't even look up. I think it's the fact that he could that turns me on. That any time he deigns to look in my direction, I'll be on display for him.

When he finally looks at me, I'm in such a heightened state of arousal that I can practically feel his gaze as though he's touching me. My nipples are painfully stiff against my top, and my pussy is drenched.

"What a shame we've run out of time to have sex, Angel."

He drops his phone next to him and moves over to where I'm sitting. He takes my chin in his hand, tilts my face up to his, and kisses me. Dante explores my mouth with his tongue as he holds my face in place. By the time he releases me, I'm aflame with desire.

"Go make dinner, Angel. When our friends leave, I'm going to eat my dessert."

He pushes two fingers into my wet pussy, and I struggle to breathe against my desperate need for him to fuck me. He fingers me for about half a minute before he sends me on my way to the kitchen, drenched and aching to be filled.

I begin to pull out dishes to cook in and vegetables to peel and chop. I know that I could have a dinner like this catered, but special occasions are the times I most like to cook. It always feels like the food tastes better when it's cooked with love. I get to spend this time preparing the food we're going to eat while we celebrate Dante's birthday.

"Need some help?" a low, melodic voice asks from near the door as I'm pulling a dish out of a cupboard, and I smile when I hear it.

I place the dish on the bench and turn to grin at Logan as I say, "Hi. You're here early."

"I knew you'd be cooking and figured I could lend a hand," he says with a smile.

I walk over to him to throw my arms around him, and he hugs me tightly. I'm happy to see him, and I could use some help with dinner. I pull a pink apron out of a drawer and throw it to him.

"Put this on. It's totally your color," I say with a laugh.

"Is that your professional opinion as a fashion expert?" he asks, and he laughs with me as he puts the apron on and ties it behind himself.

"Yes, it is."

He actually doesn't look bad in the pink apron. He's wearing jeans and a light blue shirt, so the pink complements his outfit nicely.

I pull out a second chopping board and place some carrots on it. "Peel these and cut them julienne style."

He sets to work, and I move on to slicing the chicken breasts while he does. Logan asks about my day at work, and I tell him about the stores. I enjoy chatting with him while we work on dinner. It's familiar, and we've done this hundreds of times before.

I'm seasoning the chicken breasts when I ask him, "Are you seeing anyone at the moment?"

"No. Nothing serious since Chad."

Logan was upset when Chad cheated on him, but I'm glad the asshole is well out of the picture now.

"You deserve so much better than him, anyway," I scoff.

"Thanks, I suppose," he says in an amused tone.

Chad was a complete asshole who we all hated. He was arrogant and rude but treated Logan well...until he didn't. He was caught kissing another guy at a club, and thank god Logan ended it.

"I thought I saw an article online that you were out on a date just last week?" I raise an eyebrow at him.

Logan chuckles and shakes his head at me. "I've been on some dates, yes."

I put the herb container down and step back from the kitchen bench as I turn to look at Logan. I take in his appearance with his handsome, square jaw and beautiful brown eyes. He could have pretty much anyone he wants, really.

"What's up?" he asks with a quizzical look on his face.

"You're *far* too pretty to be single," I assure him with a grin.

He laughs at me and says, "Thanks. I think so, too."

"Okay. Tell me what you want out of a relationship. I'm going to find someone to hook you up with," I say as I turn back to the chicken.

I start to run through acquaintances in my head as Logan talks, trying to think of someone who would be good enough to be with my friend. I know a lot of people, but the only woman who's really in our inner circle is Cassie, and she's out of the running.

"I definitely want someone who won't cheat on me," he says.

He gives me a look, and I cringe as I nod my head. "Obviously."

"I don't know. Someone I get along with. I think that, most of all, I want someone who wants me for me. Not someone who wants the rock star. That kind of person is getting increasingly hard to find, I'm afraid."

I sigh and nod. "I'm sure it is."

"Sometimes I'm jealous of Dante," he says as he gives me a sad smile. "He found you before we got famous. There's never been any doubt that you love him for him."

I wash my hands and wipe them dry, then walk back over to hug him again. "I get it. I consider myself lucky. I've gotten to be with you guys through all of this. Don't let anyone ever tell you that you're not amazing, Logan Ballantine. I know that there's someone out there who will love you for the amazing, unique, and wonderful human being that you are."

He squeezes me tightly and says, "Thanks, Lexi."

"You're welcome, and besides"—we break apart and head back to our cooking stations—"I'm on the case now. I'll find that person or die trying."

"Okay. But please give up before you die trying. I don't know what we'd do if we didn't have you around." He winks at me, and it makes me laugh.

We continue talking as we make dinner, and I manage to forget about the music video until we're almost finished, and I'm pulling out plates and cutlery for Logan to take out to the dinner table.

"Hey, Sexy Lexi."

Nate's voice comes from near the entrance to the kitchen as I'm standing with the items to hand to Logan.

"Hi, Nate," I say.

"Hey, Nate," Logan adds as he passes him.

Nate smiles and nods at him before turning back to me. "Smells good. Almost as good as you."

"Um, thanks," I manage to say.

He's got a cheeky smile on his handsome face as he walks over to me and pulls me into a hug. All of my nerves about the video come back as I wrap my arms around him to hug him back.

He feels good, and I like being in his arms. Guilt at my enjoyment floods through me as we break apart, and I force what I hope is a normal, cheerful smile onto my face. As though I'm not having bad thoughts about my friend.

"Anything I can do to help?" he asks.

"No, Logan's got it covered. Go relax. Dinner will be ready in about ten minutes."

"Good. I didn't really want to help with dinner. I just wanted to see your sexy ass." He winks at me.

I manage a casual laugh and say, "Was there ever any doubt?"

He leaves the room, and I blow out a massive breath of air as I bend over and rest my head on the cool marble countertop while I try to calm my now racing heartbeat. Agreeing to be in the music video with Nate was a huge mistake. It's changed something in me, and it scares me.

It's not like I've never once thought about the guys in a sexual way. They're all ridiculously good-looking, so every now and then, they'll come into my consciousness when I'm masturbating. I feel so guilty about it, though, even though I'd never do anything with them because I love Dante.

This music video feels dangerous. As though I'm taking one of those secret fantasies and putting it on display for everyone to see.

"Lexi? Are you okay?" Logan asks, and I jump before I stand up and turn to look at him.

He's still wearing his pink apron, and it makes me smile. "Yeah. I was just thinking."

"About what?" he asks with a smile.

I turn away and pull the baking dish of chicken out of the oven as I say, "Just stuff. Is the table all set?"

"Yes. Ash and Cassie have arrived, too."

"Cool," I say as I place the dish on a potholder. "Just in time."

We take the food out to the table, and my stomach flops when I realize I'm going to be stuck sitting next to Nate. I'm in between him and Dante on one side of the table, while Cassie is opposite me between Ash and Logan.

I walk around to hug both of them before I take my seat. "Hey, guys. Long time, no see, Cassie."

"Yeah, it's been a while," she laughs. "The food smells amazing, Lexi."

"Logan helped," I tell her as I smile at him.

"Lexi did most of the work. I was just her helper bee."

"Well, I look forward to eating it," Ash says as he raises his glass. "Let's toast to Dante. Happy birthday!"

We all raise our glasses and toast my beautiful husband, who thanks us all profusely. The dinner is enjoyable, and I soak in the compliments before we finish up, and Logan helps me clean up afterward.

"What would I do without you?" I ask him with a smile.

"Take twice as long and delay Dante opening his gifts?" he suggests, and I laugh.

"Probably."

We're still laughing as we head back out to the living room where the guys are hanging out. I drop into Dante's lap, and he wraps his arms around me before he kisses me passionately.

I'm heady with a combination of lust and alcohol, and Dante tastes like the whiskey he's been drinking tonight. I'm incredibly aware of the fact that I have no underwear on.

Our friends whoop and holler as we kiss, and when it ends, my cheeks are burning with embarrassment while my pussy aches.

"I think we know what Lexi will be giving Dante for his birthday," Nate says as I turn to face him. "Lucky boy!"

Nate's eyes traverse my body, and I clamp my legs together to avoid giving him a full show as he grins at me.

"The luckiest," Dante agrees before kissing me again. "I believe I have some presents to open first, though. Why don't you get them for me, Angel?"

I'm so turned on as I nod at him. "Of course, Honey."

I stand and walk over to a table in the corner of the room where the guys have left their presents and cards. There's a large, flat, rectangle-shaped present, a small cube-shaped present, and a box about three feet tall and wide.

I place the two smaller presents on the big box with their cards, and when I try to lift them, I'm surprised by how heavy it is.

I've only managed to grunt as I take the weight in my arms and turn back to Dante and our guests before Logan is at my side. "That's my gift. I'll carry it over for you."

I look up into his smiling face and say, "Thanks, Logan."

It's a relief when he takes the weight off me, and I pick the other two gifts up off the top of the box before we walk together back over to Dante. Logan places the box on the floor in front of him, and I hand him the other two gifts before I sit next to him.

Dante reads the card from the first gift, which is from Nate. I look over at him, and he's grinning from ear to ear as Dante unwraps the gift.

As he pulls back the wrapping paper, the vinyl album cover for *Diver Down* by Van Halen is revealed. It's signed by the band, and Dante gasps.

"Holy shit, Nate. Thank you!"

"You're welcome. I thought you'd love it."

Dante nods his head. "I do. It's amazing."

He stares at the cardboard cover before turning it over in his hands and then pulls the record out reverentially. He looks at it for about a minute before he carefully puts it back in the sleeve and thanks Nate again. The album is passed around, and we all appreciate Nate's gift.

"This must have cost a fortune," Cassie gasps when she looks at it.

"Yeah, it cost a bit. Dante is worth it, though." Nate shrugs then turns to grin at him.

"Well, thanks again, Nate."

I hand over Ash's gift, and when Dante opens it, he finds a black leather box. Inside it is a brown leather box with cream stitching and the Breitling logo embossed on it.

Dante's eyes widen, and he whips his head around to look at

Ash. "You got me a Breitling?"

"Maybe," he replies with a cagey smile, and Dante laughs. When Dante opens the watch box, the watch inside has a black leather band. The case is made of steel and gold, and the watch face is blue. It's stunning, and Dante is clearly pleased with it.

"It's a Navitimer, but if you want a different one, they said you can exchange it."

"No, it's amazing. Thanks, Ash."

"It's from Cassie as well," he replies with a good-natured smile.

"Of course. Thank you, Cassie," Dante amends quickly.

"You're welcome." She smiles at him.

"Okay, time to find out what the hell Logan got you," Nate announces. "I'm dying of curiosity." He leans closer to me, and I catch the scent of his cologne. "What do you think it is, Sexy?"

I look into his eyes, and his amusement is clear to me. It's a normal joke, but I shift in my seat, aware of the wetness between my legs.

"It's obviously a brand new car," I manage to joke in a casual tone.

"You're probably right. Want to bet on it?"

"I'm not *that* sure it's a car," I backtrack.

He laughs and puts an arm around my shoulders before pulling me to him for a hug as Dante pulls the big box closer to where he's sitting.

I squirm out of Nate's embrace as casually as I can, not because I dislike it, but because I like it too much. Nobody is even looking at us or giving it a second thought because I've always been touchy-feely with Nate. No, this is normal for us. My reaction to Nate isn't normal, though.

I look at my husband as he starts unwrapping Logan's present. He's the man I love, and I shouldn't be enjoying Nate's touch. I force myself to ignore Nate's presence next to me as Dante reveals the gift, a big metal box with a single display that has random characters on it.

"What is it?" Nate asks.

"It's a custom puzzle box. I had it imported from Germany."
Logan looks pleased with his gift.

"That's so cool. Thank you, Logan," Dante says.

We spend the next few hours drinking while we make sporadic attempts to open the puzzle box, which we move to the middle of the room. Logan tells us that he had to order the box months ago to get it here in time for Dante's birthday.

We're a few drinks in, and I'm tipsy when Dante removes his arm from around me as he says, "I think I see something down at the bottom of the box. Why don't you take a look, Angel?"

Heat rushes to my cheeks as I follow his instruction. I get onto my knees, but I can't see anything.

"Where?" I ask as I turn my head to look at Dante.

He allows his gaze to roam over my body for a moment before he gives me a seductive smile. "Right at the bottom. Can you see it? You probably need to get closer."

I lean down to look at the bottom of the box, and my skirt rides up my legs as I do. Cool air hits my pussy, and I grab the hem of my skirt to wrench it back down since everyone is behind me, and I don't want to flash them all.

Dante is right, and the name of the company that made the box is engraved there. There's a tiny line next to the 'L' in the name that I realize isn't part of the 'L' itself. I feel underneath the box at that point, and there's a slight lip. When I pull on it, the name section slides forward to reveal a small tray with a small device that has a switch on it.

"Oh my god. You were right, Honey!" I hold the device up to show him.

We're able to use the device to move the letters on the display and open a door in the box before we get stuck again. We don't make any further progress on the puzzle before our friends leave after midnight.

As soon as I've closed the door to our apartment behind Logan, Dante wraps his arm around my waist from behind. He pulls me hard against him as he uses his other hand to reach under my skirt.

I'm dripping wet because he's been giving me instructions for hours, and he wastes no time in rubbing my clit with his fingers.

"Mmm…I've wanted to play with you all evening, Angel."

I bite my lip to withhold a moan as Dante slides a hand into my top to play with my nipple.

"When you bent down to look at the bottom of the box, I swear I saw a flash of your pussy. It was a struggle not to get an erection," he murmurs in my ear, and I gasp.

"Really? You don't think anyone else saw, do you?"

Dante rubs my clit faster. "Possibly. It would only be if they were looking. Do you think any of our friends spend much of their time trying to get a glimpse of your pussy?"

Nate.

A shock of arousal hits me at the thought of being on display. Dante stills in his movements. "Do you, Angel?"

My cheeks burn with heat. It's partially the embarrassment of knowing I was exposed, but the thought of being seen is also hot.

"Maybe. Do you think they do?" I ask him, my voice thick with lust.

His cock is stiff against my ass as he pulls his hands out from under my clothing and walks around in front of me.

"Lift up your skirt, Angel."

I reach down to the hem to raise it to my hips, and my pussy throbs as I expose myself to his view.

"They might," Dante says thoughtfully. "You have such a nice pussy. I guess I couldn't blame them if they wanted to see it. Come with me."

He takes my hand and leads me back to the living room, where he stops next to the sofa. Dante pushes my torso down, so I'm bent over the arm of it at the end. My face lands where Logan's lap would've been a few minutes ago, and the sofa is still warm with his body heat.

As I realize this, I can't help but imagine my mouth around his cock while Dante lifts my skirt back above my hips again. I can hear him unbuckle his jeans before he pushes his stiff cock into my aching pussy.

Dante grips my hips as he starts to fuck me, and I imagine Nate walking over to where we are, so I can jack him off with my hand while I blow Logan. I clench Dante's cock tight as the dirty thoughts of being used by multiple men at once run through my mind.

It's wrong, and I shouldn't be thinking of anyone but the beautiful man I'm fucking, but the thought of it tips me into orgasm. As I come, I moan Dante's name loudly to remind myself who I love and have committed my life to.

Chapter Three

Simulated Sex Is Still Sex

A young woman with a clipboard is smiling at me. "Come right this way, Mrs. Sullivan, we'll get you into hair and makeup."

It's a bit after ten, and the guys have been here since almost five this morning, shooting the music video. I didn't need to be in as early, but I went to see them on my way in, and they looked good filming some of the shots of them playing on their instruments, even though they weren't really playing them. The video is being shot on a massive soundstage with several different scenes set up. There are people everywhere, and it's complete chaos.

"The nightclub scene is first, then the restaurant, and then the bedroom," the woman that I'm following informs me.

"I'm sorry, did you say *bedroom*?!" I ask in mild alarm.

"Yes, did you not get the storyboards?" she frowns at me.

"Oh, um, not really. It's fine. I was just surprised."

Dante definitely saw the storyboards. He knows exactly what's being filmed, so I'm sure that it won't be anything too erotic or inappropriate for Nate and me to be doing together.

I'm taken through hair and makeup before being clothed in a very short, skin-tight silver dress with sky-high black heels for the nightclub scene.

When I walk onto the soundstage, Ash sees me first and wolf-whistles at me. "Looking good, Lexi."

"Thanks, Ash," I grin at him.

Dante and Nate both turn and see me at the same time. The darkening look of arousal in their eyes is so similar that it scares me. I'm worried, not because Nate has the same reaction as Dante, but because I like that he does.

I get a glow of pleasure that he clearly finds me attractive, but I am also scared as hell by that. I've been so worried for the last two weeks that doing this music video will fuck up our friendship. I'm concerned that we're crossing some kind of invisible line with this.

The director of the shoot, James Wilson, makes his way over to me. "Okay, Lexi. In this scene, we're going to start by just having you walk across in front of the guys. Nate will notice you and start to follow while singing the first verse."

I nod and move to my position while James gives the large crowd of extras behind the guys their instructions. Then, when the music starts playing, I stride confidently across the scene, sensing when Nate begins to follow me.

"Cut!" James calls.

He gives me instructions to walk a little slower, and I do that. I walk across the nightclub a solid fifteen times before we move on to the second shot.

"Okay, Lexi. In this shot, you're going to dance with Nate while he's singing. I want you to look at him while he does. You've met this new man, and you're having an amazing night together. Do you think you can do that?"

I nod and move to stand in front of Nate, and he's instructed to put his arms around my waist while mine go around his neck. We get into this position and wait for the take to begin.

"Having fun?" he asks me while James talks to the other guys.

"My feet are starting to hurt," I complain to him.

"I could give you a foot massage if you'd like," he grins at me.

"Yes, please," I say with a laugh.

"Maybe after this scene is done." Nate winks at me.

I'm very aware of the feeling of his arms circling my waist, of the pressure of his hands against my lower back, and of just how little distance there is between us. When the music starts, Nate sings while staring into my eyes, and I follow my instruction of looking into his eyes as though he's just a hot guy I met at a club.

James tells us to get closer, and Nate moves his hard body against mine. My breasts are pressing into his chest, and I wonder if he can feel that my nipples are stiff. I'm sure that is a bulge in his jeans, and heat rushes to my cheeks.

"Are you okay, Lexi?" Nate asks me.

"Yes, this isn't weird at all," I laugh at him.

In answer, he pulls me closer against him and asks, "Isn't it?"

"No. I always dance with men who aren't my husband at nightclubs, don't you know?"

"You dance with me when we're out all the time," he points out.

"Not like this," I say, as my cheeks continue to burn.

"Well, maybe you should."

The director cuts off our conversation by calling for action, and the take begins. Nate and I start to dance together, and he looks down into my eyes as he sings to me about meeting a beautiful woman. It's strange. I can still feel him against me, and it feels as though all of my nerve endings are on fire. I glance over at Dante between takes, and he seems completely fine and not fazed by this at all.

After many takes, we finally get one that James is happy with. Nate and I are moved over to the wall of the nightclub set. I'm positioned with my back against it while Nate stands close in front of me with his arm above my head on the wall and leaning over me.

We're again left on our own while everyone else is given instructions. I don't even know what to say to the man in front of me right now because I've just been told that I'm going to kiss him.

"Should we practice our kiss while we're waiting?" Nate asks cheekily.

"Very funny." I roll my eyes at him.

"I'm only half-joking," he tells me. "It might be less pressure if we get it out of the way before everyone's watching."

"I've kissed you a thousand times." I shrug.

"In my dreams," he laughs. "Kissing me on the cheek doesn't count."

The way we're positioned, we're not that far apart, so I move my head forward and press my lips against his, the way we've been told will happen for the scene. Nate stiffens and then relaxes while I kiss him. After five seconds, I pull my head back.

"There. Now it's over with," I tell him.

The air between us is crackling with sexual tension, and when the shock disappears from Nate's face, the way that he is looking at me is downright dangerous. I'm playing with fire right now, and I'm doing it while my husband is standing less than fifteen feet away from me.

I glance over to see him looking at us with a strange look on his face, and I'm worried that he's going to be angry with me, but I don't have time to say anything before the take starts. I'm kind of glad I did kiss Nate because the cameraman is right in our faces when we do it for the shot, which is nerve-wracking.

It takes longer than I would've expected to get the take right, and I kiss Nate over and over to the point where it becomes almost meaningless and feels so natural and normal that it scares me.

I'm glad when the director tells us that we've got it and sends me back to hair and makeup to get ready for the restaurant scene. I'm tired and grateful as hell to get away from Nate for a bit.

"You did great, Angel," Dante says as he appears in the room.

"Thanks. Oh my god, is it always this exhausting?" I ask him with a groan.

He laughs at me, "Yeah, it can be."

The makeup artist is preparing the makeup they need, and the hairstylist isn't here yet, so I slip off the chair and walk over to him, wrapping my arms around his waist. He envelops me in his embrace, and it feels like coming home. I love him so much.

"Are you really okay with this?" I ask him quietly, and I hope the makeup artist can't hear me.

"Yeah, I'm fine. Are you?" he tilts my face up to his to force me to look at him.

"I guess I am. It's just weird to be kissing Nate." I shrug.

Dante drops his head so that his lips are next to my ear. "If you need to safeword, you know that you can, right?"

He looks back into my eyes, and I nod.

"I mean it. If you do that, I will shut the entire shoot down if I have to."

"Thank you," I smile at him.

"I love you, Lexi."

He drops his lips to mine, and his kiss is so familiar, I instinctively part my lips to allow him to access my mouth with his tongue. He pulls me hard against him and kisses me so passionately that I long to have him in bed with me.

I hear a cough from behind me, and the makeup artist tells me she's ready for me, so we break apart.

Dante smiles at me. "I'm really fine with it. I saw the storyboards, Lexi."

"About that—" I start to say, intending to ask him about the bedroom scene.

"I really need you now, Lexi," the makeup artist says.

"We'll talk later. I should get back to set, anyway," Dante tells me.

After I've had my makeup redone, my hair is put into an elegant updo. I'm dressed in a stunning blue cocktail dress, and I wonder where I could get this from because it's gorgeous, and I'd love for Black Lilac to be able to stock it.

Someone comes and leads me back to the set, where I take a seat at a restaurant table across from Nate. I'm so grateful for the space between us, even though he's smiling at me in a way that is simply friendly and holds none of the sexual intensity of the way he was looking at me earlier.

"Good to see you again, Sexy Lexi," he grins at me.

"Thanks, Nate," I say, ignoring his nickname for me. I don't say anything more for a few seconds before I decide to go ahead and ask him, "Hey, what's happening in this 'bedroom scene' I've heard about?"

"Didn't you see the storyboards?" he asks me.

"Nope, I've been slammed at work this week." I shrug.

"Oh, we're going to have sex," Nate tells me.

He says it casually and gives me a wicked grin before allowing his gaze to trail over what he can see of my body as I sit across from him. I hate myself for the reaction this brings to me because I find myself aroused as I'm bombarded with images of Nate in bed with me.

"Well, simulated sex, but sex nonetheless." He smirks at me, and heat rushes to my cheeks.

Dante said that I can safeword if I want to. I know that he knows the plan for the shoot, and if I get too uncomfortable, I can stop this at any time. So, I take a deep breath and nod.

"Cool. Shouldn't start too many rumors about us having an affair or anything."

"Any publicity is good publicity, right?" he grins back at me.

After we've filmed the restaurant scene, I'm taken back to have soft and natural makeup done this time, along with manufactured bedhead. I head back to the set wearing a large robe, and I have approximately a thousand butterflies flying around in my stomach.

I'm taken to the bedroom set, and it feels intimate without the hundred or so extras from the first scenes. All the guys are here, though, and plenty of crew members are in the room doing various tasks. Dante, Ash, and Logan are standing off to the side of the set and watching me walk toward them while Nate is already lying in bed. I don't know what he's wearing, but his muscled torso is exposed, and the sheets are lying low across his hips, making him appear to be naked.

"Um, is Nate actually wearing anything?" I ask the guys as I get near them.

Ash laughs, "Yeah, he is, but not much."

"Are you okay, Lexi?" Logan asks me, looking concerned.

"Yeah, I'm fine," I grimace at him.

"You don't look it," he says, frowning harder at me.

"You don't have to do anything you don't want to do, Angel," Dante hugs me quickly and then angles me toward the bed after kissing me on the head.

An assistant asks for my robe when I get next to the bed, and I untie it before I hand it to her. Nate watches me, and when he sees me in the racy red lingerie, his eyes go dark. His expression turns to one that can only be described as lust.

I slide into the bed as I have been instructed to do, and Nate says in a husky voice, "You're looking *really* good, Lexi."

I'm grateful to discover Nate is wearing Calvin Klein briefs, but I'm sure they're a smaller size than he would normally wear because they don't cover much at all. In the few moments the bed sheets aren't covering him, I catch a glimpse of an obvious bulge there.

He wraps his arms around me, and I'm surprised by how good this feels. My heart is racing, and I'm looking into his eyes while he smiles at me.

"Ready to have sex with me, Sexy?" he grins at me.

I ignore the innuendo behind his words, but I also have to ignore the spark of arousal that flares inside me.

I force myself to act as though this is totally normal when I reply. "Sure. It'll be fun."

Nate laughs, and it's melodic and sexy. I don't know what it is about me lately, but it's like a veil has been dropped from my eyes, and I'm seeing him in a whole new light. I try to remind myself that I'm married to his best friend and that he's nothing more than one of my best friends of more than a decade. I can feel him getting hard against me, and some part of me wishes that we were doing this for real.

James instructs us, "Okay, we're going to play the whole song while you guys just pretend as though you're having sex. Once we see what it looks like, we'll make any adjustments. Let's close the set!"

I'm relieved when a considerable number of crew members leave the room before he calls for action. All of our friends stay, as well as key personnel.

The music starts to play, and Nate pulls me on top of him. I can feel his very obvious erection, and his hands on my waist are shooting sparks of electricity around my body.

"You need to kiss," James calls out.

I lower my head to Nate's and kiss him softly on the lips before raising my head again.

"Cut!" James says after what must've been only thirty seconds.

I roll off Nate and onto my back. He raises his knees, which tents the sheets above him, and I realize that this is hiding his erection and find myself blushing.

"Sorry, guys, but have either of you even had sex before?" James asks us with a grin on his face. "Because right now, this is looking like a couple of mannequins who have been stacked on top of each other for storage."

"Sorry." I cringe. "I'll try to do better."

"Me, too. I've got plenty of experience to draw from," Nate adds with a grin back at James.

James walks away while chuckling, and we get back into our initial position, with Nate holding me while laying on his side. The music starts, and he rolls me on top of him again. I grind my crotch against his erection and see the mild surprise in his eyes before he slides one hand from my waist down to my ass, where he grabs me and pulls me hard against him as I continue grinding.

With the other hand, he slides it up to the back of my head and pulls me down to kiss him. After about ten seconds of kissing, my lips part, and Nate slides his tongue into my mouth. I'm in ecstasy because his hard shaft is rubbing against my clit as I grind against him, and he's a really good kisser.

I can't stop myself, and a moan escapes my lips. When it does, Nate rolls me over onto my back and braces himself above me, thrusting his hips back and forth roughly against my crotch. I've completely forgotten where we are. I've forgotten that my husband, our friends, and complete strangers are watching us. The world is reduced to Nate and me.

I can feel that I am about to come, and I'm panting for breath. Moments before my orgasm hits me, Nate drops his head to mine and kisses me hard, covering the moan that I wouldn't have been able to stop myself from making. He keeps going, and for a second, I wonder why before I realize that this is meant to be acting, and we haven't been told to stop.

We keep going for so long that I can feel a second orgasm building. My desire to be filled by Nate is intense, and I desperately want him inside of me. I kiss him with so much passion that it scares me because he kisses me back equally intensely.

"Cut!" James calls when I'm about ten seconds away from coming again.

Nate and I freeze, and we're both panting heavily. I stare into his eyes in horror as everything comes rushing back to me. Where we are. Who we are. What we're doing right now.

"That was perfect, guys. I don't even think we need another take. I'm pretty sure we got it," James announces. "Come here, and we'll watch it back."

"You're going to need to give me a second. I can't exactly stand up right now," Nate calls out and causes our friends to laugh.

I turn beet red as I roll off him and put on the robe that the assistant is holding out for me. I walk over to Dante, nervous about his reaction. Logan and Ash don't seem at all fazed by what they just watched, but I'm sure that Dante will have noticed that I actually came during that.

"Lexi, your acting skills are off the charts," Ash tells me, looking amazed.

"What about mine?" Nate's voice comes from right behind me, and I jump because I thought he hadn't left the bed yet.

Ash grins at him, "I had no doubt that you'd be able to fake sex well. I thought Lexi might struggle with everyone watching her."

"Especially since she's never had to fake an orgasm with me," Dante says with a smirk.

He gives me a meaningful look, and I know that he knows I wasn't faking. I turn bright red, and Nate laughs behind me.

"Yes, it was very convincing. Maybe you should quit running the stores and take up acting full time, Lexi," Nate tells me.

"I'll be fine, thanks. Let's just go watch the video." I roll my eyes at him, feeling the heat flood to my cheeks.

We walk over to where James is standing with Mike, the cameraman. Dante slips his arm around my waist as we do, and I'm comforted by being in his embrace. I'm a mess of emotions because I just had an orgasm given to me by a man who isn't my husband while he and a whole bunch of other people watched. Not just that, but it was recorded for posterity for the entire world to see, and we're all about to watch it together. When it's played, I feel completely exposed, knowing everyone just watched me come.

I get more praise for my 'acting skills' from James before he says with a frown on his face, "Something's a little off with it, though, and I can't figure out what it is."

I'm terrified that he's about to realize that I'm faking precisely nothing in this video when Dante speaks up from next to me.

"It's because Lexi's wearing a bra." I inhale sharply and stare up at him while he continues his thought. "It doesn't look realistic because she wouldn't be wearing a bra if they were actually having sex."

He looks down at me, and he has a very odd look on his face right now. James is responding, but I can't look away from Dante.

"You're right. Are you comfortable shooting topless, Lexi?" James asks me.

"I guess so," I say.

Dante smiles at me, "I really think it'll look a lot better for the music video, Angel."

My eyes widen in surprise because that's the magic word. He wants me to get topless in front of Nate. Oddly enough, I don't even care about anyone else in the room. It's the fact that I'm going to be exposed to Nate that matters.

"Okay, if Dante's fine with it, then I am." I shrug.

"This music video is going to break the internet," Ash laughs from behind me, and I actually manage a smile.

"Yeah, probably. People are going to lose their minds." I roll my eyes and laugh, but for a second, I wonder if this is the right thing to do.

I remind myself that I can safeword if it gets too much. I don't want to do that, though, and I feel guilty as fuck about that. I *want* to be back in bed with Nate.

"Okay, let's get you guys back on set," James says. Then he announces, "I want everyone gone from the set except for me, Mike, and Dante."

This time, even more people leave the set, and I wave goodbye to Logan and Ash as they follow the rest of the crew out, leaving me alone with Nate, Dante, James, and Mike. Dante follows Nate and me over to the bed so he can take our robes from us.

Nate gets in the bed first and asks quietly, "You really okay with this, bro?"

"Sure, the music video will be hot as hell," Dante smiles.

"You're definitely fine with Lexi acting as well as she did in that last take?" Nate swallows heavily as he asks this.

"Absolutely. She's a brilliant actress, and I guess we never knew how well she could act. You should use your best acting skills for our music video, Angel." Dante smirks at us both, and I blush.

He's giving me permission to have another orgasm during this take if Nate can get me there, and I fucking think that's a sure bet. In answer, I untie my robe and hand it to Dante before getting under the covers and unclipping my bra.

Dante takes the bra and our robes away and walks off set while I dare to look at Nate. He softly strokes my skin with his thumb under the sheets. I know nobody will be able to see that he's doing it, and I shiver. James and Mike are busy setting up the camera while talking together, but I know without checking that Dante will be watching us.

"Do you have any idea of the things I want to do to you, Lexi?" Nate asks me in a husky voice.

We can't have this conversation. It's too damn dangerous. Everything about today has a high probability of fucking up our friendship entirely.

"Nathaniel Walker," I say in a warning tone.

"What, Alexandra Sullivan?" he smiles at me.

"I assume that you mean your character and my character because this is acting," I tell him in as cool a tone as I can manage.

Nate laughs and lowers his head and says with his lips close to my ear, "You weren't acting when you came for me, and I'm about to make you do it again."

He places his hand on my ass to pull me closer to him, and I can feel that he's already hard again. At least they gave me full panties to wear instead of a thong, but that doesn't stop Nate from sliding his fingers under the band of it and grabbing a handful of my flesh. I gasp, and my skin is seared where he's touching me.

"You should've gone without panties, too," he tells me, squeezing my ass again.

I hate to admit it, but I'm dripping wet right now, and I'm pretty sure he can tell. If he can't, he'll probably figure it out when James starts the take, and I rub my wet crotch against his hard cock.

"Are you two ready for this?" James calls out, and we confirm we are. "Okay, Lexi, we're going to shoot mostly from behind or slightly to the side. We're going to do our best to keep your breasts out of the shot, and they certainly won't be in the final footage."

"Thank you," I tell him.

"Okay, action!"

The song starts playing, and almost at once, Nate and I repeat our performance from earlier. I'm on top of him and grinding against his hardness while he kisses me passionately. He leaves one hand underneath my panties on my bare skin, and I'm aching for him to slide it around to my front and finger me with it, but I know that would be going way too far. The thought of it is enough to topple me into orgasm, and Nate rolls me onto my back as we continue kissing, which hopefully covers my shaking body.

This time, James has us continue for longer than he did last time, and I wrap my legs around Nate's waist as he continues to stroke his erection up and down my covered slit. The friction between us drives me wild, and I'm coming again as the guys are singing the outro for the song.

"Cut!" James calls, and Nate rolls off me. "You two stay there, and we'll check this with Dante. It's easier than getting you in and out of bed, Lexi."

I nod, and there's no sound between us except for our panting breath.

"Was that as good for you as it was for me, Sexy?" Nate asks me.

I can't even pretend to him that I didn't enjoy that, so I don't respond at all.

"This is one of the best days of my life," he whispers in a husky voice.

He slides his hand slowly from my waist, up my torso, toward my breast. I don't move at all, and he stares into my eyes.

"Tell me no, Lexi," Nate says quietly, but I don't do it.

He places his hand on my breast and slowly strokes across my nipple with his thumb as he slips his other hand under the band of my underwear, which causes me to gasp quietly when he finds my clit.

I know that I should tell him to stop, but I can't bring myself to do it. Instead, I widen my legs slightly, allowing him even better access, and he smiles triumphantly at me when he slips two fingers inside me.

The song is coming to the end of the first chorus as the other men watch the video back, and I know we don't have long for this. Nate begins thrusting his fingers in and out of me, making me wish more than ever that it was his cock, and he begins to rub my clit with his thumb while he does. I can't stop myself from brushing my fingers against his erection as waves of pleasure crash over my body.

His erection is thick and fills my hand when I close my grasp over him to stroke him slowly, and he groans quietly. This sound breaks me, and another orgasm hits me, but there's no music or kissing to cover it this time. I bite my lip hard and stare into his eyes as my body shakes. Nate pulls his fingers out of me and places his hand on my waist again, as though nothing happened.

Nate gives me a satisfied smile and whispers, "I'm going to masturbate tonight while thinking about your 'O' face."

I blush but don't respond to that because I think that I have just royally fucked up. As the song finishes, I realize that my hand is still on his very hard cock, and I pull it back, which causes Nate to smirk at me.

"Okay, guys, that was great. I don't think we could get it better. Lexi, you've been amazing, and you're done for the day. Nate, we've still got several more shots to get for you."

Nate looks over at James and smiles, "Sure, not a problem."

Dante walks over to us with the robes, and I put mine on quickly and leave the set without saying anything more to Nate. I can't believe what I just did, on camera, but especially off. His words are ringing in my ears, and I've never felt this turned on in my life.

Dante's finished shooting for the day, as well, and we head to my Tesla. He got a lift here with Logan this morning.

"Do you want me to drive, Angel?" he asks me.

"Sure."

Once we're in the privacy of the car and driving home, Dante speaks again. "Did you enjoy today?"

"I don't know," I tell him, feeling guilty about the extra orgasm I allowed Nate to give me after the last take.

"I think you did," he smiles at me. "It's okay if you did, Angel. I told you to do it, and it was hot as hell."

I consider for a second keeping the last orgasm a secret, but I know I can't, so I confess to him, "Nate gave me another orgasm while you guys were watching the last take."

"Did he really?" Dante asks me, and I bite my lip as I nod. "Well, points for honesty, I guess. But I didn't tell you that you could have that one, so I think I'll spank you when we get home."

"How many times?" I ask.

We stop at a set of lights, and Dante leans over to kiss me roughly as he reaches between my legs, finding my wetness and stroking my clit before the light turns green again, and he stops abruptly.

He grins at me as we start to drive off from the lights, "Ten times. Then, I'm going to fuck the shit out of you like I've wanted to do all day."

Chapter Four
Being Shared

*I*t's Saturday evening, and I'm still reeling from the video shoot yesterday. Last night, I dreamed about having sex with Nate, and I feel guilty as hell for that. This morning we started a no-clothes weekend. That's when I don't wear any clothes all weekend and do whatever Dante tells me to do. He uses me for sex when and where he sees fit, and I basically spend the entire weekend feeling like a bitch in heat because I'm so horny.

I walk over to Dante, where he sits on the sofa, playing a video game. I'm carrying a cold can of Coke for him. My elbow is at my side, and it's balanced on the palm of my hand, which I hold out flat in front of me. When I reach him, I stand still nearby and hold the can out as I wait for him to take it.

Dante continues playing the game, ignoring me as I stand there. He's playing a race car game, and the screen tells me that he's on lap eight of twelve in this race track. I sigh mentally, but not out loud, and hope that it's a short track.

It takes Dante about five minutes to finish the race, and he comes third, seeming annoyed at himself for not doing better. When the race is done, he puts the controller down on the coffee table in front of himself and finally looks up at me.

Sian Ceinwen

"Good work, Angel."

He stands, and I continue to hold the can out for him, and I hope that he takes it soon because my arm is kind of starting to hurt. He doesn't. He walks around me in a circle, taking in my naked body.

"So beautiful," he says with a reverent sigh when he reaches his place in front of me again.

He takes the can from my hand, and it's a massive relief.

"Look at me, Angel."

I turn my face up to look at him and resist the urge to smile at him. He's the most beautiful man in the world. He's currently wearing jeans and a t-shirt, but I know that under those clothes is a rock-hard, muscled body, and I ache to feel him inside me.

Dante opens the can and takes a sip, then he reaches forward with it in his hand and places it against my left nipple. I gasp at the shock of the cold can against me, and he grins.

"Naughty, Angel. No reactions unless I tell you it's okay."

He twists my other nipple painfully, and my pussy aches with arousal. Pleasure and pain. Dante and I are all about it. He takes another sip of his drink, then places the can against the nipple he just twisted. I know better than to react this time, and he seems pleased.

"Stand with your legs shoulder-width apart, Angel."

I step across to do this, and I'm certain of what's coming, so I'm not surprised when he places the cold can against my clit. He holds it there for a solid ten seconds, and I want to moan, but I manage to keep it in. Dante brings the can back up to his lips and takes another sip before he turns it around and places it against my lips.

"Drink," he instructs me as he tips it up, and some of the liquid enters my mouth and makes its way down my throat. He smiles and places the can down on a coaster on the coffee table, then steps forward and kisses me while he softly rubs my clit and finally says, "You can react now, Angel."

I immediately moan so incredibly loudly. I moan to release the

41

tension from not being able to react until this point, and Dante laughs. He continues to rub my clit until waves of pleasure crash against my body, and I'm so close to orgasm when he stops.

"Please, Honey," I groan.

The same way that he calls me 'Angel' in public, I call him 'Honey.' Our pet names for each other can have dual meanings, but he knows that calling him Honey on occasions like this one is just as good as me calling him 'Sir.'

He simply steps away from me, sits back down on the sofa with a wicked grin, and says, "Maybe later."

I'm frustrated, tense, and my whole body is aching for him to make me come.

"Sit down on the coffee table, Angel."

I sit next to his can of Coke on the coffee table and face him. I spread my legs wide as I do so, and Dante goes back to his video game. He plays another race, then pauses it when his phone buzzes with a text. He looks at it, grins wickedly, and shows it to me. It's from Nate.

Hey dude. Can I come over? Fucked a chick, and I'm bored. Want to get drunk and play video games?

"I should definitely tell him that 'yes, he can.'" Dante smirks at me.

I'm not sure what the hell is going on or if I'm ready to see Nate again so soon, but fuck, I'd love an orgasm before he comes around.

"I'll have to put some clothes on," I laugh nervously.

Dante raises an eyebrow at me. "Will you?"

"Yes, Honey." I roll my eyes and say, "I cannot answer the door to Nathaniel Walker in the nude. He'll keel over and die."

"It's not like he didn't see plenty yesterday, anyway. The only reason I'm going to let you put clothes on, Angel, is because I want Nate's consent before you get naked."

My jaw drops open when he shows me the screen of his phone where he's written a reply to Nate.

Sure. Come over ASAP. Should be a good night.

"Let's go find you something to wear, Angel," Dante tells me, then starts to walk to our bedroom.

I follow him silently, in slight shock. He didn't mean that about me getting naked in front of Nate. But why am I wet and near orgasm at the thought? I mean, Nate is hot as shit, but that would fuck up our friendship for sure. Nobody can talk about it. I can't even run this by Dante because *that* would mean acknowledging it.

Yet, Dante goes specifically to the sex clothes section of our wardrobe. He pulls out a dress that is so tight and light-colored that it's practically see-through whenever I put it on. Some outfits here are nothing but mesh, so it's actually one of the tamer options.

"What are you doing?" I ask as my heart thuds rapidly in my chest and I blink at him.

"You said that you needed clothes, so I'm getting you something to wear." His eyes glint dangerously, and I know not to question further, but I do it anyway.

"We can't do this, Dante." I bite my lip, nerves threatening to overwhelm me.

"You will call me Honey," he says sternly, "and if Nate has a problem with it, he will leave. If you have a problem with it, you can safeword. You know that. I don't do anything without consent. Arms up."

He pulls the dress over my head, and when it's on, I'm breathing heavily.

"Are you going to safeword, Angel?" Dante raises an eyebrow at me.

The dress barely even covers my ass, and I'm wet as fuck. I don't know why the idea of parading around like this in front of Nate is turning me on so much, but it certainly is. Maybe it's because I need an orgasm so badly right now.

"Probably not, but I can't guarantee it. Are you trying to fuck our friendship with Nate right now?" I ask him.

Dante laughs and steps forward before he reaches a hand under the dress and swipes a finger through my dripping slit.

"I'm trying to fuck something, that's for sure. You're wet as hell, Angel. Is it me or Nate that's got you so turned on?"

"You," I breathe heavily. "Of course."

"If you say so," he says with a wicked grin as he leads me out to the living room again and instructs me to sit back down on the coffee table.

Is it just Dante that has me so turned on? This night is turning out nothing like I was expecting. I thought we would fuck, chill out, fuck again. I mean, it was supposed to be a no clothes weekend.

Now, though, I'm still feeling like a bitch in heat, but I'd be lying if I said that I'm not running through some pretty amazing scenarios in my head. Ones that involve two cocks inside me at the same time.

After about ten minutes, there's a knock at our door, and Dante looks up from his game to grin evilly at me. "You'd better go get that, Angel."

I nod my consent and walk slowly to the door as Nate knocks again.

Here we go.

I open the door and say breathlessly, "Hi, Nate."

He blinks at me, looking taken aback as he gives my body a once over. I've watched him do this to women many times. Hell, he's even done it to me before, but I've never seen him unable to respond when he did. The dress has a very low neckline, with plenty of cleavage spilling out from it. Meanwhile, my nipples are hard and clearly visible through the dress' stretchy fabric, and the dress stops barely a quarter of an inch below my crotch.

I stare back at Nate, bombarded with memories of him making me come yesterday. His features are so refined that he could only ever be described as beautiful, and he stands in front of me, wearing jeans and a t-shirt. He exudes sex at all times, and right now, I'm hyper-aware of his sexual magnetism.

"Are you coming, Nate?" Dante calls from the sofa. "Or are you going to stand there all day and stare at Lexi?"

Nate's eyes are dark, and his breathing rate has increased. He's never looked at me like this before, but I'll be fucked if I don't know that he's thinking about having sex with me right now. He looks like he wants to throw me down to the ground and have his way with me. I'd be lying if I said that I don't want him to do exactly that, too.

I step aside, and my juices run down my inner thigh as I do. I don't think I've ever been this wet before.

Nate strides over to the sofa and stands over Dante, frowning at him intensely. "What are you doing, Dante Sullivan?"

"What do you mean?" Dante looks up at him and gives him an innocent smile.

"I thought we were going to play video games, not Lexi." His voice has a strange edge to it that I've never heard before.

"Which would you prefer?" Dante asks. "I can certainly tell you which is more fun. Come here, Angel."

I'm still standing by the door, but this is a familiar instruction, and I immediately follow the command by walking over to him, where I find myself standing next to Nate. My breathing is shallow, and Nate's is as well.

"Sit on the coffee table," Dante instructs me, and I bite my lip as I take my seat and spread my legs the way I normally do. Dante gives me an approving smile, then says, "Take a seat, Nate, I'll race you."

Nate frowns and sits down on the sofa, then gasps when he sees me, "What the fuck, Dante?"

"It's a nice view, isn't it?" Dante says casually.

Nate stares at me with his mouth open. I see him simply look at my pussy, seemingly unable to do anything but stare at me.

"Are we going to play?" Dante asks him.

Nate just continues to look at me, then finally looks at Dante and shakes his head in apparent amazement. "Apparently so."

He takes the controller that Dante is holding out to him, but he's shit during their race. Probably because he looks over at me repeatedly, and I'm clearly a distraction for him.

"So," Dante says, after he well and truly wins the race, "all I need to do to beat you is have Lexi display her pussy for you. I should try it sometime when we're playing pool."

Nate grins at him as he says, "I hate you, Dante Sullivan, and that is one fine fucking pussy. Of course, I was distracted."

"Would you like a closer look? It tastes just as good as it looks."

"Are you serious?" Nate's eyebrows shoot upward.

Dante laughs. "Yeah, what did you think this was about? I'm sharing Lexi with you tonight."

Nate breathes out slowly through his teeth. "Why?"

"It seemed like you two were enjoying yourselves yesterday, and I'm feeling generous."

"You're not worried I'll steal her from you?" Nate smirks at him.

"Lexi is a grown woman with a mind of her own. You can't 'steal' her," Dante says. "I have no doubt that she'll remain mine, but I thought it might be nice to share my toy with my friend."

Nate's erection is obvious in his jeans while they have this discussion, and I desperately want his cock in my mouth. Shit. I've only ever fucked Dante, but now I'm going to fuck Nate, and I can't wait.

Nate moves off the sofa and kneels in front of me. I look up and catch Dante's eye as Nate looks at my pussy. Dante seems exultant in showing me off to his friend, the one who's always wanted me. Fuck. Does this mean he's going to make me fuck Ash or Logan sometime?

I look down at the man who has spent a decade teasing and flirting with me and realize that one of my deepest, darkest fantasies is about to come true. I also realize, with some degree of guilt, that I'm in love with Nate as well. I realize this as Nate inhales deeply and finally looks up at me.

I look down into his eyes as he whispers, "You smell amazing, Lexi."

"Thank you."

I want to kiss him. I want to fuck him. I want to tell him that I love him. I want him in every hole in my body.

He leans forward and slowly licks my wet slit from bottom to top, and I can't stop myself from gasping. I look at Dante in alarm, and he laughs at me.

"You can have reactions for him, Angel. I want him to see how you can be."

Nate slowly starts to rub my clit with his fingers, and I'm moaning now that I'm allowed to, even as he turns his head to look at Dante, "What the fuck is your deal, dude? Is this some kind of Dom/sub thing?"

"Yeah, it is," Dante admits with a shrug.

"I fucking knew it," Nate laughs, then turns to look at me. "Hot as hell and feisty as shit Alexandra Sullivan doing anything she's told to do? God, Dante, you live an amazing life. I'm jealous."

"No need to be jealous, Nate. She's yours to play with, too."

I don't know what this means, and Nate doesn't ask for clarification. He uses his thumbs to pull apart my labia, and he stares at me again. I start to squirm because it's uncomfortable to have someone stare into my vagina like this, and Nate smirks.

"What's wrong, Lexi?"

"This is weird, Nate," I tell him honestly.

In answer, he leans forward and thrusts his tongue in and out of me twice. I'm shocked because I wasn't expecting it, but his tongue feels good. Strong and muscular like the rest of him. Then he pulls his head back and looks into my eyes again.

"There is nothing weird about me wanting to appreciate the beautiful artwork that I see before me. You're amazing, Lexi. Your pussy looks as good as it tastes, and I want to commit this shit to memory because if Dante never lets me fuck you again, I'm going to be jerking off to the thought of it for the rest of my goddamn life."

Dante chuckles quietly behind him, and I look into his eyes as Nate leans forward again and begins eating me out. I see how hard Dante is, and I moan loudly, but I can't stop the name that falls from my lips.

"Nate."

In response, he moans into my pussy as he continues to eat me out.

"I think he likes hearing you say his name, Angel," Dante grins as he begins unbuttoning his jeans and pulls out his erection. "You should do it again."

I literally moan Nate's name about fifty times in a row as he makes me come twice. It's the only word that I say as Dante begins stroking his cock, and the only reason I stop moaning it is that Dante walks over to me and puts his cock in my mouth.

Nate keeps eating me, and I'm in pure ecstasy. I can barely handle the sensations that he is giving me, mixed with the feeling of giving Dante head. Dante thrusts his cock in and out of my mouth as Nate licks and sucks my clit while pushing three fingers in and out of me as well. After some time, Dante pulls himself away from my mouth, and I moan softly, wanting to suck him again.

"How about we take this to the bedroom, Nate?" Dante asks our friend.

Nate pulls his head back and looks up at Dante. He still has three fingers inside me, and he begins to rub across my clit with his thumb while simultaneously making a 'come here' motion with his fingers across my g-spot.

I come loudly while yelling, "Nate."

He turns his head to grin at me, continuing what he's doing, then looks back at Dante and says with a smirk, "Sure, why not. Do I get to tie her up in there or something?"

"If you want to." Dante shrugs. "We have tie-down points and rope."

Nate looks back at me, and my entire body is shaking now. It feels like my clit is on fire because it's so fucking sensitive. He pulls his fingers out of me and sucks his pointer finger clean before he places his middle and ring fingers near my mouth.

"So fucking tasty, Lexi. Clean my fingers."

I open my mouth and suck his fingers, tasting myself, and Nate looks pleased. As we make our way to the bedroom, I wonder if Nate is going to take Dante up on his offer of tying me down. I don't want him to. I want to be free to feel and explore while we fuck this first time, but I'll do it if it's what he wants.

"Am I getting the rope?" Dante asks as we reach the bed.

Nate walks around to stand in front of me, grabs my hand, and places it on his cock. "Nah, I want her to use her hands. But I can't pretend that the idea of Lexi tied up and free for me to use as I see fit isn't a tempting one. Again, I'm jealous as shit of you, dude."

"Maybe some other time, then," Dante says casually.

I'm stroking Nate and fucking loving that I get to do this, when he says to Dante with a warning tone, "You'd better not be fucking with me. I assumed this would be a one-off deal."

"Hey, if she's down for it and you're down for it, I don't see any reason that this can't happen again. On your knees, Angel."

Dante directs these last words to me, and I know it's a weird flex. He's showing Nate that I will do whatever he tells me to do. I also know, without being told, that today Nate can tell me to do whatever he wants me to do as well. I drop to my knees in front of Nate.

"Worship his cock, Angel," Dante instructs.

I do exactly that. I put it in my mouth and go to town. Nate is big, bigger than Dante, but not by a lot. I get a sore jaw giving Dante head, and that little bit of extra girth makes it even harder with Nate. I don't dare to stop, though. I touch my nose to his stomach and revel in the feeling of having my access to oxygen cut off.

Nate is making all the right sounds, the ones that I love to hear when I'm sucking Dante. I look up at him, and he is looking down at me as though all of his fantasies have come true.

I keep going for a long time, and I think that my jaw might become dislocated by the time Dante gives me some relief by informing Nate, "You have to tell her to stop, Nate, or she'll suck you till you blow in her mouth and keep sucking until you blow again."

"Shit." Nate looks shocked as he looks down at me. "Stop, Lexi. Stop."

I take him out of my mouth and breathe a sigh of relief, thankful as shit that Dante could tell how badly I was hurting. I rub my jaw a little, then open and close my mouth a few times.

"I didn't know. I'm so sorry. I didn't mean to hurt you." Nate looks guilty.

"It's okay," Dante tells him. "If we keep doing this, you'll learn. Lexi is very well trained. Take your clothes off and get on the bed, Angel."

I remove my dress and put it in the clothes hamper. I'd never dare to drop it on the floor, or Dante would spank me. Then, I climb onto the bed and lie with my head on the pillows, watching these two beautiful men as they both look at me with lust-filled eyes.

"Do you want her pussy or her ass?" Dante asks Nate.

"Are you fucking for real?" Nate gasps.

"Sure," Dante says and shrugs. "You're the guest. It's only fair that you get to choose."

"I can fuck her in the ass?" Nate asks, seeming shocked.

Dante laughs and says, "Yeah, if you want to."

"No, I want her pussy. I want to fuck her for the first time with natural lubrication. If there's a next time, I'm taking her ass, though."

"Okay, well, you guys might as well get started then. I'll grab the lube."

Nate climbs onto the bed next to me and hesitates before saying, "Um, can I kiss her, Dante?"

"Of course. Shit, I didn't think I'd have to tell you that. It's not like you didn't have your tongue down her throat all day yesterday." Dante smirks at him.

Nate kisses me, and it's kind of amazing. Unlike yesterday when everyone was watching us, this is intimate and beautiful and loving. I can't pretend to myself that I hadn't fantasized about it before yesterday, either. He's got amazing lips. They're big and soft, and his tongue explores my mouth. He reaches between us and strokes my clit again while I moan into his mouth.

He's still kissing me when Dante comes back from the bathroom with the lube and laughs at us. "Having fun, guys?"

Nate stops kissing me and says, "A little too much fun. I suppose we should probably fuck her now."

He lies on his back, and Dante hands him a condom that Nate opens and rolls onto his cock before I slide myself onto his erection. I've never been with anyone else, and I'm amazed at how this is the same and yet totally different from being with Dante. I look into Nate's blue eyes, and I know that I've fallen for him. I stop myself from telling him that I love him because he knows that already, and if I say it, it might break the spell of today.

"Kiss him again, Angel," Dante instructs me.

I lean down and go back to kissing Nate. He's deep inside me, and he holds me tight to him while we kiss. Cold lube drops onto my ass before Dante uses a finger to push it inside me. He keeps doing this, making sure there is plenty of lubricant in my ass and that he's able to push two, and then three fingers inside me easily before he positions himself near my entrance.

"Are you ready, Angel?" he asks.

I stop kissing Nate and say, "Yes, Honey."

Then he pushes himself inch by inch inside of me. I'm so incredibly full. Full of Nate and full of Dante. This is the best fucking feeling in the world. Once Dante is inside, he slips in and out slowly, which Nate takes as his cue to do the same. They move in and out of me in rhythm.

Nate kisses me and plays with my breasts, then pulls one into his mouth, and I moan his name again. Eventually, Dante shoots his load into my ass and then pulls out. Nate grabs my hips and fucks me harder. I can feel the cum dripping out of me and onto the sheets and wonder if Dante will spank me later for making a mess.

Finally, Nate comes deep inside me and moans my name, which sounds glorious on his lips. I collapse on top of him, and he kisses my cheek as we both pant for breath.

From behind us, Dante says, "So, Nate. Glad you sent me a text tonight?"

"Fuck, yes, I'm glad. Holy shit, Dante. That was the best thing I've ever experienced."

I'm still lying on top of Nate, and I can feel his cock inside of me. He's so thick, and I feel amazingly full. His cock jerks inside me. I squeak, then squeeze my pelvic muscles around him, and I love the sound of him groaning when I do it.

This is pure bliss. I didn't realize how much I needed Nate in my life, but I'm fucking in love with him, and a part of me that I didn't know was wounded has been healed by getting to fuck him. I lift my head and kiss him again, tenderly this time. Trying to convey the love that I'm feeling for him and also unsure what any of this means.

He kisses me back, and I'm overwhelmed by how good it feels. My lips part, and his tongue is expertly dancing with mine as he rubs my back before he grabs hold of my hair and holds my head still to continue kissing me. This is the best feeling in the world.

Dante chuckles from behind me, "I'll go shower. You two have fun."

Wow, I'd actually forgotten about Dante for a moment, and I feel guilty. I love him as intensely and deeply as ever, but I also love Nate, and Dante doesn't seem to mind that he's literally still inside me right now.

He walks out of the room, and Nate quickly disposes of the condom before he comes back to the bed with me. He pulls me tight against him, and I fucking love it. He kisses me again, and it feels amazing. I just want to fuck him every which way till Sunday, and I don't want him to ever not be inside me.

Our kiss ends, and he pulls his head back to look at me. "What the fuck is going on tonight, Lexi?"

His eyes are so blue and beautiful and full of love. I know that he has half of my heart while the other half remains firmly in Dante's possession.

"I love you, Nate," I confess to him.

"Say that again."

"I love you." I kiss him after I repeat what I said. "Don't you have something to say to me?" I raise an eyebrow at him, and he laughs.

"Yes, Lexi. I love you, too. But what the fuck? Dante is literally in the other room. Why are we saying this right now?"

I'm not sure exactly why, but I know that Dante is okay with this. I just know that my Honey would not have walked out of the room if he was not okay with us loving each other. Hell, none of this would have happened.

"Because it's true?" I ask and reach between us to stroke his cock with my hand.

He groans and lifts a hand to twist my nipple, and I can't stop myself from gasping loudly. "Lexi, do you have any idea of the things that I want to do to you?"

"I could probably take a guess," I smirk at him. "I've been thinking about them a lot since yesterday, and I'm pretty sure that I want you to do them, too."

I think he only does vanilla sex, but even though I love my Dom/sub relationship with Dante, I already know that I don't crave that with Nate. An equal relationship is what I want from him while still submitting to Dante every chance I get.

Dante walks back into the room and looks at us. "Did you two tell each other that you're in love yet, or what?"

Nate's eyes widen in shock, and I laugh, then answer, "Yes, we did."

"Good, I thought that might happen."

"What the hell is going on?" Nate shakes his head.

"Well, Nate. Here's the thing. I'm pretty sure that everyone knows you're in love with Lexi. I, however, have known for some time that Lexi is in love with you."

I'm astounded. I mean, I suppose Dante wouldn't have done this without having a reason, but I do wonder how long he's known.

"Really? I didn't realize it until tonight." I stare at him in amazement that he could've known this when I didn't know it myself.

Dante smiles. "Yeah, I know, Angel. Seeing you two together, it's soothing for me. I love you both, and knowing that it hurts you not to be together, I don't want to be the thing that's stopping you. I hate that I get to have you, and Nate doesn't. I hate that you get to have me and not Nate. I don't know how this will work, but we'll figure it out."

Nate kisses me again, and his cock is stiff against me as he reaches a hand up to play with my breast. I moan into his mouth, and I can feel his smile as we kiss.

"I'm going to go play my game some more. You two have fun," Dante says and walks out of the room.

"I can't believe this is happening." Nate breaks our kiss to tell me this and shakes his head as if he's amazed.

"I can," I say, then roll him back onto his back.

I look around to see where Dante has left the box of condoms on the side table. I grab one and roll it onto Nate's erection before I straddle him, and he groans.

"I'm going to ride you this time, Nathaniel Walker. I'm not going to lie. I've fucking fantasized about this before."

"Are you shitting me?" he gasps.

"No. I have. I shoved the fantasies deep down and only brought them out when I was *really* itching for an orgasm. I told myself they were just fantasies, but"—I squeeze my muscles around his rock-hard cock—"I realize now that it's something I've wanted for a long, long time. Shooting the video yesterday probably made this an inevitability. Did you end up masturbating last night?" I ask him as I begin to move back and forth on him.

"Yes, and again this morning," he admits. "Then I pretended it was you while I fucked some woman I met at a coffee shop. None of that came close to scratching my itch or comparing at all to the real thing."

I start to ride him harder, and it's amazing. He slides in and out of me, filling me completely, and he's staring up at me in awe. He starts to play with my breasts while I fuck him, and he tweaks one of my nipples, which causes me to moan. He reaches a hand between us to find my clit, and I gasp as he rubs it. I'm feeling so fucking sensitive after the very recent sex session.

"Are you okay, Lexi?"

"Y-yes," I manage to reply.

"Are you sure?" he rubs my clit in slow circles, and I'm wetter than Niagara Falls.

"Um, yes."

"You don't seem sure." He strokes my clit faster as my breathing rate intensifies. "Say my name, Lexi."

"Nate." I love being able to moan his name like this.

"Say it again," he grins, and at once, I moan his name repeatedly, like I did earlier once I was given permission to do it.

I shudder in ecstasy as an orgasm hits me, and I collapse forward on him, then kiss him. He holds me to him and keeps kissing me as we continue to fuck. He pumps in and out of me until he eventually blows his load inside me, and I come a final time on his cock.

"I love you, Lexi," he whispers to me.

"I love you, too, Nate."

Chapter Five

Having a Ball

ate kisses me as I lie in his arms in our bedroom. It's been four weeks since we shot the music video, and when it was released last week, the internet did go wild. Rumors are running rampant about us having an affair, but I don't even care because I'm so happy.

Two weeks ago, Nate moved into Dante's and my apartment, and we have our own bedroom, which is where we're lying in bed at the moment.

"I love you so much, Nate," I smile at him.

"I love you, too. It still feels so weird actually getting to say that to you," he replies.

I kiss him and slide my hand down his torso to begin stroking his morning erection while I do, and I break our kiss to make my way under the covers, which causes Nate to laugh.

"I don't think you love me at all. You just love sucking my cock."

I grin at him, "Yup, that's exactly it. You just happen to be attached to the most perfect cock in the world. Aren't you lucky?"

"I guess I am. Particularly since I get to put it in you on a daily basis now," he smirks at me.

He's not wrong. We've been fucking like rabbits since we got together, and Dante's joked that we're trying to make up for lost time. I've still spent plenty of nights with Dante, though, being spanked, tied up, and fucked by him. All in all, I feel satisfied as a pig in shit with this new arrangement.

I place my lips over Nate and suck him until he's as hard as steel, and my jaw is aching before I slide myself onto him.

"Mmm, you feel so good, Lexi."

I lean down to kiss him as I slide up and down on him. Our tongues intertwine, and he raises a hand to my breast to tweak and play with my nipple.

I break our kiss to moan at him, "Oh god, Nate."

"Do you like that, Sexy?"

I nod as I raise myself up to ride him. Nate got STD tested as soon as we got together, and he was negative. Because of my IUD, we don't have to use condoms anymore, and I love the feeling of having him bare inside me. Nate lifts his other hand to play with my other breast. He moves his head to one of my nipples, licking and sucking it while he tweaks my other nipple. I'm in ecstasy and feeling deliciously full with him.

As I continue to fuck him, he reaches between us to find my clit. I pant for breath as he rubs back and forth. I can feel my orgasm approaching, and I moan his name loudly.

"Nate."

He removes his mouth from my breast and lays back on the bed to watch me with lust-filled eyes as I grind myself hard on his cock and my orgasm hits me.

He continues to stroke my clit, and I gasp but keep going as my pussy clenches his cock through my ecstasy. When my orgasm fades, Nate grabs my hips and bounces me up and down on him.

I bite my lip because I'm so sensitive after I've come, but I love watching him as his face screws tight and his cock jerks when he comes inside me.

I collapse forward onto him, panting for breath, and he wraps his arms around me as he strokes my back gently.

"That was so good," I pant before I kiss his neck, which is salty with sweat.

"You're telling me," he says, and he jerks his cock inside me.

I squeal and laugh. "Cassie's going to be here soon. You probably shouldn't be balls deep in me when she gets here."

"Shouldn't I?" He gives me a wicked grin. "I think I should be balls deep in you at all times, Alexandra Sullivan."

"Maybe you should be."

I move my head down and kiss him. It's a luxurious kiss, slow and loving, with a million things passing between us. I'm so lucky to have him in my life, and I can't believe that I get to have him like this now.

We kiss for a long time before I slide off him, and we head to the bathroom. We shower together, and I clean off first before Nate gets under the water. He strokes his cock under the spray and raises an eyebrow at me.

"Want to get on your knees before I put soap on my cock?"

I grin at him. "You know me so well."

He holds my chin in his fingers and presses his lips against mine. He explores my mouth with his tongue while he reaches between us to stroke my wet clit.

Then he breaks our kiss and lets my face go as he says, "I know you're never happier than when you have a cock in your mouth."

I drop to my knees on the hard tiles and smile at his semi-hard cock. I use my tongue to lick him from the base of his cock to the head, and he groans.

"I'm probably not going to come again so soon, but I very much enjoy fucking your mouth anyway."

In answer, I wrap my lips around his glorious cock. It's so good, and I love hearing him moan my name while I give him head. The water sprays on my face now and again, and Nate leans down to play with my breasts. I reach a hand between my legs to rub my clit as he does, and I moan my pleasure onto his cock. I keep doing this until I come, then pull him out of my mouth so I can moan in a more satisfyingly loud way.

Nate laughs as he looks down at me. "I fucking love watching you come, Lexi."

"I want you to come down my throat," I moan.

"I can't guarantee it, but I'll see what I can do for you, Sexy. You'll tell me if you want me to stop, yeah?"

Even though we're only vanilla, Nate seems to have learned that he needs to be aware that I'll sometimes go further in sex acts than he expects, and after that first day, he's been worried about hurting me.

I nod my head. "Yeah, I will."

"Open your mouth, then, and give it your best shot."

I grin at him as I happily follow his instructions. He slides his cock into my mouth, and I suck him for a few minutes before he holds my face in his hands and begins to move in and out of my mouth.

My jaw aches, but I love it, and he fucks my mouth so long that my knees are aching from being on the hard tile when he finally comes down my throat. I swallow his offering and use my tongue to ensure his cock is entirely clean before I stand up and kiss him passionately.

"I love you, Nate. Thank you."

"I'm pretty sure *I* should be thanking *you*," he laughs. "I love you so much."

We get out of the shower and dry off, laughing together as we head back to the bedroom. Nate puts on a pair of jeans and a t-shirt. I don't have any clothes in this room, so I kiss him and head back to the master bedroom where Dante is relaxed back in bed looking at his phone and, if I had to guess, I'd say he'll be reading the news.

"Morning, Honey," I greet him with a smile.

"Hi, Angel."

I climb into the bed with him, and he wraps his arms around me. I rest my head against his chest and listen to his heart beating there. I've always felt at home in Dante's arms, and a sense of peace and love comes over me from being here with him.

"When do you need to leave?" he asks me.

"Cassie should be here soon, so I need to get dressed and be ready to go when she gets here."

"Makes sense. I'll let you get ready, then. You really need some clothes in yours and Nate's room," he laughs.

"But then I'd have no excuse to come in here and see my Honey," I joke.

"You need an excuse to come see me now, huh?" He raises an eyebrow at me.

"Well, no. But I like having one anyway."

I reach up and kiss him as he squeezes me tightly. I rest my head on his chest again for a few more seconds and then sigh.

"Okay, I need to get dressed."

Dante kisses the top of my head and says, "Yes, you do. I'll play with you when you get home, though."

A dart of arousal heads straight to my crotch, and I bite my lip. Dante's eyes darken, and he gives me a sexy smile.

"Do you like that idea, Angel?"

"Yes, Honey," I say, and his cock stiffens against me as I do.

He kisses me thoroughly, tweaks my nipple as his tongue explores my mouth, and then ends our kiss with a sexy laugh.

"You should go get dressed, Angel. If you stay here much longer, I might tie you to the bed, and that would be awkward when Cassie gets here."

I bite my lip again as my pussy aches with the need to be fucked by Dante, even though I've already been fucked by Nate this morning.

Dante looks at me and gives me a wicked grin. "That wasn't an order, but if it were, you'd be punished, Angel."

"Maybe you should punish me," I taunt him, and I know that I'm playing with fire.

He looks at me for a few seconds, then says, "Bend over the bed, Angel."

I scramble out of bed and bend over it with my ass and pussy on display for him when he walks behind me. I think I might be about to get fucked when Dante walks into our closet instead.

It's behind me, but I can hear that's where he's gone. I also hear him open a drawer and close it again before he comes back. He could've gotten anything. Our sex toys are in there, as well as our clothes and some storage stuff. It's probably a sex toy of some kind, but I have no clue what, and I can't turn around to see. When he comes back, he stops just behind me, and I'm panting for breath and so incredibly turned on right now.

"I really do love this view," he murmurs in a husky voice. "I can't wait to play with you later."

Disappointment floods through me. That means he's not going to fuck me right now. In which case, I'm curious to know what he has planned for me. It could be a spanking, but I don't think so. I hear him drop to his knees, and then he pushes three fingers inside me, and I can't stop myself from moaning.

He swiftly smacks my ass before he says in a stern voice, "You know better, Angel."

I'm dripping wet now. I can feel the juices running down my thigh, and the ache in my pussy is intense. Something cold and hard runs along my wet slit until it reaches my opening. I realize what it is when Dante pushes the first weighted Ben Wa ball inside me. The second one in the set follows it, and I'm completely filled.

It's *utterly* unsatisfying, and if I know Dante like I think I do, this is going to be keeping me on edge all afternoon.

"Stand up, Angel."

I stand up but remain facing the bed.

"Turn and look at me."

I can barely keep my breathing rate normal, forcing myself to display as few signs of my arousal as I can when I look at Dante. His cock is stiff in the gray sweatpants he's wearing, and I want it in my mouth.

Dante watches my gaze travel to his crotch, and he chuckles. "Oh no, Angel. You don't get my cock for a long time. Go get dressed. You can choose whatever you want as long as it's a dress or skirt with a hemline at least two inches above your knees and you're not to wear any underwear. I'll check."

Oh, fucking hell.

I nod and walk toward the closet. As I pass him, Dante reaches out and tweaks one of my nipples painfully. I have to bite my lip to withhold a moan as I walk away from him, and I swallow heavily as I enter the closet because Dante's instruction is going to leave me a mess for my afternoon with Cassie. Probably literally, since I'm going to be wet as fuck with nothing to stop me from doing it.

I pull out a tight red Chanel dress that ends three inches above my knees. It has a halter top and a boned bodice. Most importantly, it's a bodycon dress, so even if there's a gust of wind, I won't be exposed. This means I just have to hope and pray the balls don't drop out of me.

As I pull the dress on, the change in my position causes the weighted balls to move inside me, and I gasp. I'm definitely going to have to keep my reactions in check in front of Cassie.

I pull on a pair of strappy silver heels to go with the dress and grab a red Chanel handbag before I sit at my mirror to do my makeup and hair. By the time I head back into the bedroom, I'm happy with my appearance and have gotten used to the balls moving inside me.

Dante isn't here, so I head out to the living room to find him sitting and talking on the sofa with Nate. When Dante looks up and sees me, he gets a wicked grin on his face.

"Very nice. Come here, Angel."

I walk over to him and stand in front of where he's sitting on the sofa. He places his hands on my thighs just under the hem of the dress and pushes it up to my hips, so my pussy is on display for him. He leans forward and kisses my clit before he sucks it, then swipes his tongue across it, and I have to withhold a moan.

Dante pulls his head back and murmurs, "Go see Nate."

I move over in front of Nate, and he grins up at me before he does the same thing. This time, I moan my pleasure as he uses his tongue to lick my clit.

He pushes a finger inside me and feels one of the balls there before he pulls his head back and laughs. "What is that?"

"Our angel is going to wear some Ben Wa balls out on her trip today," Dante smirks at him.

"You'll definitely have fun with her when she gets back," Nate says, and waves of pleasure flood through me because he's moved his hand up to rub my clit while they talk.

"That's the plan. Let her spend the day horny as fuck and then spend the night with her tied to the bed."

I shiver in anticipation and bite my lip as I moan at the thought and from what Nate's doing to me. He pulls his hand away when Dante says it, though, and I groan softly.

"Well, she's already had an orgasm this morning. I'd better not give her another one if you want her wound up all day."

Nate gives me a shit-eating grin as he pulls my dress back down. I'm wet as hell, and my pussy is aching as he grabs my hand and pulls me down onto his lap before he wraps his arms around me. Nate kisses me passionately before he sets me down into the space between him and Dante on the sofa.

We've only been sitting there for another five minutes or so when there's a knock on the apartment door. Dante goes to answer it, and as he walks away, Nate kisses me again as he reaches under my dress to rub my clit.

"I hope you have a fun day with Cassie," he murmurs in my ear before gently nipping my earlobe with his teeth, and I moan softly.

"If I didn't think Dante would spank me for it, I'd go and get myself off in some bathroom stall while we're out," I groan.

Nate chuckles and quickly sits up, neatly smoothing my dress out as he does, just before Dante and Cassie appear around the corner. Cassie smiles brightly at me, and she looks pretty. She's wearing a white top and a short navy skirt with white heels, and her black hair is in a high ponytail.

"Morning, gorgeous. How are you today?" she asks as she leans down to hug me.

"I'm good," I tell her, trying to focus through my arousal and not give anything away.

I realize with horror that I'm probably sitting too close to Nate, and when Cassie turns to walk over to one of the armchairs, I surreptitiously shift away from him a little. He chuckles under his breath, and heat rushes to my cheeks as Cassie sits facing us.

"You're here early, Nate," she comments with a smile at him.

He shrugs casually and says, "I slept here last night."

It's not a lie, but it's not the whole truth, either. The three of us probably need to have a discussion about how and when we're going to tell Ash, Cassie, and Logan about our new relationship status. I'm not sure exactly how you drop something like this on your friends, though.

"Oh, that's cool. Did you guys go out last night? How come you didn't invite us?" Cassie asks, but she sounds only mildly interested.

"No, we didn't go out. Just stayed here and had a few drinks, then watched a movie together."

So, by 'together' he means just him and me…and by 'a movie' he means a porno.

"Sounds like fun," Cassie says.

"It was," Nate agrees. "Lexi was screaming…"

He gives me a wicked grin, and I try to remember how I would react to his flirty comments in the past.

I give him a playful shove and roll my eyes. "That sounds dirty. It was a horror movie."

Cassie laughs and shakes her head. "Okay, that makes more sense."

"Yes, it does. Shall we go now?" I ask, desperate to get away from Nate and his double entendres.

"Sure." She smiles and stands up from the armchair.

I give Dante a hug and a kiss, then turn to Nate and try to remember how to farewell him in a way that doesn't involve his tongue being down my throat.

I hug him, and he keeps his hands away from my ass but murmurs in my ear, "You were screaming my name in ecstasy, and you know it. Enjoy those balls."

Heat rushes to my cheeks as I stand up. As I do, the balls move position inside me. I squeeze my pussy tight against the aching and also to keep them in place.

We head downstairs to the parking garage under the building and get into my Tesla. I squirm on the seat as one of the balls moves inside me, and Cassie slides into the passenger seat.

"I'm so excited," Cassie says with a smile on her face.

"Me, too. Lunch is booked for twelve-thirty, so we've got plenty of time to do some shopping first."

"Awesome. I want to go to Coach." She looks over at me and asks, "Is that dress Chanel?"

"Good eye." I nod and quickly smile at her. "It's one of my favorites."

"It's gorgeous."

I get a flush of pride because this dress was a present from Nate for my birthday two years ago. It's out of season, but it means so much more to me today than it did back when I got it. Just another sign of how he's loved me for years.

"Thanks."

I don't tell Cassie about who gave it to me because I'm not sure that I should bring up the topic of Nate with her right now. I don't get the option to avoid it, though. By the time we've spent an hour shopping and are sitting at a table in Bar Verde, I've been gawked at by nearly every person we've encountered.

"Well, they all watched you basically screw Nate in that music video last week," Cassie says while wrinkling her nose when I comment on it. "I still can't believe you did that."

"The music video was hot," I point out.

"Yeah, but Nate is gross." Cassie shrugs her shoulders.

She says it so casually, and I'm incredibly offended on his behalf.

"Nate is *not* gross." I glare at her.

She raises her eyebrows and snorts. "Come on, Lexi. How many women has he fucked? Too many to count. He's a walking STD."

My jaw tenses, and I have to work to keep my breathing calm. I know for a fact that Nate is negative because I've seen the medical records to prove it. He was always cautious with his contraception when he was sleeping around because he didn't want to have any accidents anyway. He's certainly *not* a walking STD, and I would *love* to tell Cassie all of that, but I know I can't.

Instead, I say, "They were all consenting women. To my knowledge, he always used protection. There's nothing wrong with people having sex with whomever they want."

I take a sip of my wine as Cassie shrugs at me. "If you say so. I'm just glad Ashton was never like that."

"Ash fucked *plenty* of women before he met you. Maybe not as many as Nate, but he was no pure angel when he wasn't in a relationship."

"Why do you care? The whole world thinks Nate's a slut. It's not like my opinion is any different to everyone else's." She frowns at me.

My jaw tenses, and I bite out, "Nate's my friend. We've all been friends for a very long time. Sorry, but you can't talk shit about my friend and expect me to be okay with it."

There's an awkward silence, and Cassie looks away from me. I pick up my glass and take another sip of my wine as I try to calm down. She has no idea how far past the line she's gone because she has no idea that I'm in love with Nate.

She sighs and says, "Sorry. I didn't mean to offend you, and I didn't think you'd be so touchy about it." She turns to look back at me with a frown on her face. "You guys are so tight, and sometimes I just feel like an interloper. You've got all these in-jokes and stuff, and I know you and Nate are...close."

I bite back a laugh because she has no clue exactly how close we are now. I shift in my seat as I'm reminded of the Ben Wa balls. I've gotten used to their weight inside me, and when I'm not moving around, I can forget they're there.

"We are close. All of us are, but I met the guys when I was seventeen, and we've had a lot of years of being friends. You're not an outsider. We've all welcomed you in, and you're probably my best female friend. But, yeah, we've got years of jokes and stuff because we've been friends for so long. In five years, you'll forget that you ever felt this way." I smile at her.

"You think that Ashton and I will go the distance?" Cassie asks with a smile back at me.

"For sure. He once had a girlfriend for a year, but since then, he hasn't dated anyone longer than a month for years. He's happy with you, and we all love you."

It's true. For the most part, she's slotted nicely into our world, and Ash seems happy, which is all we really care about. I'm still a little annoyed at her for what she said about Nate, but I can't deny that it's definitely the reputation he has. I do wonder how that will change now that he hasn't been going out and fucking tons of women.

We finish up our lunch and head into the women's section of Nordstrom. I squeal with delight when I see the latest collection from Serenity has arrived.

"Oh my god, they're so *gorgeous*," I gush to Cassie as I look through the flowing, colorful designs.

"Absolutely beautiful. You know Heather Fletcher, don't you?" Cassie asks.

I shake my head. "Not really. Well, kind of. Nate's friends with Cruise Control, and I've met them a few times at events, but I don't know them that well myself. Hayden Vega had his wedding at Nate's estate in Napa. Apparently, it was gorgeous. Super small, though. Nate was the only one of us that got an invitation."

"Why don't you stock her line in your stores?" Cassie suggests.

I blink at her and shake my head. "No way. This is *way* too high fashion for me. I'm just a small boutique, and Serenity wouldn't look twice at us being a stockist."

"You never know if you don't ask, though."

"Maybe."

I shrug my shoulders as I pull from a rack a stunning long-sleeved dress that's fitted at the bodice and flares out from the waist.

"I'm going to try this on," I tell Cassie with a smile.

We each grab a few outfits to try on and head to the changing rooms. As I pull my dress up and off over my head, the Ben Wa balls move inside me, and I bite my lip as I clench my pussy tight to keep them in place.

I pull the Serenity dress on and head out of the changing room to see Cassie wearing a lavender jumpsuit.

"Stunning," I gasp as I take her in. "Can you zip me up?"

I turn away from her, and she zips up the dress. I turn to look in the mirror, and it's gorgeous. It's a couple of inches shorter than the dress I wore today, though, and I definitely wouldn't want to wear this in public without underwear on. It's floaty and gorgeous, but even a small gust of wind would leave me exposed.

I grab my phone and snap a picture in the mirror, using my spare hand to lift my hair to the top of my head to see what it would look like in an updo. This move lifts the dress another inch, and I can feel the cool air-conditioned air on my bare pussy.

I snap the picture while trying to control my breathing because Cassie is only a few feet away, then swallow heavily and face away from her before asking, "Can you unzip me?"

"Sure."

She unzips the dress, and I dart back into my changing room. I open my messages to Nate and send him one.

Do you like the way this dress looks on me?

I attach the last picture I took, with me holding my hair up and the skirt riding high. Sure enough, I have a response from Nate by the time I've hung the dress back on its hanger.

Buy it. It'll look great on our bedroom floor.

I laugh and then send him a reply.

I look great on our bedroom floor. Carpet burn for the win.

While I'm naked, I sit on the bench seat opposite the mirror and spread my legs. My pussy is dripping wet, and my nipples are rock hard because I'm horny as hell right now. I bite my lip and stare into the camera lens in the mirror as I take a picture of myself.

I open my messages to Dante and send him the pic along with a message.

I can't wait to come home and see you, Honey.

It's only a second before my phone starts buzzing, and Dante's name is on the screen. I swallow heavily and answer quietly because I'm aware that Cassie will be able to hear the conversation, along with anyone else who comes into the changing rooms.

"Hi, Honey."

"Are the balls still in?"

I bite my lip and nod, even though he can't see it. "Yes, they are."

"Your pussy looks very wet. Have you been touching it?"

"No. I've been at lunch with Cassie, and we're just trying on some clothes. I'll be home afterward, though."

I try to keep the information vague in the hopes that Dante gets the hint that I can hardly talk sex shit right now. That being said, if he insists on it, I can only get out of it by using my safeword.

"Okay. Well, I want you to masturbate right now with me on the phone. No noise whatsoever. You have to do it until I tell you to stop, and you're not allowed to come. Do you understand, Angel?"

"Yes, Honey," I breathe out quietly.

"I want you to say, 'Okay. I can hold on if you need me to' now, Angel."

"Okay. I can hold on if you need me to," I repeat dutifully.

"Good girl. Start rubbing your clit, Angel."

I do as I'm told and bite my lip, drawing on every ounce of willpower to keep myself as silent as I can. This is hot, and I'm on edge, waiting for Cassie to knock on the door and check on me or something, but I suppose Dante's line for me was to try and prevent that.

After about thirty seconds, Dante says, "I want you to take a video of what you're doing and send it to me."

I flick into the camera app and take a fifteen-second video that I send to him in a message before I go back to our call and put my phone to my ear again. I don't speak because he didn't tell me to do it, but he must've gotten the video because about a minute later, his voice is laced with lust when he speaks to me.

"Very fucking sexy, Angel. Rub yourself faster. I know that you're avoiding an orgasm. I want you to bring yourself to the edge, and you can only stop when you're about to come. When you're done, say, 'Oh good, you're back. I need to get going.' I trust you to do this right."

I don't dare do it wrong, to be honest. Coming here would be embarrassing, and I want to remain on edge. I close my eyes and think about Dante fucking me. I imagine him here in this changing room, with me pushed up against the wall as he thrusts into me. I bring myself as close to orgasm as I dare before I grit my teeth and pull my hand away from my pussy.

"Oh good, you're back. I need to get going."

"I want you to put your fingers in your mouth and suck yourself clean. I'll see you when you get home, Angel. I love you."

I suck my fingers clean, tasting my juices before I say, "I love you, Honey. I'll see you later."

I hang up our call and rest my head back against the changing room wall as I try to compose myself. I manage to do it, then pull on a pastel pink skirt and light blue top before I head out of the changing room. Cassie is sitting on a seat in the big open area and looking bored.

"Everything okay with Dante?"

"Yeah. It was so annoying. He had another call to take delivery or something, but he wanted to talk to me about something our accountant told him. It's the weekend. Can't I just forget the stores for two seconds?" I complain.

"Sounds frustrating," Cassie says.

"It was. Anyway, what do you think of this one?"

I turn from side to side to show off the outfit.

"It looks stunning, of course. You make basically everything look good." Cassie shrugs.

I smile at her. "Well, thanks. I think I'll get it, and *definitely* the dress."

I try on the rest of the clothes and end up getting all the outfits I pulled out. I allow the material to flow through my fingers as I hand them to the cashier. Serenity's clothes really are gorgeous, and I'm totally in love with what I've bought.

We visit a few other stores before we're ready to leave, and we take our bags to the parking garage, where we stow them in the trunk of my car. I drive Cassie to her place and drop her off before I head home.

I've had a great day with Cassie, but I am *more* than ready to be fucked by Dante. When I get home, I find the guys playing a video game together, and they both look up when I walk into the room.

"Hi, Sexy. Did you have a fun day?" Nate asks with a wicked grin.

I laugh and nod. "I did. Lots of shopping. A phone call with Dante. The usual."

"I heard about that." He smirks at me, then looks at Dante.

"It certainly brightened my afternoon," Dante says with a smile at me.

"I'll be back in a minute. I just need to put my shopping away."

I take my shopping bags to the closet and set them aside in a way that I know Dante will spank me for, but I'll put the clothes away properly later. It's worth the risk because, right now, I desperately need to be fucked.

I head back to the living room, and the guys are in a race now, so I know I'll have to wait. I drop onto the sofa in between them and cuddle into Dante's embrace as he races Nate. He smiles down at me quickly, then looks back up at the TV.

When the race is over, Dante has beaten Nate, coming second to his third, and he exits the game to the console menu.

"So, I was thinking while I was out that we probably need to tell the guys and Cassie about us sometime," I tell them.

Nate whips his head around to look at me, and I feel Dante turn his head as he looks down at me, but I stare firmly at the TV screen in front of us.

There's silence for a few seconds before Dante says, "I suppose you're right."

"Feels kind of official, doesn't it?" Nate says next to me, and I sit up from cuddling Dante before I turn to look at him.

"It does, and I'm nervous about how they'll react." I remember the discussion with Cassie at lunch about Nate and amend, "Actually, I'm nervous *as shit* about how they'll react. But I love you, Nate. This is forever, and we might be able to hide it from the world, but I don't want to hide it from our friends."

I lean over to him and wrap my arms around his waist before I kiss his soft lips.

"I want to be able to hug you and touch you in front of them. I want to be able to admit I spent last night in bed with you…but we don't need to go as far as telling them what we did in bed," I laugh.

Nate laughs too, and asks, "Are you sure? I mean, I have no problem sharing my sexual escapades with people." He sobers and looks over at Dante. "Are you okay with this?"

I turn to look at Dante as well, and he nods with a smile on his face. "Yes. I'm happy, and you guys are happy. We can tell them if you want to. I'd prefer that to lying to anyone…and I'm not just saying that because Lexi currently has her pussy on display for me, and I'd agree to anything she suggested right now," he finishes with a chuckle.

I laugh as I move back to Dante and kiss him passionately. "I love you, Honey."

He kisses me back, and I'm breathless by the time our kiss ends. Dante strokes my face softly with his hand as he looks down at me with so much love in his expression.

"Let's go to the bedroom, Angel. You've been a good girl today, and you deserve a reward."

Chapter Six
Revelations

"You're so cute when you're stressed, Sexy," Nate smirks at me.

"Shut up." I roll my eyes at him. "You're not helping."

Nate grabs my hand as I pass him while I'm pacing the living room and pulls me onto his lap in one swift movement. He places one hand on my right breast and begins to stroke my hardening nipple as he reaches his left hand underneath my skirt and between my legs, where he rubs his fingers over my wet pussy.

I rarely ever wear underwear these days, but I thought I should today. It doesn't stop him from reaching underneath the lace to find my clit, and he begins to stroke it as he murmurs in my ear, "I know exactly how to help you destress."

I moan in response, and Nate laughs as he reaches under my top. My breasts are encased in a mesh bra, and my nipples are straining against the encasing as Nate begins to rub his thumb across each of them in alternate movements.

My head is tilted back as I succumb to the feelings of pleasure that Nate is giving me. We continue in this manner until I reach orgasm, and I moan his name.

"Were you wound a little tight, Angel?"

I hear Dante's voice and open my eyes to see him smiling as he leans against the wall with his arms crossed in front of him as he watches us. From the bulge in his pants, I know that he is just as hard as Nate is beneath me.

Nate hasn't stopped stroking me. He never lets me off with fewer than two orgasms, but he laughs at Dante as he trails his tongue from my neck and up to my earlobe. He nips it with his teeth, and I gasp.

"She sure was, Dante. Seems very concerned about today. How ever can we help her be less stressed, I wonder?"

I'm teetering on the edge of another orgasm, and I know that Nate can tell because he changes the tempo of his stroking, which causes me to groan the word 'no' in disappointment as my orgasm fades away from my grasp.

Dante strides over to me, holds my face in his hand, and tilts it up to look at him, raising an eyebrow at me. "Did you just complain about being denied an orgasm, Angel?"

"Yes," I admit, hoping for punishment, because that is exactly the distraction I need today.

"Don't let her orgasm, Nate. I'll get the ropes. I think our angel needs to be tied up today."

Fuck. Yes.

As soon as I knew Dante was here, I was hoping this would happen.

"Somebody's in trouble," Nate teases me in a singsong voice.

I turn my head to face him and smash my lips against his, forcing my tongue into his mouth. We kiss passionately for thirty seconds before I end the kiss.

"You could give me some relief, you know." I whisper this because it's so against the rules, and I will cop major punishment if I'm caught.

Nate laughs. "I'm not that dumb. Besides"—he strokes me faster, at the tempo that he knows will make me come, before slowing down again—"you're so fucking hot when you're gagging for an orgasm."

"If you loved me, you'd let me come," I groan.

Nate kisses me again. "I love you. That's *why* I'm not letting you come, Sexy."

He pushes two fingers inside me and allows me to grind my hips on his hand. I'm desperate for relief. I want his cock filling me. Or Dante's cock, either work. I need a cock inside me. I don't care which hole it fills, either.

"Stand up, Angel," Dante instructs me.

I hadn't even realized he was back. I follow the instruction, and my juices are dripping down my thighs. I'm so fucking wet, and I need to be fucked.

"Strip," he commands.

I take off my skirt and top, then hand them to Nate. I peel off my panties and hand them to him as well. When I unclip my bra and try to hand it to him, though, he doesn't manage to grasp it firmly enough, and it drops to the floor.

"Whoops," he says.

I narrow my eyes at him. "You did that on purpose."

"No, I didn't. I was distracted." He raises my panties to his nose and inhales deeply while smirking at me. "Your scent is just too intoxicating."

"Naughty, Angel. You know your clothing doesn't go on the floor. Pick it up and follow me."

I glare at Nate, but I also love the shit out of this, and he knows it. He is always more than happy to helpfully get me more punishments from Dante. I bend over to pick up the bra, and Nate sticks two fingers inside me while I'm bent over. I'm not expecting it, and it causes me to squeal.

"Tut tut, Angel. Come here now."

I stand up quickly and scurry over to him. I follow him to the bedroom. I can feel Nate following me at a much more leisurely pace. It's fine for him. He's not about to get his ass spanked harder if he's not quick enough.

We pass the door to Nate's and my bedroom and head into the bedroom I share with Dante instead. Unsurprising. This is where the tie-down points are.

"You'll be spanked ten times today, Angel," Dante informs me. "Five for dropping the bra and five for not following quick enough."

I almost remind him about complaining about Nate denying me an orgasm but decide not to. I doubt he's forgotten, and I wonder what my punishment will be for that.

"Bend over the bed and count."

I catch sight of Nate, who has made his way into the room and taken a seat in an armchair by the window to watch. He never spanks me, but I don't think he hates watching it happen.

"One," I gasp as Dante smacks my ass for the first time.

I'm always grateful when he tells me to count because reactions are a no-no, but counting allows me to react somewhat. He's alternating ass cheeks, and by the time I've reached six, they're both stinging, and I'm absolutely soaking wet.

"Ten," I moan with the final hit and lie panting until Dante gives me my next instruction.

"On your back on the bed, Angel."

I climb on the bed and start to lie on my back, wincing slightly as my weight lands on my stinging ass cheeks before I lie fully down, and it eases a little. Instinctively, I hold my arms and legs out as I watch Dante go about the process of tying me down. He's hard as hell under his jeans, and Nate has unzipped his jeans and is stroking his cock.

I lick my lips as I look at it, and when Nate sees me do it, he laughs as he asks, "You want my cock in your mouth, Sexy?"

"Yes," I moan.

"How much do you want it?"

"More than anything. I want you to fuck my mouth," I tell him honestly.

"Maybe later, if you're a good girl." He smirks at me, and I resist the urge to groan in frustration.

Answering Nate's questions is fine, but expressing displeasure in what I'm told is not. Dante is tying the final knot, and I'm tied spread-eagle on the bed, unable to move as both men eye me greedily.

"Now, Angel," Dante says with a wicked grin as he trails a hand softly over my body. "You wanted an orgasm, didn't you?"

"Yes, Honey," I tell him.

I resist gasping as he leans down and takes one of my breasts in his mouth. He uses his tongue to torment my nipple, then nips it with his teeth before standing up and looking at Nate.

"Hey, Nate, did you hear our angel complain about being denied an orgasm earlier?"

"I certainly did, Dante," Nate confirms.

"I think she needs to be taught what it's like to *really* be denied an orgasm. What do you think?"

Dante is so motherfucking hot when he Doms me like this. I love being at his mercy, and I can tell that whatever he has in store for me is going to be deliciously painful.

"I completely agree. What did you have in mind?" Nate raises an eyebrow.

"Fancy licking that tasty pussy of hers?"

Nate gets a wicked grin on his face. "You know I fucking love eating her out."

"Who cares how many licks to get to the center of a lollipop? I want to know how many licks it will take for her to come," Dante says casually.

Nate walks over to me and twists my nipple between his fingers hard enough that I feel a rush of arousal straight from my nipple to my pussy.

"Less than fifty, I think." Nate leans down and kisses me, thrusting his tongue inside my mouth as he still plays with my breast before he stands up and continues. "She's so fucking on edge. I think she'll be screaming my name the second my tongue touches her."

He's probably right. Every cell in my body feels like it's aflame and as though I might spontaneously combust any minute now.

"She'd better not if she knows what's good for her," Dante smirks. "Fifty licks it is. You are allowed to come on lick fifty, Angel."

I fight back a groan as I catch sight of Nate's shit-eating grin. He's fucking loving this. He positions his head between my legs but doesn't do anything, and I can feel his breath on my pussy as he says, "You should probably count out loud, Sexy. Keep me on track, or I'll just fucking lick you forever."

Then he strokes my pussy from bottom to top slowly with his tongue. When his tongue hits my clit, it feels like an electric shock, and he was fucking right because I'm resisting the urge to shatter into a thousand pieces and scream his name.

Instead, I whimper, "One."

Nate does it again, slowly, drawing his tongue painfully across my aching clit as I pant for breath.

"Two."

I feel like I'm going to fucking die because my orgasm is threatening to hit me, and I keep having to push it back, but Nate's tongue is on me again every time I think I've managed to avoid it from hitting me. Sometimes, he will quickly bite my clit, or suck on it, and I'm in ecstasy.

By the time I'm at lick forty-nine, I'm practically delirious with lust and think that I might pass out because I'm all but hyperventilating as I count. Nate licks me one final time, and as his tongue hits my clit, I explode.

"Fifty," I manage to say before straight-up screaming as I allow my orgasm to hit.

Nate hasn't removed his head, and he's going to town on my clit as waves of pleasure crash over me repeatedly. I'm still screaming, and I can't stop. Dante pushes his cock into my open mouth and fucks my face.

My eyes have rolled back in my head, and I can barely even focus amidst the onslaught of pleasure. Dante holds my face in his hands as he fucks my mouth. Nate is giving me zero relief for my overly sensitive clit, and I feel like I might pass out again.

I'm about five seconds away from safewording because I think I've almost reached my limit when Dante shoots a load of cum down my throat. Nate lifts his head, and I swallow Dante's cum while my entire body shakes, and I can't stop it.

Nate looks concerned, but Dante lies down next to me and rests his head on my shoulder as he softly strokes my body and murmurs comforting words to me.

"Go ahead and fuck her, Nate. She needs it," he tells him.

"Are you sure? Lexi?" Nate looks at me, and I nod.

Dante wraps an arm over me and kisses my lips softly while Nate places his cock at my entrance before pushing himself inside, and I moan into Dante's mouth as another orgasm hits me from finally being filled the way I've needed for the last hour.

Nate fucks me slowly before building up to a faster rhythm, and I'm grateful when he finally comes inside me. Dante breaks our kiss so that Nate can lean down and kiss me, too, before pulling out of me.

Dante undoes the ropes, and my body is still quaking a little. Nate lies down next to me and kisses me.

"I'm going to go shower, Sexy. Thank you. I love you."

"I love you, too, Nate." I kiss him again before he walks away.

Dante pulls me into his embrace and kisses me. "Are you okay, Angel?"

"I am," I say with a nod.

"That was intense," he says.

"Yeah. So fucking good, though." My body gives an involuntary shudder.

We cuddle together as I slowly come back from where I was during that. Dante's warmth is grounding me, and I'm so in love with him. When Nate comes back from the shower, he smiles at us.

"Shower's free," he says with a grin.

"Thanks, Nate," Dante says.

Nate walks out of the room as Dante picks me up and carries me to the shower, where he washes me gently, and afterward, I'm feeling back to normal. We get dressed before going back to the living room, and any tension I was previously feeling is well and truly gone. Nate is sitting on the sofa, so I go over to him and sit on his lap before kissing him softly on the lips.

"Thank you," I say with a smile.

"You're welcome. You seem far more relaxed."

I wrap my arms around his neck and kiss him again. "Yeah, it was just what I needed."

"I'm glad, Sexy," Nate smiles at me.

I rest my head on his chest, and he wraps his arms around me, holding me close to him. He smells so good. Clean and soapy from his shower, but also that sexy as hell smell that Nate always has to him.

Dante sits down on the sofa next to us, and Nate kisses my cheek, then lifts me off his lap and onto Dante's.

"I don't think I signed up for being passed around whenever you two see fit," I tell them.

Dante kisses my neck softly, and I sigh. "Didn't you, Angel?"

He raises an eyebrow at me, and I laugh.

"Okay, I probably did. What if the others are disgusted by us?" I ask while biting my lip.

I've been really worried about this ever since we decided to come clean to our friends about our new arrangement. I just don't think that I could handle the judgment from them.

"They're not going to be disgusted, Sexy. They love us, and we love each other. If Dante is fine with it, I don't see why they won't be." Nate shrugs, but he links his hand with mine when he does.

"Exactly, Angel. Have you *ever* known Logan or Ash to be judgmental?" Dante agrees. He's looking into my eyes, and he gives me the sweetest, kindest smile as I see the puzzle pieces click into place for him. "Cassie isn't going to judge you."

"She might. She has some prudish tendencies." I cringe as I remember our discussion last weekend at The Grove.

Nate moves closer and kisses me passionately. He thrusts his tongue into my mouth in a way that turns me on and distracts me from my concerns.

"Well, if the worst comes to the worst, I'll just fuck her so that she can't claim to be perfect." He winks at me, and I laugh.

"I see how it is. Now that you actually get to fuck me, you're going to start joking about doing it with Cassie?" I raise an eyebrow at him.

He holds my chin in his hand and stares into my eyes. "They weren't jokes, Lexi. Desires? Yes. Fantasies? Definitely. A way for me to desperately avoid the fact I was fucking in love with you? One hundred percent."

Dante's arms are around me as I sit on his lap. He holds me tight, and this is the place I've always called home. At the same time, Nate is professing his love for me, and I am the fucking luckiest woman on the face of the planet to get to have these two amazing men in my life.

I smile at Nate while simultaneously regretting the years that we spent *not* doing this. "Okay, fair enough. They weren't jokes. You wanted to fuck me as badly as I wanted to fuck you for the last ten years."

I can feel Dante starting to get semi-erect beneath me. We've talked about this before, and apparently, the name for what he feels when Nate and I talk like this is 'compersion.' It means getting joy out of seeing your partner getting sex or love from someone else.

He loves both Nate and me, so when he gets to see us be happy and in love, it makes him feel good. He certainly doesn't mind when Nate gets me more punishments, but he's also happy for me to go off and spend the night having sex with Nate and sleeping in his arms instead of Dante's.

My favorite nights are when we all share a bed together. I get sandwiched between them, and it's warm and cozy and sexy and fun all at once.

Nate smiles at me. "Well, now we can fuck any time we want to."

"How about right now?" I ask him with a grin on my face.

Nate laughs. "Yes, if you really want to, but I doubt you do."

"I don't know…" I trail off and make an exaggerated thinking pose before continuing, "We do have a lot of making up to do."

Nate smiles at me and says, "I'm always more than happy to give you orgasms, Sexy, but everyone's going to arrive in about ten minutes. I'm not sure that's how you want them to find out about us."

"I'm going to be sick," I moan.

"You'll be fine, Angel," Dante laughs and squeezes me tight. "Do you want to sit back with Nate until they get here?"

I laugh, "How very generous of you to ask and not just dump me on his lap like *some* people do."

Nate slips his arms around my waist and pulls me onto his lap, which causes me to squeak in alarm because I wasn't expecting it.

"Do you have a problem with being manhandled by me, Alexandra Sullivan?" Nate growls into my ear.

"Well, yes, if you're going to do it right now because it makes me want to fuck you," I tell him.

Nate lays me on my back on the sofa, and I'm looking up into his ice-blue eyes, which are full of lust and amusement. He hovers over me, bracing his weight above me, and I'm breathing heavily.

"Later, I'm going to make you come so hard that you see stars." He grins wickedly at me.

"You've already done that once today," I laugh at him. "Don't you have any other tricks up your sleeve?"

Nate laughs and leans his head down to kiss me, intertwining his tongue with mine and allowing his weight to press me into the sofa.

"Fine. Later, I'm going to let you worship my cock until I come down your throat. Is that better?"

I lick my lips instinctively, just thinking about it, and Nate smirks at me before kissing me again. He's learned very quickly just how much I love giving blow jobs, and his cock is so glorious that I can't wait for him to follow through with this promise.

"I thought that might be more to your liking."

I wrap my arms around his neck and pull his head back down to mine. We kiss for a long time, and I don't realize how long it's been until I hear a knock on our apartment door, and I break our kiss quickly.

"Get the fuck off me," I hiss at Nate.

Nate laughs and shakes his head as he stands up and indicates to the massive bulge in the crotch of his jeans.

"And what do you think I should do about this, Sexy?"

"Oh, god, this was a terrible idea," I groan.

For many reasons. Not the least of which is because I'm desperately aching to take Nate to our bedroom and show him exactly what I think he should do about his erection.

"Are you two ready for this?" Dante asks with a grin on his face. "Because I don't think we should keep them waiting much longer."

On cue, the person knocks again, and I'm one hundred percent certain that it's Ash and Cassie because out of the three people who are coming over today, only Ash would knock twice.

Nate kisses me quickly, then says, "Sure. Just tell them I'm in the bathroom."

He walks out of the room, and I can't stop myself ogling his ass as he does.

"I think this secret is going to last about ten seconds," Dante informs me with a laugh as he walks toward the door to let in our guests.

No eyeing off Nate until after we've told our friends the news.

I chastise myself as Dante opens the door to let our friends in. Sure enough, Ash and Cassie are standing there, holding hands and smiling brightly at Dante.

"Hey, guys," he greets them. "Oh, good timing, Logan!"

Ash and Cassie walk into the apartment, followed by Logan, who must have just arrived. Cassie sees me and rushes over to hug me.

"Hi, Lexi," she smiles at me.

"Hey, Cass. How are you today?"

"I'm great. Is Nate here? We saw his Ferrari downstairs." Cassie looks around as though Nate might suddenly appear.

"Yeah, he's in the bathroom."

I force a smile onto my face, and I feel sick because how do we even tell them what we're going to tell them? It feels like it's going to change our entire group dynamic. Especially if Cassie does get all judgmental. I love her, but she has her uptight moments. I remember our discussion last weekend, and I dread the moment I have to tell her I'm in love with Nate.

Cassie sits down on the sofa, and Ash sits next to her, with Logan next to him. Dante is getting us drinks when Nate appears in the hallway.

"Hey, guys," he greets them, and his eyes flicker toward mine.

No ogling Nate, Lexi Sullivan.

But he looks so good that I want to run over to him and kiss him and drag him to our bedroom. He smiles at me, and I know damn well that he wants the same thing.

He walks over to the sofa and drops down next to me. This is not something that will arouse suspicion with our friends, though, and none of them seem even the tiniest bit surprised that he's done this.

Ash and Cassie are telling us about their afternoon at an art museum as Dante hands out drinks to everyone. Nate subtly rubs my back with his hand, and when I stiffen, he stops quickly.

"So, we have some news that we want to tell you all," Dante says when there's a lull in the conversation.

He's sitting next to Nate, and I'm back on edge as everyone's heads snap up to look at him.

"Oh my god, you're having a baby!" Cassie exclaims, and I cringe.

"Um, no." I shake my head.

"Shit, sorry. I just assumed." Cassie flushes red.

"I can see how you got there," Nate laughs and turns to look at Dante. "Good choice of words, bro."

Dante nods. "Sorry, guys. No, Lexi and I aren't having a baby. It's…other news."

He looks at Nate and me. We probably should've planned this out better. We didn't even talk about who would deliver the news.

"Not it," I say without thinking, and Nate bursts into laughter when I do.

"Yeah, not it, either. Continue on, Dante." Nate grins at him.

Dante rolls his eyes but is smiling as he does it.

"Okay, what the fuck is this news?" Logan asks. "I feel like I'm seriously out of the loop."

"You're not the only one," Ash shrugs.

"Right, well. I don't know how to say this, and these two are useless, so I'll just tell you, I guess. Nate and Lexi are in a relationship."

There's silence when Dante stops talking, and I watch my friends' faces. No disgust, just confusion, and they kind of do this thing where they look at me, then look at Nate, then look back at Dante.

"I'm sorry, I don't understand," Logan says with a frown on his face.

"They're together now. Like...romantically," Dante answers him.

Cassie gasps. "Oh my god, you're getting a *divorce?*"

"But you guys have been together for almost ten years, and you finally got married, and what the hell? Did you two fucking *cheat* together?" Ash is glaring at both Nate and me when he asks this last question, and I wince at the disdain he shows us.

"No, no. Guys, no. It's not like that," I say. "Nate and I didn't cheat."

"As if I ever would've fucked Lexi without Dante's permission," Nate says, which causes another long silence.

I see them still trying to put it together in their heads, and I know that I should clarify this a little more, but before I do, Ash speaks again.

"So, you two broke up, and then Nate, what, took Dante's place before his side of the bed was even cold?" He raises an eyebrow at us.

Dante laughs, which causes everyone to look at him, and he looks thoroughly amused as he informs them, "Lexi and I aren't broken up, are we, Angel?"

"No, we're not." I smile at him as my love for him floods through me, and I smile.

I turn to our friends, hold up my left hand, and wiggle my ring finger, heavy with diamonds on both the engagement ring and the wedding band that Dante gave me when we got married.

"See?"

I think that I can tell the exact moment that Logan understands what our new situation is like because his expression clears and changes from one of concern to one of happiness. Nate must have been able to tell as well because he snakes a hand around my waist and pulls me into him.

I know that Ash and Cassie aren't quite there yet, and I'm still worried that Cassie will be judgy, but I also can't resist leaning into Nate and enjoying the comfort of being in his arms. I notice Cassie's eyes widen when I do, and she immediately looks over at Dante. Probably to check if he's okay with this.

"So, you're sharing?" Logan asks.

Ash and Cassie whip their heads around to look at him, then back to look at Dante, who nods with a smile on his face.

"I can't say that I'm overly surprised." Logan shrugs.

Dante laughs. "I know, right? Nate's been trying to get in Lexi's pants for over a decade."

He nudges Nate with his elbow, and Nate laughs at him. "Yeah, I never really thought I'd actually manage it."

I'm starting to really get worried about Ash and Cassie. They don't seem to have fully gotten on board like Logan seems to have done. I catch Cassie's gaze and smile ruefully at her. She doesn't look upset, just confused.

"What does he mean about sharing?" she asks me.

Oh, god. Bless her fucking soul. She hasn't clued in yet.

"Well, I'm in a relationship with Dante, and I'm also in a relationship with Nate. I'm in love with them both." I shrug.

"Are you okay with this, Dante?" Ash looks at him.

Dante smiles at him. "I'm really, really okay with it. They're happy, and that makes me happy."

"So, you're sleeping with both Dante and Nate at the same time?" Cassie asks me with her eyebrows raised.

I laugh and can't help smirking, "Well, not always at the same time, but sometimes."

"I see." Cassie breathes out slowly, then her eyes widen, and a red flush comes to her face as she turns to stare at me. "How long has this been going on?"

I get the feeling that she's just remembered our conversation at The Grove as well, and I admit, "Since the day after we shot the music video."

"Why didn't you tell me last weekend? I was"—her eyes flick to Nate, then back to me—"completely unaware of your situation when we were talking about Nate."

He chuckles and asks, "Would knowing that Lexi's my girlfriend now have changed whatever it was you discussed, Cassie?"

"Uh, yeah. Just a little," she snorts.

"It's all good. That conversation was kind of the catalyst for us telling you guys, though." I sigh heavily and tell them, "Look, we know that this is an unusual situation, to say the least. We're all really happy, though. We're obviously not going to tell the world, or probably even our families, but we don't want to lie to you guys and keep secrets. I mean, eventually, you might start to wonder why Nate is *always* at our apartment."

"Nate lives here now?" Ash asks.

"Yeah, I do." Nate kisses my cheek and squeezes me tightly. "I've been living here for three weeks now, and I love it."

"Well, I'm happy for you guys." Logan gets up and walks over to hug me and says with a smile, "If you're happy, I'm happy for you."

"Thanks, Logan," I say as I hug him back.

His hug is comforting, and I squeeze him tightly before I let him go. Ash and Cassie both give us hugs and congratulations before the conversation moves on. We spend the evening hanging out and playing pool before our friends leave, and Nate joins Dante and me in our bedroom for the night. I can't imagine life ever getting better than this.

Chapter Seven
A Room With a View

I pat purple glitter eyeshadow on my lid with my finger as I sit in front of my makeup mirror to get ready for the movie premiere we're attending tonight.

"You look gorgeous." Dante walks over to me and drops his head to kiss my neck.

"Thanks," I say with a smile at him in the mirror as he walks toward our closet.

My hair is up in a ponytail, and I've swept some of it back to wrap around the hair tie, so it looks like I've used my own hair to tie it up. My purple eye look will go well with the purple dress I plan to wear tonight, and I use a glossy lipstick in a reserved shade so it doesn't take away from my shadow.

Dante is dressed in a gray suit and putting on his shoes as I enter our closet. When he stands up and looks at me, his eyes darken as he smiles.

"Take off the robe."

I untie and slip it off while I keep Dante's gaze before I drop it in the hamper. He walks over to me and places his hand on my stomach before he walks around me in a circle, trailing his hand across my skin as he does.

"You know what I'm going to tell you, Angel," he murmurs as he reaches my front again.

My skin zings with electricity where his fingers touch it, and he draws a path up between my breasts to the top of my bra. He hooks one cup with his pointer finger and pulls it away from my breast.

"I don't want you to wear underwear. If you didn't have this bra on, your breast could be in my mouth right now."

Wetness pools between my thighs at the thought of being in public without underwear. I've done it before, and it was hot as shit, but the risk of being exposed at something like a movie premiere is intense.

"What if someone sees?" I bite my lip and clench my thighs tight against the ache I feel at the thought.

Dante frowns at me. "Are you questioning my decision?"

"No, Honey."

"Good." He drops to his knees and yanks my panties down to my ankles. "Because I want this pussy accessible all night." He looks up at me and gives me a smug smile. "You don't seem to mind the idea of people seeing you."

He's right because I'm dripping wet, and to illustrate this point, Dante pushes two fingers into me easily.

"So wet. So ready to be fucked."

I hold back a moan as he leans forward to tongue my clit, and I thrust my fingers into his hair as he brings me to the brink of orgasm before he stops. I pant for breath and blink down at him as he looks up at me with a wicked grin on his face.

"Take your bra off, Angel. Question me again, and there'll be punishment."

I shiver at the thought as I reach behind myself to unclip my bra. I drop it in the hamper before I step out of my panties, then bend over to pick them up and put them in the hamper as well.

Dante's cock is stiff in his trousers as he looks me over, his gaze traveling slowly over my body. "I can't decide what to do with you. I could tease you and keep you excited all night, which would mean this pretty makeup and hair you've done would stay intact. I could use your mouth, but I'd get lip gloss all over my cock. I could also fuck you stupid and have you go to this premiere with messy hair and makeup along with being full of cum."

I gasp softly in horror at the thought. It's hot, but I also absolutely do not want that. I know without a doubt that I will safeword in a heartbeat if Dante chooses that option.

He raises an eyebrow at me. "Not a fan of that idea?" He strides over to me and carefully takes my chin in his hand before tilting my face up to look at him. "You're mine to play with however I see fit, Angel. Do you agree?"

"Yes, Honey," I murmur.

My heart races in my chest, and despite my aversion to the concept of attending a movie premiere in such a state, my pussy also aches at the thought.

"Maybe I should just fuck you on the red carpet instead." Dante reaches between my legs to rub my clit. "It's not like the entire world hasn't watched Nate give you an orgasm."

I pant for breath as my ecstasy builds, and I remember Nate pleasuring me on the music video set.

"I'm feeling generous, so I'll let you choose today, Angel. Would you like me to fuck you on the red carpet, or would you like me to stop doing this before you come and fuck you when we get home?"

He's got a wicked grin on his face because he fucking well knows that there's no real choice here for me. I get slow torture today.

"Stop now, please, and fuck me later."

He continues to rub my clit. "Are you sure?"

"Yes, Honey."

Dante lowers his mouth to my breast and swirls his tongue around my nipple. My orgasm is building, and I'm not sure if he intends to give me one or if I'll be punished if I come. I can't stop the moan of pleasure that comes from my throat as I come perilously close to coming.

He stops what he's doing and shakes his head at me. "Naughty, Angel. No reactions. Follow me."

I follow him out to the bedroom, and he sits on the edge of the bed. He looks beautiful and sexy as hell, with his erection straining against the confinement of his trousers. Sometimes I forget that he tortures himself as well when he edges me like this.

"Get over my knee so I can spank you. If you don't want your hair and makeup ruined, you'd better be careful."

I do as instructed and turn my face away from the bed, so nothing smudges my makeup. Dante's cock presses against my pelvis, and I wish he was inside me right now.

He rests one hand gently on my back and says, "Count to ten."

His other hand comes down hard on my ass cheek, and I gasp, "One."

As Dante continues to spank me, my pussy gets even wetter, and the need to be fucked grows with each hit. By the time he's finished, I would probably take the option of being fucked on the red carpet if it was back on the table.

"Ten," I say, and Dante's cock jerks underneath me.

I want it in my mouth. I want it in my pussy. I want it in my ass. I need something, anything, to satisfy the desire that's burning me up as though I'm on fire.

I get nothing, though, and Dante says, "Go get dressed, Angel. We need to leave soon."

I can barely walk back to the closet. My juices are dripping down my thighs, and as soon as I'm out of sight, I grab the towel I used after my shower from the hamper and use it to wipe myself dry.

As I walk past the mirror to get my dress, I pause and check my reflection. My makeup and hair are still in place, which is a relief. After I've pulled on my purple dress and silver shoes, I pick out a silver bag and slip my powder compact and lip gloss into it.

I stop in front of the mirror again to check myself out. I look red-carpet ready, except that my body is still on edge and filled with an ache to have sex. My face is flushed, and my nipples are hard pebbles against the thin fabric of the dress.

If Dante keeps me aroused the entire trip there, the whole world will be looking at pictures of me like this when they hit the internet. It's not a turnoff, though, and the embarrassment I feel at the thought makes my cheeks even redder while my pussy gets wetter.

I head to the living room, where Dante is sitting and looking at his phone. "Sit on the coffee table, Angel."

I follow his instruction and lift the skirt of my dress as I spread my legs wide. Dante gives no reaction, just watches me do as he said, then looks back down at his phone. He's still ignoring me when Nate walks into the room.

He's wearing a royal blue suit, with a white shirt that has the top button undone. He looks gorgeous, and his eyes immediately head toward my pussy.

"I do love this view," he says to Dante with a grin as he drops onto the sofa next to him.

Dante finally deigns to look at me, and he nods. "Yes, it's very nice."

"Are you planning to fuck her before we go?"

"No. Not until we get home. You can if you want to, of course," Dante offers.

Nate chuckles and turns to look at me. "You look ready for it, Sexy. Do you want to be fucked?"

"Fuck yes," I confirm.

My pussy clenches as Nate gets up and walks over to me. I'll just fuck him carefully so my makeup doesn't get ruined. I desperately need the relief of an orgasm.

He stands in front of me and takes my hand, which he places on the bulge in his trousers. "I could do with an orgasm before we go, that's for sure."

I stroke him through the fabric and bite my lip as his cock grows in size, straining against the material. Nate unbuttons his pants, then unzips them and drops both them and his briefs to the floor, freeing his erection.

"I think Lexi can wait, though. I'll just use her mouth to get what I need." His eyes glimmer with amusement as I groan softly. "Want to swallow my load before we go, Sexy?"

I nod and take his cock in my mouth while I look up at him. I begin to move back and forth on him, sucking him and licking the head of his cock occasionally. Nate reaches down and holds my breast, using his thumb to stroke the nipple that's hard against the fabric of my dress.

When he moans in ecstasy, my pussy clenches against the ache and need to be filled. I reach around and grab his tight ass cheeks in my hands as I take him as deep as I can so my nose touches his stomach.

His cock jerks in my mouth, and he moans, "Fuck yes, Lexi."

I have the strong urge to pleasure myself while I do this, but I resist the temptation. By the time he comes, Nate is slightly thrusting his hips back and forth to fuck my mouth. I don't think he's even aware he's doing it because his head is thrown back, and his eyes are closed while he moans my name.

His cum shoots into my mouth, salty and warm. I swallow it and suck every last drop from him before I remove him from my mouth and tongue the head to be sure. There's a slight sheen to his cock from my lip gloss, and I like that I can see the evidence of what I just did.

Nate pulls me up to standing and kisses me. "That was so good. Thank you."

"You're welcome." I use my thumb to rub off the lip gloss I've left on his lips, and he kisses my thumb as I do.

I touch up my makeup before we leave for the premiere, and there's no sign of our sexual activity when we climb into the limousine that will be taking us to the event once we pick up our friends.

Nate gets in first, and I follow him inside. He sits me on his lap along the side of the limo as it takes off toward Logan's apartment building.

"Are you cold, Lexi?" Nate asks as he takes my breasts in his hands and strokes my nipples with his thumbs.

I turn to roll my eyes at him. "You know very well that it's because I need a good fucking and not because I'm cold."

"If you say so. I thought it was just chilly." He winks at me.

Dante reaches underneath the skirt of my dress, and his fingers find my wet pussy. "I think she's telling the truth." He pushes his fingers in and out of me a few times before he pulls his hand out from under my clothing and holds it up to display his wet fingers. "She's very wet. Taste yourself, Angel."

I suck my juices off his fingers while I look into his eyes to see his satisfaction at me completing his request. They continue to torment me as we approach Logan's building.

When the limousine stops in front of it, Dante chuckles, "You'd better sit on the seat, Angel. We should try to be appropriate for our company now."

I slide over his lap to sit on the seat next to him about thirty seconds before the car door opens and Logan's smiling face appears.

"Hey, guys," he says as he gets into the car and sits on the seat next to me.

My breathing is still shallow, and I'm self-conscious of my stiff nipples as I hug him in greeting.

"Hi, Logan," I manage to say as casually as I can.

He blinks at me, and heat rushes to my cheeks. It doubles when he looks me over, and his gaze hovers at my chest for a fraction longer than anywhere else. My nipples are clearly visible against my dress, and my pussy aches at the knowledge that Logan can see them.

"Are you looking forward to the movie?" Dante asks, and it manages to distract Logan from the view I present right now.

He looks past me to my husband and smiles. "Yeah, it should be good."

I blow out a breath of air slowly as they continue their conversation. I'm not sure why the thought of being exposed to people is so hot, but it is. I'm so horny that I just want to turn the limousine around and take Dante and Nate back to our apartment so we can fuck.

Hell, with the way I'm feeling, I'm about five seconds away from jumping on one of their cocks right here in front of Logan. I shift in my seat as I squeeze my thighs together to try and ease the ache between them.

"You're quiet," Logan says to me after we've picked up Ash and Cassie.

Everyone else is talking about the trip Dante, Nate, and I are planning to Nate's estate in Napa in two weeks' time.

I can't exactly tell him that I'm quiet because my pussy is probably drenching the car seat underneath me, so I say, "I'm just tired."

"Everything good with the stores?"

I nod. "Yeah, I'm just at the end of organizing a big deal with a new supplier. It's been full-on. What about you? Are you seeing anyone yet?"

"No, because my friend promised she was going to find me someone, and she hasn't yet," he teases me.

"I'm struggling to find any good candidates," I admit.

I have been trying to find someone, but my social circle is small. The ladies at work are lovely, but all of them would certainly want the 'rock star.' Logan deserves someone who can see past that.

"Welcome to my world," he groans.

"Yes, well, it's your fault for being a hot, rich rock star," I scold him playfully. "I'm sure plenty of people would happily fuck your brains out, but it's finding someone who will do that for the right reasons that I'm finding difficult."

I look over at where Cassie is sitting with Ash. As much as I like her and she's a good friend, I have to admit that she does seem to like the perks of Ash being a rock star. He's happy, though, and Logan wants something different.

He laughs and gives me a cheeky smile. "Trust me, I'm more than capable of finding people to fuck my brains out if I want them to. I don't need your help with that."

"Duly noted. Well, I'll be on the lookout tonight. Maybe I'll come up with a questionnaire for people to fill out. Make sure they have the right intentions toward you."

"Sounds like a plan. Will it be an online questionnaire, or are you hiding a stack of papers somewhere around here?" he teases me.

Tonight is probably my best chance of finding someone for Logan. Another celebrity isn't going to care about his fame. They'll have their own money. Maybe they can see him for who he is.

I grin back at him. "Okay, well, maybe I'll have to forego the questionnaire. Still, I bet I can find someone for you."

"I won't be holding my breath," he says in a dry tone.

We walk the red carpet as a group, and I'm grateful that my arousal has dampened, so even though I'm still wet, my nipples are no longer rock hard.

Occasionally, Cassie and I are asked to stand to the side so the guys can be photographed without us. The guys also go over to some fans that are here and sign autographs for them.

We're about halfway to the venue when a reporter asks, "Dante, what do you say about the rumors that your wife is having an affair with your best friend?"

His arm is around my waist, and he tenses slightly but maintains his composure as he turns to smile at Nate before looking back at the reporter.

"I trust both Nate and Lexi." He smiles down at me with love in his gaze before he turns back to them. "They're not having an affair. I loved having my wife star in our music video, and it was great having her on set."

"Lexi, what was it like pretending to have sex with your friend?"

"Awkward at first," I say with a casual laugh. "With all the people on set watching and doing multiple takes, you get used to it. Don't expect to see me starring in a movie anytime soon, though."

"She did us a favor by agreeing to appear in our music video," Ash adds.

We move along the red carpet, and only one other person asks about the rumors. When we get inside the venue, Nate moves over to me with a grin on his face.

He lowers his head to my ear and murmurs, "If only they knew I had my cock down your throat an hour ago."

"I'm sure they'd love to know that." I look up at him and raise an eyebrow. "Want to go back out there and tell them?"

"Probably not a good idea." He puts an arm around my shoulders and hugs me. "Will you sit next to me for the movie?"

"Sure," I agree.

He lets me go, and I take Dante's hand as we head toward the theater. There are a few celebrities around, and we talk to some of them, but everyone is coupled up.

Finally, we approach April Conway. The guys know her a bit from some music events they've been to. She's pretty much the world's biggest solo act, but she's from Chicago and is filming a movie in LA at the moment. She's currently talking to Julia Shepherd, who's the star of the movie we're here to see.

"April, hey," Ash says as he hugs her.

She smiles at him. "Ash! Hey, guys. It's so good to see you here."

April hugs each of the guys, and as she hugs Logan, I realize that she's single. Maybe I could set her up with him. She's stunning, with shoulder-length blonde hair, blue eyes, and a great figure.

"Guys, this is my friend Julia. She's the star of this movie."

Nate nods at her. "Nice to meet you, Julia."

She gives him a beautiful smile as she clearly checks him out. I'm surprised when I get hit by a stab of jealousy. I know he won't sleep with her, but it's weird having someone check out the man I love in front of me.

I think she might be single, too. She's blonde like April, but her hair hangs long and straight to her waist. She's wearing a tight, glittery sky blue dress and looks gorgeous.

As we talk to the women, I consider both options for Logan. April has always been nice, but she doesn't live here. She's also busy touring a lot of the time, and now she's moving into movies as well. Logan deserves someone who will be here in LA with him, so he doesn't have to have a long-distance relationship.

Julia is based in LA but would be away a lot for filming. She also shoots frequent looks at Nate that I dislike. Not just because it makes me uncomfortable, but because she hasn't given Logan a second look. He needs someone who will look at him the way she's looking at Nate. He shouldn't be anyone's second choice, and it feels like that's what he would be if he dated her.

I look at his pleasantly smiling face, and he doesn't seem interested in them, either. I position myself next to him as we say goodbye to the women and walk away from them.

"What about April or Julia?" I ask as we walk toward the candy bar.

He glances back at them and shakes his head. "I'm not really into blondes that much."

"Oh, *now* you're going to get picky?"

He nudges me with his elbow and gives me a grin. "Julia seemed more into Nate than me. I'll pass."

"Fair enough." I sigh. "Well, there's still plenty of candidates here, I guess."

I've ruled out every man and woman who's single that we've spoken to by the time we make it into the theater, and it's frustrating. I end up sitting between Nate and Logan, and I look over at Dante, who's next to Nate.

I think this is the first event like this where I haven't sat next to him. I mouth the words 'are you okay with this?' to him, and he smiles at me before he whispers something to Nate, who laughs.

He leans his head toward mine, and I lean over to him so he can tell me in an undertone, "Dante said he's fine not sitting next to you as long as I keep you on edge during the film." I give a short, sharp intake of breath, and Nate gives me a wicked grin. "Just wait until the lights go down."

I shift in my seat as a shot of arousal goes straight to my crotch. Nate chuckles, and he's true to his word when the cinema goes dark. He places his hand on my thigh and slides my dress a few inches higher.

It's dark in the cinema, but not that dark. Luckily, everyone in the vicinity knows about Nate and me.

He leans over to whisper to me, "I'm imagining myself sliding my hand under your dress and fingering your wet pussy."

I swallow and bite my lip as Nate sits up again. He's looking at the screen, but he's drawing patterns on my thigh with his pointer finger, and my skin zings with electricity where he's touching me.

By about an hour into the movie, I'm a mess. Nate keeps whispering dirty things to me, and he's moved my dress high enough that I can feel the cool air-conditioned breeze on my bare pussy.

I have no idea what's happening in the film. I'm just focused on my arousal and Nate next to me. As the movie nears the end, I happen to look to my right, and my gaze meets Logan's. He's got a strange look on his face, and I don't know what it is until his eyes dart to my thigh before they return to my face. Heat rushes to my cheeks as I realize that he's been watching Nate tease me.

He leans across and whispers in my ear, "Sorry. I was trying to mind my own business, but you guys have been a bit obvious."

"All good." I force a smile at him and pull my skirt down as I wish that the ground would swallow me whole.

This time, Logan's eyes move quickly to my chest before coming back to my face. I fold my arms over the rock-hard pebbles that my nipples have become, and Logan looks abashed at being caught looking at my breasts. I stare firmly at the screen as Logan speaks quietly in my ear again.

"Sorry, Lexi."

"It's fine," I whisper back.

I look over at Dante and Nate, who are both watching us with interest. I turn back to the screen, my arms still folded over my chest and my cheeks burning with heat.

Less than a minute later, Nate whispers to me, "What did Logan say?"

"That you're being too obvious," I chide him as quietly as I can, and he chuckles.

He reaches down and hikes my skirt back up, higher than before, so that there's only a small amount of fabric stopping me from being exposed. My breath catches in my throat, and my pussy throbs with arousal. I can't stop myself from turning to look at Logan, but he's staring straight ahead at the screen, and I do the same.

Nate goes back to drawing patterns on my leg, but this time he draws them on my inner thigh, just below where the hem of my dress is sitting. His finger is mere inches from my pussy, and I have the strong urge to spread my legs so he can pleasure me, regardless of where we are.

It's a relief when the movie ends, and Nate pulls my skirt back down before the lights come up in the theater. I desperately want to skip the after-party and go home with Dante and Nate, but we take shuttles to the event instead.

I can barely look Logan in the eye, but after I've had a few drinks, he comes to the bar as I'm getting a refill for my drink. After he's gotten one as well and we're on our way back to our group, I brave a conversation with him.

"Hey, sorry for what happened during the movie."

"All good." He gives me a cheeky grin. "It was very interesting to watch."

"The movie?" I purposely misinterpret his comment, and he laughs.

"Yes. I've always seen Julia's character with her husband, so it was strange to see her with that new male lead."

I take a sip from the cocktail I've been drinking. "Did it make you uncomfortable?"

"Not really. It was just a change. I'll get used to it, no doubt."

I feel like we haven't seen enough of the guys lately. Since I got together with Nate, I've spent all my spare time fucking him, and I could count on one hand the times we've hung out as a group.

"Hey, you should come out to Napa with us," I suggest.

Logan's eyebrows raise. "Are you sure?"

"Yeah, we haven't all been out there in ages. Ash and Cassie can come, too. It'll be like old times."

"You should check with the guys. You're going in two weeks, aren't you?" I nod my confirmation, and he says, "I've got a family dinner on Friday, but I could come to stay Saturday night."

"That would be awesome." We reach the group, and I announce, "Logan's going to come to Napa with us. Can you guys come, too?" I ask Ash and Cassie.

"To Napa in two weeks' time?" Cassie asks, and I nod. "No can do. Ash and I are going to my cousin's wedding."

"Damn. That sucks. I thought we could all hang out."

"It was a good idea," Dante says with a smile at me. "You can still come if you want to, Logan. We're just planning to get away from LA for the weekend."

"I did tell Lexi that I can only come for Saturday night, but I don't want to intrude on your weekend away." Logan shrugs.

"Don't be stupid. If you don't come out to my estate to hang out, I'll quit the band because I'll be so offended," Nate jokes.

Logan laughs. "We wouldn't want that. Sounds like fun, then. It'll be good to get away."

I spend the rest of my time at the party trying to find someone suitable to set Logan up with. Either he or I rule everyone out, though. Most people are already in relationships, and others we know have a history of cheating. Of the remaining candidates, Logan isn't attracted to anyone I think is worthy of him.

As the limousine makes its way toward Ash's apartment building to drop him and Cassie off, I tell Logan, "God, that was depressing. You're awesome. How come there was no one for me to set you up with at that party?"

"And now you see why I'm not seeing anyone," he cringes. "Also, because the two people I might have been interested in, you thought 'wouldn't be a good fit.'"

"Christine is a massive gossip who tells me everyone's business the second I start a conversation with her, and Tom lives in the UK. I don't want you to have to do long-distance."

"I would move there if it worked out," he says, and I glare at him.

"No way am I going to be the reason you move countries. The guys would have me hanged, drawn, and quartered for my part in it."

Logan laughs. "I'm just teasing you. This has basically been my life for the last three months."

"Don't give up yet. You're amazing, and the right person is out there."

"Thanks, Lexi." He hugs me, and I smile as I hug him back.

When we've dropped Ash and Cassie off, the limousine starts toward Logan's apartment. I lean my head against the seat and close my eyes.

"You look tired, Angel."

I nod my head, and Nate chuckles, "I know how to wake her up."

He rests his hand on my thigh, and I stiffen as I open my eyes to look at him. I look over at Logan, who is watching us, before I turn back to Nate.

"Did you enjoy the movie, Logan?" Nate asks as he pushes my dress up.

He doesn't push it up as high as he had it in the theater, but I still feel exposed, especially when Logan laughs.

"It was good. I have to admit that you groping Lexi all through it was mildly distracting."

"Whoops. Sorry about that. I just couldn't resist."

Nate moves my dress a little higher, and it gets harder to breathe. My nipples are rock hard again, and I'm wet. I don't want to look at Logan to see his reaction, and my cheeks burn with heat.

"Fine by me," Logan says. "I said to Lexi that it'll be an adjustment seeing you with her as well as Dante, but I'm sure I'll get used to it."

The conversation moves on, and Nate doesn't push my dress up any further. I do catch Logan glance at my chest as he says goodbye to me and gives me a hug.

"I think our angel likes being on display. Don't you, Nate?"

Nate kneels on the floor of the limousine in front of me and pushes my dress up to my hips before he spreads my legs wide.

"Her pussy is drenched, so I would say she does."

"I always thought that you had exhibitionist tendencies, Angel. I've never had a chance to test them like this before. Very interesting."

Nate drags his finger down each side of my pussy, and he avoids touching my clit or even inside my lips. I moan softly, and he grins up at me.

"Almost home, Sexy Lexi. We'll fuck you as soon as we're there."

Nate leans forward and begins to eat me out as Dante slides along the car seat to be next to me. He kisses me passionately, and our tongues intertwine as he lifts a hand to my breast to stroke my hard nipple.

"You've been a good girl tonight, Angel. Come for Nate."

I lean into Dante as Nate tongues my clit, and I moan loudly as I give way to the pleasure that rocks my body when my orgasm hits. Nate doesn't stop and continues to eat me until we arrive at our apartment.

Dante pulls my dress off over my head the moment we reach our bedroom. He strides into the closet with it while Nate kisses me. He reaches between my legs to stroke my clit while his tongue explores my mouth.

Nate breaks our kiss as I almost reach another orgasm, and he pushes me toward Dante, who claims my mouth for a moment before he pushes me onto the bed. He's naked, and he buries himself inside me in an instant.

I gasp as I finally get the satisfaction of having a cock in my pussy. Dante thrusts roughly in and out of me for a few minutes before Nate's cock appears near my mouth. I take him in my mouth and suck him as I wrap my legs around Dante's waist.

Nate reaches down to tweak and pull my nipples while Dante uses his fingers to rub my clit while he fucks me. I'm lost in lust as my pleasure builds, and I come again about a minute before Dante does. He pulls out, and Nate moves to take his place to fuck me.

He's eager as well, and I meet his thrusts with my own.

Dante's voice reaches my ears as he says, "Are you thinking about being looked at, Angel?" He tweaks my nipples in turn. "You looked so hot tonight with these nipples hard and showing the world how horny you were."

I pant for breath as the knowledge of being exposed rips through me—Logan's inability to stop himself from looking at my chest on more than one occasion. We're just friends, and he was unable to resist the temptation, which is hot as shit. Logan's face when I caught him looking at my chest is in my mind when Nate comes inside me, and another orgasm hits me as he does.

Chapter Eight
A New Player

"Logan!" I exclaim as he appears in the doorway to the room where Nate and Dante are playing pool together.

I haven't seen him since the movie premiere, and I've been looking forward to this weekend. Logan's been on my mind a lot, but I wouldn't admit it aloud. A few times when I've been fucking Dante and Nate, I've pretended Logan was watching us. I kind of want that to happen for real, but I don't know if it will.

"Hi, Lexi." Logan smiles at me.

He greets the guys, then grabs a beer from the fridge before coming to sit next to me on one of the stools at the side of the room.

I put my arm around him to hug him before asking, "How was the drive from San Francisco?"

"Not bad. It feels like forever since I've been out in Napa."

I nod because he's right that it's been too long since we've been out here. "We should all come here way more often. I love it here."

"Me, too." Logan smiles at me. "So, how are things going?"

He nods toward the pool table where Nate is soundly kicking Dante's ass, of course. I smile as I watch the two men that I love more than anything in the world joking with one another as they play their game.

"Really good. I've never been happier, and I think it's the same for them."

"I'm glad," Logan says and takes a sip of his beer.

"When you found out, you said that you weren't surprised. Why?"

Logan turns to look at me, and he doesn't reply at once, but I know that he does this. He thinks things through before giving a response. A smile comes across his handsome face before he answers.

"Well, I was surprised, but also not surprised. Nate's been in love with you for years, and I think that if I'd thought about it, I'd have known you were in love with him. You two have acted as though you were a couple. The only thing you didn't do was have sex. I'm assuming that's changed now, given your behavior at the movie premiere." He gives me a wry grin.

I smirk back at him. "Yeah, we've done it once or twice."

Logan laughs, "I'm sure. Well, yeah. Once I realized what the hell it was that you guys were actually telling us, it made complete sense to me."

"Thank you for not judging us," I say, sincerely meaning it because his friendship means so much to me.

"Given that you guys have always been accepting of me and my sexuality, I'm hardly going to judge someone for what they do in the bedroom." Logan winks at me and takes another sip of beer.

Nate has just beaten Dante in their game, and he looks over at Logan and me as we sit and talk together.

"You want to play, Logan?" he asks.

"Of course," Logan grins back at him.

I head over to the bar and am starting to make myself a rum and Coke when Nate wraps his arms around my waist from behind me. I know it's him because I've started to learn his touch almost as well as I know Dante's.

"Hi," I say with a smile as Nate drops his head to kiss my neck. "Did you want something?"

He pulls me hard against him and says, "Always."

I put the bottle of rum down and turn so that I'm facing him. Dante is setting up the game of pool, and Logan is watching us with mild curiosity.

"Logan's looking at us," I tell Nate.

He grins at me. "Does that bother you?"

In answer, I place my arms around his neck and pull his head down to meet mine. We kiss for half a minute, with Nate pressing me against the bar behind me. I can feel his cock start to harden, and I know that if Logan wasn't here, Nate would have no problem with bending me over and fucking me where we stand. I'm wet as hell at the thought of it.

"I guess I'm breaking, Nate?" Logan calls out, and he sounds amused.

Nate kisses my lips softly before replying, "Sure, go ahead."

I hear the sound of pool balls hitting one another and smile at Nate. "Okay, go play pool. I need a drink to cool off."

I turn back to the bar, and Nate smacks my ass once before walking away, which causes me to squeal, and he laughs. It's strange to be flirting and making out with Nate in front of Logan. I mean, I've made out with Dante in front of him more times than I can count, but there's something about doing it with a man that's not my husband that feels thrilling.

I finally have my drink in hand, and I turn to face the room. Dante is sitting on one of the stools now, and he smiles at me.

"Come here, Angel," he says, and a smile spreads across my face as I walk toward him.

I sit down on the stool next to him, and Dante kisses me passionately, for possibly longer than I just kissed Nate, and I'm breathing heavily when he stops. I turn to watch the men playing pool, and Logan is watching us again, looking curious.

"What's up, Logan?" I ask him because I know that he won't generally offer up his thoughts uninvited.

He smiles at me and says, "Okay, can I ask you guys some questions?"

"Of course," Dante laughs, and Nate nods while lining up to

sink one of the balls on the table.

"I just watched Lexi make out with Nate, and then less than a minute later, she's making out with Dante. Aren't either of you jealous about that?"

Nate stands up from his shot as the yellow number nine ball falls into the pocket across from him and shakes his head. "Nope. I just consider myself lucky as shit that I get to be with her at all."

He looks over at me, and I blow him a kiss. I fucking love him so much that my heart hurts because we've had each other in our lives for years and haven't been able to have what we have now. I regret so much that we didn't do this sooner.

Logan nods and then looks over at Dante, who shakes his head as well. He has his arm around me and is softly stroking my arm with his hand while we watch their game.

"No jealousy here, either. It was far more painful to watch Lexi and Nate love each other without getting to be together sexually than it is to watch them be openly in love. I get so much joy out of being able to facilitate them being together. It would be selfish of me to keep them apart and watch them suffer for it."

"It's certainly an interesting dynamic," Logan comments as he moves toward the table for his turn. "Is it okay if I keep asking questions?"

"Sure," I smile at him. "You know you can ask us anything."

Logan looks thoughtful while he takes his turn and doesn't sink any of his balls.

"Do you all sleep together?" he asks.

"Dante and I have a bedroom, and Nate and I have a bedroom, too," I tell him.

"How do you decide who you sleep with? Is there a schedule?"

Nate sinks one of his balls and laughs at this question. He looks over at Logan with a grin on his face.

"Do you think I would have a schedule for sex?" he asks as he raises an eyebrow at Logan.

"Fair point," Logan laughs back.

"We just go with whatever everyone is feeling and wants to do.

Sometimes I sleep with Dante, and sometimes I sleep with Nate. If either of them really needed me, I would switch in a heartbeat." I look into Dante's eyes and smile at him, then turn back to Logan. "As for sex, it's the same as any relationship. Whenever we want it, we have it."

"Or Dante tells us to do it, and then we have no choice but to want it," Nate adds with a laugh.

I glare at Nate. The whole kink aspect of my relationship with Dante has remained a secret for almost ten years, and Nate has barely managed to keep it for ten days.

"What the hell does that mean?" Logan asks.

Dante laughs, and I'm surprised when he answers with the truth, "Lexi is my sub. Nate sometimes helps me with her punishments, and he always has a choice because I'm big on consent. So far, he's never chosen not to, though."

I feel like I can't breathe as Logan looks from Dante to me and then to Nate. I feel exposed and as though I'm standing naked in front of him as he thinks through the secrets that we've revealed to him.

"How did I not know this?" he asks.

"It turns out they're very sneaky, Logan," Nate laughs. "She doesn't call him 'Sir,' she calls him 'Honey' and he calls her 'Angel.'"

It's like a lightbulb has gone off above Logan's head. His mouth drops open, and he turns his head to look at where I was previously standing at the bar before he turns to look at me again. I'm sure that he's rethinking a shit ton of nights out together when Dante has Dommed me in front of them all.

"I can't believe it," Logan says, shaking his head.

"Hey, at least she was wearing clothes when you were told," Nate smirks at him as he sinks the eight-ball to win their game.

"Wait, yeah, how did you find this out?" Logan asks him.

"Dante invited me over to their house, and Lexi answered the door wearing practically fucking nothing."

Nate smiles at me, and his eyes glaze over for a second. I'm sure he remembers that night, and I'm wet as fuck talking about all of this with Logan.

"Anyway, he ordered her around a bit, and I put two and two together sometime around when she was sitting on the coffee table with her legs spread wide and no underwear on."

Logan's mouth is hanging open, and he stares at me. I know that he is thinking about the image that Nate has put in everyone's heads. Dante and Nate have both seen it in person, but I can tell Logan is imagining it, and I'm horny as shit because I know that he's thinking about my pussy.

"If you guys have finished playing pool, maybe we could play some poker now?" Dante suggests. "We can keep talking while we do."

"Sure, sounds good," Nate agrees, and Logan nods.

I finish my rum and Coke, and we all get another round of drinks. I catch Logan looking at me and smile at him. We walk out of the room, drinks in hand, to the room with Nate's poker table in it.

"Have we blown your mind today?" I ask him.

"Ah, yeah, just a little." He grins at me and shakes his head. "I'm just processing it."

"I did that, too…while my tongue was in her pussy," Nate says this while looking in my eyes, and I'm unsure what's happening right now.

I'm wet as hell, my nipples are hard and completely visible against my top, and I'm literally aching to be fucked. I feel like we've crossed some invisible line with Logan, and I'm not sure where we're headed. Or maybe I am, but I don't know for certain that's what's going on.

We sit at the poker table, and I sit between Logan and Nate. Dante sets up the game and shuffles the cards.

Before he deals them out, he looks at us all and announces, "We're playing strip poker, of course."

"What?!" I exclaim.

"I thought it went without saying," Nate says with that shit-eating grin that he gets on his face whenever Dante is Domming me, and it's going to result in sexual benefits for him.

"Are you up for it, Logan?" Dante asks him.

My heart is in my throat. Consent. Dante is asking so much more than just about this game, I think. He doesn't need my consent. It's a foregone conclusion because I can safeword if I don't consent.

Logan takes a swig of beer and then says, "Sure, it sounds like fun."

He looks at me in a way that he has never looked at me before, and it turns me inside out. Logan is sexy as hell. I know this. His eyes are molten pools of chocolate, and it's obvious that he's aroused. Like me, he probably has been since we first started talking about sex. I start to think about what he would look like naked, and I hope like hell that his poker game is lacking today.

"This isn't fair," I say cheekily. I watch for a reaction from Logan when I inform them, "I'm not wearing any underwear. Two bad hands, and I'll be naked."

Desire flares in Logan's expression, and Dante laughs, "You'd better hope for good luck, then, Angel."

Our game begins, and I lose the first hand. I'd already thought this through, and I take off my engagement ring and drop it on the table in front of us with a smirk.

"That's cheating!" Nate protests.

"Hey, I'm wearing it." I shrug.

Dante grins, "I'll allow it. Trust our angel to find loopholes, huh."

The next few rounds go by, with shoes and socks being removed. I take my wedding ring off and my earrings out one by one amidst Nate's protests about them. Then, the fun really begins. I have pants and a t-shirt before I'll be naked. The guys are each wearing jeans, a t-shirt, and, presumably, underwear. Either way, flesh will be exposed on the next hand.

Logan loses to Dante's pocket aces and stands up to remove his shirt. I watch him lift it slowly over his head, and his rippled muscles are exposed as he does. I've seen Logan topless a thousand times before, but never like this, with sexual tension crackling in the air around us. Never with me imagining him buried deep inside me and fucking me into oblivion.

"Enjoying the view, Angel?" Dante asks me as we're betting on the next round, and I blush because I've just been peering over at Logan, thinking I was being subtle about it.

"I think she is," Nate says. "Do you like Logan's body, Sexy?"

I shrug. "Meh. He's okay, I guess. I really couldn't judge without touching it to see how it feels."

"Go on, then," Logan says as he turns in his chair to face me and my eyes widen.

I look over at Dante, who is smiling in amusement and gives me the tiniest nod of his head. I turn my body to face Logan and reach a hand forward to place it on his chest between his pectoral muscles. I slide it softly down his body, over his washboard abs, and stop when I reach the waistband of his jeans.

There is a very impressive-looking bulge there, and I want to give him head. I still have my hand on his stomach, and I raise my eyes to look into his. Both of us are panting for breath, and Logan's eyes are hooded.

"I think our angel likes Logan's body, don't you, Nate?" Dante asks him.

I drop my hand, and my cheeks burn with heat as I turn to face the table while Logan chuckles softly next to me. Nate reaches over, slides his hand under the waistband of my pants, and his fingers find my drenched pussy.

"Given how wet she is"—I moan softly while he rubs my clit—"I'd say that you're right," Nate announces.

He pulls his hand out of my pants but doesn't move it away from me. Instead, he leans further toward Logan.

"Want to taste her?" he asks him, and I gasp.

Logan doesn't hesitate. He wraps his lips around Nate's fingers and sucks my juices off them while looking at me. I think that I'm going to die. I realize that Logan is bisexual and just how hot it would be to watch him give someone head because fuck me, he is hot as hell.

Nate pulls his fingers out of Logan's mouth slowly, then leans back in his chair and winks at Logan. "Dude, you must give a hell of a blow job because that technique was hot as shit."

"Thanks. I've been told I'm all right at it," Logan grins at him.

I lose this hand with a two-pair to Nate's straight, and he grins wickedly at me as I stand to take my top off.

"Oh, no. I won your top," he tells me. "It's only right that I get to take it off you."

We all look at Dante, who nods in agreement, "That definitely sounds fair."

"Arms up, Sexy," Nate instructs me.

I raise my arms above my head as Nate stands and places his hands at either side of my waist, then slowly begins to lift my shirt. He spreads his hands across my chest as he lifts it so that he is rubbing my skin the whole way. He pulls it up so that it's sitting above my breasts and holds his hands on my breasts for a minute, softly stroking my nipples with his thumbs as he does before he lifts my top the remainder of the way over my head.

We sit down, and I'm fucking soaking wet. My pants have literally got a massive damp patch at the crotch, and I am nothing but a ball of nerve endings and a need to be fucked. Logan wins the next hand, getting Dante down to his boxers, and everyone can see his erection when he does.

All three men are staring at my chest frequently, and my nipples are taut and painful. Nate wins the hand after that, taking Logan down to his boxers and revealing a very impressive erection when he drops his jeans.

On the next hand, I have a king and a queen in my pocket. When Dante makes the flop, it's a king, a queen, and another queen. I know with my full house that I'm not losing my pants on this hand, and I bet big.

Logan matches me, and I laugh. Dante and Nate both fold, and after the river, Logan calls my all-in bet.

"What do you have in your hand?" I ask him.

"Oh, no, Lexi Sullivan." He grins at me. "I called you. I want to see what you've got."

He's looking at my chest again when he says this, and I laugh.

"You won't like it, but I'll enjoy seeing you drop those boxers."

I flip my cards over, and Nate whistles, "Nice hand. Got it on the flop, too."

"Show me what you've got, Logan," I say seductively to him, and I can't wait to see him naked.

I'm surprised when Logan laughs, "This is probably going to hurt."

He flips over pocket kings, and my jaw drops.

"Full house, kings over queens. I've got you beat," he informs me.

I swallow heavily and stand to take my pants off, but as I reach my hands to the button of my trousers, Logan shoots a hand out to pull mine away.

"Nate got to take your top off when he beat you. Doesn't that mean I get to take off your pants?"

I'm literally panting for breath, and I'm dying for an orgasm now. I want Logan to take off my pants. Hell, I want him to do a lot more than that.

"That only seems fair," Dante informs us.

As though he was only waiting for Dante's permission, Logan kneels on the floor in front of me. He undoes the button of my trousers and pulls the zip down agonizingly slowly. He reaches behind me and slips his hands into my trousers, places his palms over my ass cheeks, and begins to squeeze and rub them.

I moan softly, looking down into his gorgeous brown eyes, and he pulls my pants down so that my ass cheeks are exposed. Then, he brings his hands around to my front, slides one into my pants, cups my pussy, and squeezes it quickly before he pulls my trousers to my ankles.

I'm standing naked in front of Logan Ballantine, and I am fucking loving the shit out of this. He lifts my left leg, slides my trousers over my foot, and places it down out further than my hip. He does the same thing with my right leg so that I'm standing with my legs spread wide, completely exposed to him.

Logan looks up at me and smiles an erotic smile as he casually tosses my trousers aside before he moves forward and uses his hands to spread me further before he kisses my clit softly. He pulls his head back and looks up at me again.

"You're beautiful, Lexi," he says, then he puts his head back between my legs and begins eating me out.

It's amazing. He's really good at this, and the waves of pleasure wash over me. I start to feel unsteady on my feet, and before I can even voice this, Nate is standing behind me. He wraps his arms around me to hold me up and places his hands over my breasts, thumbing my nipples as I turn my face to his to kiss him passionately.

We're standing like this when my orgasm hits me, and I moan into Nate's mouth. Logan stands up, and Nate breaks our kiss, then pushes me against Logan, who crashes his lips against mine to kiss me, too. I can feel his erection pressing against my stomach, and I can't wait to get my lips around it.

It's strange kissing Logan. He's good with his tongue, as I just found out, and I am more than enjoying this. However, I have time to wonder what this all means for our friendship. Then, he reaches between us and begins to stroke my sensitive clit, and I don't have any time for more thought. Nate takes my hand and places it on the erection that's straining against Logan's boxers. I begin to stroke him with the soft silk between our skin, and Logan groans.

Dante's voice cuts through my lust-filled daze as he tells us, "You know, there's a perfectly good sofa a few feet away from you."

"Good point," Logan laughs as Dante drops the deck of cards from our long-forgotten poker game on the table.

Logan removes my hand from his cock before linking it with his and pulling me over to the sofa. Nate holds my other hand as he follows us. When we get there, Logan turns to face me, looking in my eyes as he drops his boxers and finally frees his cock from his briefs.

It's a beautiful sight to see, and I'm eager to wrap my lips around it. Logan drops to sit on the sofa and strokes it while looking at me.

"What do you want to do now, Lexi?" he asks.

I drop to my knees immediately, and Nate laughs behind me. "Lexi loves sucking cock, Logan."

"Hey, me too!" Logan winks at me.

"If I died with a cock down my throat, I'd be a happy woman," I tell him as I circle my tongue around the head of his shaft.

"Mmm, what a way to go, though," Logan agrees.

I laugh as I wrap my lips around his beautiful erection, and he moans in response. I think this is what I love about giving head. The power I feel when I'm making them moan like this is intoxicating. The giving of pleasure to my lover…well, lovers now, I guess. I look up at Logan's face and am struck by his beauty.

How have I taken his looks for granted for so many years? This man is ridiculously handsome, and it's like I've never *seen* him before today. He's staring down at me and looks entranced by what he's seeing. He softly strokes my head while I continue to blow him, and it's nice.

I feel Nate's hands on my hips as he pulls me back, so I move onto my hands and knees and continue to suck Logan as I do. Nate places his cock at my entrance and slowly presses it into me, filling me inch by inch, and I groan onto Logan's erection as I'm completely filled by Nate, who holds himself there and doesn't move yet.

I need to be fucked, and I wiggle my hips, which causes Nate to laugh. "Just let me enjoy this moment for a second, Sexy. I'll fuck the shit out of you in a minute."

I groan and keep doing what I'm doing. Logan reaches down to start playing with my breasts, and I feel pleasure rocking my body. Nate doesn't move his hips, but he does reach around me to rub my clit. I pop Logan out of my mouth and rest my face next to his cock as my orgasm hits me, and I scream. When my orgasm ebbs, I put Logan back in my mouth and go back to my task.

"God, this is amazing," Logan groans.

"You're fucking telling me," Nate replies as he *finally* begins to fuck me, and I'm in ecstasy.

"This is definitely not how I thought today would go," Logan laughs.

I didn't expect it, either. I thought that *maybe* Dante or Nate would show me off, and I'd enjoy Logan's response to it. This is so much more than that.

I increase the suction on his cock and press my nose to his stomach as Nate thrusts into me and am rewarded with Logan's laugh turning into a moan of pleasure.

"I thought it might go this way," Dante says with a shrug as he drops onto the sofa next to Logan.

We all pause mid-movement, and all our eyes are on him. My mouth is full of Logan's cock, and my pussy is full of Nate's. I am currently being spit roasted by two men who are *not* my husband, the man who apparently expected our day to turn out like this. Dante has gotten naked as well and is stroking his erection as he looks at us. Clearly, he's happy to wait for his own turn to use my body.

"You thought it would go this way?" Logan asks, then strokes my head softly, and I begin sucking him again.

"I guess once I started sharing Lexi with my friends, I just couldn't stop. Why should you miss out on her awesome blow jobs?"

"You're the best friend a man could ask for, Dante Sullivan," Logan grins at him.

Nate laughs, "I'd like to point out that I'm sharing her with you, too. She's as much mine as she is Dante's."

My heart feels like it might explode at this declaration. I love that he loves me as much as he does. I love that none of us would deny his claim. My love for Nate is equally weighted with my love for Dante.

"Well, thank you, too." Logan laughs. Then he moans as I increase the speed of my head as I move up and down on him, "I'm going to come."

That's all the warning I get before I feel his cock spasm and he shoots his load into my mouth. I suck him dry and lick his cock clean before he leans down and kisses me passionately.

"Thank you, Lexi. That was the best blow job I've had in ages. And I've had some fucking great blow jobs."

He winks at me, then shifts across on the sofa, allowing Dante to take his place, and I know my task, at once placing my lips over his shaft. Logan has leaned back against the sofa and is watching us.

"God damn, this is the best fucking show ever," he announces, and I'm pleased by his words.

He moves off the sofa and climbs under me, clamping his lips around one of my breasts, which causes me to moan as he simultaneously reaches between my legs to rub my clit while Nate pumps in and out of me. It doesn't take long for this amount of stimulation to bring me to another orgasm. My insides spasm around Nate's cock, and he gives way to his own orgasm.

Nate shoots his load inside me with a groan of, "Fucking hell, I love you."

He pulls out, and Logan keeps rubbing my clit and playing with my breasts as I pant heavily with Dante in my mouth.

"Come sit back on the sofa, Logan," Dante says.

Logan gets up and looks curiously at Dante before sitting down again. Dante has him sit sideways on the sofa so that I can sit in his lap with my legs down the length of the sofa. Dante lifts my leg over the back of the sofa so that I'm spread wide before he enters me.

In this position, cradled by Logan as Dante fucks me, I can feel Logan starting to get hard again. He has his arms wrapped around me and is playing with my breasts. Every now and then, he'll kiss me, and I'm in orgasmic bliss by the time Dante dumps his load in me.

Logan is hard as a rock underneath me, and I don't even have to ask to know that I'm going to fuck him, too, today.

Sure enough, Dante asks through panting breaths, "Have you been STD-tested recently, Logan? Or do we need to get condoms?"

"I'm negative. I got tested after Chad cheated on me and I haven't been with anyone since."

"Okay. Well, we're all negative as well, so you can go ahead if you want to," Dante tells him.

As soon as Dante is out of me, I turn to straddle Logan, and he slides inside me easily.

"Fucking hell, Lexi. You feel amazing," he groans.

I kiss him, sliding my tongue into his mouth, and am rewarded with him kissing me back even more intensely than he kissed me before. He's probably the best kisser I've ever come across, and this is brilliant.

"Who are you fucking, Angel?" Dante asks me.

"Logan," I answer.

"Make sure he knows that you know who you're fucking, then. Say his name, Angel."

Logan raises an eyebrow, but I know better than to not follow an instruction that Dante gives me, so I say Logan's name again while I look into his eyes. I moan his name a thousand different ways, and he kisses my neck and plays with my breasts and occasionally kisses my mouth, but mostly just lets me moan his name as I fuck him desperately to yet another orgasm.

When it hits me, it's intense as shit, and I scream and drop my mouth to Logan's, moaning his name one last time before we kiss. He kisses me through my orgasm, grabs my hips, and begins to fuck me...hard. I wish I were bent over something because I can sense that Logan has the ability to rock my world, and I want him to really *fuck* me, but I'm not calling the shots here, and I am satisfied with the way he thrusts roughly in and out of me until he's spilling his seed in the same place Nate and Dante did before.

I collapse on his chest, and he wraps his arms around me before kissing the top of my head. "That was so fucking good."

Chapter Nine

Dabbled In It?

I lay on Logan, panting hard, and squeeze his cock with my pelvic muscles. I don't want to move. I'm exhausted and in post-orgasmic bliss as I lift my head to kiss Logan again. He slips his tongue into my mouth, and I'm amazed again by just how good he is with that tongue, both when giving me head and also when kissing me.

I slowly get off him, feeling every inch of him sliding out of me as I do, and then I feel cum dripping down my leg as I stand up.

"Argh! Someone get my pants, please?" I groan.

Nate swiftly grabs them and throws them to me so I can put them on. He laughs as he looks over at us.

"I'm probably going to have to double my maid's salary if I'm going to expect her to clean cum stains out of the carpet and sofa."

"Whoops. Sorry, Nate," I cringe.

He strides over to me and pulls me against him, dropping his lips to mine and kissing me while he brings a hand up to play with my exposed breasts.

"No need to apologize, Sexy. I fucking love you, and you're worth the cleaning bill."

I place my arms around his neck as I continue to kiss him, allowing him to play with both my breasts as I do. When our kiss ends, he pushes me in Dante's direction, and he kisses me as well.

"Why don't you and Logan go and clean up in his bathroom?" Dante suggests.

I raise my eyebrows at him. "Really?"

"Yeah, you probably need a shower, and Logan can help you get clean. Can't you, Logan?"

We both look over at him, and he's giving us a strange look, but he nods his consent. He looks amazing, sitting completely naked on the sofa, his softening cock glistening with my juices, and I want him in my mouth again.

I watch him as he stands and walks over to me, linking my hand in his, and we walk away from the other two. I turn to look at them as we go, and they're both smiling at me. No jealousy in either of their expressions, just love and lust.

Logan and I walk up the stairs, and when we reach the landing, he turns right to head toward the room he always uses when he stays here. When we're inside, we just stand there for a second in silence.

"Well…" Logan says and trails off.

"So, that happened," I laugh.

Logan catches my eye and laughs as well.

"It was really good, though," he tells me.

"You're telling me. I came about a thousand times and left a mess on Nate's sofa."

"What does this mean, though, Lexi?"

He doesn't go to the bathroom. Instead, he makes his way to the bed and relaxes back on it, with his back leaning against the bedhead as he looks at me. Logan looks beautiful, sexy as hell, and I'm amazed because I've never thought about him that way before.

"I don't know," I admit as I climb onto the bed and sit next to him. "Like, with Nate, as soon as we did it, I just knew that I had always been in love with him and that we were always meant to be together. I love you, too, but it's never been like that for us."

Logan smiles and teases me, "Gee, thanks."

"Come on, have you ever thought about me in that way?" I nudge him with my elbow.

He looks over my exposed breasts, and his voice drops to a seductive, husky tone when he says, "Are you asking if I've ever imagined fucking you?" I nod my confirmation, and he admits, "I have on occasion, yes. I sure as shit will more often in the future now."

I give him an equally provocative stare as I commit the image of him naked in front of me to memory. "Same here."

"I'm just worried that if it all goes sideways, then the band will be fucked up. As much as I would love to fuck the shit out of you every day of the week, the band will always be my priority."

I shudder at his words and the arousal that the concept of fucking Logan on the daily brings to me. How the hell is it that just a few hours ago, I didn't think of him as anything other than as one of my closest friends? What we just did has changed our friendship forever.

"What if we just, I don't know, see how it goes?"

Logan laughs, "Do you even know me, Lexi Sullivan?"

"Okay, fair point. Well, we can talk to the other guys and see what they think. They sent me up here with you, so I think it's safe to say that so far, they're not jealous of the idea of me being with you."

"Really? You think they thought we'd have sex?" Logan seems surprised, and it's kind of cute.

"Aren't we?" I ask him as I raise an eyebrow at him.

Suddenly, the air between us is thick with sexual tension, and I have the pleasure of seeing Logan's cock stiffen in response to my question. He swallows heavily, and his eyes roam my body again.

"Are we?" he asks, but he raises a hand to begin tracing around my areola.

He doesn't touch my nipple, but it causes desire to flare throughout my body.

I bite my lip as I nod at him. "Yes, we are. I want you to fuck me. Hard."

A slow smile comes across Logan's face, and he tilts his head to the side as he looks at me and watches for my reaction when he finally tweaks my nipple and rolls it between his thumb and forefinger.

"Is that so?" he asks.

"It is. Are you up for it?"

Logan moves over me and places his lips around my nipple. He swirls around it with his tongue, which causes me to moan before he moves over and straddles me across my thighs then begins undoing my pants.

"I'm going to eat you until you scream my name," he informs me.

"Awkward. Are you sure you want to do that? I've just had three men come inside me." I cringe.

Logan raises an eyebrow at me. "Do you think I haven't tasted cum before?"

I blush because, of course, he has, and he laughs at me as he unzips my pants and pulls them down and off before spreading my legs and not hesitating for a second to stick his tongue deep inside me as he rubs my clit.

There is something that is hot as shit about him eating from my cum-filled pussy. I'm struck again by the desire to see him give a blow job. He's so good with his tongue, he could probably give me tips.

He swirls his tongue over my clit, and my ecstasy builds as he moves his mouth back down to thrust his tongue in and out of me again. He immediately goes back to stroking my clit with his fingers, and I'm amazed by how good this is.

It isn't long at all before I can't stop myself moaning, "Logan."

He keeps doing what he's doing, and my orgasm hits me. Once it does, Logan moves up to kiss me, and I can taste the salty cum mixed with my juices while we kiss. It's completely erotic, and combined with Logan's expert kissing technique, I'm enjoying myself immensely.

"So, you want me to fuck you hard, huh?" Logan asks me when he breaks our kiss.

"Yes, please. Sometimes, I like it rough, and it felt like you were holding back before."

"How rough?"

My eyes widen. If he has to ask, then that means he goes hard enough to need clarification. I'm curious as shit about just how hard that is, but it's our first day fucking. Hopefully, not our last, though.

"That depends. I can always safeword with Dante, and we use the traffic light system as well. You can do whatever you want to me, really, but do I need a safeword?"

Logan blows out a breath of air. "What's your safeword?"

"Pineapple."

"Do you promise to use it?" he asks me.

I blink at him. "What the fuck do you mean?"

"Promise that you'll use it if it gets too much. I need to know that you'll use it."

Okay. Now, I'm starting to get a little scared. I'm also wet as fuck and desperate to be used by this gorgeous man in every way, shape, and form.

"Yes. I promise that I'll use it."

Desire flares in Logan's eyes and he leans down and bites my nipple. Not softly. I squeal as the pain hits me, followed by the pleasure as it ebbs.

"I'm going to use your fucking body, Lexi." Logan sticks three fingers in my pussy and roughly fucks me with them. "I'm going to stick my cock in every one of your holes, and you're not getting another orgasm until I've come inside you."

I. Am. Dead.

It's always the quiet ones.

"Tell me that you're mine to use," he instructs.

"I'm yours to use, Logan."

I'm dripping wet and, fuck, even just saying it is hot. Saying his name. Everything about this is driving me wild, and I am immediately aching for an orgasm.

"Good girl," he says, and his praise does things to me.

Logan holds my face in his hands and begins to fuck my mouth. His cock slides in and out, and I love it. This is the goddamn best. He holds his cock in my mouth with it pushed all the way in so my nose is touching his stomach and my access to oxygen is cut off. My eyes start to water, and I actually fucking love this. He pulls his cock out of my mouth, and I gasp for air, but I'm sad his cock is gone.

Once I've caught my breath, Logan does it again. Fucking my face, first, then holding his cock down my throat before removing it and allowing me to catch my breath. I am in next-level ecstasy, in complete subspace, and have given myself over to the experience.

He repeats this process four or five times before he decides he's finished with my mouth. Logan flips me over without warning, and I'm panting with my face in the pillow. He pulls my ass cheeks apart and sticks his tongue in there.

I gasp because I've never had anyone do this to me before. Dante and I have done some serious anal training, and I'm well versed in taking a cock in my ass, but I've never had someone stick their tongue in me with zero concern. It's not unpleasant, and soon I'm squirming and rubbing my clit against the bed.

"Do *not* come, Lexi," Logan growls at me.

He smacks my ass hard, and I squeal, but, fuck, I'm even closer to coming now. He lowers his head to keep doing what he was doing, then he dips his fingers into my drenched pussy several times and uses my juices to lube up my asshole. He fucks my ass easily with one finger, then adds a second one.

"Mmm, you've done anal before, I'm guessing."

"I have," I breathe, unable to say more.

"I'm going to use a condom, so I can fuck your pussy straight after," he informs me.

He gets off the bed, and after a few seconds, he's back before I feel him pushing into my ass. I groan, and Logan leans down as he quickly shoves himself in the rest of the way, which causes me to gasp.

"You still want it rough, Lexi?" he growls into my ear.

"Yes. So much yes," I confirm.

It's true. This is one of the best sexual experiences of my life so far, and I do *not* want to stop. Logan takes that as his cue and begins to fuck my ass with fast, hard strokes. He doesn't attempt to give me any pleasure. This is for him, and I'm delirious with lust. I know that whenever I eventually come, it's going to be one fucking hell of an orgasm.

"Get on your hands and knees," Logan tells me, and I do as he instructs.

He continues to fuck my ass but reaches underneath me to roughly grab and twist my breasts and nipples as he does. After a couple of minutes, he stops torturing my breasts and reaches between my legs to stroke my clit.

"Holy fuck," I scream.

"Did I tell you to talk?" he asks and uses the hand that isn't rubbing my clit to smack my ass cheek hard right before he thrusts roughly into me again.

Oh my fucking god. I could tell that he would be able to rock my world, but this is better than I could've imagined. Not being able to come and knowing that he is using my body to get off is making me incredibly hot.

Logan pulls out of my ass, and I expect him to thrust in again. After only a second, he plunges hard into my pussy, and I gasp. I can feel that the condom is gone, and this is the best fucking feeling in the world.

He grabs my hips hard, digging his fingers into my flesh as he begins to pound me so hard that I bounce off him as my ass cheeks smash into his stomach when he thrusts into me. No words could possibly describe how good it feels to have him fuck me as hard as he does, simultaneously pulling me back toward him with his hands as he thrusts forward into me with his hips.

Logan flips me over onto my back and puts my legs onto his shoulders before thrusting into me again. I'm staring into his chocolate brown eyes, and this is amazing. His eyes are dark with lust, and I fucking love this so damn much. He's deep inside me, and my legs are stretching as he leans forward, the slight pain adding to the pleasure he's giving me.

He starts to stroke my clit as he continues to fuck me, and I'm panting loudly. I don't think that I can possibly stop myself from coming if he keeps doing this.

"Don't you dare," Logan warns me, and I wonder if I said that out loud or if he could just tell.

The fear of my orgasm adds to my arousal. I know that it's going to be huge, and I want it more than anything. He hasn't stopped rubbing my clit, and I'm worried because I'm so close. I don't think that I can stop it and my eyes widen as I reach the very brink of orgasm.

Logan stops completely. He stops rubbing my clit. He stops fucking me. I blink at him, and I pant loudly. After about ten seconds, my orgasm fades away completely. I'm staring at Logan, and I don't dare say a thing. He smiles at me and then begins fucking me, impossibly harder than before.

He slams into me, drops my legs from his shoulders as he leans down to kiss me, and continues to pound me hard as he does, and I feel my orgasm returning, not as intensely as before, and I can keep it at bay, but fuck he is such a good kisser.

Logan grabs a fistful of my hair, holding my face against his as we kiss. He ends our kiss and leans back to fuck me while he rubs my clit again. It's painfully sensitive, and my orgasm rushes back with a vengeance.

"I said no, Lexi," Logan says sternly.

I'm about to fall apart because I can't stop my orgasm for much longer, especially not when he won't give me any relief, and he continues to rub my clit. He leans down and bites my nipple again, which causes me to gasp. The pain breaks the immediate threat of my orgasm, though.

Once the pain has gone, the pleasure it leaves behind is incredible, and Logan swirls his tongue around my nipple. His constant rhythmic pounding is intense amidst the other sensations that he's giving me and the fear of not being able to stop my orgasm.

Right when I'm on the brink of it again. Logan stops once more. He waits and watches me until I'm able to breathe semi-normally, waiting even longer than last time so that my orgasm is well out of reach before he starts up again.

His fucking is different this time—animalistic and rough. He claims my lips with his, forcing his tongue into my mouth, and even his kiss is different. He is taking his pleasure from me. I am his, and I love that. I feel his cock spasm, and he comes inside me, but he doesn't stop fucking me. He groans, and his jaw tenses, but he leans back to keep going while he returns to rubbing my clit with his thumb.

"Now."

His single-word instruction is enough to see me shatter into a thousand pieces as I embrace the orgasm that I have pushed away this entire time. My eyes roll back into my head, and I scream louder than I think I've ever screamed in my life. I scream his name. I scream obscenities. I moan, and I wail as Logan continues to fuck me and continues to rub my sensitive clit.

Multiple orgasms roll over me. I'm light-headed, and I can't stop the sounds coming out of me. I wrap my legs around his waist, and he thrusts into me roughly one last time and then holds himself there as I ride out the last of my orgasms.

I drop my legs and lie panting, staring at Logan in awe. I've never had an experience like that before. He has ruined me. I belong to him now, as surely as I belong to Dante and Nate. There is no coming back from this.

He drops down and kisses me softly, tenderly, as if he knows what I have just realized.

"Was it good, then?" he asks me with a smile on his face.

"I can't even explain how good that was." I shudder, and his smile widens.

"I'm glad."

"Where the fuck did you learn to do that?" I shake my head.

He's still inside me, and he pulls out, then brings me close to him for a cuddle before he replies.

"I've dabbled in BDSM," he tells me.

"Dabbled?" I raise an eyebrow at him and laugh. "You fucked me as if the world was ending tomorrow."

He smiles at me. "I don't do it full-time like you and Dante. Only in the bedroom, and only if I'm asked. You seemed like you wanted it."

"Have you ever had someone safeword?" I ask him out of curiosity.

A pained look crosses his face. "Yeah, I have. I've also had someone not safeword when they should have. I felt like a piece of shit."

"Whoa." I place my palm against his cheek. "I'm sorry that happened. I promise that I will safeword if I ever need to."

"This is a thing now, isn't it?" Logan smiles at me.

"Yeah. Sorry, but there's no going back after that. I'm yours, and you will definitely have to fuck me regularly."

Logan kisses me, and it's a sweet and loving kiss. He wraps me in his arms, and I feel my heart grow and expand, and space is made there for me to love him, too. It's strange and unexpected because even after we had sex earlier, I didn't think that I could love him like this. He breaks our kiss and chuckles as he looks at me.

I raise my eyebrows at him. "What?"

"Did you actually find someone to be in a relationship with me?"

I laugh as well and check off his criteria. "Let's see. I don't want you because you're a rock star. I don't want you because you're rich. I like you for the person you are and not because of those things. I mean, I guess the only thing is that I'll be sleeping with two other men as well. Is that a dealbreaker?"

"It's not cheating if I agree to it, and I'm okay with it as long as it's only Dante and Nate."

"It's definitely only Dante and Nate," I say and press my lips to his again.

We kiss for a long time, and Logan softly strokes my body, then we get up and make our way to the shower. Logan washes me the way that Dante does after a particularly intense scene, and I can tell that he has experience with aftercare. He holds me in the shower and kisses me again.

When we get out, he towels me dry before drying himself. He puts on briefs, a pair of jeans, and a t-shirt, then takes my hand and leads me out of the room.

"Should I get some clothes on?" I ask him.

Logan looks me up and down, then smiles at me, "No."

I grin at him as he links his hand in mine, and we start to make our way downstairs.

"So, what will the rules be if we're going to keep doing this? Will you do that to me every time we have sex?" I ask him.

"I could if you wanted me to,"— I shudder at his words — "but it's not my go-to move."

"Will you do it to me sometimes?" I blush as I ask him this.

We're halfway down the stairs. Logan stops walking; he wraps his arms around my waist, pulls me to him, and kisses me.

"Sure, I can do that to you sometimes," he smiles at me. "Now that you've promised me that you'll safeword, I'll do it if I feel like it or if you specifically ask me to. Do you have any hard limits?"

"None that we've found," I shrug at him.

I'm looking in Logan's eyes, and I see his eyes darken when I tell him this. The endless sexual possibilities are laid out before us, and I'm excited to discover some of them with him.

"Good to know. Well, then, we might as well start now. You're not wearing clothes for the rest of my time here. I want you to be accessible at all times."

As if to make this abundantly clear, he moves me over to the banister and bends me over it. My breasts are hanging on the other side of the railing, and I've already started breathing heavily. Logan presses up against me, reaches his hand between my legs, and slides two fingers inside me, which causes me to groan loudly.

I see movement downstairs, and Nate appears in the main foyer, followed shortly by Dante. They look mildly surprised, but their expressions change quickly to ones of arousal. Logan doesn't stop what he's doing to me.

"Having fun with her, then?" Dante asks with a grin on his face.

"Definitely," Logan replies as he starts to rub my clit with his thumb. "Just so you know, I've told her she's not allowed to wear clothes until I leave. I don't give a shit if she puts clothes on the second that I'm out the door, but I want her naked as long as I'm in the house."

Dante nods and looks at Nate. "Noted. Sound good to you, Nate?"

"Yeah, except the part where she ever puts clothes on," he agrees with a grin on his face.

I'm panting loudly and am dying from the way they're talking about me. I had thought that maybe I was done for sex for the day, but Logan has me back in a level of ecstasy that has me aching to be fucked again already.

He pulls his fingers out of me and shoves them into my mouth. "Taste yourself, Lexi."

I suck him as though I'm giving him a blow job, and he chuckles.

"She's so fucking sexy," Nate says from below us.

"She really is. Thanks for sharing her, guys."

Logan takes my hand again and begins to lead me down the stairs.

"We heard you had quite a bit of fun. I don't think I've ever heard Lexi be that fucking loud in my life," Dante laughs.

I gasp and stare at Nate as we reach the bottom of the staircase because a long time ago, he said that he'd soundproofed this house. "I thought you said that these rooms were soundproofed."

Nate laughs and walks over to me, pulling me into his embrace and kissing my neck. I melt into him and feel completely at peace being in his arms.

"Of course, I didn't soundproof all my fucking bedrooms, Sexy. I just said that to tease you and because I like talking about the idea of you screaming in ecstasy. Now, I've heard it, seen it, experienced it, and just heard it again while Logan apparently fucked you senseless."

I blush when he says this. "You guys heard me from down here?"

"Yeah, we did. What the hell did you do to her, Logan?" Nate laughs and looks at his friend.

"She said she wanted it rough, so I gave her what she wanted." He shrugs.

Dante laughs, "I can see that. Orgasm denial?"

"Yup. I edged her twice before I let her come. When she did, she came like a freight train." He smirks at me, and I laugh.

"So yeah, Logan and I are a thing now. I hope you two are cool with that?"

I look up at Nate as I say it. For some reason, I feel like he has more reason to be jealous than Dante does. He's newer to this, and adding Logan means taking away from time that he can be with me.

Nate smiles at me. "I get that whole 'compersion' thing that Dante was talking about now, Sexy. I love you, and I love Logan. Seeing you two go off and getting pleasure from one another was hot as shit."

"But it means less time that I get to be with you." I bite my lip.

"I'm sure you'll make time for me, and I'm also sure that you'll let me join in sometimes," he grabs my ass and squeezes it.

"So, what are we going to do now?" I ask them.

"We thought that maybe we could watch a movie," Dante says.

We all go to Nate's theater room. I sit on Nate's lap as the movie starts, but we're not watching it. He's kissing me heavily and fingers me to an orgasm within minutes. The other two men are watching us instead of the movie, as well.

"Come here, Angel," Dante says, and I follow the instruction instinctively.

I curl up on his lap, but he doesn't touch any of my erogenous zones, just keeps me on edge with soft touches of my arms or legs or face and with kisses that are soft and sweet. As a result, I'm burning with the desire to have him touch my pussy or my breasts.

Dante's eyes are glued to the screen, though I doubt he's really watching it. He's a pro at pretending to ignore me while focusing solely on me. It drives me wild, though, because I never *really* know if he's paying me any attention or not.

I try to watch the movie, but I'm just itching for Dante's next touch. By the time the movie ends, I'm aching to be fucked by any one of these three men, if not all of them.

Chapter Ten
Pool Time

"Maybe we should have some drinks?" Nate suggests when the movie ends, and the other men agree.

"I want to drink someone's cum," I complain, and they all laugh.

"Oh, you will. Don't you worry, Angel," Dante smirks at me.

Nate gets us all drinks once we've made our way to a sitting room with a large sofa in it. I'm sitting on Dante's lap, and he's still just teasing me with soft touches.

"So, what's it like giving head?" We're on the second round of drinks when Nate asks the question, and he's looking at Logan, not me.

Logan looks surprised. "Why do you ask?"

"Well, Lexi seems to fucking love it, and you agreed with her before. I'm curious what's so good about it." He shrugs.

"It's just a lot of fun for me. I get to see my partner in ecstasy from what I'm able to do to them. It's also a challenge to see if I can make them come, just with my mouth," Logan looks at me, and I nod.

"Would you blow me?" Nate asks.

My eyes widen, and the air in the room gets thick with tension. I'm unsure if it's sexual or not. Dante has stilled in his movements as he strokes my arm, and we're both watching the other two men as they have their discussion.

Logan tilts his head to the side and looks at Nate in mild curiosity. "Is this a theoretical question or an actual one?"

"Theoretical...for now." Nate shrugs, and my eyebrows fly up on my face.

"I see. What makes you ask?"

Nate grins and admits, "When you sucked my fingers earlier, I got *really* curious about what your blow jobs are like."

"I don't think you could handle it," Logan laughs.

"Want to make a bet?" Nate shoots back quickly.

There is definitely sexual tension in the air now. I'm probably making a fucking mess on Dante's jeans because I'm horny as shit and desperately want to see Logan suck Nate off.

"I mean, if you really want me to do it, I will." Logan shrugs.

I can barely breathe as I watch Nate consider the possibility.

"Is it a good idea? I mean, we just started this whole thing with Lexi. Should we complicate shit like that?" Nate asks.

Logan smiles at him. "If you're not sure, then it's probably not a good idea."

"Can you just do that finger-sucking thing again to help me decide?" Nate grins at him.

I'm mildly surprised when Logan actually moves closer to him on the sofa. He picks up Nate's hand and puts his pointer and middle fingers into his mouth. Whatever he does to him causes Nate's eyes to go dark and become hooded. I know this look; Nate is hot as fuck and turned on like mad.

Logan does this for almost a minute, sucking Nate's fingers as though he's trying to get him to shoot a load of cum down his throat, and by the end, Nate is actually groaning in satisfaction. His erection is straining against his jeans, and Logan is also hard.

"So yeah, it's a bit like that," Logan says as he takes Nate's fingers out of his mouth.

There's an eerie silence, and both men pant heavily as they stare at one another. This is going to happen. I know it is, and I'm excited as hell to see it. Nate doesn't say anything. Instead, he undoes his jeans and lifts his ass to pull both those and his boxers down to his ankles, freeing his massive erection.

Logan gets onto his knees in front of him, and he looks up at Nate. "Are you sure?"

"Fuck yes, I'm sure. Just blow me already," Nate growls.

Logan places his lips around Nate's cock and begins to give him head. Nate groans, and I'm amazed by how much pleasure I get from watching this happen. Seeing Nate receiving sexual pleasure from someone that isn't me, someone that I love as much as I love him, and knowing that they're both getting ecstasy from one another makes me hot as hell.

I lower my hand to my clit, and Dante doesn't stop me. I start to finger myself as I watch the sex show these two beautiful men are giving me. They seem to have forgotten us, though. Logan is looking up at Nate as he moves his head up and down on Nate's shaft, and they're staring at each other. The only sound in the room is the sound of Logan's blow job and Nate's noises of ecstasy.

It's a surprisingly short amount of time before Nate growls, "Fuck, I'm going to fucking come, Logan."

Logan closes his lips tightly over Nate's cock, and I see Nate's face contort as he shoots his load into Logan's mouth. Logan uses his tongue to clean Nate's cock, and I'm plunging my fingers in and out of my pussy as I watch this happen. Yup. Just as fucking hot as I thought it would be.

I rush over to Logan and smash my lips against his, thrusting my tongue into his mouth, and am thrilled when I can taste Nate's cum. He looks surprised, then wraps his arms around me and pulls me down on top of him as he lays back down on the floor. We kiss for about a minute before we stop.

"Did you like that, Lexi?" Logan asks me.

"Seriously. Hottest fucking thing I've ever seen. You need to give me some tips," I grin at him, and I can feel his erection straining against his jeans underneath me.

"You don't need any tips; your blow jobs are just fine. Trust me. I'd know," Logan grins at me.

"Thanks for the endorsement," I laugh.

We sit up, and Logan pulls me into his lap. We look at Nate, who is sitting where Logan left him, pants around his ankles and with a slightly stunned expression on his face.

"Are you okay, Nate?" I ask him.

He looks at me and blinks. "I think so. Am I gay now?"

"No, Nate, you're not gay. Assuming that you still want to fuck Lexi," Logan laughs from behind me.

"Oh, I *always* want to fuck Lexi," Nate says and grins at us.

"Then, at best, you're bi. I'd say it's more likely that you're heteroflexible and just really like blow jobs. Unless you enjoyed my blow job *because* I'm a guy, and that's what turns you on. It's fine to be curious, and it's fine to just enjoy sex," Logan shrugs.

"And if I'm thinking that I would have no problem with you doing that to me again?" Nate actually blushes when he says this.

"Then I would still think the same thing and that I'm just *really* good at giving head," Logan grins at him.

As he says this, he lowers his hand between my legs and begins to rub my clit. I come almost immediately because I was so close anyway, and Logan laughs.

"I think Lexi might have enjoyed that more than both of us, Nate."

Nate turns to me, still looking slightly dazed. Logan is dipping his fingers in and out of my pussy at a leisurely pace, and I can tell that he has no real intent on giving me another orgasm.

"Thank fuck I still want to fuck the shit out of you, Lexi," Nate says. "Otherwise, I would literally change teams for more blow jobs like that one."

Logan laughs, "Not all guys give blow jobs as well as I do. It's a talent of mine. Trust me, I've had some shitty blow jobs from guys, and Lexi is up there with the best of the ones I've ever gotten."

He uses his free hand to turn my face to his and kisses me. Once again, I'm amazed at how skillfully he uses his tongue...apparently, that skill extends to sucking cock, too.

"Well, thanks again," I say with a grin.

Nate pulls his clothes back on, and the conversation moves on to more mundane topics. As almost the antithesis to Dante earlier, Logan continually fingers me and plays with my breasts while we're talking. He doesn't acknowledge it at all, doing it as though it's absentminded, but I know without a doubt that everything he's doing to me is deliberate.

The only clue is the fact that he is hard as a rock underneath me. Any time that I try to get him to finger me faster, he will still completely. If I moan or make any sound other than regular conversation, he also stops. He is teaching me the rules for this game as we play it, and I love it.

I need to figure out what I can do to make him give me an orgasm, but I feel like there is nothing. It is purely up to him as to when I can come. I look at Dante, who is watching us with an amused smile on his face. It's interesting that he's not jealous of someone else Domming me like this. I know that he would never intervene and give me an orgasm.

Nate, however...

I look at him, and he is watching us with great interest. I know that I can get an orgasm from him if I play my cards right. As long as I don't do anything to make either Dante or Logan deny me.

"Can I sit with Nate?" I ask Logan.

He turns my face to look at him. "Why?"

"He looks like he might want my company," I say, trying hard to keep the lust out of my voice.

"No."

Dante is the one who denies me, and my head snaps up to look at him. He gives me a wicked grin in return.

"Nice try, Angel. You know better than that, though."

Damn. Dante knows me too fucking well. I almost stick my tongue out at him in defiance, but being a brat never got me anywhere good.

I hear Logan chuckle, "I almost fell for that, too. Naughty, Lexi."

Logan slows his stroking of me to a painfully slow pace, and I groan in frustration.

"What did she do wrong? I want her to sit with me," Nate says, and he looks confused.

"Lexi wants to sit with you so she can get you to give her an orgasm," Dante tells him. "She knows that Logan isn't ready to do it, and I'd never step on his toes by doing it, but she thought she'd be able to convince you to."

Nate looks surprised, then laughs. "God, this whole BDSM thing is beyond me, but I fucking love watching you guys torture her."

He walks over to me and kisses me fully on the mouth, then drops his head to my breast and sucks and plays with it for thirty seconds before stopping.

"They're right. You're naughty," Nate says, then drops his head to my ear and says quietly, "if you sleep in my bed tonight, I promise to give you a thousand orgasms before morning."

I moan out loud and nod. I think that after being Dommed all day by Dante and Logan, a night in Nate's bed will probably be what I need.

Logan must have heard what Nate said because he gives me a wicked grin and says, "Well, if Nate's promised you a thousand orgasms before morning, I don't see any reason that Dante or I need to give you any before bedtime."

I feel the immediate response that my body has to his words. He is promising me extreme orgasm denial. We have hours before bedtime, hours during which these men will torture me so that I'm practically coming the second I'm in Nate's bed.

"Sorry, Sexy. I didn't mean to get you in trouble," Nate says, but he's grinning.

"You'll get the easiest orgasm from her ever the second she's in your bed, Nate," Dante laughs, then looks at me. "Make no mistake. You will not orgasm until you're in bed with Nate tonight."

As soon as he says this, Logan begins to stroke me faster, and my eyes widen because this will one hundred percent make me come.

"No, Logan," I say without thinking.

He pushes me off his lap so that I'm lying face down on the carpet and smacks my ass hard.

"Don't tell me no. Ever. You safeword, or you do whatever I tell you to do."

"Yes, Logan," I whimper as he smacks my ass again.

"And when I'm Domming you, I want you to call me 'Sir.'"

"Yes, Sir," I moan.

My pussy is drenched and aching to be filled. Bedtime seems so far away, especially when Logan smacks my ass a third time and flips me over, spreading my legs and diving between them in one swift movement. He tongues me until my breathing rate increases and I'm a millisecond from exploding into orgasm.

He sits back up, pulls me up to him, and sits me back in his lap as he did before. He goes back to stroking my clit slowly, but I'm so on edge that I think that even this might make me come any minute now. Logan stops and twists one of my nipples painfully hard, holding it twisted for a few seconds before letting it go.

Goddamn, I want him to fuck me again. I know without question that neither he nor Dante will be fucking me until tomorrow, though. This goes on for about ten minutes, and I'm dizzy with lust.

"Come here, Angel."

Logan drops his arms, kisses my neck, and pushes me off his lap so I can stand up and walk over to Dante.

"Yes, Honey?"

He pulls me onto his lap so that I'm straddling him and kisses me deeply. I get the usual feeling of homecoming from being in Dante's arms, and despite my high levels of arousal and frustration, I feel at peace.

"We're going to go swimming," Dante announces.

"We are?" Nate asks.

"Yes, and if Lexi is a good Angel and does everything she's told,

I'll let her drink my cum before bedtime. What do you think, Logan?" He looks over at Logan, who is watching us with eyes full of lust.

"Sounds fair. She can have mine, too. Nate's as well if he wants it. Though, in my experience, he probably does." Logan smirks at Nate, who flips him the bird, and Logan laughs.

We make our way to Nate's indoor pool. On the walk there, hands are on me almost constantly. All three men kiss me sporadically, and fingers are pushed inside both my pussy and my mouth.

When we get to the pool, I relax a little as things go back to some sense of normality. We swim and play games as usual until Logan grabs me and takes me to the spa. He lifts me up and out of the spa so that I'm sitting on the edge.

He spreads my legs wide and instructs me, "Sit there."

Logan sits on the opposite side of the spa, and I'm wet as shit. His hand disappears into the water, and I can tell from the movement of his arm that he's stroking himself slowly while he looks at me.

"Have you had a good day?" he asks me.

"Yes," I reply, and my voice is thick with lust.

Logan looks up into my eyes and smiles at me, "It's been quite a day, huh."

"You could say that," I laugh.

Logan stands and moves over to me so that we're face to face on my side of the spa. He puts his lips against mine and kisses me slowly and passionately. I can feel the arousal and desire wash over me, and I long for him to fuck me, but I know that he won't.

"I can see why Dante Doms you full-time. You're a lot of fun to play with," he grins at me.

I beam with pride at his words. "Thanks. I try."

"As I said, I don't do it all the time. Normally, it's only really in the bedroom. But with you, it feels like everywhere is our bedroom."

His eyes are hooded with lust, and I gasp as he quickly twists one of my nipples before dropping his hand to begin stroking my wet clit. Logan kisses me again as he does, bringing me to the edge of orgasm before he stops touching me except for where his lips are against mine.

I'm so close to coming, and I'm delirious with lust. Logan steps closer to me, and I wrap my legs around his waist as we continue to kiss. His hard cock presses against my clit, and it feels so good that I'm done for. I don't have time to stop it as my orgasm crashes over me. I moan into his mouth as I come, and my body shakes.

Logan keeps kissing me until my body stops quaking, then he laughs, "Well, that was a mistake."

"I'm sorry, your cock just felt so good against my clit," I say, biting my lip.

It still does. I can feel his thick shaft pressing against me, and I want it inside me more than anything. I want him to flip me over and fuck me hard and fast and fill me to the brim with his cum.

"Hey, Dante, you'd better come here," Logan calls to him, and I cringe.

Dante looks up, and both he and Nate swim over to the spa to join us.

"What's up?" Dante asks.

"What punishments do you normally give Lexi?"

"It depends on what she's done, but as a general rule, it's spankings. Unless I feel like getting creative because she's done something unusual. Did you come, Angel?" I nod my confirmation, and Dante raises an eyebrow at me. "I see."

"To be fair to her, I knew she was too close. I thought I'd stopped soon enough, but the tiniest bit of contact with her clit set her off," Logan laughs.

"Well, in that case, she can probably just be spanked. If you think it's okay, she can still give us blow jobs before bedtime. Otherwise, I would have denied her those."

Logan nods, and I'm so thankful that I'm still going to get to give them head. I would've been so sad to miss out on that.

Logan looks into my eyes, and I think I might die from how

much I want him to fuck me right now. "I'm going to spank you twenty times, Lexi. Then, you're going to suck me until I come down your throat."

"Yes, Sir," I say dutifully.

"Bend over the side of the spa."

The other two men have taken seats opposite us, and I slip off the side of the spa, turn around, and bend over it. The tiles around the spa are cold against my nipples, and the air is cool against my ass in comparison with the warm water swirling around my legs. I feel deliciously exposed as I wait for Logan to begin my punishment.

He smacks my ass so hard that I jump. I knew he'd be rougher than Dante. The few times he's spanked me so far have been hard, so I'm excited to get a proper spanking from him. He alternates ass cheeks the same way Dante does, but even by the fourth hit, both of my cheeks are stinging as badly as they do when Dante's finished one of my punishments.

My juices are dripping down my thighs, I'm so fucking wet, and Logan keeps spanking me. I love it. Fuck, I love him. I'll have to tell him sometime. Today, I've gone from loving him as someone who has been one of my best friends for fourteen years to loving him as surely as I love Dante and Nate. He has claimed me as his own, and every time he spanks one of my ass cheeks, it solidifies that fact for me.

When he finishes, he bends down and kisses each of my cheeks before pulling me upright and sitting down where I was before. His cock is at full attention and looks glorious. He pulls me to him and kisses me deeply. I try to put all of my love for him into this kiss. Now is not the time to tell him that I've fallen in love with him today.

"You can take my load now, Lexi," Logan informs me, and I nod.

I kneel in front of him and place my lips around his shaft. It's wonderful and velvety smooth, and I love it so much. He groans his pleasure, and I'm exultant in that sound. I keep going until I feel his cock pulse, and I suck him dry. I swirl my tongue around his head, ensuring that I've cleaned him of every last drop before I remove him from my mouth and smile up at him.

"Good girl," he tells me and pulls me up so that he can kiss me.

"Is it my turn now?" Nate asks.

Logan laughs, "See? You're not bisexual, Nate, just a big fan of blow jobs."

"Hey, there's nothing wrong with being bisexual. One of my best friends is bisexual, don't you know?" Nate grins back at him.

"I heard he gives *really* good blow jobs," Logan winks at him.

I'm watching them have this conversation and really fucking hoping that at some point, I'll be treated to a repeat performance of Logan giving Nate head sometime when Dante catches my attention.

"Nate asked a question, Angel."

I look at Dante and feel a painful ache between my thighs. I desperately need to be fucked, and he is giving me permission to suck Nate's cock. Giving head is definitely the next best thing. Hell, it's probably my favorite sex act.

I turn to Nate, who has already moved to sit on the side of the spa and is waiting for his turn. I make my way over to him, and he slides his hands around my waist and pulls me hard against him, slipping his tongue into my mouth as he kisses me.

He reaches between us and begins to rub my clit while we kiss, and I've started to get worried that I might come again when he ends our kiss and smiles at me.

"Fuck, I love you," he says as he leans back on his hands and angles his hips, so his erection is prominently on display for me.

I drop to my knees as I did for Logan and take him in my mouth. All three of them are well-endowed, but Nate is definitely the biggest of the three men. His cock is long and thick and perfect. I love it so much in my pussy, but it definitely makes giving him head harder. My jaw aches so much quicker with him, but I relish it, and it's a delicious pain.

Nate places a hand on my head, and I look up at him as I bob up and down, delighting in the ecstasy that is obvious in his expression. When he comes, I love feeling his hot seed spill into me and clean his cock of every last drop before I remove him from my mouth. He kisses me before I sit back down in the spa and wait for my next instruction.

"Not that it's a competition," Logan says with a cheeky grin at Nate, "but who's better?"

"Yeah, as if I'm going to answer that question," Nate smirks at him. "Is it your turn now, Dante?"

"She's had plenty of cock for now, especially since she was meant to be punished for coming too soon, not rewarded for it," he grins at Logan.

"What can I say? I wanted my cock sucked. What's the point in having a toy if you can't put it to good use?" Logan laughs, and I shiver at him referring to me as his toy.

Dante must have noticed because he smiles at me, "Do you like the idea of being Logan's toy, Angel?"

"Yes, Honey," I reply automatically.

"Well, this has been an interesting day," Dante laughs. "I expected the sex, but I did not expect Logan to turn out to be a second Dom for Lexi, who would also blow Nate on the side."

Logan grins at him. "Yeah, I thought I'd come here. We'd play some pool and drink some alcohol. I did *not* expect to fall in love with your wife before the day was done."

He says it so casually, and my eyes snap up to meet his. I'm staring at him in shock, and I don't know how to respond or if I'm even allowed to. I want to look at Dante for permission, but I can't take my eyes away from Logan's, and he smiles at me.

"Come here, Lexi," Logan says, and I move over to him, following the command by instinct and stopping in front of him. "Do you have anything you want to say to me?"

"I love you, too, Logan."

He kisses me, and my heart feels like it's going to explode because it's so full with these three men. Logan strokes my back softly, and it's a sweet and loving kiss. I love belonging to this man because he's amazing. Our kiss ends, and Logan bends me over the side of the spa again, positioning himself behind me.

"I'm going to fuck you now, Lexi. You don't get to come. Understand?"

"Yes, Sir."

"If you come, you don't get to spend tonight in Nate's bed. You'll be in mine. What do you think that will be like, Lexi?"

I'm bombarded with a thousand erotic images of spending the night in Logan's bed, but I know that if I come right now, tonight will mean nothing but torment with zero release for me.

"No orgasms," I answer his question, both confirming that I won't come now and that I know what my punishment for tonight will be if I do.

"Good girl."

He pushes himself inside me, gripping my hips tightly. I'm wet as hell and more than ready for this. Logan begins to fuck me just as hard as he did earlier. I grip the side of the spa to hold myself steady as he plows into me repeatedly. Thankfully, he doesn't touch my clit because I know that if anyone did, I would shatter into a thousand pieces and come immediately.

Logan groans as he fucks me and asks, "Do you belong to me, Lexi?"

"Yes, Sir," I confirm.

"Are you my toy?" he asks.

"Yes, I am, Logan."

"That's right. I can fuck you any time I want to, and you will not come unless I think it's okay, or Dante thinks it's okay. You can't just go running off to Nate for relief. Your orgasms belong to Dante and me."

I groan because I'm about to fucking die. This man can bring me to the brink of orgasm with his words alone.

"Do you have a problem with that, Nate?" Logan asks him.

I can't see Nate's face, but I can practically see his shit-eating grin, "As long as I can give her orgasms when *I* want to, I have no problem with you guys making sure she's gagging for it by the time I do."

Logan hasn't stopped his constant pounding of my pussy while they have this conversation, and when he speaks again, I can hear that he's facing me again.

"Of course. I'd never prevent you from giving her an orgasm. I just want her to know that she can't go seeking one when I don't want her to," he leans down to growl into my ear, "and if she tricks you into giving her one, she'd better hope like hell that I don't find out."

Waves of pleasure hit me, and I know that I'm going to have an orgasm any second now. I fight the urge with everything that I have. I want to spend tonight with Nate, fucking and coming and fucking again. I'm relieved when Logan's cock spasms, and I feel him come before he stills inside me. My relief is short-lived as he spins me around and sits me on the side of the spa before spreading my legs.

"Now, Lexi, we can't have you dripping cum in the spa. That would be unsanitary. I'd better make sure you're cleaned up before you get back in."

My eyes widen as I realize exactly what he means, and I know that I'm going to come if his tongue even touches my clit for a second.

"Unless you'd like to taste my cum, Nate?" Logan grins over his shoulder.

"Fuck off," Nate laughs.

"Just checking," Logan says and then lowers himself to place his face between my legs.

He sticks his tongue inside me and begins eating me out. His tongue doesn't touch my clit, but I'm incredibly fearful that he will. He licks every part of my pussy, cleans me out entirely, and traces all around it except for my clit. I'm in ecstasy right now. I can't stop myself from moaning with pleasure, and Logan reaches up to twist my nipple painfully when I do.

I like it a little too much, so about half a minute later, I moan again and am rewarded with Logan twisting the other nipple even harder. Good to know. When he does touch my clit with his tongue, I almost come at once. I moan loudly, and Logan painfully squeezes my nipple, keeping my orgasm at bay.

I'm able to withstand him licking my clit for almost a minute before I have to moan again, and Logan twists my nipple, pushing my orgasm back. I hope and pray that he'll stop, but he keeps going. I can barely keep my wits about me enough to moan and have him twist my nipples when I need him to.

After several minutes, the nipple twisting isn't working as well anymore. I'm not sure how much longer I can withstand this. I groan loudly, and Logan doesn't twist my nipple this time. I'm terrified because I'd been relying on that, and my orgasm is rushing in. I gasp in fright, and Logan stops immediately.

"Okay, I think you're clean enough to get in the spa now."

I pant for breath and just stare at him as he grins at me. Logan grabs me and pulls me into the spa, where he sits me on his lap and wraps his arms around me.

"I love you, Lexi," he whispers into my ear, and I sigh in contentment.

I lean my head back against his chest and revel in the joy that washes over me at being here, in his arms, and in love with him. I look at the two other men that I love as they smile back at us.

For now, it seems as though my torture is over. The men pass me back and forth as we talk about general things in our lives. They kiss me when they feel like it and keep me wrapped in their arms. I'm at peace and completely loving it.

Chapter Eleven
Dinner and Bedtime

When we get out of the pool, we rinse off in the shower before the guys get clothes on, and I make us all dinner. I find it erotic moving about the kitchen naked while completing this mundane task.

"It smells great. Is there anything I can do to help?" Dante asks when I'm almost finished cooking the meal.

"If you could take the plates and cutlery out, that would be great," I smile back at him.

He does this for me and then comes back into the kitchen. This time, he walks over to me and presses me against the refrigerator. The stainless steel is cold against my back, and I'm holding kitchen tongs in my hand because I was about to get the chicken out of the oven.

Dante claims my lips with his and kisses me passionately. My body burns with excitement and arousal as Dante reaches his hand between my legs to begin stroking my clit. I manage to hold back a moan as he continues to kiss me, but I can tell that he's not attempting to get me as close to coming as Logan did earlier. He just wants me back on edge after the long break I've had from being tormented.

It's working, though. I'm back in that state of arousal and aching to be fucked again, needing more than anything to have the relief of an orgasm. Dante must be able to tell because he ends our kiss but keeps stroking my clit and grins wickedly at me.

"You know the punishment if you come earlier, Angel. Not until you're in bed with Nate."

"Yes, Honey," I smile back at him and bite back another moan of pleasure.

I've fallen back into our old rules of no reactions, I realize. I've been so wild today. I'm surprised Dante hasn't been punishing me, but I suppose his rules only apply with him. We'll need to talk it through at some point, I suppose. For now, I'm having a lot of fun finding them out as we go, though.

Dante is still stroking my clit, and he starts to play with my breasts as well. My orgasm approaches rapidly, and I'm concerned that I will actually come. He kisses me again and explores my mouth with his tongue. Everything about Dante is familiar and wonderful. His touch is comforting to me, but my fear of coming too soon is strong, and he knows exactly how to bring me to pieces if he wants to.

He pulls his head back and watches me through lust-filled eyes as he strokes me faster, and I can't stop myself from panting to try and catch my breath.

"You're not going to come, are you, Angel?"

"No, Honey," I pant at him.

Dante keeps stroking, and I fight hard with the orgasm that is threatening me now.

"Are you sure?" he asks me with a grin on his face.

"Yes, Honey, I'm sure. I'm not going to come."

I hope to god this is true, but it feels like a lie because I am so fucking close that I know that if I allowed it, my orgasm would crash over me in less than a heartbeat.

Dante finally stops stroking my clit and grins at me. "Good to hear. You'd better serve dinner up, then."

He walks out of the room, and I bend over the bench and

breathe heavily as my orgasm washes away from me. Thank fuck he stopped when he did. I get the chicken and vegetables out of the oven and take them out to the dining table, where the men are seated and waiting for me.

I sit next to Dante, opposite Logan, who is next to Nate. Both men seem unable to stop themselves from ogling my chest while we're eating our dinner, and I'm wet just knowing that I have this effect on them, even though they've had plenty of opportunity to play with my body all day long.

Halfway through eating his dinner, Dante pushes his plate aside and says, "Come here, Angel."

I'm surprised, but I stand and take the single step needed to bring me next to him.

"Sit on the table," he instructs me, indicating to the empty space where his dinner plate was until a moment ago.

I blink but climb up to sit where he indicated. The tablecloth is warm underneath my ass from the radiant heat of his plate, and I place my feet on either side of his legs on the chair. Dante begins to slowly caress my thighs and then my labia before he pulls my lips apart and leans his head down to place his tongue in my pussy.

When he starts licking my clit, I almost explode at once. I find it such a turn-on to have him eating me as though I'm literally a part of his meal. Also, knowing that Nate and Logan are watching him do this adds to my arousal. But I know that I absolutely cannot come from this.

Dante has slipped two fingers inside me as he tongues my clit and slowly fucks me with them. My breathing becomes ragged, and I know that I am so close to coming that I'm scared I can't stop it from happening. He keeps going for thirty more seconds before he stops, places his hands on my hips, and pulls me down from the table.

"Sit in your seat, Angel."

I can barely walk, and the ache between my thighs is intense. I'm longing to be fucked, but I also desperately need the orgasm that is hovering on the horizon for me. I sit down and can barely focus on eating the food on the plate in front of me.

"Are you enjoying your dinner, Dante?" Nate asks him with a smirk on his face.

"It's very tasty, that's for sure," Dante laughs back.

"I'll have to try some later," Nate says and looks at me as though he wishes his tongue were buried in my pussy right now.

We finish our dinner and clear up before heading to the sitting room for after-dinner drinks. Dante holds my hand as we walk there. It's strange because, aside from the fact that I'm naked, this feels like any of a hundred nights we've spent hanging out with Nate and Logan.

But the way those two men look at me when I sit on Dante's lap is decidedly *not* like any of those hundred other nights. Plus, I know that tonight I'm going to fuck Nate's brains out, and Logan has literally claimed me as his toy to play with.

As we talk, Dante slowly trails a finger around my nipples, drawing a path from one to the other and back again. Eventually, he places his pointer finger and thumb around one nipple and rolls it between them, not missing a beat in the conversation as he does.

The same as Logan did earlier, he's doing these things to me as though they're absentminded. The other two men are watching every single movement, though they're also continuing the conversation as if nothing is happening. Dante holds my breast in his hand and rubs his thumb across my nipple before he lets go and drops his hand between my thighs.

He starts slowly rubbing my clit, and I'm wet as fuck right now. I find myself back in that state of arousal with an orgasm approaching within seconds of him touching me, and their prediction earlier that I would come the second I'm in Nate's bed is almost certainly going to come true.

Dante is hard as steel underneath me, and I'm grateful when he stops rubbing me and says, "You can give me head now, Angel."

I slide off his lap, turn to face him, and drop to my knees. I watch eagerly as he undoes his jeans and drops them and his briefs to his ankles, exposing his erection for my pleasure. I wrap my lips around him and begin to suck him off. He groans his approval of what I'm doing to him, and I'm pleased as hell.

I know exactly what Dante likes and how to make him come, so it isn't long before I get the enjoyment of having him blow into my mouth as he moans my name. I swallow everything and make sure he's clean before I pull my head back to look up at him.

"Well done, Angel. I think that might be a record," Dante grins at me.

"I had to try and beat Logan's time from earlier," I wink back at him.

Logan laughs, "It was very impressive, I must say. Come here, Lexi."

I smile as I follow his instruction, and he has me sit on his lap facing him, and his erection presses against me.

"It's almost bedtime," Logan says and looks down at my pussy as he begins to stroke my clit with his thumb. "Does that feel good, Lexi?"

"Yes, Sir," I reply.

"Do you want to come, Lexi?" he asks me.

"Yes, Sir, but I know that I can't."

"Good girl."

Logan slides his thumb into me and begins to thrust it in and out while he uses his other hand to twist my nipples, which causes me to moan. He does this longer than I can stand. He somehow manages to take me to the brink of orgasm every time he's done this to me today, and I'm so fucking close to coming that I feel like I might expire from trying to stop it.

Logan stops what he's doing abruptly and pulls my face to his to kiss me. It's deep and tender and soothes the nerves that are frayed from the fear that I might come too soon.

"I'm taking her to bed now," Nate announces from next to us on the sofa. "I'm more than ready to fuck her."

Logan breaks our kiss and smiles at him, "Okay, okay. You go have your fun with her."

He kisses me again, and this time it's rougher and more

passionate, but every one of his kisses is amazing. I want his tongue back between my legs right now. He holds my chin with his hand and turns my face to his, and is looking deeply into my eyes.

"You have until I wake up in the morning, Lexi. When that happens, I'm going into Nate's room, and I will drag you back to my bed, where I will have my way with you. Understood?"

I shiver in anticipation and fight the urge to come just from the thought of all the things he could do to me.

"Yes, Sir," I smile back at him.

He kisses me again, then pushes me off his lap. I walk back over to Dante and kiss him again before linking my hand in Nate's as we walk out of the room. Once again, I look back, and I see no jealousy on either man's face as we walk away. Both men have obvious erections and are looking at me with desire and longing.

"Damn, this whole BDSM thing is intense, isn't it?" Nate observes as we walk up the stairs.

"Yeah, you could say that. I fucking love it, though," I laugh.

"Do you wish I did it to you?" Nate asks.

We've reached the landing, and I slip my arms around his waist and kiss him passionately. He pulls me against him and kisses me back. I love him so much that it hurts, and I need tonight with him.

"No, Nate. You're perfect the way you are. Dante is not as hardcore a Dom as Logan is. I don't think I could've done it full-time for a decade if he was, and being able to come and be with you is exactly what I needed tonight, so thank you for offering," I smile at him.

He smiles down at me, "I love you. You know that, right?"

"I'd kind of gotten that feeling, yes. Now, are you going to give me the orgasm I so desperately need, or am I going to get into your bed and give it to myself? I just need you to be there if I do so I meet the criteria of 'in bed with Nate,'" I inform him.

"They're right—you're naughty, and you find loopholes," he laughs and takes my hand as we continue toward his bedroom.

"Hey, a girl's gotta do what a girl's gotta do," I grin at him.

Nate opens the door to his room, and it's dark and quiet. He picks me up, and I squeal because I wasn't expecting it, then he strides over to the bed and throws me down onto it.

"So. You want an orgasm, huh?" Nate grins at me.

"Yes, please. Oh my god, yes," I confirm.

"I think I can manage that."

Nate has a very obvious bulge in his pants, and I can't wait for him to fuck me. He spreads my legs and places his face between them to lick my clit. Dante wasn't wrong, and I come within thirty seconds. It's a relief to be able to embrace my orgasm when it hits me so surprisingly quickly.

"You were just a tiny bit worked up, huh," Nate smirks at me as he rubs my clit with his fingers.

"Nathaniel Walker with the understatement of the year," I laugh back at him.

His eyes are dark with lust, and he tells me, "Well, nine-hundred and ninety-nine orgasms to go, Sexy."

I laugh and then groan when he puts his head between my legs again. Nate brings me to orgasm several more times before he stands up and removes his clothes. He lies next to me on the bed and kisses me deeply. We make out for a long time and enjoy each other's bodies as we caress one another while we kiss.

"So…what now?" Nate asks as he rolls onto his back, his erection pointing toward his chest.

"I think you know very well, 'what now,'" I say and lick my lips.

Nate laughs, "Of course."

I place my lips around his cock and begin to suck him. He groans his satisfaction, and I try to count up how many times he's had his cock sucked today. A shot of arousal darts to my pussy when I get the image of Logan sucking him in my head.

"Let me eat your pussy while you do that," Nate tells me in a husky voice.

I move so that each of my knees are either side of his head and go back to sucking him as I lower my pussy to his face. I groan in ecstasy when he begins to eat me out again because it feels so good.

Nate gives me another orgasm, and he slightly thrusts his hips to fuck my mouth as I suck him. I'm enjoying this so much, but I'm also aching to be fucked.

I take him out of my mouth and ask, "Can we fuck now, please?"

"Sure," he laughs after removing his mouth from me.

I spin around so that I'm over him and slide myself onto his cock. Every single inch of him feels glorious inside me, and I close my eyes and throw my head back as I moan my pleasure.

"Feel good, Sexy?" Nate asks.

I open my eyes and look at him, a slow smile coming across my face as I see the beautiful man that I'm fucking looking back at me with such love and lust.

"Better than good." I drop my head to kiss him. "You feel amazing."

We start to fuck while we're kissing, and I'm in ecstasy. He feels so good deep inside me, and I'm thrilled to finally have him filling me. I start to fuck him harder, moving on him in a frenzy, and he laughs.

"Whoa, slow down, Sexy. We've got all night. Logan won't be in to do bad things to you until morning," he smirks at me.

"Don't you start Domming me, too," I laugh.

Nate rolls me over so that I'm lying on my back, and he's on top of me. "I don't have any desire to do that. Just to reap the benefits of it happening. But, I want to take my time with you while you're mine."

I just about come from the way he claims me as his own. He fucks me slowly, taking his time to explore my body, using his fingers to rub my clit and give me orgasms while we have sex. Nate plays with my breasts and kisses me, and this experience with him is so pure and amazing that I fall impossibly deeper in love with him.

When he eventually comes inside me, I come around him in sync, and it's beautiful. We go to his shower to wash off before heading back to the bed together. I lay with my head on his chest, listening to his heart beating.

"Thank you," I tell him as I raise my head to smile at him.

"For fucking you? I should be thanking you," he laughs.

"I needed that. Today has been intense as shit," I sigh a contented sigh as I remember how on edge I've been.

It's been a wild day, and I absolutely loved it, but this time with Nate has been perfect.

"I had my cock sucked by my best friend. I know exactly what you mean." He gives me a wry grin.

My eyes widen at the memory. "It really was the hottest thing I've ever seen."

"I'm glad you enjoyed it," he says while stroking my side softly with his hand.

"It seemed like you did, too," I smirk at him.

"More than I thought I would, that's for sure." Nate shakes his head in apparent amazement. "Logan's *really* good at giving head."

"Better than me?" I raise an eyebrow at him.

"Different," he tells me. "You're both just as good as one another, but it was different with him. With you, I'm also thinking about fucking you and enjoying your body. With Logan, it was just…he's very, very good at it."

Nate is blushing now, and I laugh, "I, for one, hope that it happens again."

"Noted." Nate kisses me. "In the meantime, I believe I still owe you over nine-hundred orgasms?"

"Can I take an IOU?" I ask him. "I'm completely wrecked."

Nate smiles and kisses me again as he pulls me into his warm embrace. "Of course, Sexy. It's been a fucking full-on day for both of us. I'm just happy to have you here with me tonight."

He turns the light off, and I lie in the quiet darkness and listen to his breathing. It really has been a full-on day. I never imagined when Logan was visiting today that it would turn out the way it did.

"You're really not jealous of Logan?" I ask Nate.

"Were you jealous when he gave me head?"

"I think you know I wasn't," I laugh. "Considering I want it to happen again, and I kind of want sex again just from thinking about it despite the fact that I'm tired as hell."

Nate laughs, too. "Okay, so why weren't you jealous?"

I think about it and decide what exactly I liked so much.

"Well, I love you both, and seeing you getting pleasure from each other was hot as hell. Also, it's not like I wasn't getting plenty of attention. It didn't detract from anything, just added to it."

"That's pretty much how I feel about you and Logan, too," Nate says.

"Yeah, but tomorrow morning he's going to come in and take me away from you."

"I could join in if I wanted," he says.

"Are you sure about that?"

Nate laughs, "Yeah, both of them told me at different points today that they didn't want me to feel like the BDSM stuff would restrict me or interfere in my relationship with you."

I'm grateful for this. As much as I love being their sub, I also love being Nate's equal.

"Thank you," I say, rolling over to face him so that I can kiss him. "I hope you know that you're as important to me as they are."

"Are you sure I'm not *more* important?" he asks me, and I can tell that he's smiling even though I can't see his face.

"Well, of course. I mean, you're the most important person in the world, after all," I laugh.

Nate kisses me again. "I'm glad you can admit it. Go to sleep, Sexy. I get the feeling that you're going to need your energy for whatever Mister Ballantine has planned for you tomorrow."

I roll over and curl up against Nate, feeling safe and secure in his arms. He kisses my head and pulls me closer to him. Tiredness washes over me, and it's not long before I start to drift off to sleep, feeling content and happy.

Chapter Twelve

Safe as Houses

I wake to the feeling of being lifted up by strong, muscular arms. "What's going on?"

"I told you that you had until I woke this morning," Logan says in a husky voice.

I can instantly feel the wetness between my legs and an intense ache, along with a desire to be filled.

"Of course," I say, as Logan strides through the door to his bedroom and kicks it shut behind him.

He drops me on the bed unceremoniously in the dark room before walking over to the curtains and ripping them open. I blink rapidly against the painfully bright light as Logan returns to the bed.

"Much better. I can see my toy to play with it now."

I shudder at his words, and a satisfied smile crosses his lips. He pulls out some pink rope that I recognize as belonging to Dante. Logan takes the end of it and trails it across my nipples. They're painfully stiff, and my breathing rate increases.

Logan leans down and swipes his tongue back and forth over one of my nipples as he drags the rope down and drops it on my pussy, which feels ominous.

He moves his lips next to my ear and growls, "I'm going to tie you spread wide open and use my toy however I want to."

I'm overcome with lust, and I can barely breathe as Logan does exactly that. He binds my hands together, then pulls them roughly over my head to tie them to the headboard of his bed.

He takes my ankles and spreads them wide, tying each to the corner of the bed with a quick-release cuff before he checks my position and grins wickedly at me. "I think you can go further."

Logan releases the cuff on my right leg and wraps his fingers around my ankle before he pulls me further down the bed, and it causes my arms to stretch. A dull ache forms in my muscles, and I smile. He ties my right leg back up, then moves to my left leg and releases it as well, only to tie it back up so wide that I feel like I'm doing the splits.

"What am I going to do with you now?" he ponders.

I don't know if I should reply, so I keep my silence just in case. Logan opens a drawer next to the bed and pulls out some things that he places on the table. He takes a set of nipple clamps out to put them on my nipples, and I bite my lip as I watch him. He tightens the clamps more than Dante normally would, and it's painful but also correlates directly to the amount of desire I have for him to fuck me.

When he's done that, Logan takes a large butt plug that I recognize and lubes it up with a generous amount of lubricant as I realize that Dante must have provided him with these supplies. The butt plug is the biggest one we own, and Logan positions his face between my legs. He presses the butt plug against my asshole and slowly begins to insert it as he places his lips over my clit and sucks on it.

My body can't tell which feeling to focus on, and everything becomes muddled in my brain. The pain in my nipples, the pleasure in my clit, and the pain in my asshole. Logan keeps licking my clit, but also uses his spare hand to stick two fingers inside me and stroke my G spot while he continues to push the butt plug in further.

I gasp as the butt plug approaches its widest point, and Logan pauses its movement to allow me to adjust but continues eating me out. After about fifteen seconds, he puts pressure on the base of the butt plug again and pushes it until I can feel it's all the way inside me.

Logan nips my clit with his teeth and, when I squeal, he grins at me, "I was told you know better than to react."

"Yes, Sir," I say and bite my lip.

"It's fine. I enjoy your reactions."

He licks my pussy again as he keeps fingering me, and my orgasm rapidly approaches. He hasn't told me that I can't have one, so I don't even attempt to avoid it.

"Sir," I moan as it hits me.

He doesn't say anything, just walks out of the room and closes the door behind him, leaving me tied where I am. I almost come immediately from the anticipation of his return.

I can feel my juices dripping onto the bed by the time the door opens five minutes later, and Logan walks back into the room with a grin on his face.

"That's a beautiful sight to see," he murmurs as he walks toward the bed.

Logan pulls his t-shirt off over his head, then drops the sweatpants he's wearing to the floor, freeing his erection. He climbs onto the bed and braces himself over me before pushing his cock inside me.

He kisses me passionately as he fucks me. Logan doesn't hold back, fucking me roughly. I can't move, and I'm in ecstasy from being filled with both the butt plug and Logan.

After he fucks me for a while, Logan pulls out of me, then moves to pick up a small pink vibrator from the pile of sex toys. He switches it on, and without warning, he holds it directly against my clit.

I moan loudly, unable to stop myself, and Logan laughs, "Do you like that, Lexi?"

"Yes, Sir," I gasp my response as he turns the vibrator's speed up.

It isn't long before my body is shaking through another orgasm, and my eyes widen as Logan doesn't stop the vibrator. Instead, he turns it on to its highest setting while keeping it firmly placed against my clit.

The third, fourth, and fifth orgasms come in quick succession, and I start to feel dizzy. Logan tugs gently on the chain holding the nipple clamps together, which causes darts of pain through my nipples, at odds with the pleasurable sensations in my clit.

I scream loudly as a sixth orgasm hits, and I begin to see black spots at the edge of my vision. Logan shows no sign of removing the vibrator, and I scream again as waves of pleasure rock my body and the black spots increase.

"*Pineapple!*" I shriek as loudly as I can.

Logan yanks the vibrator away from my clit and switches it off in an instant. He drops it on the bed and quickly removes the nipple clamps before he looks down at me with a concerned look on his face. My body is still shaking sporadically, and I pant for breath.

"Are you okay, Lexi? Do you need me to untie you?"

"I'm not sure if I'm okay, but I don't think I need you to untie me." I blink a few times while I try to clear my mind as I shudder again. "Can you just cuddle me for a minute?"

He still has a frown on his face as he lies down next to me. He kisses my lips softly and rests his head on my shoulder as he places his arm over my stomach and softly strokes my side with his thumb. His arm doesn't go anywhere near any of my erogenous zones, and it's calming. My heart and breathing rates get slower as we lie together.

I turn my head and kiss the top of Logan's head as I smile at him. He's so beautiful, and I love him so much. We've been in each other's lives for so long, and I love getting to know him in this new way.

"I'm sorry, Lexi," he says quietly.

"Hey, that's what the safeword is for. I think I'm okay to keep going."

He lifts his head to look at me with his beautiful chocolate brown eyes. "Are you sure?"

"Yeah, I am. If you want to, of course. I'll safeword if I need to."

He kisses me again, softly and tenderly, before he pushes his tongue into my mouth to kiss me more passionately. He traces a line up from my stomach to my breast, where he thumbs my nipple as he kisses me.

I moan against his mouth, and I wish that I could hug him right now, but the pleasure is flooding back into my body, and Logan's cock is stiffening against me again.

He breaks our kiss and moves his mouth to my other nipple, licking and sucking it while he lowers his hand to my pussy. He pushes his fingers in and out of me, and I moan my satisfaction as my desire for him to fuck me builds.

"Sir," I moan.

He lifts his head and smiles at me. "I can't believe how much fun you are to play with." He leans down and bites my nipple, which causes me to gasp. "I also can't believe I've spent years *not* fucking you."

He pulls his fingers out of me and rubs my sensitive clit. He watches me carefully as I gasp, and it takes less than a minute before I come for him.

Logan puts the nipple clamps back on my breasts before he straddles me and looks down at me with a satisfied smile on his face. His cock looks glorious, stiff, and pointing to his stomach.

"Open your mouth, Lexi."

I do as I'm told, and Logan pushes his fingers into my mouth. Instinctively, I suck him as though I'm giving him a blow job, and I can taste my juices on his fingers as I do.

He pulls his fingers out of my mouth with a popping sound, and we both laugh, then he moves forward and positions his cock near my mouth. He pushes his cock between my lips and begins fucking my mouth.

He hasn't been doing this for long when I realize that he's definitely not going as hard as he did yesterday. I wait another minute to make sure he's not just easing into it. When he doesn't get any rougher, I frown and kind of shake my head at him.

He pulls his cock out of my mouth at once and asks, "Do you need to safeword?"

"No," I laugh. "You're going easy on me."

He gives me a chagrined smile and says, "I suppose I am. You're definitely okay?"

"I will be as long as you fuck me properly," I tease him.

For a moment, I forget that he's my Dom now, and I fall into the usual relationship we've had for years. I recognize my mistake when he raises an eyebrow at me.

"I see." He moves away from me and shakes his head. "Do you think that's the way you should talk to me when you're my toy?"

"No, Sir." I cringe.

"Exactly. What happens to naughty subs who try to tell their Dom what to do?"

I swallow and bite my lip. "We get punished."

"Correct." He moves all the way off the bed and tilts his head to the side as he looks at me. "Now, what should I do with you? I can hardly spank you right now."

I know this is a rhetorical question and that I absolutely need to hold my tongue. Logan bossing me around is putting me firmly into subspace, and I love it. I can't wait to see what he does to me, and I'm dripping wet as he observes me lying tied up in front of him.

"I think the answer is obvious, of course. You don't get to come again for this scene."

I almost groan aloud because Logan has already proven that he is very adept at tormenting me with orgasm denial. I swallow heavily and nod at him.

"Yes, Sir."

"Open your mouth."

I do as he says, and he pushes his cock into my mouth. He fucks it much harder than he was before, and it's far more satisfying, but now I can't come no matter how good it feels. Logan holds my face in place, and I love him doing this. I choke on his cock a couple of times, and he keeps going for a long time. When he moans my name loudly, it pleases me immensely.

After a while, he pulls his cock out of my mouth and leans down to kiss me. I close my eyes and enjoy the sensations of everything as he tugs on the nipple clamps. It sends sparks of arousal shooting throughout my body, and I'm in ecstasy. He moves down to my pussy, and I clench against the ache I feel. I need to be fucked, but more importantly, I know that he's going to bring me to the brink of orgasm.

Sure enough, he buries his face in my pussy, licking and sucking my clit while he pushes his fingers in and out of me. I pant for breath and desperately fight the arousal that I feel. I know that there is a huge risk that I'm going to come, and I know that I'm not allowed to. This heightens my ecstasy, and Logan looks up at me with a wicked gleam in his eye as he continues to eat me out.

I can't help but squirm as I fight against the orgasm that threatens to crash over me. I focus on the aching in my arms and legs from being tied up for so long to try and avoid it from hitting me. I'm grateful when Logan lifts his head, and I pant heavily as I watch him move up again.

He leans down and bites my nipple as I moan, "Sir."

He smirks down at me as he finally pushes his cock inside me and reminds me, "Don't come, Lexi."

I nod as he braces himself over me before he begins fucking me. Again, he does it roughly, and I fucking love it. I wish I could come, but I also wish my hands weren't tied up. I want to touch Logan, and I want to rub my clit as he fucks me so that I can come while he fucks me as hard as he does.

Unfortunately, I can't, and it's both frustrating and satisfying. I love being used for Logan's pleasure, and when he leans forward to kiss me, he's at an angle that means his groin grinds against my clit when he buries himself deep inside me. This, combined with his kiss, causes my ecstasy to increase.

It takes everything I have to avoid coming while he fucks me, and I clench my pussy hard around his cock while I try to stop my orgasm from hitting me. Logan's eyes widen, and he thrusts roughly into me. His cock pulses inside me as he comes, and he collapses on me while he pants heavily against my neck.

After a minute, he lifts his head and kisses my lips softly with a smile. "Very good, Lexi."

I feel like I'm wound as tight as a spring. My orgasm has well and truly faded, but I'm still wildly aroused and aching for release. Logan pulls himself out of me and removes the nipple clamps. I gasp as he does, and the blood flow returns to them with a shock of pain.

Logan removes the butt plug, then moves on to untying me, releasing each of my legs first before he unties my hands, and I shake my limbs to get the blood flow to return. Logan drops the ropes next to the bed, along with the nipple clamps, and climbs onto the bed next to me.

He pulls me into his embrace and kisses me softly. "I love you, Lexi."

"I love you, too, Logan," I tell him with a smile.

He strokes my back as he cuddles me, and I wrap my arms around him; his skin is warm and soft, with hard muscles underneath. I love him so much, and it feels as though every experience with him deepens our connection further.

"I'm going to go run a bath. I'll be back in a second, okay?" he asks, looking into my eyes as he does.

"Sure," I tell him with a smile.

He disappears into the bathroom, and I hear the water start to run before he appears again. He cuddles me in the bed, making me feel safe and loved before he takes my hand and leads me into the bathroom. Logan takes me into the shower and cleans me off quickly before leading me over to the bath.

Logan gets in first and has me sit in front of him. He wraps his arms around me, and I relax against his chest. He kisses my cheek, and I smile as I close my eyes. The warm water is soothing, and he has put some kind of scented bubble bath in the tub. I feel completely at ease, and my love for him is almost overwhelming.

"Can you believe that this is happening?" I ask quietly.

"Not really," he says with a laugh.

"You said you'd fantasized about me before. Do you remember when?" I ask out of curiosity.

He chuckles, and the sound reverberates in his chest underneath me. "After the movie premiere, obviously. You were so clearly aroused all evening, and it was a big turn-on."

I kiss him, then admit, "I thought about you when I was fucking Dante and Nate after we got home. What about before that, though?"

"I didn't do it frequently. There was one event a couple of years ago when you wore this sparkly rainbow dress. You were showing it off to us, and you spun in a circle. The dress flared out, and I happened to get a glimpse of your black thong."

I remember the night he's talking about, seeing it in my head as he talks about it, and I'm wet listening to his version of the event.

"I thought about it every time you talked to me that night. I couldn't help it. The dress also showed off a *lot* of cleavage. As soon as I got home, I masturbated while thinking about you. Then I felt guilty as hell because you were Dante's girlfriend at the time, and I shouldn't have been thinking about you that way at all."

I turn in the bath as much as I can to claim his lips with mine before I tell him, "That's so fucking hot. Any other times you can think of?"

I turn back to my previous position with a smile on my face. Logan trails a hand up my stomach and starts trailing patterns over my breasts as he talks, increasing my arousal as I listen.

"Sure. Remember when we all went to Tahiti?"

I nod and then gasp when his wet finger trails over my nipple before he talks again.

"You wore these tiny bikinis every time we went swimming. I'd be shocked if both Nate and Ash didn't use you as masturbation material on more than one occasion that trip."

My eyes widen, and my body stiffens because I'd never even considered the idea of Ash masturbating while thinking about me.

I would bet my entire bank account that Nate did, but Ash? It makes me worry that he's been left out of this, and I'm not sure how he and Cassie are going to react when they find out that I'm now in a relationship with Logan as well.

"What's wrong?" Logan asks.

"Do you think Ash and Cassie are going to react badly when we tell them about us?"

I bite my lip in concern, and Logan immediately stops playing with my breast before he squeezes me tightly against him. He kisses my head as he cuddles me, and I feel him shake his head.

"No. They were fine when you told them about Nate. I don't see any reason they'd react badly when we tell them about us. I love you, Lexi, and you love me. We're both consenting adults. I think that, like when you told them about Nate, they'll just be concerned that Dante is okay with it."

As he speaks, my body relaxes again. "You're right. Given we're happy and in love, they can't judge us for that. I was *so* nervous to tell you guys about Nate." I chuckle as I remember that day. "They tied me up and fucked me to calm me down before you guys arrived."

Logan's cock jerks underneath me, and he goes back to playing with my breasts. "Did they, really? It's a shame I missed it. Speaking of you being tied up, I believe I owe you an orgasm from before? Since you were such a good girl when I denied you for your punishment."

As he says it, he trails his hand down from my breasts to my pussy. He kisses my neck as he begins rubbing my clit.

I spread my legs as wide as the tub will allow and moan softly, "Oh god yes, Logan."

He grasps my face with his hand and turns my head to the side so he can kiss me. His tongue explores my mouth as he continues rubbing my clit, and he drops his hand from my face to my breasts as we kiss. It isn't long before I'm moaning into his mouth as my orgasm hits and my body shudders.

Logan ends our kiss and kisses me softly on the lips one more time before I settle back against him. He wraps his arms around me again and, with my post-orgasm glow surrounding me, I feel completely at peace here with him. My eyes drift closed, and I listen to the sound of our breathing in the bathroom.

We lie together for a long time, and I luxuriate in being in Logan's arms. It's a wonderfully calming experience, especially now that I've had an orgasm and I almost fall asleep.

"Lexi?" he asks.

"Hmm?" I murmur, leaving my eyes closed.

"The water's getting cold. Do you want to get out, or do you want me to put more water in?"

I sigh and laugh. "I suppose we can get out. I'm going to get all wrinkly if we stay here much longer."

Logan laughs as well, and I stand and get out of the bath. He pulls the plug, then gets out and uses a towel to dry me. I love the hot sex I get with my Doms, but I'll admit that sometimes I love aftercare almost as much. Being treated as though I'm a perfect, beautiful thing to be cherished is amazing. Logan is as good at it as Dante always has been.

He takes my hand and leads me back into the bedroom before laughing. "We'll probably need to change the sheets."

"I'm just making cum stains all over Nate's house, apparently," I chuckle.

Chapter Thirteen
Pool Time II

*L*ogan throws on a pair of jeans and a t-shirt, then leads me out of the bedroom and downstairs. He takes me to the kitchen, where I sit at the bench while he makes us toast and cereal. He gets some juice and slides onto the stool next to me to eat.

"Whenever we find the guys, we should probably talk about what we plan to do," he says.

"What do you mean?"

"Well, I was meant to go home today. I don't know how long you guys were planning to be out here." He raises an eyebrow at me.

"Oh, yeah, we were going home today as well." I nod at him.

We finish eating and put the dishes away. Logan takes my hand, and we walk through the house and end up back in the pool area, where we find the guys in the gym working out. I bite my lip when I see Dante doing pull-ups. His muscles tense, and he's covered in sweat as he raises his head above the bar before dropping down again. He does about five before he drops to the floor.

"Hey, guys," he says with a smile, then his eyes darken with lust as he looks over my naked body. "Have you had a fun morning, Angel?"

"Yes, I have." I nod and squeeze Logan's hand with mine.

Nate's been doing bicep curls, and he smirks at me as he walks over to drop the dumbbell on the rack. "I bet you did. Logan stole you away from me before I woke up, and my cock hasn't even been sucked today."

"I bet if you ask Logan nicely, he'll do it for you," I tease Nate.

Nate shrugs. "Well, if you're not going to do it, I might have to."

"Do you want to work out with us, Logan?" Dante asks.

He nods. "Sure. I'll grab my workout gear and be back."

He kisses me, then leaves the room. Dante walks over to me and pulls me hard against him. He kisses me passionately as he grabs my ass to press me harder against him.

"You can come shower with me when I'm finished, Angel. Until then, sit on that chair at the side of the room as though it's the coffee table." He tweaks my nipple quickly before I walk away.

My pussy is immediately aching, and I'm completely drenched. I sit, exposed for the men to watch in between their exercises, though Nate basically never looks away from me, and I think he might be using me as inspiration to keep going. By the time Dante finishes his workout, I'm aching to be fucked again.

He grabs his workout towel and wipes it across his face. "I'll see you guys later."

"We were going to talk plans, weren't we, Logan?" I ask.

Logan chuckles. "I think Dante's got plans for you, Lexi. We can talk later."

"Did you just question my decision to take you upstairs, Angel?" Dante raises an eyebrow at me.

I blink at him, and he's got a familiar wicked gleam in his eye. I can't resist nodding my head because I want him to spank me. It's his go-to punishment, and I could do with a spanking this morning.

"I see."

He picks me up and throws me over his shoulder in a fireman's carry, and I squeal because I wasn't expecting it. Dante smacks my ass, and the stinging pain causes a shock of arousal to my pussy. He carries me out of the gym and upstairs to the bedroom he and I have always shared on visits to Nate's estate.

Dante drops me on the bed, and I'm reminded of not just Logan doing it this morning, but a thousand other times Dante has manhandled me like this. We've fucked in this bedroom so many times when visiting Nate's estate.

"Bend over the bed, Angel."

I'm *so* fucking wet as I follow his instruction. The air is cold on my ass, but the bed is soft and warm as I wait for Dante to follow through on my punishment.

"So…how many times should I spank you for questioning my decision?" Dante asks, but he doesn't say my name, so I know it's rhetorical.

This is definitely a stretch, and I know that he's doing this for me because if I'd said I wasn't questioning him, he wouldn't have offered the punishment. I've discovered that I prefer spanking to orgasm denial as punishment, that's for sure, and I love that I'm learning things about myself this weekend.

"I think ten will be fine," Dante says. "You should count, Angel."

"Yes, Honey."

I bite my lip, and I'm so turned on when he smacks my ass for the first time.

"One," I moan.

He smacks my ass again, and I flinch at the stinging sensation. "Two."

By the time he's finished, my ass is hot and sore. He's spanked me harder than he's ever done it before, and I wonder if he was inspired by watching Logan do it in the pool yesterday.

"On your knees, Angel."

I grin at the instruction but wipe the smile off my face before I turn around and dutifully drop to my knees in front of Dante.

"Worship my cock."

He's hard as hell, and I pull his gym shorts down, freeing his stiff erection. I wrap my lips around him and take him in my mouth. He looks down at me with so much love and lust in his expression as I suck him, and I enjoy this so much. He's so familiar and beautiful. His cock makes its way down my throat, the way it has on so many occasions before, and I revel in giving him this pleasure as he moans his satisfaction. I suck him for a long time, but I'm used to this with Dante.

My jaw starts to hurt after a while, and Dante finally says, "Stop, Angel."

I pull him out of my mouth and resist the urge to stretch my jaw to ease the pain. Dante pulls me up to standing and kisses me passionately. He pulls me against him as we kiss, his hard cock pressing against me as his hands roam over my body.

He reaches between us and rubs my clit as he walks me backward to the bed. When the back of my knees hit the mattress, Dante breaks our kiss and pushes me down, so I'm lying on my back on the bed. He drops to his knees in front of me, and I bite my lip as I watch him.

Dante puts a hand on each of my knees and spreads my legs wide. He pulls me forward on the bed, so my ass is right at the edge, and pushes my legs even further apart before he buries his face in my pussy. I work hard to control my breathing as arousal floods through me.

I'm sure he can tell because Dante lifts his head and says, "You can react, Angel."

I moan loudly when he lowers his head again and begins eating me out. He pushes his fingers in and out of me while he licks and sucks my clit, and I gasp when he nips it gently with his teeth.

"Dante," I groan in satisfaction.

He continues what he's doing, and I'm lost in ecstasy as I enjoy the sensations he gives me. The world is reduced to Dante and the things he's doing to me. His familiarity and the love I have for him swirl in the air around us as he does the things he knows will make me come, and when I inevitably do, he doesn't stop what he's doing to me. I'm treated to multiple orgasms before he gives me any relief, and I pant heavily for breath as he moves forward to position himself over me.

Dante kisses me, and our tongues dance together as he pushes his cock inside me. I wrap my legs around his waist as he fucks me, and he smiles at me as he wraps his arms around me and lifts me up from the bed.

I gasp in surprise as he carries me over to the wall and slams me against it. He thrusts roughly into me, and the wall is cold and hard against my back. Nothing gets me hotter than Dante manhandling me, and I love when he does unexpected shit like this. I tighten my legs around his waist, and he pounds me repeatedly.

He lowers his head to my breast and licks and sucks it while he fucks me. I moan loudly and wrap my arms around his neck, holding on for dear life while waves of ecstasy rock me. Dante holds himself still as his cock jerks, and he grunts roughly when he comes deep inside me. He presses his lips against mine and kisses me passionately while he explores my mouth with his tongue. When our kiss ends, we look at each other while we pant heavily.

"Was that good, Angel?"

I nod and say, "So fucking good, Honey. I love you."

Dante kisses me again, then eases me down to the floor. My legs are weak from how tightly I was holding onto Dante with them, and I do my best not to make a mess as we head to the bathroom.

Dante turns the warm water on in the shower and smiles at me. "Get in, Angel."

I do as he instructs, and he proceeds to wash every inch of me. He kisses and caresses my skin before he washes each body part. When I'm clean, he holds me tight under the warm spray and kisses me gently. His tender kiss is soothing, and even though our scene today wasn't intense, I very much enjoy Dante's attentiveness to me right now.

We get out of the shower, and he towels me dry before he dries himself and gets dressed in jeans and a t-shirt. He takes my hand and leads me out of the room. I've gotten used to being permanently naked since the poker game, and I love that any one of my three men can access me at any time now. It makes me wonder how things will be when we get back to LA, though.

I'm unsurprised when we find Nate and Logan playing pool when we get downstairs. Of all the guys, these two love the game the most. Nate's the best at it, Logan's the worst, but they probably love the game equally.

Nate's currently bent over the other side of the table to take a shot, so I walk over to Logan, who smiles at me as he wraps his arm around my waist. He lowers his head to mine and gives me a slow, luxurious kiss.

"Hi," he murmurs when our kiss ends.

"Hi," I repeat with a smile.

Nate stands up from where he's failed to sink the red number eleven and smirks at me. "No 'hi' for me, Sexy? Your turn, Logan."

I stride over to Nate and wrap my arms around his neck before I smash my lips against his. He's the only one of these three men that I haven't fucked today, and I'm disappointed by that.

He sets his cue against the wall and lowers his hands to my ass before he pulls me hard against him. He breaks our kiss and smiles at me.

"Hi, Sexy Lexi."

"Hi, Nate."

His stiff erection presses against me, and I wish that it was in my mouth. Unfortunately, Logan distracts Nate.

"Your turn, Nate," he calls.

I sit on one of the stools nearby, and Dante gives me a wicked grin and asks, "Is that how you sit, Angel?"

Dutifully, I spread my legs wide. Immediately, Nate looks up from where he's lined up to take a shot on the other side of the table. When he sees me, he bites his lip and accidentally hits the white ball with his cue. It rolls about six inches before coming to a stop without hitting anything.

"Two shots to me." Logan laughs and then winks at me. "Thanks for the assistance, Lexi."

"That's not fair," Nate complains.

Logan takes his turn and manages to sink the purple number four. "How is it not fair? I have to try to focus while my toy has her fine pussy on display for us, too."

A dart of arousal heads straight to my crotch when Logan calls me his toy, and I'm sure he knows what he's doing because he smirks at me.

I remember Dante's comment about having me display my pussy for Nate to see if he could beat him at pool. I wonder if it would work for Logan, who is even worse at the game.

Nate lines up for his next shot, facing away from me, so I lower my fingers to my pussy and begin rubbing my wet clit.

"Nate," I moan in my best 'I need to be fucked by you' voice, right as he pulls his arm back to take his shot.

Sure enough, he fumbles the shot, and the white ball hits one of Logan's instead of Nate's. He turns to look at me with a frown on his face.

"This isn't funny, Lexi," he growls.

I'm still rubbing my clit, and I give him a seductive smile as I ask, "Isn't it?"

"No."

I slide off the stool and walk slowly over to Nate as Logan sinks another ball. Nate might be frowning at me, but his gaze still roams over my naked body as I head toward him, and he's hard as hell now.

I unzip his jeans and reach into his underwear to stroke his cock as I look into his bright blue eyes and raise an eyebrow at him. "Come on, Nate. You're the best pool player. Surely my pussy can't be *that* distracting, can it?"

"Lexi," he moans softly, and I give him a wicked grin.

"Yes, Nate? Did you want something?"

"You on your knees in front of me for a start," he says in a voice laced with arousal.

"Deal. I'll get on my knees for you and suck your cock every turn, and we'll see if you can keep up to your usual standards of pool playing," I tease him.

I'm still stroking his thick, hard cock, and he looks down at me with pure lust in his eyes as he murmurs, "Fine. Do it, then."

I grin in satisfaction because this will be an immense amount of fun for me. Even more so if Logan manages to actually beat Nate. He's pretty terrible at pool, though, so it's still a long shot.

I pull Nate's jeans and underwear all the way down and off, then toss them aside. His cock is pointing toward his stomach, and I lick my lips, eager to suck him, but I have to wait until it's his turn. Nate pulls his top off over his head and drops it on his other clothes.

"It's just weird to only be wearing a top," he laughs.

"Your turn, Nate," Logan says in a husky voice, and I realize that this is turning him on, too.

While Nate looks over the pool table, I glance at Logan and see a telltale bulge in his jeans. I follow Nate to the other side of the pool table and drop to my knees in front of him.

I take his cock in my mouth while he lines up for his shot. The pool table is right behind me, and my head hits it as I move back when he leans forward to hit the ball. I don't care, though, and I keep sucking him as I swirl my tongue around the head of his cock.

He groans softly, then says, "Not good enough, Sexy. I still sank the nine. We need to move."

I suck him for another couple of seconds, then slowly draw him out of my mouth. "Fine."

I follow him to the end of the table, and as we pass Logan, I trail my hand over his crotch and squeeze his cock.

He wraps his fingers around my wrist, pulls my hand off his cock, but also pulls me hard against him. He kisses me expertly while he uses his spare hand to rub my clit for thirty seconds before he ends our kiss.

"Off you go. Nate's waiting for you to suck his glorious cock." Logan winks at me.

"It is pretty fucking nice, isn't it?" I agree with a grin as I pant for breath, arousal flowing through me.

I take my position in front of Nate again and start by sucking his balls as he lines up, which makes him groan before I take his cock in my mouth. I take him as far as I can, pressing my nose to his stomach as I squeeze his ass cheeks with my hand, and he curses above me.

"For fuck's sake!"

"Having trouble focusing, Nate?" Dante asks in an amused tone, and I assume Nate's fucked up his shot.

Since it's Logan's turn, I don't stop what I'm doing, slowly pulling Nate out of my mouth before I slide him back in again.

He puts his hand on my head, and I look up at him to see him looking down at me, clearly enjoying the pleasure I'm giving him. "Yeah, it's a little difficult to focus. Lexi's mouth is only the second-best place for my cock to be compared to her pussy."

"What about her ass?" Logan asks.

Nate reaches down to play with my breasts while I continue to suck him and says, "I love her ass, but her pussy is better, and I love how much she loves sucking cock."

I increase the suction as I slowly pull my mouth backward on his shaft, and Nate groans while I swirl my tongue around the head of his cock again. I plunge forward to press my nose against his stomach and hold my head there with his cock down my throat as I revel in his groan of satisfaction.

I manage to repeat this process three times before Logan chuckles and says, "Your turn again, Nate. Unless you want to just forfeit this match and concede that I'm better at pool than you are?"

I don't stop what I'm doing, and Nate is moaning in ecstasy now, but he says through panting breaths, "No. I'm fine."

"You don't sound fine," Dante says, and he sounds amused.

Since Nate hasn't told me he needs to move to take his shot, I don't stop and, instead, continue to worship his cock. When he shuffles sideways slightly and bends forward, I barely even need to lean across to keep doing what I'm doing.

Whatever happens with Nate's shot, though, causes Dante and Logan to burst into laughter before he looks down at me and says, "You're lucky you're fucking hot, Lexi."

I look up and lock eyes with him as I continue blowing him. I reach my hand between my legs and begin rubbing my clit while I do it and when Nate sees me do it, his cock jerks in my mouth. It doesn't take long before I'm moaning in ecstasy on Nate's erection.

"Your turn again," Logan says from the other end of the pool table.

Nate doesn't move, but he raises his cue, and I hear it hit a pool ball before he says, "No, it's really fucking not." He looks down at me and places his hand on my head as I keep doing what I'm doing. "Finish this game, Logan. I want to fuck Lexi over my pool table."

He pulls his cock out of my mouth and pulls me up to standing before kissing me passionately. When he ends our kiss, he spins me around and bends me over the pool table before thrusting into me from behind. I manage to see Logan sink the black eight ball before I close my eyes in ecstasy. I grab hold of either side of the pool table as Nate pounds into me.

After about thirty seconds, I gasp in surprise when I feel someone move underneath me, followed by a tongue on my pussy. I open my eyes and look to my side to see Dante sitting and stroking his cock in the same place he's been for some time, so I know it's Logan underneath me.

He's so ridiculously good with his tongue, and he uses it on my clit expertly to bring me to orgasm in record time while Nate fucks me.

"Holy fuck," I moan as my body shakes, and I grip the pool table for dear life as Nate continues to plow into me.

Logan doesn't stop what he's doing, and it extends the waves of my orgasm, which I ride through until Nate comes inside me. He grips my hips tightly and buries himself deep inside me when he comes.

"Fucking hell, Lexi," he groans and then kisses my back before he pulls out of me.

I'm only empty for a second before Logan takes Nate's place behind me. He pushes himself into me, and I groan in satisfaction as he fills me.

He fucks me for a minute before Dante appears next to me. He lifts my head to kiss me roughly while holding my face in place.

"Get on your hands and knees, Angel."

Logan pulls out of me, and I feel a little unsteady but manage to get down on my hands and knees. Logan wastes no time in grabbing my hips and entering me again to continue fucking me.

Dante pushes his cock into my mouth, and I feel enjoyably full with both men fucking me. I'm moved back and forth between them as they fuck me in rhythm until Logan's cock jerks inside me when he comes.

His tongue is on my pussy straight away, and I groan on Dante's cock. Logan eats me out, again not caring that I've just had two men come inside me, and he rubs my clit with his fingers.

I give in to the ecstasy I feel and enjoy the sensations Logan gives me, along with the enjoyment of giving Dante head. After a while, Logan moves his tongue from my pussy to my clit, and it doesn't take long at all for him to bring me to orgasm after that.

I come just before Dante groans my name and blows in my mouth. I suck him dry and ensure his cock is completely clean before I remove him from my mouth.

I flop onto my back and pant for breath. Logan lies next to me and pulls me into his embrace to kiss me. I wrap my arms around his neck as I kiss him back and then smile at him when our kiss ends.

"I love you, Lexi," he says and then laughs. "It's still kind of weird to say that."

I nod my head in agreement. "It is, but I love you, too. I've never been happier. I loved you for years, and this is just a different kind of expression of that love."

He looks at me with his beautiful chocolate brown eyes, and I'm struck by how amazing he is and how lucky I am to have him in my life.

"I'm glad I came out here this weekend," he says with a smile.

"Do you think it would've happened at some point anyway, if

not this weekend?" I wonder aloud.

"I think it would have," Nate says with a laugh nearby.

I look over and smile at him, but as much as I love lying here in Logan's arms, we should probably discuss logistics for our return to Los Angeles, and lying on the floor to do it probably isn't practical.

I sit up, and Logan follows suit, kissing me one more time before he stands and heads over to his clothes to get dressed.

Dante and Nate are already fully clothed, and Dante says, "I agree, Nate. We've all been so happy that when Logan said he was coming out here, I thought I'd just be open to whatever happened. If that was sex, it was sex. If that was something more, it was something more. If that was just a fun, platonic weekend with a friend, that was fine as well."

I have so much love for this man who loves not just me so deeply but also his friends deeply enough to allow us to have this unique relationship.

"Thank you, Dante," I say in a choked-up voice, and he smiles at me.

Logan links his hand in mine as we walk to the living room. He sits on the sofa and pulls me down onto his lap. Dante sits on our right, and Nate sits on our left.

"Lexi told me you guys were planning to go back to LA today?" Logan says once everyone's settled.

Dante nods. "Yeah, we are. Lexi's got work tomorrow, and we've got that meeting with the label."

"Makes sense," Logan says with a smile, then looks up at me. "So, what's the plan for us when we get back?"

I realize that he won't be living with us, and it makes me sad, but I also understand that Logan is very practical and even jumping into this is big for him. Unlike Nate, he's not likely to want to move into our apartment right this minute.

"I guess we'll just need to plan our nights together a little more than I do with Dante and Nate." I smile at him. "I can come over to yours a couple of nights a week, and maybe you could come to ours on the weekend or something?"

"I think we can make that work." Logan pulls my head down to kiss him, and he explores my mouth with his tongue before he ends our kiss.

This weekend has been so unexpectedly beautiful. I'm actually excited to go back to Los Angeles and start this new life with Logan as one of my partners. I'm sad he won't be living with us, but I'm sure it's something we can work toward in the future.

Chapter Fourteen

Taking Stock of the Situation

I wake in Dante's arms when my alarm goes off on Monday morning and smile at him. "Morning, Honey."

"Good morning, Angel. Did you sleep well?"

A smile creeps across my face before I nod. "Yes. I dreamed about the weekend and all the stuff we did...plus some stuff we didn't."

His cock is stiff with his morning erection, and he presses more firmly against me. "Want to reenact some of them now?"

"I mean, sure I *want* to"—I laugh and shake my head—"but I have to get to work early this morning. We've got a shipment coming in at the Rodeo Drive store, and I need to help the ladies do inventory."

"Fine. I guess I'll just have to sort myself out," he teases me.

He knows he could always instruct me to blow him, so I know he's not actually upset by the fact I don't have time this morning, and I smile at him. "I'll sort you out after work."

"No, you won't. You're going to Logan's tonight," Dante points out.

I bite my lip and frown at him. "Shit, you're right. Do you want to have sex now?"

"No, Angel. You need to get to work." He wraps his arms around me and squeezes me tight. "I don't want you to be late, and I'm not upset that you're going to Logan's tonight. I love you."

His reassurance is definitely welcome because I was worried he would be upset, and I realize that this new situation will take some getting used to. I kiss him and allow myself to relax in his warm embrace for a few moments before my alarm rings again. I kiss Dante and get out of bed to go get ready.

I shower quickly and head to the closet to get dressed because, ideally, I'd like to be there when the shipment arrives. I smile as I pull on the colorful Serenity dress I bought when I went to The Grove with Cassie, along with some pastel pink heels. I pull underwear on just in case it's windy today and smile at my reflection once I've done my hair and makeup.

I really do love this dress, and I've been unable to get Cassie's comment about Black Lilac stocking Serenity's clothes out of my head. I know it's a long shot, but I think I might follow it up as soon as I get a chance. As Cassie said, you never know if you don't ask.

I head back into the bedroom, and Dante's eyes darken when he looks at me. "I like that dress, Angel. You look sexy. Are you wearing underwear?"

"Sadly, yes. I don't want to risk a sexual harassment lawsuit at work." I laugh as I lift the hem of the dress to flash him my matching pink underwear.

"Very nice. Have a good day at work, Angel, and have fun with Logan tonight."

He holds his arms wide, and I climb onto the bed to kiss him and give him a hug.

"Are you sure that you're not jealous of all of this?"

He looks down at me and shakes his head. "I'm really not. I love the guys as much as I love you, and I honestly would've done this sooner if it had occurred to me."

"What made you do it out of the blue?" I ask out of curiosity.

He's quiet for a moment as he seems to consider my question, and I wonder what finally tipped it for him.

"I knew Nate had feelings for you. On some level, I also knew you had feelings for him. You were both so close, and some people would probably have called your friendship an 'emotional affair.' I didn't mind, though, because it never affected my ability to get what I needed from our relationship. I also would never have wanted to deny either of you that source of comfort."

He kisses my lips softly and smiles before he continues talking.

"When Nate suggested you play the part of his lover in our music video, I could see how it excited you. I was excited, too. The thought of seeing you with him turned me on, so I instructed you to do it. On the day, he made you come twice—no, three times"— he smirks at me—"and I don't think there was any turning back from there. I didn't want to cling to some concept of monogamy at the detriment of everyone's happiness. I knew a bit about the concept of polyamory, and I decided to embrace it."

I kiss him again, and I'm so in love with this man who I once thought would be the only man I would ever love like this.

"What about Logan? You said to us that you thought we would have sex?"

Dante shrugs. "I didn't think it would become what it already has, but I'm also not surprised. I wouldn't ever have offered you up to any random stranger. It's Logan, though, and he's been one of our best friends for a long, long time. If we were all happy, I didn't see any reason that he wouldn't be happy as well if he joined us, even just for sex if that's all he was interested in…and I was pretty sure he would be interested from the way he was looking at you at the movie premiere."

He smiles at me for a few seconds as he squeezes me tightly in his embrace, but then he frowns and sighs.

"I probably should've spoken to Nate about it first, but he ended up partially initiating it, so I took my cues from him and assumed he would be okay with it."

"And you're not jealous of Logan Domming me?" I laugh and shake my head. "I found it curious that you weren't."

Dante gives me a wicked grin. "All I see are far more interesting ways for you to be teased and tormented, Angel. But no, I'm not jealous. Logan and I talked about it on Saturday night after you and Nate went to bed. We're both happy to 'share custody' of you, so to speak. God knows we've worked together for over a decade, so collaborating on sexual punishments is hardly a big leap. If you're worried about going to Logan's tonight, don't be. Nate and I will be fine here, and tomorrow I promise to let you worship my cock to your little heart's content."

He kisses me again, deeply and passionately this time, as he slips his fingers under my dress to rub my clit through my underwear.

He breaks our kiss, and I pant for breath as he asks, "Don't you need to get going?"

"Uh-huh," I moan softly.

"Off you go, then," Dante says with a smirk at me as he pulls his hand out from under my dress.

"Not fair," I moan.

He chuckles, "Life's not fair. Go to work, Angel. You don't want to be late."

Since he used my nickname, and I really don't want to be late, I climb off the bed and make my way into the hallway. Before I leave the apartment, I peek into Nate's and my bedroom. It's dark in there, and he's obviously sleeping, so I leave him alone and head out.

I get a coffee and a muffin for my breakfast on the way to the store and arrive just before eight. The store manager, Jasmine Adams, has already arrived, and she smiles at me when I walk in.

"Morning, Lexi. I *love* that dress!"

"Thanks, Jazz." I grin at her. "It's from Serenity's latest collection."

"Oh my god, I saw the collection online. The clothes are to die for"—she gestures to my dress—"I mean, clearly they're to die for."

"I got a few outfits, but yeah, I could totally have bought the whole collection and been a happy woman," I admit.

We talk for about fifteen minutes, and Jasmine brings me up to speed on everything with the store. We're in her office going through some numbers when one of the salesgirls comes in to tell us that the shipment has arrived.

We head out to greet the delivery driver and check off the boxes against the purchase order. These clothes are for the new season, and they've come from a supplier that I managed to snag a deal with a few months ago. They have deals with multiple designers, and the profit margin on this shipment is huge, so I'm excited.

Jasmine and I sit in the storeroom to open the boxes and take inventory of the clothes. I know that I could leave this to her, but I like to be involved, especially in important shipments like this.

We've been at it for an hour, checking items off against the list of what was ordered, when my phone pings with a message from Nate.

You left without saying goodbye this morning.

I feel guilty that I didn't say goodbye, so I quickly send a reply.

I'm sorry. You were sleeping, and I didn't want to wake you.

I glance over at Jasmine, but she's not paying any attention to me, and it's not like she'd know who I was sending messages to anyway, even if she were.

For future reference, you can always wake me. Preferably with your mouth around my cock.

I shift in my seat as I read his message because it has an immediate effect on me. Heat rushes to my cheeks as I write my response.

Noted. I'm at work, so I probably shouldn't tell you all the things I want to do to you when I see you tomorrow.

I almost groan out loud when his next message comes through because he's sent a picture of him in bed. The sheets are low around his waist, just above his pelvis, and his cock is tenting the sheet above him. His ice-blue eyes are piercing into me as he stares into the camera lens, and I don't think he's ever looked more like a rock star than he does in this picture.

But what am I meant to do about this problem, Sexy Lexi?

Jasmine walks over to me with a list in her hand, and I gulp quickly as I lock my phone and drop it face down next to me.

"I think this box is missing five outfits," she says with a frown on her face.

I raise my eyebrows and ask, "Really?"

My phone buzzes next to me, and I cringe, but Jasmine doesn't look at it, and I'm grateful it's face down.

"Yeah, five of these blue dresses aren't in there." She indicates to them on the list.

My phone buzzes twice more as I look through the list, and I wonder what Nate is sending me. The blue dresses should be in the box, but everything else is ticked off on the list except for them. I count the dresses and, sure enough, Jasmine is right, and we're five short.

I frown because that isn't good, but mistakes do happen sometimes. "Okay. Highlight it, and we'll make sure they're not in any of the other boxes."

"Can do."

She heads back to where she was and starts hanging the clothes from the box on racks, and I pick up my phone to look at it.

What I need is a lover to suck me dry.

Someone who loves nothing more than being on her knees in front of me.

Know anyone like that, Lexi?

I bite my lip and type out a reply.

You're going to be the death of me. Yes. I wish I were there to suck your amazing cock today. Call Logan because I'm busy at work, and you're going to get me in trouble if anyone sees my phone.

Almost immediately after the message shows that he's read it, my phone starts ringing, and Nate's name is on the screen.

"Yes, Nathaniel Walker?" I answer with a laugh.

Jasmine looks up with a look of surprise on her face.

Obviously, she knows I'm friends with all of Wicked Stallion. Basically, everyone in the world knows about our friendships, but I know she still gets starstruck whenever Dante comes into the store. Most of my employees do.

"Is that going to be your default answer whenever you can't give me head now?" he asks, and he sounds amused.

"Maybe. You seemed to enjoy it."

I shift in my seat as I remember Logan giving Nate head. I definitely want to see that again. Maybe I can give Logan head while he does it next time.

"If I recall, you enjoyed it quite a bit, too," Nate says in a husky voice. "I wish you were here sucking my cock right now. I'm imagining it while I'm stroking myself, though."

"I see. That seems like fun," I say casually.

Nate chuckles, and he sounds so sexy as he pants for breath in my ear before he asks, "Is someone in the room with you, Sexy?"

"Yeah. I'm busy doing inventory with Jasmine at the Rodeo Drive store."

"Fair enough. I'll talk to you later, then, Sexy Lexi. Have a fun day at work. I love you."

I almost repeat the phrase without thinking but manage to catch myself in time and instead say, "Okay, I'll talk to you later."

I hang up with the sound of Nate's panting breath echoing in my ears. I blink at my phone for a few seconds before Jasmine speaks.

"I can't believe you know Nathaniel Walker and all of Wicked Stallion."

I laugh and shake my head at her. "You've met Dante about a hundred times, though."

"Yeah, but it's weird seeing my boss in gossip magazines because she had sex with her husband's best friend in a music video and then hearing you just casually chatting to him on the phone."

Heat rushes to my cheeks again, and I say, "It's not weird to me because we've been friends for so long. The guys are awesome."

"I have to ask...what's Nate like in person? He's *ridiculously* hot." She gives me a cheeky grin. "Maybe you could snag me an introduction?"

"Okay, well, to answer your question honestly. In-person, Nate is *ridiculously* hot." I grin at Jasmine as I repeat her words back to her. "He's got these amazing blue eyes, and he basically just oozes sex. Everything he says seems sexual, and just one look from him is enough to turn you on."

I realize that I'm waxing poetic about him because I love him and that I don't sound *at all* like a woman with a husband who is talking about her platonic friend. So I laugh casually and roll my eyes as I draw on Nate's reputation to cover my slip up.

"Which is why he sleeps with *so* many women. They just throw themselves at his feet because he's so damn hot. I've lost count of the number of women I've seen him hook up with. He'll disappear for an hour and come back with a smile on his face without the woman he disappeared with. Trust me, Jasmine, you don't want an introduction. I'm lucky Dante is nothing like that, just hot as fuck but totally committed to me."

"Yeah, I guess I'll pass on that introduction," Jasmine agrees with a laugh.

I feel like a traitor to Nate for making him out to be the same guy he's been in the past when I know very well that he's just as committed to me as Dante is and that he's not fucking around anymore.

On cue, my phone pings with a message from Nate. He hasn't written anything, just sent another selfie, this one with his cock exposed and cum that has squirted onto his stomach. I swallow heavily and clench my pussy against the aching arousal I feel there.

I type a reply and have to work to keep my breathing rate normal.

I wish I were there to lick you clean.

As I hit send, Jasmine asks, "What about Logan, then? What's he like?"

An amazing Dom who I can't wait to see tonight.

"He's really nice and doesn't really sleep around. He had this awful boyfriend that we all hated, but thank god he dumped him during the last tour. I think he might be seeing someone at the moment, though," I say casually, then grin at her. "And I *know* Ash is because she's basically my best friend."

"What's the point in knowing someone who's friends with a band if she can't hook you up with anyone suitable?" Jasmine teases me.

"I believe the point is me paying you a mighty fine paycheck every month," I joke, and we laugh together.

When we've finally finished the inventory of the delivery, everything was there except for five of the blue dresses and another box which was missing two purple skirts.

I tell Jasmine, "I'll email the supplier and let them know so they can either give us a credit note or organize the delivery of the items."

I help Jasmine prepare the merchandise to be put on display in the coming week, and we do some other work in her office for the rest of the day, talking and laughing together. This was the first store I ever opened, and Jasmine was one of my first employees, so I trust her to know what she's doing, but I still like to have oversight.

By four-thirty in the afternoon, I'm more than ready to leave and go to Logan's, and I say with a smile, "I'll see you guys tomorrow. Great work today, Jazz."

"Thank you for helping. Most bosses would dump it on me and then bitch about the missing items as though I stole them or something."

I widen my eyes and gasp, "*Did* you steal them?"

"Yes. There's a big clothing black market, and I'm the ringleader, don't you know?" she jokes with a grin at me.

"I always suspected as much," I laugh back at her.

I head out the back of the store to my Tesla, and I send Logan a message.

On my way!

I smile as I put his address in the GPS. I'm excited to see him, and I have butterflies in my stomach when I think about him. It's weird to feel this way about Logan, but I also love it.

Just as I'm about to drive away, his reply comes through.

Send your location through to me.

I raise an eyebrow but do as he asks. I assume it's so he's aware of when I'm going to arrive because I take the elevator upstairs to his apartment, and when the doors open, he's standing in front of them and waiting for me. He's wearing a pair of jeans and a shirt, looking sexy as fuck, and I'm horny as hell at the sight of him.

"Hello, Alexandra. When you come to my apartment, I want you to take off your clothes immediately and put them in this basket." He indicates to a wicker basket sitting next to the elevator doors. "Do you understand?"

I'm so fucking wet just from this small instruction.

I swallow heavily and nod as I drop my overnight bag next to me and begin to remove my clothes. "Yes, Sir."

"I want you to spend two minutes or less wearing clothes in my apartment. You have up to a minute to get undressed when you arrive and a minute to get dressed when you leave." He points to a camera above us. "I'll check the footage to make sure. If you take too long, you'll be punished."

Fucking hell.

I think that I might just come right now, and I scramble to remove my clothing as quickly as I can. My training from Dante kicks in, so I fold it and place it neatly in the basket before turning to look at Logan.

"You're also not to wear underwear when you come here. I don't want to see it in the basket unless there's a reason." He smiles at me. "If you have your period, these rules don't apply. You get an exception, and I'll get you ice cream or whatever it is you might want instead."

I can't help but laugh. "Could you be any more perfect?"

"I don't know, Alexandra. Could I?"

"Maybe. It depends on what you have planned for me tonight," I tell him, arousal coating my voice with lust.

He gives me a slow, sexy smile. "Plenty."

He walks over to me and begins tracing around my areola with his finger. He uses his other hand to trail down over my stomach and down to my pussy, but he diverts from his path and continues down my left leg instead of touching it, and I groan in disappointment.

"I love playing with my toy. I have an entire night to play with you, too. I have lots of things I want to do to you, Alexandra Sullivan."

I shiver in anticipation because as he's been talking, he's continued to touch me but is avoiding my erogenous zones. He links his hand with mine and leads me through his apartment. I expect to go to the bedroom that I know is his, but instead, he takes me to one of the spare rooms.

I find it filled with a bed as well as bondage and sex paraphernalia, and I gasp, "Oh my god, *we* don't even have half this stuff. You even have a tantra chair? Why do you have all this stuff? I thought you weren't into full-time kink?"

"I'm not," he laughs. "I paid a fortune to have this delivered and set up today, so I could have my wicked way with you tonight. You bring out my inner Dom, and I love it." He lowers his head to my ear and growls, "I'm going to do anything I want to you, Alexandra, because you're my toy to play with. However, I see fit."

I can feel my juices dripping down my thigh. Logan is hard in his jeans, and I want to be used by him more than I want to keep breathing. He takes me over to a stockade and flips open the shackles.

"Get in."

"Yes, Sir."

I get onto my hands and knees, place my wrists into the shackles, and rest my torso on the chest pad. The ankle restraints are a little close, though, so Logan has me stand up and he adjusts both that and the neck restraint before I get back down.

When I'm in position after Logan has locked the ankle, neck, and wrist restraints with padlocks, I feel deliciously exposed and vulnerable to Logan's every whim.

He stands in front of me where I can see him and pulls his shirt off over his head. I delight in seeing his muscled body, with his smooth tanned skin and his torso tapering down to his waist in a 'V.' His jeans are riding low, and his hip bones are visible just above the waistband.

He drags a chair over in front of me, unbuckles his belt, and drops his jeans and underwear to the floor before kicking them aside. He sits on the chair and begins stroking his stiff erection slowly.

"What should I do with my toy, I wonder?" His eyes are dark with lust, and he tilts his head to the side as he considers me. "You look very pretty right now, Alexandra. Are you aware that I can do anything to you, and you can't stop me?"

"Yes, Sir," I breathe.

"Will you use your safeword if you need to?"

"Yes, Sir," I agree.

He doesn't say anything for another few minutes, just looks at me while he strokes his cock, and I'm dripping wet. Eventually, he stands and walks over to me before he fucks my mouth. I'm in ecstasy but aching to have my pussy filled by him instead of my mouth.

He pulls himself out of my mouth but doesn't fuck me. Instead, he walks out of my field of vision before moving in front of me again. He's holding a large blue dildo and a bottle of lube.

"Since neither Dante nor Nate is here tonight, I figured I needed some assistance to ensure you get properly fucked. Open your mouth."

I do as instructed, and Logan puts the dildo in my mouth. It's big, probably bigger than Nate, and, given the bottle of lube in Logan's hand, I have my suspicions about what he wants to do with it. Sure enough, once I've sucked it for a minute and my jaw is firmly aching, he takes it away and moves behind me.

He pushes it in and out of my pussy a few times before he says, "You need this cock in your ass. Don't you, Alexandra?"

"Yes, Sir," I moan.

Cold lube drops on my ass, and Logan slowly pushes the dildo inside me. I gasp at the painful stretching feeling, and, to my surprise, he presses a vibrator against my clit. I come almost instantly, and he pushes the dildo in a little further. When the dildo is all the way in, he removes the vibrator from my clit, and the pleasurable feeling disappears, leaving only the mildly painful feeling of being filled by the dildo.

Logan moves back to the chair and sits again. His cock is rock hard now, and I'm filled with the desire for him to fuck me. Every cell in my body craves Logan, and I lick my lips as I watch him stroke his cock. He pulls out his phone and takes a picture of me before he stands and takes pictures from different angles.

I think he's purposely left his phone off silent so that I will hear the camera shutter noise it makes each time he snaps a pic. My nipples are painfully hard and, as he takes a picture from the side, he leans forward and twists one roughly. That is enough to cause an orgasm to rock my body, and I moan his name as I come.

"I love that you can come just from this, Alexandra. You're going to come so many more times tonight before I fuck you." I moan softly, and he chuckles. "I think it's time for me to try out my new paddle on you because you wore underwear here today. Do you think it's unfair that I'm going to punish you for a rule you weren't aware of?"

A little.

I don't say that, though, because I'm so fucking horny and can't wait for Logan to give me a punishment that *doesn't* involve denying me an orgasm.

"No, Sir."

"That's what I thought."

Logan gets a leather paddle that he shows me before he uses it to good effect on my ass cheeks. Each one gets five hits that I count out before he stops and takes another picture.

The slow torture continues for hours, with Logan using different tools on me, and he brings me to orgasm too many times to count before he finally pushes his cock into my pussy. He fucks me with both his erection and the dildo in my ass. His timing is impeccable, but of course, he *is* a drummer, so I shouldn't be surprised. The feeling of two cocks inside me is amazing, and I wish there were a third in my mouth, but the dildo has nothing on Logan's actual cock, which is warm and silky smooth as he pounds me from behind.

I burst into a thousand pieces when I come around his cock, and I squeeze him tight with my pussy just before he blows his load inside me. His hands grip my hips, and his body jerks as he shudders while he orgasms inside me.

Our panting breaths echo in the room around us as I bask in my post-orgasm glow. My body is aching from being in this unusual position for so long, and I don't think I've ever felt happier.

Logan pulls out of me and starts cleaning up. I gasp as he removes the dildo from my ass, and he leans down to kiss each of my ass cheeks before he walks away. He's back after a few seconds with a key to unlock the padlocks, and when I'm finally free of the stockade, he helps me stand before he puts a hand behind my knees and another behind my back to lift me up and carry me out of the room.

I'm surprised because I'd expected we would clean up in the bathroom I know is attached to this room, but I wrap my arms around his neck as he carries me to his bathroom instead.

He cleans me in the shower, showing as much love and attention to me as he did over the weekend, and I'm in awe of this man.

"You're so beautiful, Logan," I murmur in a reverential tone as he's on his knees in front of me, washing my legs.

He smiles up at me and says, "I could say the same thing to you, Lexi."

Hearing my name makes me realize that he only used my full name during sex, and I've learned another unspoken rule from him tonight. He finishes cleaning me and holds me tight as he kisses me passionately.

We order Chinese food for dinner and curl up in bed together to watch a movie while we eat. When it's finished, Logan kisses me for a long time, and it's just as good as ever. I rest my head on his chest and listen to his heart beating there. The heart that I know belongs to me.

"When will we tell Ash and Cassie?" I ask him.

"I'm not sure I'm ready to do that."

I can't stop my body from stiffening, and I lift my head to look up and into Logan's eyes.

He smiles back at me and says, "I'm sure about you, Lexi. I'm sure about us. I just need some time to get used to this situation before we do that. Is that okay?"

"Of course." I kiss his lips softly. "We have forever to tell them because that's how long I want to be with you."

Chapter Fifteen
Revelations II

"They're going to guess if we invite them here," I point out to the guys. "It's how we told them about Nate."

I'm sitting naked in Logan's lap while he sits in an armchair as we discuss the possibility of telling Ash and Cassie about our relationship.

"Will they, though? I mean, we all hung out together here two weeks ago, and they didn't seem to think twice about it," Nate points out.

"I think you're overthinking this, Angel," Dante chuckles.

I look down at Logan. "You specialize in overthinking things. Am I doing that?"

"A little." He squeezes me tightly and kisses my neck. "But if you'd be more comfortable having me invite everyone to my place, we can tell them there instead."

I smile at him and kiss him passionately before turning back to the guys. "Thoughts?"

"Fine by me." Nate shrugs and looks at Dante.

"Me, too. However, you two want to do it works for me." He gives me a wicked grin and says, "Not it."

Nate laughs, "Not it, either."

Before I get a chance to say it, Logan quickly adds, "Not it."

He pulls my head down to his and kisses me deeply before adding, "But I'll help you tell them because I'm nice like that."

"Gee, thanks." I grin at him.

Logan's hand drifts between my legs, and he begins to slowly stroke my labia but avoids my clit entirely before he says, "An added bonus to telling them at my place is that I'm led to believe you could be very nervous and need some calming down before we do it. The sex room is perfect for that."

As he finishes talking, he finally rubs my clit, and I moan as the pleasure hits me. It's been almost two months since Logan and I got together, and I've spent a *lot* of time in that room since then. A couple of times, Dante has even joined us there, which was an incredible amount of fun. We've gotten into a routine, and I spend Monday and Thursday nights at Logan's while he comes to our apartment on the weekends.

Nate and Dante both watch with interest while Logan brings me to orgasm. I enjoy the attention but eventually close my eyes and moan Logan's name as waves of ecstasy roll over me.

After I've finished, Logan lifts his fingers to my mouth and says, "Suck my fingers clean, Alexandra."

I suck him as though I'm giving him a blow job, and I look over at Nate as I do it because I can't help but remember Logan's blow job out at Napa. Nate has an obvious erection and is clearly enjoying the show.

Logan takes his fingers out of my mouth and holds my face in place as he explores my mouth with his tongue while he kisses me.

When our kiss ends, I bite my lip and ask, "Would you blow Nate again if I asked you to do it?"

"Why always the hypothetical questions about this?" Logan raises an eyebrow at me. "Are you asking me to do it or not, Alexandra?"

"Yes," I murmur.

"If he's okay with it, then yes. I would do anything for you. Nate's cock is amazing, and I would personally enjoy sucking him dry if he'll allow it."

We turn to look at him, and I can tell he's turned on. His cock is still hard, and if he didn't want this, I know that wouldn't be the case. Sure enough, he swallows heavily and nods.

"Yes. I won't say no to a blow job from you, Logan."

Logan gives him a wicked grin. "Good to know."

Nate flushes red. "Only because Lexi wants to see it."

"Sure, sure. Whatever you say, Nate," Dante chuckles.

"Maybe he should suck *your* cock sometime, and you'd see why I enjoy it so much." Nate shrugs.

My eyes widen, and I stare at Dante because I'd never considered that possibility. He notices my reaction and laughs harder.

"Maybe my birthday gift to you can be a blow job from Logan to me, Angel," he says with a grin.

Logan winks at him and tells him, "I'd be down."

"Noted," Dante laughs. "But for now, I believe it's Nate who gets the honor."

I slip off Logan's lap and walk over to where Nate's sitting on the sofa with him. This time, I want to be a part of the action. I drop down on the sofa next to Nate and kiss him passionately. I hear the sound of Nate's belt being unbuckled and break our kiss to look down at what Logan's doing.

Nate lifts his ass, and Logan pulls his jeans down to his ankles but doesn't touch his underwear. Instead, he puts his hand on Nate's cock and begins to rub him through the soft material.

Nate groans softly, and the air around us is thick with sexual tension. I can barely stand how hot it is to watch Logan do this, especially knowing how good he is at making me come. I love that Nate is going to experience his skill again, and I'm so fucking happy that I get to witness it, too.

Logan starts to stroke him faster and then leans forward to kiss his cock through his underwear, which elicits another groan from Nate. I watch Logan tease him, doing things that he knows will get him harder and more aroused before he actually does the act itself, and I love this. It feels as though Logan is more comfortable this time, and so is Nate.

I lower my hand to my pussy, and I'm surprised when Logan bats it away. He drags his tongue up Nate's shaft from base to tip and then turns to give me a wicked grin.

"You can't touch yourself, Alexandra. Only Nate or I can if we want to."

He moves over and tongues my clit for thirty seconds while using his hand to go back to stroking Nate through his underwear. I moan my satisfaction, then groan when he takes his mouth away.

Logan finally pulls Nate's briefs off him and exposes his thick, hard shaft to everyone's view. "You really do have an amazing cock, Nate. I can't pretend I haven't imagined doing this again since Napa."

"I might have thought about that blow job once or twice," Nate says.

He flushes bright red and looks down at my pussy. As if to reassure himself that he still wants it, he reaches over and begins fingering me, bringing waves of pleasure to me as Logan grins at us.

"If it helps, I still don't think you're even bi, Nate. I think we all know that you're an incredibly sexual person. I'm good at head. I can give you pleasure, and you enjoy that. There's still nothing wrong with that. It's different to being sexually attracted to me outside of the pleasure I give you."

"I know. It's just weird to get hard when I think about you," Nate says. "It's only when I think about that day, though. It's not like I'm jacking off to pictures of you or anything."

"I'm assuming you've done that to pictures of Lexi, though," Logan says with a grin.

Nate chuckles and nods. "Only every night she's at your place."

"Yeah. I highly doubt you're bi, but if you do ever want to jack off to pictures of me, feel free. In the meantime..." Logan trails off and lowers his head to Nate's cock.

He wraps his lips around his shaft and starts sucking him. Nate moans and looks down at Logan before he turns to me. His expression is one of pure ecstasy before he moves his head forward and claims my lips with his. I can still hear the sounds of Logan's blow job, and it's incredibly erotic to me. Nate reaches his hand between my legs again to rub my clit, and he breaks our kiss before he goes back to watching Logan.

As much as I enjoy kissing Nate, I'm glad because I want to watch this, too. Nate's breathing rate increases, and I can tell he's about to come, but Logan pulls him out of his mouth and begins to stroke him slowly with his hand.

"What the fuck?" Nate gasps as he glares at Logan. "I was about to fucking come."

"I know."

Logan smirks and continues to slowly stroke him as he moves his mouth to my pussy again. Nate's still rubbing my clit, so Logan thrusts his tongue in and out of me, and I'm in ecstasy. When Logan reaches a hand up to twist one of my nipples, I'm done for, and I moan both of their names when I come. Nate pulls his hand away from me, and Logan nips my clit with his teeth, which causes me to squeal before he moves back to his spot in front of Nate. He takes him back into his mouth and sucks him while playing with his balls. Nate pants for breath as Logan brings him to orgasm.

This time Logan doesn't stop, and Nate moans, "Logan, I'm going to fucking come."

Logan moves his head up and down on Nate's shaft faster, then stops as Nate's cock jerks, and I watch Logan swallow his load. Logan pulls Nate's cock out of his mouth slowly, then swirls his tongue around the head. He laps up every last drop of Nate's cum, and I'm jealous because I want to be the one swallowing cum. At the same time, that blow job was even hotter than the last one.

I get my wish after a few seconds because Logan growls, "Open your mouth, Alexandra."

I do as instructed, and Logan stands and drops his jeans and briefs to the floor. His cock is rock hard, and he thrusts it into my mouth. I don't get any option to tease him or worship his cock because Logan fucks my mouth roughly. He holds my face in place as he plows in and out of me, occasionally stopping with his cock down my throat, which causes me to gag before he pulls out to let me catch my breath.

I love it when he does this, and he knows it. He looks down at me, watching me, and I lock eyes with him. I'm unable to look away from him as I ride the waves with him to his orgasm. When he shoots his load down my throat, he holds his cock in my mouth until he's stopped coming. Like he did for Nate, I use my tongue to clean every last inch of him.

"Come here, Angel."

I almost forgot Dante was here, but I stand and walk over to him as he instructed me to do. His pants are already around his ankles, with his erection pointing toward his stomach, ready and waiting for me. I straddle him and ease myself onto him, groaning in satisfaction when he fills my wet pussy.

He pulls my head down and kisses me while I ride him. He uses his hands to tweak and pull my nipples as well as rub my clit while we fuck, and it isn't long before I come on his cock. When I do, he grabs my hips and bounces me up and down harder, our moans filling the air in the room until Dante pulls me down roughly and holds me there while he comes inside me.

Dante takes me to the bathroom to clean up, and it's not long before we're back in the living room with the other two men. I sit on Dante's lap this time and snuggle into his embrace as we talk.

Logan looks at me and asks, "When are we going to do this, then?"

"Next weekend?" I suggest. "I've been feeling really awkward around Cassie because I can't be honest with her. Same with Ash."

"I definitely didn't like feeling as though I couldn't go near you when we hung out the other week," Logan admits. "I never get jealous of Dante and Nate being with you normally, but I've been jealous of them whenever we were around Ash and Cassie because they could be with you, and I couldn't."

Logan's eyes are downcast as he confesses this to us, and I scramble off Dante's lap to climb into Logan's. I wrap my arms around his neck and kiss him.

"They'll know next weekend, and we'll never have to hide it from them again," I promise him.

He looks at me with his beautiful chocolate brown eyes and says, "I feel like a dick because I'm the one who wanted to wait to tell them anyway."

"Nobody begrudges you for wanting to wait until you were comfortable, Logan," Dante assures him.

"And I'd be jealous if you guys could be near Lexi, and I couldn't, too. That's totally normal," Nate adds.

Logan smiles at them. "Thanks, guys. What would I do without you all?"

"Suck one less cock?" Nate asks with a wicked grin at him, and Logan bursts into laughter.

*****

We're all at Logan's apartment on Saturday afternoon. Today's the day we're going to tell Ash and Cassie about Logan and me. I don't know if I'm more or less nervous than I was the day that we told them about Nate.

"It's different this time," I point out to the men sitting on the sofa in front of me.

I'm naked and sitting on Logan's coffee table with my legs spread as we have this discussion. I'm pretty sure Nate is paying zero attention as he stares at my pussy, but Dante and Logan are far more restrained.

"How so?" Logan asks, though his eyes do flicker to my pussy, which is dripping with wetness.

"Well, the precedent has been set now. They're going to understand pretty much straight away, so that isn't a concern. However, it does kind of tie us four together and leave Ash on the outskirts with Cassie. I worry about what that dynamic will do for the band." I sigh and chew my lip in concern.

"I won't lie. That was part of what I've been worried about." Logan nods at me. "But we're happy together, and, regardless of whatever our relationship status is, Ash will always be our best friend. Nothing will change that, and I hope he knows that."

I frown at him. "I guess so. I'm just nervous and worried."

"Would you say that you're 'stressed' about it?" Logan asks with a wicked gleam in his eye. "Because I was led to believe that tying you up and spanking you might help in such a situation."

"Do I get to see the infamous sex room I've heard so much about?" Nate asks with a grin.

"If you want to," Logan laughs.

"I want to dine on Lexi's pussy. Right now, I don't give a fuck about Ash or Cassie or even the band. You guys know I struggle to focus when she sits like that," he complains.

"And I struggle to focus when I know your cock is hard and ready to be sucked. We all have our problems," Logan teases him with a wink as he looks at Nate's obvious erection.

Nate looks back at him with a smirk on his face. "If you're fishing for compliments about your oral skills, I think I'll need you to blow me a few more times before I can truly assess them."

We all stare at him for a second, and I can't tell if he's serious. I always notice the sexual tension in the room when it's between Logan and Nate, but I don't really notice it any other time. Maybe because I find it so fucking hot. I know I'm dripping wet right now just from watching them talk about it.

"You only need to ask," Logan murmurs in a husky voice.

Surprisingly, Nate looks at me and asks, "Do we have any rules in this relationship?"

I blink at him for a few seconds as I try to understand what he's saying. I have tons of rules. Ones with Dante. Ones with Logan. Not really any with Nate, though.

"I'm not sure what you mean," I tell him.

"I assumed I wasn't allowed to fuck anyone else when we got together, but what about Logan?"

There's a small gasp from Logan's direction, but I'm staring wide-eyed at Nate, trying to wrap my head around this question.

"You want to fuck Logan?"

Even asking the question has me squirming in my position on

the coffee table. I can see it in my head, and it would be the most erotic thing ever to watch these two beautiful men have sex.

"I'm not sure. I might get curious about that at some point." Nate flushes pink. "At the very least, I know I like his blow jobs. I'm pretty sure we all know that, and we also all know he likes giving them. So what are the rules? Do you have to be there whenever it happens?" He turns to look at Logan. "Same questions for you. Do you only want to do it when Lexi is in the room?"

Logan swallows heavily as Nate looks at him. I don't want to answer because I want to know Logan's desires first.

"I'll happily suck your cock any time you like. Lexi or no Lexi. You only need to ask."

Both men are breathing heavily as they stare into each other's eyes, and it feels as if some boundary or line has been crossed with them. Almost as if they've just started a new and different relationship between themselves.

Logan looks at me, and his arousal is obvious. His cock is stiff in his jeans, and I know he's turned on.

"Lexi's opinion matters, though. If she doesn't want us to do anything without her, then I'll respect that."

I love these men, and I definitely don't want them fucking anyone other than me. Each other, though? I feel like we all love each other so much that I would never deny them taking pleasure from one another if they wanted to do it.

"I would like to be there for any firsts, but only because I find you two being together hot as shit. If you do actually fuck, don't think I don't want to witness that." I say it very seriously because it is serious to me. Although, I can't help but grin as I add, "Also, if Nate ever blows you, Logan, I one thousand percent want to be there." I stop smiling and say seriously again, "But if you two want to have some kind of sexual relationship together, I'm okay with that. I love you both, and I would never deny you that—wow, I think I get why you let Nate and Logan fuck me, Dante."

I turn to stare at him, and he smiles at me. "Pretty much. Your logic sounds very similar to mine. I love you. I love them, everyone's happy. It's not like I don't get what I want and need from you."

We fall silent, and Nate looks strangely at Logan. "Does *this* make me bi?"

"If you want to identify as bisexual, Nate, just identify as bisexual. If you still don't think you're attracted to me other than sex, you can identify as heteroflexible. I think classing yourself as heterosexual would probably be a stretch at this point"—Logan laughs—"but your sexuality is your own, really. I can't give you the answer because it's yours. You identify however you feel comfortable. You also don't have to label it if you don't want to."

"Until Napa, I had never once thought sexually about a man. Now I would happily drop my trousers and have you suck my cock any day of the week. It's just weird for me because I always thought I was straight." Nate shrugs his shoulders.

"As I said, you don't need to label it unless you really want to. You can be curious, and I'm happy to explore your sexuality with you and do whatever you want to do. There's no pressure to be anything other than what you are or do anything other than what you want. Don't feel ashamed if you're curious about what it would be like if we fucked. Maybe you'd like it, and maybe you wouldn't. If you don't like it, we'll stop."

I am absolutely making a mess on Logan's coffee table and maybe even the carpet. The possibility of them fucking is ridiculously hot, and I want to be there if it happens. Hell, I want to participate.

But what they're talking about is *their* relationship, not mine, so I offer, "If you are serious and want to experiment, Nate, I don't have to be there. I know I said I want to be there for any firsts, but I don't have to be. Whatever you're comfortable with is fine by me. I guess my only rule is no outsiders. Just us. Forever."

Nate comes over to me and kneels in front of me so that we're eye to eye. "I love you, Lexi Sullivan."

He kisses me, and I wrap my arms around his neck as he explores my mouth with his tongue. We kiss for a minute before it ends, and we both pant heavily as we look into each other's eyes.

"I think I would be more comfortable if you were there the first time—*if* it happens. That way, if I'm not into it, Logan can feel less shit about himself because I know you'll still want to fuck him into next week."

Logan chuckles and nods. "That's definitely something I can count on."

I blow him a kiss and, as I do, Nate moves down to begin eating my pussy. I thrust my fingers into his hair and throw my head back in ecstasy as pleasure rocks my body. After I've come, he kisses me again, and I can taste myself on his tongue.

"Let's go to the sex room, Logan," Nate says in a husky voice while he looks into my eyes. "I think we should make Lexi scream."

I bite my lip in anticipation as Logan and Dante laugh, and Nate holds my hand as we follow them to the room. Unlike the day we told the guys about Nate, I'm not tied down today. Nor am I punished for anything. The four of us share the large bed in the room, and each of the men takes turns fucking me while I occasionally suck one of them or stroke their cock with my hand.

I'm lost in a haze of lust and love as they fill all of my holes. They work in concert, pulling out of me and moving away when they come too close to prolong the experience. Meanwhile, I get no such relief and am given orgasm after orgasm, my body shaking and rocking with each one.

By the time we finish, I'm exhausted, and I collapse on my back on the bed. Nate cuddles into me, pulling me against him, while Dante spoons me from behind.

Logan lies down behind Nate and asks quietly, "Is this okay, Nate?"

"Yeah. I don't mind," Nate murmurs as he kisses me.

I feel Logan's arms reach over Nate to touch me as well, and I smile as I close my eyes before I drift off to sleep. When I wake again, it's from Dante kissing me softly. I'm not sure where Logan and Nate are, but I'm sad that they're not here anymore.

"Sorry to wake you, Angel, but Ash and Cassie have arrived. You need to shower and get dressed, beautiful."

I blink at him and frown. "Huh? Where are my clothes?"

"In the bathroom. Nate got them for you when the guys arrived. They've gone to entertain them while we shower."

All of my post-orgasm bliss seeps away, and my nerves return as I nod. "Of course."

Dante takes my hand and leads me to the bathroom attached to this bedroom, where we shower. He still cleans me, but he does it much more quickly than usual. I put on the top and skirt that I wore here today, and I'm assuming the rule of me only being clothed for two minutes in this apartment is being waived, though I still don't have any underwear on.

When we walk into the living room where everyone else is, Cassie looks up at me with a concerned face. "Are you feeling better, Lexi?"

"Huh?" I ask without thinking.

"The guys said you weren't feeling well."

I glance over at them and nod. "Yeah. All good. What are you guys drinking?"

"Bourbon. You want me to get you a drink, Lexi?" Logan asks with a smile at me.

I nod back at him. "Sure, thanks."

I sit between Dante and Nate, but I wish I could sit with Logan. That would be suspicious, though. I remember that I'm apparently 'it,' so I need to try to find a good time to tell them what we're going to tell them, and I have a thousand butterflies in my stomach.

Nate puts his hand on my knee and strokes my leg, which is comforting. When Cassie looks over and sees us, she gives me a smile and waves me over to where she's sitting with Ash. I drop down next to her on their sofa, which puts me closer to Logan, who is sitting on an armchair on the other side of Ash, and I'm instantly soothed by being closer to him.

"How are things going?" Cassie asks quietly.

"Good," I say with a smile back at Nate.

"You seem happy," she comments.

"I really am."

"Well, I'm glad. I can't pretend I wasn't shocked when you told us, but I've watched you guys over the last couple of months, and everyone's happier than I've ever seen you. It totally makes sense, too, because it was so obvious that you two were in love. I even commented on it to Ashton a couple of times," she laughs.

I laugh as well and nod my agreement. "Yeah, it did make sense with Nate, and we were in love for years. Sometimes love can surprise you, though."

I glance over at Logan, my beautiful third partner, who surprised me with the swiftness that he stole my heart after so many years of platonic friendship. It didn't make sense, but it's no less right for us than it is for Nate and me.

"I'm happier than you could even know," I tell Cassie as I look back at her.

"What do you mean?" she asks as she raises her eyebrows at me.

I bite my lip and nod.

No time like the present, I guess.

"Excuse me, Ash?" I say in a normal tone, interrupting his conversation with Logan.

"Yes, Lexi?" he says with a smile as he turns to look at me.

I can feel the tension in the room from the three men who know what I'm about to say, but Ash and Cassie just look at me with curiosity in their expressions.

"We have something to tell you," I say, unwittingly echoing Dante's words from the last time we did this.

"I'm not going to even attempt to guess this time," Cassie tells me with a grin on her face.

"You might be able to," I say with a chagrined smile at her.

"So…apparently I get to be 'it' this time. Um, remember how I'm in a relationship with both Dante and Nate at the same time?" I ask and swallow heavily as I do.

Cassie frowns at me. "Uh, yeah. We were literally just talking about it."

"Of course we were. Well, anyway...um, Logan is my partner now, too."

Both Ash and Cassie blink at me a few times, then look between Logan and me as if they're watching a tennis match. To illustrate my point and make it easier for them, I stand and walk over to Logan, where I turn to face them before I sit on his lap. He wraps his arms around my waist and kisses my cheek.

I know there's no confusion about what the situation is like this time, which makes the silence in the room even eerier.

"This won't change anything," Logan says from behind me. "We're all happy. I love Lexi, and she loves me. Dante and Nate are both okay with it."

"It won't change anything?" Ash is the first to speak, and he has a frown on his face. "Look, I'm happy for you guys, but isn't there a huge risk that this will all blow up in your faces and ruin the band?"

Logan laughs and shakes his head. "Do you think *I* haven't thought this through, Ash? Me, of all people, doing something without thinking about the possible consequences? I wouldn't take the risk if it wasn't worth the reward."

He squeezes me tightly, and I smile, then lean down to kiss him quickly.

"What if the press finds out? You know they'll have a fucking field day," Ash says.

"We're being good in public. Hell, even you guys clearly had no clue the other week that Logan and Lexi are together," Nate points out.

There's silence for about a minute before Ash sighs and looks at us with a resigned smile on his face. "Look, I really am happy for you guys. It's an adjustment, but so was finding out Lexi and Nate are together. I can't pretend that I'm not worried about the possible fallout for me if this all goes south, but I also wouldn't want to deny you guys any happiness in the meantime."

I hop off Logan's lap and walk over to hug him. "Thanks, Ash. I love you, and I'm glad you're being so understanding."

"I love you, too, Lexi. Apparently, I'm the only member of

Wicked Stallion who isn't *in* love with you now," he says with a laugh.

"Trust me when I say that I've got more than enough men, and I'm running short on platonic friends now, so you're basically a unicorn." I grin at him.

I turn to Cassie to hug her as well, then realize she hasn't actually given us any congratulations like Ash did. She's staring at me with a strange look on her face.

"Why?" she asks quietly.

"Huh?" I frown at her, then look at Ash to see if he has any insight, but he looks as confused as I am.

"You said before that you'd been in love with Nate for years. Why Logan? Why now? It doesn't make sense."

I step back from Cassie as she's talking and stand a few feet away as I shrug my shoulders at her. "I don't know. He came out to Napa, and one thing led to another. We've been friends for years, so it wasn't a huge leap from that to falling in love."

I turn to smile at Logan as I remember the day he marked me as his own. I belong to him, and he belongs to me. Dante, Nate, Logan, and I are all entwined with one another. Friendship and love and lust; we've become a family of our own unique design.

"I'm sorry, but I still don't understand." I turn back in time to see Cassie shaking her head. "You've been with Dante for almost a decade, and now you're suddenly collecting men as if they're some kind of trophies or something? It doesn't make sense."

I didn't expect this reaction from her, and I don't know what to say. I hadn't expected her to be judgmental of us, especially not after the conversation we were literally having right before I started this one.

"I'm not 'collecting' them, Cassie. I'm in love with them. All of them. I don't know how else to explain it. We're all happy. Can't you be happy for us?" I swallow heavily against a lump that's formed in my throat.

"I don't know," she says quietly. "This is all too weird. Can we go, Ashton?"

She turns to look at him, and he looks stunned. "Um, I guess we can?"

"I'm a little uncomfortable here right now," she tells him.

"Okay." He sighs and frowns at us. "I guess we'll see you guys later?"

Cassie turns back to me and stands as she says, "Look. I'm happy for you, I guess. I just think it's strange, and I don't get why you're doing this."

She walks away toward the elevator without another word or a goodbye for any of us. Ash looks torn as he watches her leave, then he turns back to me.

He hugs me and says, "I really am happy for you guys." He lets me go and sighs before he says quietly, "Just give Cassie time. She'll get used to it, I swear. We've been friends for years, and all I want is for you guys to be happy. If this is how you're happy, then I'm happy as well, okay."

I nod at him, but I can't stop a tear from falling because I feel like shit after Cassie's reaction to our news.

"Ash, are we going or not?" she calls from the direction of the elevator.

"I'm sorry, Lexi," Ash says and gives me another hug, squeezing me tightly before he lets me go.

As soon as he does, Logan is in his place, holding me in his embrace as Ash says goodbye to him, Dante, and Nate. I watch Ash walk away feeling utterly bereft. These were the only two people in the world that we trusted with our secret, and I truly thought they would both be happy for us.

The delayed reaction from Cassie that I'd expected to our initial news cuts me deeply because this time, I never saw it coming.

Chapter Sixteen

The New Normal

"*L*et me see what you're wearing tonight, Lexi," Logan says with a smile as he walks into the closet I share with Dante. He's wearing ripped jeans and a tight t-shirt that shows off his muscles. His hair is wet and slicked back from his forehead, and I want to fuck him so badly right now...then again, I *always* want to fuck him this badly.

"Is it this? Because I very much like this outfit." He grins as he takes in my appearance.

I'm wearing a matching lacy black bra and thong set but nothing else at the moment.

"No," I say with a laugh. "I don't plan on going to your concert in my underwear."

"Good, because I don't like when you wear underwear. Take it off, Alexandra," Logan murmurs.

I'm instantly wet, and I groan aloud before I point out, "It's too risky in public, Logan."

I realize my mistake too late as Logan strides over to me. He doesn't say a word, but he spins me to face where my clothes are hanging up, takes my hands, and places them on the rail.

"That's not your safeword, Alexandra. Count."

He smacks my right ass cheek hard, and I say, "One."

He does it again, and I continue to count. I get ten to my right ass cheek before he does ten to my left. My cheeks are burning, and I'm dripping wet, so I know that even if he hadn't told me to take off my underwear, I would've had to change it anyway.

Logan places his lips near my ear and growls, "Take off your underwear, Alexandra."

I do as instructed, and I hope that he's going to fuck me, but I doubt that he will because Logan is an expert at holding off on that until I'm delirious with lust.

Sure enough, he says, "Pick a dress to wear."

I go immediately to a bodycon dress that will be tightly fitted and keep me from being exposed.

"Not that one," Logan says.

I turn to look at him, and he's leaning back against the drawers across from me with his arms folded across his chest and a smirk on his face.

I try another one, only to hear, "Not that one, either."

I'm tempted to make him decline every one of my suitable dresses, but I'm also sure that if he figures out what I'm doing, I'll be punished. My ass cheeks are still stinging, so I pull out one of the Serenity dresses. This one has cap sleeves and also flows from the waist out, but the skirt is a little longer than the other dresses I got from Serenity, and I'm grateful that Logan makes no noise of disapproval.

I pull the pale blue dress on and ask Logan, "Can you zip me up, Sir?"

"Sure," he murmurs.

He moves over to me and pulls the zip up before reaching under the skirt to find my wet pussy. He rubs my clit, and I moan softly as the pleasure from what he's doing hits me.

"You're so wet, Alexandra. Do you want to come?"

"Yes, Sir," I moan.

"How badly do you want it?"

"More than anything, Sir."

He pulls his hand away from me and sucks his fingers clean as he looks at me. "Tasty as ever. You don't get to come until I decide the time is right. Now isn't the time."

I bite my lip to withhold a moan because I'm wet, I desperately need an orgasm, and I'm probably going to make a mess of this dress tonight. I'm actually concerned that I might be exposed in public, too. We're going to a charity concert, and Wicked Stallion is one of the bands performing a set. It's an outdoor venue, and I'm going to have to keep a tight hold of this skirt if I don't want the entire world to see my pussy.

Logan looks me over and then gives me a wicked grin. "Come with me, Alexandra."

I follow him out to the living room, where Nate and Dante are talking. They've already gotten ready for the concert and are looking hot as fuck, but I'm also horny and biased.

"Looking good, Sexy Lexi," Nate says with a grin.

"Want to help me torture her, Nate?" Logan asks.

"Um, I'm not sure. What did you have in mind?"

Logan laughs. "Not literal torture. I thought that maybe you would let me blow you today. Lexi's not allowed an orgasm for a while, but that doesn't mean I can't give you one—"

"While you make her watch," Nate finishes with that shit-eating grin he gets on his face.

"Exactly." Logan licks his lips and looks at the telltale bulge in Nate's jeans. "You down?"

"Yeah, I'm down. Come here, Lexi. I want to make sure you get a really good look at this," Nate taunts me.

When I reach them, Logan lifts my skirt and says to the guys, "Look how wet she is."

The cold air hits my bare pussy, and it aches as I'm exposed to the view of all three men.

"Do you wish you were the one about to suck Nate's cock, Angel?" Dante asks.

"Yes, Honey," I admit.

Logan drops my skirt and says, "Sit next to Nate."

I do as instructed and watch as Nate pulls his jeans and briefs down to free his now hard cock. Logan takes him in his mouth, and Nate moans his satisfaction.

Instinctively, my hand drifts to my pussy because I want to rub my clit, but Dante's voice stops me. "No, Angel."

I bite my lip, and I'm concerned that I might spontaneously combust from watching what's happening in front of me without me getting any relief. Logan slowly pulls his mouth off Nate's cock after touching his nose to Nate's stomach, then looks at me.

"Having fun, Alexandra?"

"Yes, Sir."

"Good." He grins wickedly at me, then turns to Nate. "Can I kiss you, Nate?"

Nate blinks at him, then shrugs. "Sure."

Logan moves up, and I almost fucking die when he kisses him. I know how good a kisser Logan is, and he slips his tongue into Nate's mouth. I'm pretty sure Nate's enjoying it because, after a few seconds, he puts his hand behind Logan's head and thrusts his fingers into Logan's hair as he kisses him back.

I'm a complete mess, and I desperately need an orgasm. I squirm in my seat as Logan ends his kiss with Nate and moves back down to his knees.

He looks at me and grins. "No, Alexandra."

He takes Nate's cock back in his mouth and continues what he was doing until Nate blows his load and moans, "Logan."

Hearing Nate moan Logan's name in ecstasy, not just a warning that he's going to come but an actual moan, is almost my undoing. Logan leans back on his heels and pants for breath as he stares into Nate's eyes.

"Was that good, Nate?"

"Yes. Want me to return the favor? You look like you could use some relief."

I swear to god that my heart has stopped beating. I didn't expect this. I'm pretty sure Logan didn't either because his eyebrows almost fly off his face in surprise.

"Are you sure?"

Nate shrugs and nods as he stands up and pulls his briefs and jeans up. "Yeah. You've blown me, what? Three times now? I figure I probably owe you one. If I don't like doing it, I'll just get Lexi to finish you off."

He smirks at me as he buckles his belt and moves aside to let Logan sit where he was before. As Logan gets his cock out, Nate looks at me, and I can barely breathe at all, unable to believe this is really happening and lost in a daze of ecstasy.

"Lift your dress up, Lexi. I want to see if you're enjoying this or not," Nate tells me.

It's not an instruction from Nate, but I'm so lost in everything that I do it automatically, and I bite my lip when I see their reaction to me.

Nate moves in front of me and trails his tongue from the bottom of my pussy to the top, swirling it around my clit a few times and bringing me incredibly close to orgasm before he stops.

"Very tasty," he murmurs. "Now, Lexi. Let me see what you love so much about sucking cock." He moves back in front of Logan and smiles up at him. "You have a very nice cock, Logan."

"Yeah, yeah, it's not as big as yours. Be grateful now when you're sucking it because it'll hurt your jaw less. If I ever fuck you with it, though, you'll see that it isn't just size that matters," Logan laughs.

There's so much sexual tension between them that I'm roughly a million percent certain that Logan is going to fuck Nate sometime. Or vice versa. I swallow heavily and clench my pussy because I'm aching so intensely to be fucked from the show they're providing for me.

"Good to know," Nate murmurs in a husky voice.

They stare at each other for another few sexually charged seconds before Nate lowers his mouth to Logan's cock. He doesn't take him fully in his mouth, though. Instead, he swirls his tongue around the head of Logan's cock as he uses his hand to stroke the shaft.

Logan moans and looks surprised as he watches Nate with wide eyes. I'm completely entranced by this sex show. Nate looks up at Logan, who continues to make noises of ecstasy as he stares down at him, and Nate finally takes him all the way in his mouth.

"Fuck, Nate. That feels so good," Logan moans.

Nate takes him out of his mouth but goes back to stroking his shaft with his hand as he grins at Logan. "Does it?"

"Yes," Logan gasps as he bites his lip.

Nate stops what he's doing, takes his hand off Logan's cock, and shrugs. "Cool. I'm done now. Maybe Lexi can take over for me or something."

"Oh." Logan blinks at him and nods. "Sure. Sounds good, I guess."

Nate gives him a wicked grin and laughs as he starts stroking Logan's cock with his hand again. "I'm kidding. I just wanted to pay you back for that time you edged me. I do want to see if I can make you blow, but I don't think I want to swallow your cum, so can you give me a heads up when you're about to do it?"

"Uh-huh," Logan agrees, and the single word turns into a moan. A few seconds later, he manages to say, "I can do that."

"Good."

Nate leans down and wraps his lips around Logan's cock again. The sound of him sucking Logan fills the air in the room, along with Logan's noises of ecstasy. I'm enthralled by watching these two beautiful men.

I need to be fucked. I need an orgasm. I need so many things, and I struggle hard against the desire to touch myself. Watching them in clear ecstasy as Nate gives his first blow job and Logan receives that pleasure from him is intense. I'm glad I was here for this, even though it's absolutely having Logan's desired effect of tormenting me.

I look over at Dante out of curiosity, and he smiles at me. He doesn't have an erection, and I find it strange that he wouldn't be as wildly turned on by this as I am. He has far more self-control than I do. Unlike Nate, he's also able to ignore my pussy and keep his arousal under control when I sit on the coffee table.

"As always, I'm not sure who is enjoying this more, Angel. You or the guys," Dante says in an amused tone.

"Me," Logan moans as he thrusts his hips slightly toward Nate's mouth, seemingly unable to resist the motion. "Definitely me."

Nate puts his hand on Logan's taut stomach and slowly pulls his mouth off Logan's cock. He looks up at Logan but doesn't say anything before he moves up to stare into his eyes. They both pant for breath as they look at one another before Nate presses his lips softly against Logan's.

He kisses him twice like this before he thrusts his fingers into Logan's hair and deepens their kiss. This is even more erotic than watching Nate give him head. I think it's the connection that turns me on. Kissing is more than sex somehow, and this time I see Nate push his tongue into Logan's mouth first.

I don't know how long they kiss, but it's longer than I expected them to do it, and I squirm in my seat, wishing that I could get some release. Eventually, Nate breaks their kiss and moves down to Logan's cock again. This time, he moves his head back and forth quickly, gripping Logan's cock with his hand and stroking him at the same time.

After a couple of minutes, Logan growls, "I'm going to come, Nate. Get your fucking mouth off me if you don't want to swallow my load."

Nate pulls his mouth off him with a popping sound and pumps Logan's cock with his fist, continuing the same rhythm that he had when he was sucking him while he stares up at him. It isn't long before Logan's cock spasms and cum squirts onto his stomach.

Nate strokes him slowly a few more times until Logan's finished coming, then grins at him and asks in a husky voice, "I did okay, then?"

"Nate," Logan pants.

"Yes?" He raises an eyebrow at Logan.

"You did okay, yeah."

They silently look at each other for a few seconds, and something passes between them. The same way that I knew that our time upstairs in the bedroom at Napa had changed things with Logan and me, I can see the shift in their relationship happen in front of me. My heart is so full of my love for them, and I don't think I've ever been happier.

After a few more seconds, Logan turns to look at me, and he says in a husky voice, "Clean me up, Alexandra. I can't go to our concert like this."

Nate moves aside, and I take his place in front of Logan. I begin by taking his softening cock in my mouth and ensuring that every last drop of cum has been removed. He's semi-hard again when I move up to his stomach. I begin to lick the cum off it and gasp as I feel the cold air on my pussy.

I look back to see that Nate has flipped the skirt of my dress up and over my hips. As I clean Logan, Nate tongues my wet pussy, but he avoids my throbbing clit and doesn't satisfy me at all.

"That's enough. I'm clean now," Logan murmurs to me.

I move away from the smooth skin that I've been licking just because I want to and not because there was any cum left on it. Nate pulls my dress back down and sits on the sofa next to Logan.

"May I come now, Sir?" I ask.

I've never asked for permission from Logan to come before. I've always waited for him to give it, but I'm *so* on edge that I can't even think straight, let alone fathom the idea of doing anything other than being fucked right now.

He gives me a wicked grin and shakes his head. "Now is not the time, Alexandra."

Dante chuckles and says, "Come sit with me, Angel."

I walk over and sit on his lap. Immediately he begins a slow torment of softly touching me but not going anywhere near my erogenous zones.

"We have to leave in twenty minutes. You guys timed that well," Dante comments.

"I timed nothing. That was very unexpected," Logan laughs.

"I'm going to say it. I don't think we should mention any of *this*"—Nate indicates back and forth between himself and Logan— "to Ash and Cassie."

I stiffen and nod as I cringe at him. We haven't hung out with them since we told them about Logan. The guys have been in rehearsals for the concert with Ash, and I sent Cassie a couple of messages, but she hasn't responded.

"I hate that it's causing issues. I love you guys, and we're so happy. I'm so hurt that Ash and Cassie aren't happy for us," I admit.

Dante squeezes me tightly and says, "Ash is happy for us, Angel. He's told us all several times."

"Apparently, Cassie's just an uptight prude who thinks it's 'wrong' that you're sleeping with Logan now as well," Nate says in a cold tone.

I'm only mildly surprised to have this confirmed because it's what I expected. "Did Ash tell you that?"

"He didn't exactly phrase it that way, but it's the vibe I got from what he said. He also said to give her time, and she'll come around."

"I don't get it. She took a minute to understand what we were telling her with Nate, but once she understood, she was fine. I thought we were friends, but now she's icing me out and apparently thinks I'm 'wrong.'" I sigh and frown at the carpet in front of us.

"Come here, Lexi," Logan says in a soothing voice.

I walk over to him and sit on his lap, and he wraps his arms around me. He uses one of his hands to brush my hair out of my face, and he tucks it behind my ear as he gives me a beautiful smile.

"We know what's between us, and I love you with my whole heart. Most people aren't used to relationships like ours. They think you should only love one person and completely ignore the fact that they themselves love multiple people. Friends and family, as well as their chosen partner."

He kisses me softly and hugs me to him before pulling back to look into my eyes again.

"Honestly, I've thought about it a lot lately, and I think she's probably feeling a bit scared and threatened."

"Huh? Why?" I ask in confusion.

"Think about it from her perspective, Lexi. You've known us all for over a decade, and you've known Ash just as long as you've known me. We weren't in love until we took our friendship to the next level in Napa. She's probably scared that you'll do the same thing with Ash."

My jaw drops open, and I stare at him for a few seconds before shaking my head. "But I'm not interested in Ash like that."

"And you weren't interested in me like that until I went out to Napa. You love Ash exactly as much as you loved me then. Hell, you probably love him the same amount as you love me now. It's just a different kind of love. For Cassie, she likely has a very real fear that you will decide to 'collect' him because she doesn't understand that it's not about that."

I look away from Logan and stare out the window as I think about what he said. I do love Ash as deeply as I love the rest of the guys, but he's always been like a brother to me, nothing more. Then again, it's definitely true when Logan says that's how I used to feel about him. Now I can't imagine living my life without him. I just don't see Ash in that way, though, and I'm disappointed that Cassie might think I would betray her like that.

I shake my head and look back at Logan. "I know what you're saying, but it's different. For a start, you were single. I would never try to break them up or cheat on her with him. Ash is happy, and that's all I want for him."

"You don't have to convince me." Logan smiles at me. "I wouldn't even say any of that to her if I were you. She'll probably get defensive about it if you do. Just keep it in your mind and give her time, like Ash said. Once she sees that there's nothing to worry about, it'll all go back to normal."

I wrap my arms around his neck and press my lips to his. He kisses me, using his tongue to explore my mouth as he gently strokes my back with his hand.

"Well, back to our new normal. Where I get to love you, Nate, and Dante as much as I do, and we all get to be happy...and apparently Nate gives you blow jobs," I say with a cheeky grin at Logan as our kiss ends.

Logan nods and winks at me. "It's the very best kind of normal, that's for sure." He hugs me again and says quietly in my ear, "It'll be okay, Lexi. We love each other, and that's all that matters."

"Sorry to interrupt, but they're here. We have to go," Dante says from nearby.

I know that we're going to have to be on our best behavior for the rest of the night, so I take this moment to cling to both Nate and Logan in the elevator ride downstairs.

I sigh when the elevator dings and say to them, "I love you guys."

"Alexandra." I turn to look at Logan as we all exit the elevator, and he murmurs, "Don't think I've forgotten that you need to have an orgasm when the time is right."

I swallow heavily and bite my lip because, amidst the conversation about Ash and Cassie, my arousal has diminished. It comes rushing back to me at Logan's words, and he gives me a satisfied smile as he runs his hand down my back. He barely brushes my ass as we make our way out of the front of the building.

We're being driven to the event in a big white van with blacked-out windows. Ash and Cassie are coming with us, and as we approach the vehicle, my nerves increase. I had thought they might bail, but questions would be asked if the band didn't arrive together, so I'm glad they didn't.

"Hi, guys," Dante says in a cheerful voice as we get into the car.

Logan and I are at the back of the group, so when we get in, I sit in a seat next to him at the front of the van. I immediately regret my decision when I look behind us at the group, and Cassie frowns deeply at me. My jaw tightens, and I sigh softly, then look up at Logan. He smiles down at me, takes my hand in his where no one can see, and squeezes it tightly.

"How are you guys? Looking forward to the show tonight?" Ash asks.

"Definitely. It's been good performing again. I can't wait to get on tour," Nate says.

I look out the window and let the conversation happen around us. I'm surprised when I feel Logan's hand on my thigh, and I gasp softly. Logan smiles and surreptitiously slides his fingers higher up my leg, underneath my dress. The tips of his fingers brush my wet pussy, and I bite my lip as I do my best to avoid any kind of reaction so nobody in the van will know. Luckily, I've had years of practice keeping my reactions under control with Dante.

Logan lowers his lips to my ear and murmurs, "Is now the time, Alexandra?"

"Fuck, I hope not, Sir," I breathe, and I try my best to keep my voice so low that Ash and Cassie can't hear.

Logan chuckles quietly. "It's okay. Now isn't the time."

He rubs my clit with his fingers slowly as he brings his lips to mine and kisses me. I've forgotten where we are, and I'm lost in the pleasure that Logan is giving me. He explores my mouth with his tongue, and I wish that his tongue was on my pussy instead.

There is a loud and obvious cough from behind us, though, and we end our kiss before we look at our friends. Four very different expressions greet me when I look at the rest of the people in the van. Nate is obviously turned on by watching us make out. Dante looks annoyed, and I'm sure he's frustrated that we might cause a problem.

Ash's jaw is tight, and he looks concerned as his eyes flicker between us and Cassie, whose expression could only be described as disgusted. Her lip is curled, and she has a deep frown on her face as she looks at us. I feel guilty that I got so lost in this moment with Logan that I forgot to behave better.

Sure enough, Cassie snarls, "Could you two maybe not do that? Thanks."

"They can do whatever they want. Get over yourself, Cassandra," Nate says with a roll of his eyes.

"You would say that. I'm sure you've had your tongue down her throat today, too," Cassie snorts.

Ouch.

"Cassie, can you stop?" Ash glares at her. "We've talked about this. They're all happy."

"And you said that I wouldn't have to watch them do shit like this if we only saw them in public places." She turns her glare to him instead of us.

Ash flushes pink and glances at us before looking back at Cassie. "Yeah. I, uh, did say that. But we're not in public right now, so they can do whatever they want."

I remember what Logan said earlier and sigh before I say quickly, "It's fine, Ash. I'm sorry, Cassie. You're obviously uncomfortable with my relationship with Logan. We'll keep that in mind in the future."

Logan squeezes my hand as Cassie huffs and crosses her arms over her chest before she turns her head to look out the window without saying anything in response to me. Ash cringes as he looks at her, then turns to look at me again.

I mouth the words 'it's fine' to him and shrug my shoulders before I give him a smile, which he returns. I turn to face the front of the van, and the conversation between Ash, Dante, and Nate starts up again, even if it does sound a little forced.

Well, I guess we're in for a fun evening.

Chapter Seventeen

Connections

We're backstage at the venue, and the vibe is amazing, even though there's tension within our group.

"Hey, guys. How are you doing this evening?" Isaac Meade, Wicked Stallion's manager, greets us shortly after we've arrived.

I'm holding Dante's hand and playing the role of the dutiful wife who doesn't fuck any of his friends ever, but Cassie's still been shooting daggers at me for the last half an hour.

"Great, Isaac." Ash smiles at him. "It should be a good night."

"It really should," Isaac agrees. We talk with him for a few minutes before he looks at his phone and says, "Let me know if you guys need anything. Cruise Control arrived a little while ago, and I should probably go check on them."

"Of course. I'll have to catch up with them later," Nate says with a smile.

Isaac walks away, and I turn to Nate because I've just been reminded of the Serenity clothes. "Hey, do you know if Heather is here with them?"

"I'm not sure. Why?" He raises an eyebrow at me.

I shrug my shoulders. "I love her clothes and would really like to talk to her."

He pulls out his phone and says, "I'll check." He sends a message before smiling at me when he gets a reply. "Yeah, she's here."

"Oh, that's awesome."

"I'll introduce you to her at the after-party," Nate promises, and I smile at him.

"Thanks, Nate."

"Any time, Sexy."

Cassie glares at me, and I cringe as we head toward the area where the guys' instruments are set up. Travis Murphy bustles over to us with a big smile on his face. He's in his late thirties and big in country music. It's also his charity that we're here to support.

"I'm so glad you guys came tonight. Thank you again for agreeing to participate."

"We're more than happy to, Travis," Dante assures him. "Your charity does great work feeding homeless people. We'd have to be real dicks to not want to help you out."

Travis gives a good-natured laugh. "You say that because you don't know how many people said no to participating."

"Well, we're here. That's all that really matters, isn't it?" Nate says with a grin, and Travis laughs.

"Of course. Well, thanks again, guys. Tony will let you know when it's time for your set, and we can party afterward."

"Partying is my specialty," Nate laughs.

We talk with a few other bands but don't see Cruise Control. There are some media outlets that have been allowed backstage, and the guys do a few interviews while I stand to the side with Cassie.

During one of the interviews, I turn to her. "Could we maybe talk?"

"What do you want to talk about, Lexi?"

She doesn't turn to look at me, just stares firmly ahead at the men in front of us as they smile for the cameras.

"Are you not my friend anymore or something?"

"Of course I am," she says stiffly.

"It doesn't feel like it. You haven't replied to any of my

messages since I last saw you." I know Logan said I shouldn't mention it, but I can't help asking, "What is your problem with"— I glance around us and lower my voice a few decibels—"Logan and me?"

Cassie finally turns to look at me before she shrugs. "I've told you. I think it's weird. It doesn't make any sense, and, quite frankly, I don't think it's right. But, hey, you do you."

"What's not 'right' about it? Dante's fine with it." I frown at her.

"So that makes it okay to just sleep with whoever you want whenever you want? You made this excuse that you and Nate have been in love forever. Then suddenly, you want to be like, 'oh, Logan and I have loved each other for years,' as well. I call bullshit on the whole thing, but whatever. I don't really want to talk about it."

Her jaw is set, and she turns back to look at the guys for a few seconds. I don't know what to say or how to explain it to her. I'm pretty sure Logan is right, and I shouldn't even try to do it, but she speaks before I can think of anything to say anyway.

"I do want to be your friend, Lexi, but you make it very hard when you decide to do something like this. I can't support what you're doing. It's wrong."

Ouch.

There it is. She's confirmed exactly what Nate said to me earlier.

"Ashton is my boyfriend, and he's friends with you guys, so I have no choice but to be around you. It doesn't mean I have to think any of what you're doing is okay."

"But you were *fine* when it was Nate," I say in an exasperated tone.

I take a breath and lower my voice again because even though no one is really close enough to listen, I should be careful with what I say.

"You only reacted badly when it was Logan," I point out.

I want her to confirm that he was right with what he suspected, and she's threatened by the situation, but I'm also a little worried that I'm pushing her too hard on this.

Cassie snorts. "I wasn't as fine with you and Nate as you might think. I accepted it because Dante was fine with it, and so was Ashton, but I feel like you're taking advantage of the situation. How would you feel if Dante was having sex with me? Would you be fine with that? I bet you wouldn't. No. You want these men to be yours like they're trophies, but they're not allowed to be with anyone other than you. It's greedy."

Greedy?

Now we seem to be getting to the heart of the matter. She has no clue what she's talking about...or that I watched Nate and Logan blow each other mere hours ago.

I can't exactly say that, though, so I tell her, "I see. Well, now I know how you feel, I guess. I'm not sure what to say, but nothing is going to change. I love them all, and they all love me. Nobody is unhappy in this situation except you. So maybe you should fix your issue because I can't fix it for you."

I stride away from her to go get a drink and take a breather. As I'm grabbing a bottle of water from a table that has some drinks on it, I catch sight of Cruise Control. They're from Chicago but recently signed with Meade Management, and they've been spending a decent amount of time in LA lately since their latest tour ended.

Sure enough, Heather is with them, along with the wives of the rest of the band members. I'm feeling annoyed after my conversation with Cassie, though, so I don't want to go and try to talk to Heather right now. I unscrew the lid of my bottle and take a sip of my drink as Cruise Control is greeted by some other people who are backstage, and they start talking with big smiles on their faces.

Travis' voice comes from the stage through the sound system, and he announces, "Thank you so much for coming out tonight! We've got some great artists here to support the cause. Feed Well Los Angeles has multiple soup kitchens around the city, and we're committed to opening three more in the coming year, so please give generously. First up tonight, we've got Arctic Blaze."

The crowd cheers, and I sigh as I make my way back to the guys and Cassie. They've finished the interviews and are standing in a group of people, talking and laughing as the first band for the evening takes the stage. Ash has his arm around Cassie's shoulders, and she's smiling up at him. Dante, Logan, and Nate are all talking animatedly as I move to Dante's side.

He puts his arm around me and smiles down at me. "There you are. I wondered where you'd gone."

"I went to get a drink," I say as I hold up my bottle of water.

He leans down to kiss me, and I snuggle into him. Cassie seems to be avoiding my gaze, but Ash gives me a smile along with both Nate and Logan. I force a smile back at them and try to enjoy myself.

"When are you guys on?" I ask Dante.

"Tony said about half an hour," he says.

I'm looking forward to their set because I always love watching the guys perform, but I know that this will likely leave me alone with Cassie. Sure enough, as they warm up with their instruments, we're left to ourselves. Soon after, they're introduced and head onstage.

Both Cassie and I move to the area to the side of the stage where other family and friends of bands that are performing have congregated to watch the show. We stand awkwardly together as Nate takes the microphone and smiles his sexy smile at the crowd.

"Hey, LA! I hope everyone's having a great night. We're Wicked Stallion, and we're so happy to be here to support Feed Well Los Angeles. Let's rock!"

They start playing "Honey Killer," and I try to ignore Cassie's presence. There's a cool breeze blowing, so I hold my skirt tight as I watch them perform. Nate's voice is velvety smooth as he sings, and I'm entranced by watching him. Logan takes his shirt off before the second song, and Nate does the same after it. I wish Dante would, but he rarely goes topless when he's performing.

Their third song is a love song that Dante wrote for me, and

Nate sings it to me. He rarely looks away from me, and I can't help but watch him because I love him so much. As he's singing the final verse, Cassie speaks in my ear.

"Do you know how sick it is that you're standing there drooling over a man who isn't your husband?"

"So much for 'I'm happy for you guys,' I guess," I say in a dry tone.

"The more I think about it, the more I realize how wrong it is. Being around you today has confirmed it for me."

I want to have a go at her and tell her that she's being a judgmental bitch, but now is not the time, and I definitely don't want to cause any issues with Ash. So I work my hardest to keep my temper.

"You know what? You don't need to talk to me about this anymore. You've made your position very clear, and I get it," I say while trying to focus on the guys performing in front of us and also trying to keep my skirt from blowing up and exposing me to the world.

"I don't think you do. Did your wedding vows mean nothing? You swore to be faithful to Dante, and you apparently don't give a shit about that anymore."

I clench my teeth and try to maintain the last thread of my temper, but I make the mistake of looking at her, and she's got that disgusted look on her face again.

I narrow my eyes at her and can't resist saying, "Look, if you're worried that I'm going to sleep with Ash or something, don't be. We're just friends."

To my surprise, she gives a condescending laugh and rolls her eyes at me. "As if he ever would."

It doesn't come across as her being sure of Ash remaining faithful, but more as though she thinks I'm so disgusting that he wouldn't consider it. This annoys me because the reason I don't think it would happen is that I know Ash is a good man, and she doesn't deserve him.

I choose to take her words at face value when I respond.

"Exactly. Neither of us would do that because he's with you."

"So if we weren't together, you *would* sleep with him, then?"

I sigh in exasperation and shake my head. "You're missing the point, and I'm not sure if you're doing that on purpose, but it's fucking annoying. Ash is nothing but a friend. That's it. I have no interest in him sexually, whether he's in or out of a relationship."

"Just like Logan," Cassie snorts.

I raise an eyebrow at her. "So it *is* me being with Logan that makes you uncomfortable."

"I didn't say that."

"You didn't have to." I turn back to the stage and say, "I'm done with this conversation. I want to focus on the men I love performing."

I don't say it, but I include Ash in that. I watch him as he plays the guitar. He's just as beautiful as the other men, with his blonde hair and blue eyes, singing along with the chorus. I'm not attracted to him, though. I would happily get on stage and fuck any one of these men, but not Ash.

I'm kind of reeling after my conversations with Cassie today, though. Ash might think that she'll come around if we give her time, but I really don't think she will. Even if she does, I'm personally feeling done with her.

She's free to have her opinions, but she's basically tried to be as insulting as she can to me today, and I don't need that in my life.

Onstage, the guys finish singing the song, and Nate takes the microphone out of its stand and asks, "Who here has seen the 'Heavenly Promises' music video?"

The crowd erupts into cheers, and Nate grins at them, then looks over at me before giving me a cheeky wink and then turning back to the audience.

"If you liked the video, I want to hear some screams for the gorgeous Lexi Sullivan, who we all know is half the reason it was so hot. The other half being me, of course," he finishes with a smirk on his face.

The screams from the crowd multiply, and Cassie shakes her

head next to me but doesn't say anything.

Nate announces, "This is our last song for tonight. Sing along if you know the words."

They launch into the song, and I'm reminded of the day we filmed the music video. I think Nate is, too, because he looks at me frequently, and I can hear the arousal in his voice as he sings. I bite my lip as I look up at him and think about the way he gave me an orgasm for the first time. He's given me so many since then, and I could never have imagined what that day would lead to.

The guys are putting on a good show, and the crowd is into it. Nate struts around the stage as though he owns it, and he sings into Ash's mic with a grin on his face before he heads back to his own to finish out the song.

The crowd goes wild, and as they near the end of the song, I head backstage again, not caring whether Cassie follows or not. I arrive back there just as the guys are coming offstage, sweaty and exhilarated, with big grins on their faces.

"You were great, guys," I say with a smile.

Dante puts his arm around my shoulders as Ash walks behind me. I assume to see Cassie.

"Thanks, Angel."

We head over to get some drinks, and as we walk there, Nate asks quietly, "Did you like my dedication to you, Sexy Lexi?"

"Yes. I'm sure it won't fan the flames of the rumors we're having an affair *at all*," I tell him with a laugh.

"Definitely not." He grins at me.

"Cassie wasn't a fan of it," I murmur to him.

"I bet she wasn't. I actually don't give a flying fuck about her, to be honest." He shrugs his shoulders.

"Unfortunately, Ash does. So we should probably try to be civil, even though she's been a raging bitch to me."

He stops walking and turns to look at me. "She has?"

I look around us. Dante and Logan are still walking ahead of us, and no one else is around. So I nod my head at Nate.

"Yes. But now isn't the time to talk about it, and I don't want to cause trouble with Ash. I don't want anything to do with her, though."

Nate pulls me into a hug and whispers in my ear, "I love you, Lexi. Don't ever forget that."

"I want to kiss you," I murmur.

He squeezes me tight and quickly kisses my head before he lets me go. "Yeah, me too. Later…and you can suck my cock as well."

"Promises, promises," I say with a laugh.

We catch up to the guys, and we get drinks before heading out to where Cassie and I were watching the show earlier. I dance with Dante as we sing along to the music, but I keep my distance from Logan and Nate. It's about an hour before Cruise Control takes the stage, and I sing along to "Rules to Break" when they play it. It's one of my favorite songs, and I'm glad I got to see them perform it live.

Nate moves over to me and asks in my ear, "Want me to introduce you to Heather?"

I look around and see three women nearby. Heather Fletcher is one of them. She's got blonde hair and is stunning. Currently, she's laughing with a brunette woman who I recognize as Lita Ciccone, the fiancée of Cruise Control's lead guitarist. Tatiana Vega, the woman who recently married the drummer, is with them. She's short with ice-blonde hair that's hanging to her waist as she dances to the music, and she's holding a toddler with bright blue eyes who's wearing headphones and smiling as she wriggles in Tatiana's arms. I can't see Ariana Knight, the lead singer's wife, who had an even smaller baby backstage.

"Not right now," I tell Nate and shake my head. "They look like they're having fun, and I don't want to interrupt them."

When their set is over, Cruise Control joins the growing group of bands, friends, and families enjoying the concert in our area. By the time Travis takes the stage as the last act of the evening, we all cheer as loudly as the rest of the concertgoers.

I'm a little bit frustrated because, in the past, I wouldn't have hesitated to dance with either Nate or Logan at an event like this.

Certainly not the way I would now, but I hate that they're so close, and I feel like I can't be near them.

Cassie has been shooting me daggers all evening, and I'm trying not to let it get to me, but it's really fucking hard. It also makes me feel like I can't go and talk to Ash, either. The only comfort I have is that I get to spend the evening in Dante's arms, at least. To the world, he's the only man I love, and I need to keep it that way.

When the concert is over, everyone heads backstage again, and we're grouped up. A few people are drinking and talking, and Nate comes over to me.

"Come with me, Sexy Lexi."

He takes my hand and leads me away from our group and over toward Cruise Control. They're a short way away, talking to Travis and his wife, Dolly.

"I figure since they've got the babies here, they might not be coming to the club with us," Nate says under his breath as we approach them. "So this might be your only chance to talk to Heather."

He smiles down at me, and I'm filled with my love for him. The fact that he's gone out of his way to introduce me to her just because I expressed an interest reminds me of why I love him so much.

"Hey, guys," Nate says as we reach their group, and he simultaneously drops my hand.

Hayden Vega, their drummer, grins at him. "Nate. I've been meaning to come to see you. Why did you ask about Heather?"

"Huh? What about me?" She looks over from a conversation she was having with Ariana and gives both Nate and me a once over. "Nathaniel Walker." She smiles at him. "How are you, darling?"

"I'm great. Have you met Lexi before? She's Dante's wife." He smiles at me, then looks back at Heather. "She's—"

"Wearing one of my dresses," Heather says with a big smile at me, and heat rushes to my cheeks.

I've met so many famous people because of the guys, but I'm a bit star-struck by Heather because I've been wearing her clothes so much lately. Tonight she's wearing a beautiful blue dress and an amazing diamond heart lock necklace that I can't help staring at.

I pull myself together and say as casually as I can, "Yeah, I am. Your collection is so good. I think I bought half of it."

"Which half did you think wasn't good enough to purchase?" she asks with an eyebrow raised at me.

"Um, none of it. I just liked some pieces more than others," I say quickly, horrified at the question.

Heather laughs and shakes her head. "I'm kidding, Lexi. I don't expect people to buy every item in my collection."

"I actually have a chain of women's clothing stores in LA," I tell her. "So I'm big into clothes."

"Oh, really? Where are they?"

I blink at her. Maybe if she sees one of the stores and likes it, she might consider allowing us to stock her line. I don't want to just hit her up for it right now, though.

"I've got three. Rodeo Drive, Beverly Center, and Orange County," I tell her.

"That's really cool. What's your style? I assume it's good," she says with a grin as she nods to my dress.

I laugh and say, "Yeah, basically this kind of style. I'm always looking for new and cool designs to stock.

"Interesting. Sounds awesome. I'll have to come to check one of your stores out sometime," Heather says.

"You're more than welcome to visit anytime. Just let Nate know or something, and I'll make sure I'm at the store you want to visit."

"That's silly," Heather laughs. "Give me your number, and I'll call you. What do you think, Ariana? Are you up for a shopping trip?"

She turns to her friend, who laughs and indicates to her stomach. "I'm still trying to lose the baby weight, so I don't feel like buying anything, but I'll come to see your skinny ass try on clothes."

"I'll babysit if you want to go while we're still in LA," Lita offers.

Heather smiles at her and says, "Thanks." She looks back at me. "There you go. Can we come to the Rodeo Drive store on Monday or Tuesday?"

"Absolutely. I look forward to it." I grin at her. After we exchange numbers, I say, "Well, I guess I'll leave you guys to it. Are you coming to the club?"

"Some of us are," Heather says with a smile. "I'll see you there."

I turn to Nate, who's talking to the band, and put my hand on his arm to get his attention. He stops talking mid-sentence and looks down at me.

"I'm going back to Dante and the guys," I say with a smile at him, and he nods.

Big party buses take us from the venue to a club in downtown Los Angeles. We all pile out and head inside before being led through to a VIP area that's packed once we all enter it.

The club has a great vibe, and I head to the dance floor with Dante for a few songs before we get drinks and head back to the VIP area.

"Lexi, hey," Heather says as we're passing her.

She's standing with the woman who I know is the drummer's wife.

We stop, and I smile at her. "Hi, again."

"I'll be over with the guys, Angel," Dante says and kisses me before walking away.

Heather smiles at me. "That's so cute. Angel is Harrison's nickname for me, too."

She looks over to where her husband, Harrison Fletcher, is standing nearby as he talks to Sebastian Fox and Hayden Vega.

"I'm not sure if we've met, but I'm Tatiana Vega," she says and holds her hand out to me.

I nod as I shake her hand. "I'm Lexi Sullivan. My husband is the bass guitarist for Wicked Stallion. You got married at Nate's estate earlier this year, didn't you?"

"We did. It was lovely out there," she says as she gets a faraway look on her face.

I think about my last visit to Napa a few weeks ago and can't help the heat that rushes to my cheeks. The guys and I had sex in nearly every damn room at the place, but these ladies don't need to know that.

"It really is. Dante and I go out there as often as we can."

We talk for about twenty minutes before I head over to where the guys are. Cassie is with them, and I stand next to Dante. I cuddle into him while avoiding her gaze as he talks to Ash.

To my surprise, Logan smiles up at me from where he's sitting on a sofa next to Nate in front of us. "Sit with me, Alexandra."

Immediately, my pussy aches at the sound of my full name coming from his lips, and I'm reminded of the fact I have no underwear on. My need for an orgasm comes rushing back, but it clashes with the awkwardness of Ash and Cassie being here.

Nonetheless, Logan used my full name, so I drop onto the sofa in between him and Nate.

"We'll be back in a little bit. I'm just going to talk to Isaac," Ash says after a few minutes.

"Gee, I wonder why he desperately needed to get away from us," Nate says in a cool tone.

Logan casually throws an arm around my shoulders and looks down at me. "It's not my fault if Alexandra is so sexy that I want her to sit next to me."

He's obviously had a few drinks, and my own alcohol consumption has lowered my inhibitions, even though I know we're meant to be behaving in public. My breathing rate increases as I look into his gorgeous brown eyes, and he keeps my gaze as he drains whatever drink is in his glass.

"Would you guys mind going to the bar for a refill for me?" he asks while still looking at me.

"Sure. Have fun, Angel," Dante says, and he sounds amused.

I can't look away from Logan, though. Nate takes the empty

glass from Logan and chuckles as he leaves with Dante. To my surprise, Logan removes his arm from around me and removes the jacket he's wearing. He drops it on my lap before he puts his arm back around my shoulders.

"*Now* is the right time, Alexandra," he murmurs in a husky voice as he spreads the jacket out a little so it reaches my knees.

I gasp softly and ask, "Now?"

"You'll need to be very quiet. We're meant to be good in public. So be a good girl, Alexandra. Come for me, but do it quietly."

He reaches his hand under the top of the jacket and pulls up the skirt of my dress underneath it. I swallow heavily and look out over the VIP area as casually as I can while Logan's fingers find my wet pussy. Only his jacket is preventing the entire VIP area from seeing what he's doing to me, and I moan softly as he rubs my clit.

"Quiet, Alexandra."

I look up at him, desperately trying to prevent myself from moaning in ecstasy at the pleasure he's giving me. It takes all of my willpower to stop myself from doing it, and the world is reduced to Logan and me. I lean into him as he uses his fingers to give me the orgasm I've been aching for since he arrived at our apartment today.

When it hits, I look away from him and over at the dance floor as I try not to pant too hard or scream his name. But I can't stop my body from shuddering as the ecstasy floods through me.

Logan pulls my dress back in place before he removes his hand from under the jacket and smiles at me. "You're gorgeous, Lexi." He places his lips next to my ear and murmurs, "I love you."

Dante and Nate return a couple of minutes later, and Dante hands Logan his drink before he sits next to me. I snuggle into him and turn my face up to his to kiss him.

"Did you have fun while we were gone, Angel?"

"Yes, Honey. I definitely did," I tell him with a satisfied smile on my face.

Chapter Eighteen

Opportunity

I'm at the Beverly Center store on Monday afternoon when my phone rings, and I see Heather Fletcher's name on the screen.

"Hi, Heather. How are you feeling after Saturday night?"

She seemed to be having a very good time when we left just before one in the morning. She was dancing with Harrison and seemed quite drunk.

She sounds amused when she responds. "I spent yesterday morning in bed while cursing my life. God knows how my friends with kids do it. Though, I suppose they skipped the club, which would've helped. How are you?"

"Good. We left a bit earlier, and I wasn't too hungover yesterday."

In reality, we fucked for hours when we got home, and I was as tired yesterday morning as if I'd been clubbing all night long.

I wonder if Heather's calling because she wants to come to the store today. I was kind of hoping to leave soon to go to Logan's. Still, if Heather wants to visit today, I'll head to the Rodeo Drive store.

"Anyway, Ariana and I were thinking of coming to your store

tomorrow. Will you be there?"

"Yup, I can be. That's not a problem. I look forward to seeing you again."

"Awesome, see you then." We end our call, and I smile at Sherry, the manager of this store. "Heather Fletcher and Ariana Knight are going to the Rodeo Drive store tomorrow."

"Oh my god, seriously?" I nod my head at her. "Any chance Jasmine wants to take the day off? I'd be happy to take care of the store for the day."

I laugh and shake my head. "I doubt it, but I'll ask her."

I pull my phone out and send Jasmine a text.

Heads up. Heather Fletcher and Ariana Knight are coming in tomorrow. Make sure the store looks amazing, not that it doesn't always look amazing. Sherry said to let you know that if you want the day off, she's happy to cover for you.

It's about five minutes later when her reply comes through, and I burst into laughter when I read it.

Any chance they'll be bringing their sexy husbands with them? I could do with some eye candy since you don't bring yours in enough. Tell Sherry that I could be on my deathbed, and I would still work tomorrow.

"Sorry, Sherry, she says she'd work tomorrow even if she were on her deathbed."

"Ah, well. It was worth a shot. That's pretty cool. Did you meet her at the concert on the weekend? I saw pictures of you guys online."

I nod and smile. "Yeah. Nate knows Cruise Control, and he introduced me."

"Your life is amazing," Sherry gushes.

"It's pretty good. Speaking of which, I have a man waiting for me to come home to him. So I'm going to take off early today," I tell her.

"Lucky you. Tell Dante I said hello," she says with a laugh.

"I will," I tell her, even though I won't because it's Logan who I'm staying with tonight.

I send a text to Jasmine as I head out the back to my Tesla.

I doubt they will be. I saw them on the weekend, and they're definitely very sexy, but they didn't seem interested in a shopping trip.

By the time I've arrived at Logan's apartment building, Jasmine has replied.

That's a shame. I'll see you tomorrow. The store is sparkling.

I laugh and text her that I'm glad as I take the elevator upstairs to Logan's apartment. As soon as I'm inside, I set my phone on a table nearby and quickly strip off my clothes, which I fold and place neatly in the wicker basket.

I find Logan sitting in his favorite reading chair by the large floor-to-ceiling windows that give us a brilliant view of Los Angeles.

"Hi, Logan."

He looks up from his book and smiles at me before he puts a bookmark in it and sets it on the table next to him. He spreads his arms wide, and I climb into his lap. He wraps his arms around me and kisses me. I melt into his embrace and enjoy the feeling of being with him as he does.

"I missed you last night," he murmurs in a husky voice when our kiss ends.

"Me, too. I'm here now."

He trails his gaze over me from head to toe and gives me a sexy smile. "Yes, you are, Alexandra."

That simple action is enough to set my senses on fire. My nipples are painfully hard, and my pussy is wet.

"We have a long time before dinner. What should I do with you until then, Alexandra?"

"Fuck me, Sir," I say and swallow heavily.

His cock is hard in his jeans underneath me, and he lazily strokes his hand over my exposed flesh but doesn't go anywhere near my breasts or pussy.

"Is that what you want?"

"Always, Sir."

"I see. Well, you interrupted me in the middle of a chapter, so you'll need to wait. Kneel and be patient, Alexandra."

A thrill runs through me when he asks me to do this. I get off his lap and kneel at the side of his armchair. He picks up his book and opens it before setting the bookmark aside. For the next twenty minutes or so, he doesn't look at me as he reads his book. The only indication that I'm still on his mind is that he occasionally strokes my head affectionately.

With every minute that I kneel there, my anticipation builds, and I become more eager for whatever it is that Logan is going to do to me when he's ready. Finally, he puts his book aside again and looks down at me.

He stands and moves in front of me before holding his hand out. "Come with me, Alexandra. I feel like playing with you now."

I swallow heavily and take his hand as I stand, relieving the mild ache in my knees from kneeling in one spot for so long.

He leads me to the sex room and says, "On the bed on your back. I'm going to tie you up today."

I hold my arms and legs out as he ties me up. Then he walks over to some drawers where he keeps certain items, and he comes back with a blindfold. The room turns black as he ties it over my eyes.

"Can you see anything?" he asks.

"No, Sir."

"Good. Be patient, Alexandra. I'll be back."

I hear the door to the room open and close, and I lie in the silent darkness as I wait for Logan to return. I have no idea how long he will be or what he's gone to do. My pussy is wet and aching, and I need him to come back and fuck me, but I get the feeling that today's scene is going to be a long one, and I'll be waiting a while for some relief.

The door to the room opens, and a gust of cold air flows over me before it clicks shut again. Logan's footsteps get louder as he walks over to me, and I hear him set something down nearby on the bed, but I have no idea what it is.

"My toy lying there and waiting for me to play with it is such a beautiful sight to see," he tells me in a husky voice.

I gasp when I feel an icy cold wetness against my nipple. It takes me a second to realize that it's an ice cube. Logan trails it around my nipple and across my body to my other breast. As he torments my other nipple with the ice cube, he lowers his mouth to my first breast and laves my nipple with his warm, wet tongue.

He spends the next few minutes trailing the ice cube around my body and following the path with his tongue. He only presses it to my clit for a few seconds before taking it away, but I don't get the pleasure of his tongue on my clit, and he presses the ice cube to my lips after he takes it away.

"Suck this, Alexandra."

By the time the ice cube melts in my mouth, my breathing is shallow, and I'm on edge, waiting to see what he does next, and I tense when I hear what I'm pretty sure is a lighter being used. There's silence for a few seconds before I gasp and flinch as something hot stings my stomach just above my pubic bone. It happens a few more times before I realize that it's candle wax. We've used this before, but having my sight removed has made this more erotic and mysterious.

"Sir," I moan when he touches another ice cube to my nipple.

This is immediately contrasted with the stinging hotness of some wax to my other nipple. I'm lost in pleasure and pain as Logan alternates the two sensations and his tongue for a while. Whenever he's finished with an ice cube, he has me suck it until it melts in my mouth. I don't know if he runs out of them, but eventually, he stops using them, and I don't feel any more of the stinging wax.

The sound of his phone taking a picture comes from nearby, and I'm drenched at the knowledge that he'll have this. He's told me in the past that he uses pictures of me to masturbate often, and I love that he does.

Logan drips a thick, sticky substance on me in a strange pattern, and I'm not sure what it is or what he's doing. He trails it over one nipple, but not the other, and around my body in some kind of zigzag pattern, stopping just above my pussy. The telltale sound of a picture being taken comes a few times before there's silence again.

I realize that what he's poured on me is something edible when Logan's tongue follows the same path. I assume he's done this to avoid the drips of wax that have hardened on my body. He spends a decent amount of time licking and sucking my breast before he continues on his path around my body.

When his tongue reaches the end of the trail, he continues on the next half-inch to reach my clit, and I can't resist the urge to moan when he tongues it. He pushes his fingers into me as he does and twists my nipple with his other hand. It doesn't take long at all with this amount of sensation for him to get me to come. Logan doesn't stop, though, continuing what he's doing until I've had two more orgasms.

He moves off the bed, and I think he's taking off his clothes because he climbs on again a few moments later. I feel his presence and the warmth of his body as he positions himself over me. He pushes his cock into me as he claims my lips with his. He fucks me slowly while kissing me, and he takes his time with me.

I'm lost in a haze of ecstasy by the time he comes inside me as he grunts, "Alexandra."

He holds himself inside me until he's finished coming and kisses me as he does, with his body shuddering a few times before his orgasm ends.

"Close your eyes," he says after he gets off me.

"Yes, Sir."

I close my eyes, and the room brightens behind my eyelids as he takes off the blindfold.

"You can open your eyes now."

I blink a few times as my eyes adjust to the light, and I smile as I watch Logan untie me. As he's untying one of my arms, I see the items sitting nearby and realize it was honey that he used on me after the wax. When I've been released, he picks me up and carries me to his bathroom. He never washes me in this room's bathroom at the end of a scene. He always takes me to his room to take care of me.

It takes a while for him to clean me off from the wax and honey. When he's done, he holds me tight in the warm shower and kisses me softly. Once we're dry, he takes me into his bed, and I cuddle into him.

"How are you feeling, Lexi?" he asks.

"Good," I tell him with a satisfied smile on my face.

"I'm glad."

He squeezes me tightly, and I relax into him. I rest my head on his chest and listen to his heartbeat, which is rhythmic and beautiful, just like him. I don't think I'll ever tire of spending time with this man.

We lie together in bliss for a long time before Logan speaks. "I miss you on the days you're not here."

"I miss you, too."

"I don't think we can keep this arrangement up long term," he says.

My blood runs cold, and I sit up to stare at him. "You don't want to break up with me or anything, do you?"

"Lexi, no."

He chuckles and shakes his head before he kisses me and pulls me back into his embrace.

"I love you and Nate and Dante. Our relationship is amazing. I mean that living separately isn't going to work long-term. I want to be with you more frequently than this. Even if you don't spend the night in my bed, I'll still get to be with you more often."

He sighs and swallows heavily before kissing me again.

"I get jealous of Dante and Nate when you're there. I get lonely here without you guys. At least they have each other when you're here with me."

"And on nights when I'm with Dante, you could do stuff with Nate," I tease him.

He chuckles and says, "Maybe. If he wanted to. But it's just the company. I feel like we've become a family, and I don't like living without my family. I'm looking more and more forward to the weekends when we can be together."

"I'll admit that I do like Friday and Saturday nights the best," I confess. "As much as I love coming here, having everyone together is so much better."

"Correct, but not having my own space kind of sucks for me."

Moving Nate into our apartment was easy because we had a guest room that we turned into his room, but there's no spare room to make Logan's.

"We could turn the office into a room for you," I suggest.

"We could, but we wouldn't have the sex room, then."

I sigh and nod at him. "Well, let's talk to Dante and Nate about it on Friday when we go to Napa."

"Okay," He says and squeezes me tightly.

A smile plays at my lips as I tell him, "Remember when you told me you'd 'do that to me sometimes?'"

Logan surprises me when he rolls me onto my back, and his body weight presses me into the mattress as he kisses me passionately. His tongue explores my mouth, and he fists his hand in my hair. I wrap my arms around his neck as I kiss him back. A thrill runs through me that he really is mine now. For so many years, we've just been friends, but now I get this side of him as well.

He ends our kiss and pulls his head back to stare into my eyes as he smiles at me. "In my defense, I didn't know that you'd turn out to be the best toy in the world."

"Who else have you done this with?" I ask out of curiosity.

Logan raises an eyebrow at me. "You want to have the ex conversation?"

"I was just wondering. I mean, I only had one boyfriend before Dante, who I gave head to. So I literally only have one ex since I'm married to Dante."

Logan moves over to sit up with his back against the pillows, and I move up, so I'm sitting next to him.

"I've had a few one-night stands. I don't know if you know this, but I'm a rock star," he says with a grin at me, and I laugh.

"I'd noticed," I murmur as I trail my hand over the muscular arm next to me.

"Not as many as Nate, of course, but I expect it's not the groupies you want to know about. Do you remember that girlfriend I had, Chloe?"

I nod as I look at him. They dated for about a year, but it ended a couple of years ago.

"She got me into kink. As I said, we only did it in the bedroom, not full-time. I think she might have wanted to go full-time, but I didn't particularly want to. She would ask me to do it, and she was into some pretty intense things. Degradation, breath play, pain. It got more and more extreme as time went on."

He looks away from me as he continues talking, and I stare at his beautiful face in profile. He has a sad frown and talks in a low, choked-up voice.

"I was uncomfortable doing some of the things she was asking me to do, so it was my fault. I should've put a stop to it and known my own limits. She did safeword a few times, so I trusted her to do it. The last day we were together, we had a really intense scene. She seemed into it, so I didn't think twice about anything I did, but I took it further than usual. I stopped as soon as she froze, but I didn't need a safeword to realize I'd fucked up when she started screaming and crying hysterically."

The same way I did so many months ago, I place my palm on his cheek and turn his face to mine. "I love you, Logan. I'm sorry that happened. Please tell me if you're ever uncomfortable with anything we do. I'm not interested in doing anything that makes you uncomfortable, and I'm not into anything that hardcore, really."

"I will. As I said, I blame myself because I should have told her my limits. Once I was in that zone and doing it, though, I wanted to satisfy her needs, so I would do anything for her. That's why I took it too far, and I felt like shit. I didn't do BDSM after that until Napa."

I'm relieved when he smiles at me, and I can see how much he loves me.

"When you asked me to fuck you roughly, I still wasn't sure if I was going to do it with you, even though I knew you and Dante did." Logan chuckles and shakes his head. "The second Nate mentioned your 'code,' so much stuff made sense in my head. Especially because I'd been in that type of relationship."

"Well, back in the day, we couldn't exactly tell you guys I was Dante's sub." I give him a chagrined smile.

Logan looks over my exposed breasts, then slides his hand between my legs underneath the bedsheets. He finds my wet pussy and begins to rub my clit as he gives me a wicked grin.

"Maybe you should have. We could've been doing this a lot sooner."

I bite my lip and moan softly as I spread my legs to give him better access.

"We definitely should've been doing this a lot sooner," I agree.

Logan watches me with a satisfied smile on his face as he brings me close to orgasm before he stops what he's doing and kisses me instead.

"I'm glad you decided to do kink with me," I tell him, even as I suffer the consequences of him toying with me because my pussy is aching.

"Me, too." Logan kisses me again softly as he pulls me into his arms.

I rest my head on his chest and smile when I hear the rhythmic beat of his heart. I love him so much, and I want to officially be his.

"I'm yours to do anything with, Logan," I say quietly.

He chuckles and kisses the top of my head. "That's not exactly news to me."

"Anything," I repeat as I turn to look at him. "Dante and I have a CNC agreement, and I want one with you, too."

Logan's eyebrows raise. "Consensual non-consent?"

"Yes. I'm giving you my consent to play with me however or with whoever you want. I'm yours."

"I love you, Lexi."

Logan takes my chin in his hand and tilts my face up to his.

He kisses me passionately, his tongue exploring my mouth as his hand drifts between my legs again. He rubs my clit as he watches me through hooded eyes.

He drops his head and bites my bottom lip with his teeth before he growls, "You are mine, Alexandra. Your sole purpose as my toy is to bring me pleasure, and I will do anything I want to you whenever I want to do it."

I gasp at his words, and it's so erotic knowing that I'm at Logan's whim. I love the idea of him using me, and I moan as my ecstasy builds.

My orgasm is so close when Logan stops again, and he watches me as I pant for breath. I blink at him as I stare up at his sexy face with the wicked grin he has on it.

"What do you want for dinner?" he asks casually.

I shake my head. "I don't care what I eat. I care what you eat, and I'd like to be your dinner."

He chuckles and kisses me. "Noted. I feel like Thai."

He orders the food, and when it arrives, we sit next to each other at the dining table to eat it.

"So Heather and Ariana are coming to the store tomorrow. I'm hoping that Heather will consider us as a stockist for Serenity."

"That's a brilliant idea. I've met Cruise Control a few times, and they're pretty down to earth. Surely, she'll say yes. I mean, you're offering to help her sell more clothes."

I love how loyal he is to me, despite the fact it would be perfectly acceptable for Heather to turn down the idea of us stocking her clothes.

"Hopefully, she will," I tell him with a smile as I take a bite of my pad thai.

When Logan's finished his dinner, he picks up a napkin and wipes his mouth with it before saying, "You'll have to let me know how it goes. In the meantime"—he sets his plate to the side, leaving an empty space on the table in front of him—"I'd like to taste one of the other dishes that is on offer tonight. Sit on the table, Alexandra."

I bite my lip as his words cause an immediate, intense ache in my pussy. I climb onto the table to sit in front of him the same way I did with Dante in Napa months ago, and Logan gives me a sexy smile as he looks up at me. He spreads my legs wide, pushing my feet off the chair so they're dangling off the table as he moves forward in his seat.

I wait impatiently for him to use his amazing tongue on me, but he takes his time. He uses his hands to gently stroke my skin while he kisses and licks my inner thighs, getting closer and closer to my sweet spot. When he finally reaches my pussy, I'm delirious with lust and aching for relief. I break the moment he tongues my clit, and I come after only seconds. He continues to eat me out, using his skillful tongue and fingers to keep me in ecstasy until he's satisfied with what he's done.

He pushes his chair back and drops his jeans and briefs to his ankles as he looks into my eyes. Without saying anything, he pulls me off the table, spins me around, and bends me over it. He grabs my hips and pushes his cock inside me. The glass of his dining table against my chest is a cold contrast to the fire flooding throughout my body as Logan pleasures us both.

I have no control in this situation. I'm lost to the ecstasy and love I have for Logan, and all I can do is hold on and enjoy the ride.

*****

I'm at the Rodeo Drive store late Tuesday morning, and Jasmine is obviously nervous about the upcoming celebrity visit.

"It'll be fine, Jazz," I say with a laugh that hides my own nerves.

I haven't mentioned to Jasmine that I'm hoping to stock Serenity, so it's merely the celebrity factor that has her on edge. We get more than a few celebrities in the store, but Jasmine is a fan of Cruise Control and often plays their albums, and I realize she's got it on now.

"Shit. Turn off *Cards Have Been Dealt*," I say quickly. "It looks tacky if we're playing the album when they arrive."

Jasmine cringes. "I didn't even realize. I'll put on a random playlist instead."

A man in a black suit walks through the door, followed by Heather, Ariana, and April Conway. I groan internally because despite Jasmine's efforts, I approach the three women just as one of Cruise Control's songs, "Rules to Break," starts playing.

"I swear to god, I didn't do that on purpose," I say with a laugh.

Heather grins at me and laughs as well. "I'm sure you didn't. It's one of my favorite songs, anyway. I hope you don't mind that I brought April with us."

Heather moves aside, and I smile at the singer. "Yes, we've met a couple of times. It's good to see you again, April."

"It's good to see you, too. I've been to the Orange County store a few times. I didn't know you owned these stores," April says and flicks her blonde hair behind her shoulder as she smiles back at me.

I nod at her. "Yeah, I've got three stores in total. It's nice to see you again, Ariana."

Heather has wandered off to a rack of clothes nearby and flicks through them, which leaves me alone with her friends.

"Nice to see you, too. I'm told everyone had a good time at the club. I'm too old for clubs these days," Ariana says with a laugh.

"You're five years younger than me," Heather scoffs.

"I feel five years *older* since I had Carys," Ariana groans. "What's it like to sleep through the night? Remind me, please—no wait, don't. I don't want to remember."

We all laugh, and I say, "Well, I'll be at the counter if you need any help."

Ariana sits on a long, flat sofa that we have for customers to wait on while Heather and April browse the store. Heather doesn't take long to pick out a massive armful of clothes to try on.

As some regular customers enter the store, their eyes widen when they see April, and I say to one of the salesgirls, "Can you please take care of the new customers?"

She nods and rushes over to them. I spoke to the staff this morning and said that Jasmine or I would look after Heather and

Ariana and that we'd like them to see to any regular customers.

"Want me to hang these in a room for you?" I ask Heather as I approach her.

"That would be awesome, thanks. Harrison always tells me that I buy too many clothes, but they're just so pretty, and we've been so busy lately that the only new clothes I've had were ones I made myself," she jokes as she hands me the pile of clothes.

"Surely, that's not a hardship. Your clothes are amazing, particularly the dresses and skirts. I love that they all have pockets."

Heather bursts into laughter and nods. "Yeah. When I was designing the last line, I swore that I would never make a skirt or dress without pockets again. Some styles are a challenge, but if it doesn't work with pockets, I don't want to make it."

"She caved to our friend Lita's *very* persuasive arguments that women should have pockets just like men do," Ariana says with a laugh.

"Hey, I'm always happy to admit when I'm wrong, and besides"—Heather pulls a lip balm out of the pocket of her dress and rubs some on her lips—"it's very useful."

I laugh as I head to the change rooms and hang up the clothes she's selected. I'm curious about what she likes and have a look through them as I'm hanging them up. There is one pair of trousers, but she's chosen five dresses, two skirts, and three tops to try on as well.

Most are from the shipment I secured from the new supplier, and I'm satisfied with myself because Heather clearly likes the clothes as much as I did when I sourced them. She even picked out the blue dress that we were originally missing, but has been selling well after the supplier quickly rectified their mistake.

Heather appears just as I've finished my inspection, and she asks, "What do you think?"

"They'll all look perfect on you. You could be a model," I say truthfully.

"No way," she says as she shakes her head at me. "I'm much happier designing clothes than walking a runway, but thanks."

I notice that she's wearing the beautiful diamond heart lock necklace again as I leave her to try on the clothes, and as I predicted, when she comes out in the first dress, it looks stunning on her. Ariana and April both give their compliments, and I see one of the other customers take a picture of her.

I walk over to them and give them a polite smile as I say quietly, "Hi. I'm so sorry, but we have a store policy not to take pictures of other customers. I need you to delete that photo and, if you do that again, I'll need to ask you to leave."

"I wasn't taking a picture of anyone," she says in an annoyed tone while not bothering to keep her voice down.

"I see. Well, nonetheless, that is our policy. So I'm just making you aware. Delete the photo, please." I fix her with a cold glare until she opens her photo app and deletes the photo, then I turn to the salesgirl. "If you need my assistance, just come get me."

I know she'll understand this to mean that if she sees them do that again, I won't hesitate to turf them out of the store. I head back to near where Ariana is sitting, and Heather is back out now and wearing a skirt and top.

"Thank you," Heather says quietly.

"It's not a problem." I shrug my shoulders and smile at her.

April tries on a few outfits, and she comes out in her second outfit as the other group of customers makes a few purchases and leaves the store.

To make things simpler, I say, "Danielle, you can take your lunch break now. Can you please put the closed sign up as you leave?"

She nods and heads to the door as Heather says, "Oh my god, you didn't need to close the store for us."

"It's fine. We get a few celebrities in here, so we do it occasionally."

Heather shakes her head and says, "We're not celeb—damn you, April."

"As if you're not famous, anyway. Sorry to ruin your day," April laughs.

They spend another half an hour in the store before Jasmine rings them up. Heather goes first and has five bags of clothes. Two bodyguards have been standing near the entrance this whole time, and one comes over to her.

"Would you like me to take some of those, Mrs. Fletcher?"

"Yes. Thanks, Cal."

He takes the bags off her and heads back to the entrance while Heather turns to smile at me.

"Sometimes it's nice having a bodyguard on hand to help out," she says with a laugh.

"I'm glad Dante's never needed one. The paparazzi aren't anywhere near as bad to us as they've been to you."

I quickly stop talking because I doubt Heather Fletcher, of all people, needs me to tell her how badly she's been treated by the paparazzi in the past.

She gets a tight smile on her face and says, "Yeah. Well, I hope for your sake that they never are. I wouldn't wish it on anybody. Anyway, thank you for being so accommodating. I love your store. Do you buy the clothes yourself, or do you have a buyer?"

"I do it. I probably should give the task to someone else, but I'm so attached to the brand I'm building that I'm not ready to let go of it."

Heather laughs and nods. "Hey, if anyone knows what you're talking about, it's me."

I figure there's no time like the present for me to ask her if she'd consider us as a stockist for Serenity.

Butterflies fly around in my stomach as I say, "Speaking of which, I guess. Would you consider us stocking some of your line?"

I swallow heavily as I watch her take in my question, and she raises an eyebrow at me. "You waited until I was leaving to ask that?"

"I was waiting for the right time," I admit.

"Well, when I'm heading out the door isn't the right time," she says, but she laughs as well. "We can talk. I'd definitely consider it because I love your store and, speaking of brands, it fits right in with mine. I'm hardly going to turn down someone who wants to sell my clothes."

"That's exactly what Logan said," I exclaim without thinking.

"Smart man," she says with a wink at me.

She opens the large purple handbag she has hanging over her shoulder and rifles through before handing me a business card. It's very nice, made from fancy thick, black linen card stock with the Serenity logo embossed on the front and her contact information on the back.

"Send me an email, and we can work on the details."

As soon as Heather and her friends have left the store, I flop on my back on the sofa and stare at the roof as I announce to Jasmine, "I can't believe that just happened."

Chapter Nineteen

Happy Birthday

It's Friday night, and we've just arrived in San Francisco on my birthday. We get into a rented Range Rover with blacked-out windows to drive to Napa. Nate gets into the driver's seat and drives to the furthest corner of the airport parking lot before he parks the car.

"I hope you don't think you'll be wearing clothes, Angel," Dante says in a husky voice next to me.

"Of course not, Honey," I murmur as I unbuckle my seatbelt.

All three men watch as I pull the pink Serenity dress I'm wearing up and off over my head. I wasn't wearing any underwear anyway, so I'm completely naked and very wet.

"Lie on my lap," Dante tells me.

I do my best as he shuffles into the middle seat, and my legs rest on the leather car seat while my crotch is on Dante's erection and my breasts are on Logan's hard cock. The sound of my heavy breaths fills the car, and I'm aware that Nate is watching this from the front seat.

"Now, when we get to Napa, we need you ready and able to take a cock straight to your ass, Angel. Which means we need to plug you until we get there so we can stretch your asshole ready for someone's cock."

"Yes, Honey," I manage to breathe out.

Dante moves in his seat, I assume to get the butt plug and lube, but I don't care because I'm distracted when Logan unzips his jeans underneath me and frees his cock.

"Suck me, Alexandra."

"Yes, Sir."

I take his cock in my mouth at once and begin giving him head. It gives me something to focus on while Dante drips lube on my asshole. I don't focus on the pain as he begins pushing the butt plug into it; instead, I focus on the enjoyment I get when Logan moans as I take him as far into my mouth as I can.

Dante strokes my wet clit and keeps putting pressure on the butt plug as he pushes it inside me. Once it's all the way in, Logan takes hold of my head and begins thrusting his cock into my mouth. I'm no longer giving him head. Instead, he's fucking my mouth. All I can do is suck him as much as I can and try to get my breath when I get the opportunity.

"Don't you dare make a mess in this rental car, Angel," Dante growls. "If a single drop of Logan's cum doesn't go down your throat, I'm going to spank you."

I kind of want Logan to blow his load all over the vehicle when Dante says that, but I don't get a chance to do that because Logan holds his cock down my throat when he comes. I swallow his load and remove my mouth, but he keeps stroking until a small amount of cum seeps from the head of his cock.

"You missed some, Alexandra," he murmurs with a wicked grin at me.

I look up at him as I swirl my tongue around the head of his cock to lap up the final drop of his cum. As I do, Dante smacks my ass hard, and the stinging sensation sends a shock of arousal to my dripping pussy.

He smacks my ass five times and says, "Sit up and buckle up, Angel. Keep your legs spread."

He pulls one of my legs over to him, and Logan does the same with my other leg. I can barely catch my breath as I pull my seatbelt over myself and strap in. On the hour-long drive to Napa, Dante and Logan kiss me, finger me, play with my breasts, and generally keep me in a state of high arousal.

By the time we arrive, I'm dizzy with lust. We enter the house then head to the living room. I'm reminded of the first weekend I fucked Logan, and I'm happy to be back here.

Ash and Cassie are visiting tomorrow to celebrate with us, not that I really wanted Cassie to come here. Nate didn't, either, and we're both hoping that she doesn't show tomorrow. Ash has been sending us messages that he's really sorry about how she's reacted to our relationship and that he hopes we can all be friends. So I didn't want to put my foot down, but I'm glad she's not here on my actual birthday, even though it means Ash isn't here.

We head to the living room, and I've almost reached the sofa when Logan says, "Stop, Alexandra."

I halt in my tracks, and he walks over to me as Dante drops on the sofa and Nate sits on an armchair nearby, facing us.

Logan says from behind me, "I believe you're ready for a cock in your ass. Bend over and hold your ankles."

I have to stop myself from gasping in surprise because I wasn't expecting this. I do as instructed and lean down to hold my ankles. It takes a second to steady myself, but I'm deliciously exposed like this. My nipples are rock hard, and my pussy is wet and aching while the butt plug in my ass stretches me, preparing me for Logan's cock.

He walks over and stands behind me before the sensation of the butt plug moving hits me as Logan tugs it out of my ass. I'm stretched further again as its widest part makes its way out of my asshole, and I gasp when it does.

I watch Logan's legs as he walks off to the side of the room, then he comes back to stand behind me again. The blood is rushing to my head, but it has nothing on the intense desire I have for Logan to fuck me right now. Cold lube drips on my ass, and I bite my lip in anticipation.

"Such a pretty sight to see," Logan murmurs as he sticks a

finger in my asshole. "My toy is ready for me to play with it."

He sticks a second finger in and pushes them in and out of me a couple of times before he pulls them out and grabs my hips. I gasp as he sticks his cock in my ass, and it turns into a groan as he fucks me roughly. He pulls me back onto his cock, and if he wasn't holding my hips so tightly, I think I might fall over. I hold on to my ankles and resist the urge to put my hands on the floor for more stability.

Logan pounds my ass, and I'm stretched tight around his thick cock. The room is filled with our panting breaths and moans as he fucks me until he gives a final rough thrust into me and holds himself there while he comes.

When he's finished, he pulls out and says, "Kiss me, Alexandra."

I stand and turn to him. He keeps one hand on his cock, holding the condom he used while fucking me on himself as I kiss him.

"Come sit with me, Sexy," Nate says when our kiss ends, and I move over to straddle him.

He kisses me deeply, and our tongues intertwine. I wrap my arms around his neck as his cock stiffens underneath me. My pussy is aching, and I desperately need Nate to fuck me right now.

To my surprise, he ends our kiss and says, "Turn around, Lexi. You'll want to see this."

I blink at him for a few seconds, then turn on his lap to face the sofa. I gasp softly when I see that Dante has his pants around his ankles as he strokes his stiff cock and he looks at me.

"Happy birthday, Angel. Do you want to come here to watch this or stay there?"

I realize when Logan gets on his knees in front of him that, even though they gave me gifts this morning in LA, he and Logan are also giving me the gift he promised me weeks ago.

"Oh my god, yes. I'll come there."

I scramble off Nate's lap and rush over to sit next to Dante on the sofa. I kiss him, and he takes one of my breasts in his hand and plays with it before turning to look down at Logan.

"Okay, go on, then. Let's see if you're as good as they say."

"Oh, he is," Nate says in a husky voice as he walks over to us.

He's hard in his jeans, and I'm unsurprised when he gets his cock out to start stroking it as he sits next to me. Logan takes Dante's cock in his mouth, and I lick my lips as I watch him do it. I want to suck Nate's cock, but I also don't want to miss this. Nate pulls me onto him and expertly slides his cock into me as we watch them, which makes me gasp.

"Do you like that, Lexi?"

"Yes," I moan, loving the feeling of his thick cock filling me.

I wrap my arms around his neck behind me as I lean back against him, which pushes my breasts forward, and Nate places his hands on them. He thumbs my nipples as he fucks me slowly, and we watch Logan blowing Dante.

"What do you love more? Me fucking your tight, wet pussy, or Logan giving your husband what is probably the best blow job of his life?" Nate growls in my ear.

On cue, Dante moans in satisfaction as Logan takes him deep in his mouth, and I lower my hand to my clit to rub it as Nate fucks me.

"I don't know," I gasp.

Dante leans across and kisses me, thrusting his tongue into my mouth and taking one of my breasts in his hand as Nate drops his hand to my clit to take over rubbing me.

I'm lost in the thrill of it all. The three men I love connected with one another and connected with me. I give in to the sensations, and it doesn't take long for me to come.

I don't even know whose name I moan in my ecstasy, but Nate keeps fucking me, and Logan is still blowing Dante. I break our kiss and watch as Logan does what he does best—using his tongue and mouth to give someone an inordinate amount of pleasure.

As I watch them, Nate kisses my neck, then begins fucking me harder while he watches them as well. I had thought that maybe Dante wouldn't enjoy this, but even though he doesn't seem as into it as Nate is when Logan blows him, Dante seems unable to stop himself from groaning his satisfaction at what Logan's doing.

Sure enough, he eventually groans, "I'm going to come, Logan."

I'm not sure if that sends Nate over the edge, but he pulls me roughly down on him and comes deep inside me as I watch Dante's body shudder when his orgasm hits. I love seeing him blow his load into Logan's mouth while Nate does the same inside me. Logan cleans Dante's cock with his tongue, and Dante shudders as he does.

Logan smiles up at him, then stands and faces me as he strips off his clothes and tosses them aside. Nate's still inside me, and he twists and thumbs my nipples as we watch Logan, who lies on the floor on his back.

"Sit on my face, Alexandra."

I think I might die with pleasure as I pull myself off Nate's cock and kneel over Logan's face. I drop myself down, so I'm on him, and he wraps his arms around my thighs as he begins eating me out.

I'm a mess as Logan uses his tongue both in my pussy and on my clit. I ride his face in ecstasy, and when I come, Logan grips my thighs harder so I can't get off his face. I moan my satisfaction as he holds me in place, and I'm lost in a daze of lust as I grind my pussy on him. My clit is unbearably sensitive, and it doesn't take long before I come again.

Logan pushes me up and off his face before saying, "Come kiss me, Alexandra."

I turn around to lie in his arms as he kisses me passionately. We're both panting for breath and, when we finish our kiss, I look into his beautiful eyes and smile at him.

"Was that good, Lexi?" he asks.

I nod at him and kiss him softly. "Yes, it was."

"I'm glad." He squeezes me tightly and holds me in his embrace for another few minutes.

When he lets me go, I look over at the sofa. Both men are

dressed now, so I move over to cuddle Nate, and he kisses me. Finally, I settle myself on Dante's lap and kiss him as well.

"Happy birthday, Angel. Did you enjoy your present?"

I laugh and tell him, "Very much. Did you enjoy it?"

"I didn't dislike it, but I probably won't do it again unless you ask me to."

"Interesting. I don't want to see it if you're not into it. I think part of what I love about seeing Nate and Logan is that they're both so into it," I say as I turn to smile at them.

Nate gives me a wicked grin, then moves closer to Logan, who is clothed now. He puts his hand on the back of Logan's head and presses his lips to Logan's. They kiss for about half a minute before Nate ends their kiss.

"Well, that was a nice surprise," Logan says with a laugh.

"Maybe tomorrow night I can show Lexi how much I like your mouth on my cock?" Nate suggests.

I squirm on Dante's lap, and I very much look forward to this. I'm spending tonight with Dante and had planned to spend tomorrow night with Logan.

"I think that can be arranged. Do you have room in your bed for Lexi and me tomorrow night?"

"Absolutely, I do."

The air is thick with the sexual tension between them, and they kiss again, with Logan reaching between Nate's legs to rub his crotch as they do. My pussy aches as I watch them kiss, especially with how casually they exchange sexual pleasure with one another now. I love them so much, and I love this for them.

When their kiss ends, Logan removes his hand and says with a grin, "Good to hear."

I'm very excited for tomorrow night, but I'm also reminded that Logan and I wanted to talk about the living situation, and this seems like an appropriate time to do that.

"So, Logan and I were talking on Monday about him living separately from us. It sucks only seeing him twice a week and the four of us only getting to all be together on weekends, but I'm not sure there's enough space in our apartment for him to move in."

"Couldn't you turn the office into a room for Logan?" Nate asks.

"That's what Lexi suggested," Logan says, and I can't help but laugh. He smiles at me, then shakes his head at Nate. "It would still be cramped, and it means there's no office for anyone to use, plus I like having the sex room."

There's silence for a few seconds, and I turn the problem over in my brain. The only solution I can see is for us to get a new place together. I just don't see a way for us to stay where we are as a group.

"Nate, what have you done with your apartment since you moved in?" I ask him.

"It's been empty. I thought maybe I could lease it out or sell it, but I haven't done it yet," Nate admits.

"So, if Logan moves in with us, we're going to have two empty apartments just sitting there. Wouldn't it make more sense for us to sell all three apartments and buy something together?"

The guys all look at each other and then back at me. I know that what I've just suggested is huge, but we've known each other for well over a decade. Plus, Nate's living with us anyway.

"You would do that for me?" Logan asks.

"It's not even a question," Dante says.

I look up at him, my heart full of so much love and gratitude that he initiated and welcomed these men coming into our relationship. Having them in our lives in this way has made us all so much happier, and I might never have had that if Dante hadn't encouraged it in the beginning.

"Yeah, I don't give a fuck about selling my place, as long as we have a pool table in the new one," Nate tells Logan with a grin.

"And a poker table as well," I add with a smirk at him.

Logan shakes his head. "You guys are amazing. Okay, then. I guess we'll start looking for places when we get back to LA."

I slide off Dante's lap and walk over to straddle Logan. "I can't wait to have you living with us."

*****

I'm sitting on Nate's lap on the sofa in the living room when Ash and Cassie arrive the next day. Dante goes to the door to let him in since I'm with Nate, and Logan is busy cooking dinner for us all.

He slides his hand up underneath my dress, and when his fingers reach my pussy, he murmurs, "It's such a shame you're wearing underwear."

"I didn't want to risk it. We'll have to be quiet tonight," I point out to Nate.

I'm very much looking forward to Logan and me sharing a bed with him this evening. We didn't think when we planned to spend tonight together about the fact that Ash and Cassie would be here tonight.

"Will we?" Nate asks with a wicked grin on his face.

I can't help but laugh and say, "We probably should."

I press my lips against his as he squeezes me tightly to him while we kiss. There's a cough from nearby, and we break apart before we turn to look at the entrance to the room. Dante is standing there with Ash and Cassie, who is sneering at us.

"Hi, guys," I say and give them a bright smile.

A part of me wants to move off Nate's lap to make Cassie more comfortable, but I'm not going to. It's my birthday celebration, and I'm not going to spend the evening accommodating her instead of enjoying my men.

"Lexi and Nate, hi," Ash says with a smile as he comes over to us. "Happy birthday, Lexi."

I stand and give him a hug while Cassie heads over to sit on a two-seater sofa nearby, ignoring us completely.

"Thanks, Ash." I hug him before I smile at him and say, "I'm so glad you came out here today."

Less glad that Cassie actually came with him, but that can't be helped. I settle myself back on Nate's lap, and he wraps his arms back around me as I do. Ash sits next to Cassie and smiles at us.

"Have you guys been out here long?" he asks.

"We arrived yesterday and spent the night here," Nate says, and he smiles up at me before looking back at our guests. "Do you guys want a drink?"

"Sure. I'll have a beer. Cassie?" Ash looks at her as she sits stiffly next to him.

"Whatever. I don't mind."

There's an awkward silence for a few seconds before I slide off Nate's lap, and he walks off to get drinks for everyone. Instinctively, I move over to Dante and sit with him instead. Cassie glares at me, and I assume she dislikes the ease with which I switch between showing affection to the men I love.

Nate gets the drinks, and we drink them while the guys talk, and Cassie shoots me dirty looks. It's so bizarre that she's flipped entirely and become this person. I always knew she had a tendency to be judgmental, but I find her attitude completely disconcerting. She's become an entirely different person, and it makes me worry for Ash.

Eventually, I can't stand it any longer, and I say, "I'm just going to go see how Logan is doing with dinner."

I kiss Dante quickly, then stop and lean down to kiss Nate, where he's sitting in an armchair nearby on the way out of the room. He puts his arms around me and deepens our kiss before he ends it. I can see the amusement in his expression before he pulls me into a hug.

"You're such a shit-stirrer," I whisper in his ear.

"Yup," he chuckles.

I kiss his cheek when he lets me go and walk out of the room without looking back at Cassie to see her reaction. I manage to hold it together until I get to the kitchen, but as soon as I'm safely there and well out of the earshot of everyone else, I burst into laughter.

Logan looks up from where he's putting the garlic lamb chops in the oven and raises his eyebrows at me. "What's so funny?"

"Nate practically mauling me on the way out the door, which I'm sure Cassie loved."

Logan shakes his head as he closes the oven door and turns to look at me. "Don't antagonize her, though."

"Hey, I didn't do it," I say with a pout.

"No, but you did come in here laughing about it."

He holds his arms out, and I walk over to enter his embrace. Logan wraps his arms around me and kisses me passionately. The scent of the garlic lamb chops fills the air, and when our kiss ends, I smile up at him.

"Dinner smells good."

"Thanks. It should be ready in about ten minutes."

"Do you need any help?" I ask him.

"Sure." He smiles at me and kisses me quickly before he lets me go.

I help him to finish off the dinner, and we take the food out to the dining table.

"Take a seat. I'll go get the guys," I say and give Logan a quick kiss.

When I reach the living room, the guys are talking, and Cassie is sitting next to Ash with a sullen look on her face. I can't help but wonder if she's always been like this, and I just hadn't noticed.

"Excuse me, everyone," I say with a bright smile. "Dinner's ready."

I lead the way back to the dinner table and sit down next to Logan. Nate sits next to me, and I end up across from Ash rather than Cassie, which is something of a relief. I eat the lamb chops, which are delicious, along with the pasta Logan has served with them.

"How was work this week, Lexi?" Ash asks with a smile when we're nearing the end of dinner.

"Oh my god, it was amazing. Heather Fletcher came in, and she even brought April Conway with her along with Ariana Knight," I tell him with a big grin as I take a sip of the red wine Logan served with dinner.

"That's cool."

"Yeah. Nate introduced me to her last Saturday." I smile brightly at him, grateful for the introduction, then turn back to Ash. "We're going to talk about the idea of Black Lilac stocking Serenity."

"Wow, that's an awesome idea," Ash says with wide eyes and a smile at me.

"It was *my* idea," Cassie huffs as she glares at me.

I turn my gaze to hers and smile at her as I say as civilly as I can, "Yes, it was. I really am very grateful that you thought of it. Which I would've happily told you if we were on speaking terms right now."

The tension in the room is so thick that it could be cut with a knife. I've acknowledged the elephant that we've all been ignoring since Ash and Cassie arrived today, and as much as I don't regret it, I also don't want to cause problems between the guys and Ash.

"I see," Cassie says coolly, but she doesn't make any further comment.

There's an awkward silence in the wake of her words, and Dante says, "This dinner is delicious, Logan. Thank you for cooking it."

"You're welcome. It's my birthday gift to Lexi." He turns to smile at me.

I can't help but laugh and say, "I thought your birthday gift was"—I manage to cut myself off before I finish, 'your blow job for Dante' and struggle to think of something to say, but fail miserably and end with—"never mind."

"What did you think his birthday gift was, Lexi?" Cassie asks in a far too innocent tone.

The tension is back, but I refuse to play her games, so I say, "Something he gave me last night."

"Sex," she mutters under her breath and turns to look at Ash.

He looks back at her and frowns. "Cassie, it's fine. Can you please just let them be happy?"

"We shouldn't have come here. You know I'm not okay with this."

"No, *you* shouldn't have come," Nate snarls. "Ash should've left you in LA and come on his own. You're a guest in my house, and you're very much wearing out your welcome right now."

She turns to look at him, her jaw set and shooting him a death stare. I think she might say something more, but she shrugs her shoulders instead.

"Sorry. I'll just shut my mouth about your little arrangement, I guess."

Nate opens his mouth to speak, but I place my hand on his arm and turn to look at him, "No, Nate. It's okay. Ash and Cassie are here to celebrate my birthday, which I appreciate."

"Which reminds me," Ash says, with a tight smile on his face. "We haven't given you our present. While everyone's finishing their dinner, I'll go get it."

"Awesome, thanks," I say with a genuine smile at him.

"I'll come with you. I'm done here." Cassie wipes her mouth with her napkin and drops it on the table before walking away with him.

It's as though a blanket has been removed from over my head, and I can breathe freely again once she's left the room.

"Fuck, when did she get so bitter?" I ask quietly.

Nate snorts and shakes his head. "Uh, yeah. Have you not noticed her being a bitch to me basically the entire time she's been dating Ash?"

"Really?" I turn to stare at him.

"Pretty much. She's made a few comments to me that were borderline nasty. I assumed she was just a judgmental prude about me sleeping with so many women, but now I know for sure."

I cringe as I remember the day we talked about Nate when we went shopping at The Grove. "Yeah, I'd believe it."

"Just try to ignore her, Angel. Don't let her ruin your night," Dante says before he leans over to kiss me.

He and I head to the living room while Logan and Nate clean up from dinner, and they've already joined us before Ash and Cassie come downstairs with my present.

"What took so long?" Nate asks.

He's sitting alone on an armchair, and I'm in between Dante and Logan but cuddled into Dante. I figure that Logan was right, and we shouldn't antagonize Cassie any more than we already have.

"We were just having a discussion," Ash says with the same

tight smile he had on his face earlier.

I can imagine what their conversation was about, and I'm grateful that Nate doesn't ask the question. I know Dante and Logan would know better, but Nate really doesn't have a problem pissing people off.

"Anyway, happy birthday, Lexi," Ash says, and he gives me a genuine grin.

He hands me a small, rectangular present wrapped in silver wrapping paper with a red bow.

"Ooh, I'm excited," I tell him as I take the present off him.

I pull the bow off and set it aside on Logan's lap, and he laughs. After I unwrap the present, I set the silver wrapping paper on Dante's lap. Inside is a blue velvet box. I know that Ash has gotten me some kind of jewelry, but I don't know what yet.

I open the box and gasp, "Holy shit, Ash. It's gorgeous!"

Inside the box is a stunning white gold necklace with an openwork oval link chain. On the end of it is hanging a beautiful coat hanger pendant covered in brilliant round diamonds. I've never seen anything like it.

"Flip it over," Ash says.

I turn the coat hanger over and see that engraved on the back in a tiny script are the words 'Happy birthday, Lexi.' I shake my head and swallow against a lump in my throat because it's such a thoughtful gift, and I love it so much. I stand and stride over to where Ash is sitting next to Cassie, then lean down to wrap my arms tightly around him.

"Thank you so much. I love it."

"You're welcome," he says as he hugs me back.

I kiss his cheek before I walk back to sit next to Dante again. I take the necklace out of the box, and Dante helps me put it on. I can't wipe the smile off my face as I reach up to touch the pendant again.

"It's so perfect, Ash."

"I almost had them put a little dress on it, but I didn't know if you'd want a pendant that big," he grins back at me.

"Oh, that would've been adorable, too. No, this is definitely unique and gorgeous. I'm so happy with it."

Before Ash can say anything else, Cassie says, "I'm tired. I think I'll go to bed. Are you coming, Ashton?"

He looks surprised as he frowns up at her. "No. It's not even nine yet."

"I'd really prefer it if you came to bed with me," Cassie says through clenched teeth.

"Or what, Cassie? Do you think Ash might have an orgy with us down here while you're sleeping or something?" Nate scoffs.

"Are you asking if I'm uncomfortable with my boyfriend being alone with a slut who sleeps with three men and would be more than happy to make it four?"

She asks it in such a casual, querying tone that I can barely believe she actually called me a slut. My mouth drops open, and I don't know what to say. On some level, I expect any of the three men I'm in a relationship with to be the ones to defend me, but it's none of them who speaks next.

Ash says in a cold, calm voice, "Cassie, it's over."

Everyone stares at him, and Cassie's mouth drops open. She blinks at him several times and shakes her head.

"No. You don't mean that."

"Yes, I do," he says firmly.

Cassie's head whips back and forth between Ash and me before she snarls, "So, you do want to fuck her after all."

"No, Cassie. I don't want to sleep with Lexi, but if you think that you can insult my friend and get away with it, then you're sorely mistaken. We've discussed this almost nonstop since they told us about Lexi and Logan, and I'm tired of it. This is simply the last straw. I'll help you get your things, and you can take the rental car back to the airport tonight. I'll get you a ticket for a flight back to LAX."

She shakes her head again and says, "You don't really want to break up with me. I'm sorry I said that about Lexi. I didn't mean to say it."

"You're not sorry you said it, Cassie. You're sorry that I won't accept you trashing my friend. You're sorry that I don't have any desire to be in a relationship with someone who can treat the people I love like garbage. I've let it go on for too long because I thought you would come around, but I can see that you won't. I'll say it again. It's over."

He stands and begins to walk out of the room, and Cassie calls out, "Ash, please don't do this."

"It's already done, Cassie. I'm going upstairs to get your things. You can come with me, or you can not come with me, but I'll get Nate to call the cops if you don't leave this house in half an hour."

He turns and strides out of the room, and I watch him go. I feel so conflicted because a part of me feels guilty that he broke up with her because of me, but I'm also grateful that he stood up for me and did that. He deserves better, but I really wish that things had been different. I always liked Cassie but, apparently, she just had me fooled.

This is confirmed when she snarls at me, "This is all *your* fault."

"I told you that you were the only one who had a problem with it. Have a nice life, Cassandra Foster."

She storms out of the room, and half an hour later, she and Ash appear again as they walk past the entrance of the living room toward the front door. Cassie is sniffling, and Ash is walking stiffly, with his head held high.

There's quiet murmuring from their directions before the sound of the front door slamming shut rings out from the hall.

About a minute later, the sound of a car taking off quickly can be heard, and another few seconds after that, Ash appears at the entrance to the living room.

He sighs heavily before looking at me. "I'm so sorry, Lexi. I should've broken up with her as soon as she started trying to keep me away from you guys."

I get up and walk over to hug him. "It's okay, Ash. I'm not mad. Thanks for standing up for me."

"You're one of my best friends. I could never let her speak to you like that." He shakes his head as he moves back to the sofa he had been sitting on with Cassie before. "She's been incredibly jealous since you got together with Logan. I should've known she wouldn't get over it, but I kept telling myself she would."

Now that Cassie is gone, I don't hesitate to sit on Logan's lap while Ash is talking, and Logan smiles up at me before looking over at our friend. "Are you okay, Ash?"

"Yeah, I'm fine. I thought I loved Cassie, and before all this, I'd been thinking about maybe proposing to her. I should thank you guys for making me see her true colors before I made a big mistake, I guess."

"How about we get drunk and play some pool before bed?" Nate suggests.

Ash laughs and nods. "Yeah. Alcohol is definitely a good idea." His phone buzzes in his pocket, and he looks down at it. "Ugh. It's Cassie."

Ash ignores the text, and we head to the games room to play pool. By the time he's ignored three more texts, she calls him.

"Hello?" he answers the phone as Nate waits for him to take his turn in their game of pool. "No, Cassie. I bought you a plane ticket for a reason. I can't make you leave Napa or even San Francisco, but I can refuse to let you back into this estate. I honestly don't care where you go, to be honest, but I'd definitely appreciate it if you'd return the rental car. Either way, I'm not speaking to you again, and I'm going to block your number now. Goodbye."

He ends the call and presses a few buttons on his phone before he looks up at us.

"I guess it's going to be like that. I'm prepared to pay whatever fee if she doesn't return the car. I just want her gone." He shrugs his shoulders. "I think I need to get drunk, though."

We have a few drinks and play pool, but it's clear Ash isn't in the mood to party, and he goes to bed after only playing a few games.

"Night, Lexi. I'm sorry your birthday party was ruined," he

says before he goes.

I give him a big hug and say, "It's not your fault at all, and I've had a good night. I love you, Ash, and thanks again for sticking up for me."

"Any time, Lexi. I wish it hadn't been necessary."

"Me, too." I pull away from him, and a thought occurs to me. I chew my bottom lip as I ask, "You're not going to regret this and blame me, or the guys are you? My biggest worry has been that all of this will affect the band."

He looks down at me and gives me a reassuring smile. "Never, Lexi. You and the guys mean more to me than Cassie ever did."

I watch him walk away, and I've never been more grateful to have such a loyal friend. The day that Nate asked me to be in their music video might have changed everything, but what hasn't changed is the amount of love that I have for the members of Wicked Stallion. Our relationships might have shifted, but that has remained constant.

Epilogue

"Remove your dress, Alexandra. You've been wearing it for far too many hours," Logan says after we've said good night to Dante and made our way to Nate's room with him.

I pull my dress off over my head, fold it, and set it neatly aside. Both Logan and Nate stare at my body with obvious signs of lust in their expressions.

Logan steps forward and trails his finger across my flesh, over the tops of the cups of my lace bra. "The only thing I don't like about having Ash here is that you have to wear clothes."

"All the best toys come packaged, though. Don't they, Logan?" Nate asks with a grin as he moves around behind me.

"I suppose they do," Logan says with a laugh.

Nate wraps his arms around me from behind and toys with the band of my thong. His cock is hard against my ass, and I have an intense need to be fucked.

"Sometimes it's hard to get the package open, but when you do"—he slips his hand into my underwear and starts rubbing my wet clit, which causes me to moan loudly—"it's glorious."

I lean my head back against his chest, and as Nate continues what he's doing, Logan pulls my bra cups under my breasts. My nipples are stiff and painful as Logan lowers his mouth to one of my breasts and twists the other nipple painfully with his hand.

"Sir," I call out at the sharp pain.

It turns to a moan when the pain ebbs away and combines with the pleasure from his tongue on my nipple as Nate strokes my clit.

Logan moves his mouth up to mine to kiss me, and as he presses his body against mine, I realize that the back of Nate's hand must be rubbing against Logan's cock. I'm lost in a daze of ecstasy, and this knowledge tips me over into orgasm. I moan into Logan's mouth as he kisses me. His skillful tongue tangles with mine as my body shudders and waves of pleasure roll through me.

Nate pulls his hand out of my underwear while Logan continues to kiss me, and Nate pulls my panties to the floor. I step out of it as Logan ends our kiss. He removes my bra and hands it to Nate as Logan places his hands on my breasts and thumbs my nipples.

When Nate comes back to us, he's removed his clothing and is naked now, too. His thick, hard cock is jutting out in front of him, and I bite my lip as I look at it. Despite my orgasm, my pussy is aching, and I'm desperate to be fucked.

"So, what should we do now?" Logan asks with a smirk at me.

He turns to Nate, who has moved right next to him, and they press their lips together. Logan reaches between them to place his hand on Nate's cock, and he strokes him as they kiss. The room is filled with the sound of their heavy breathing when their kiss ends, and Logan continues to stroke Nate while he looks deeply into his eyes.

"Is this what you want, Nate? Or do you want me to suck you until you blow down my throat?"

Nate groans and shakes his head. "Can you stop for a second? I can't think straight when you're doing that to me."

"Sure," Logan says and immediately removes his hand from Nate's cock. He raises an eyebrow at him. "I didn't think it was a difficult question, though."

Nate swallows heavily and just stares at Logan. There's silence in the room, and I watch them have this discussion, eager to see what happens next.

"I was thinking that maybe we could try fucking tonight and see if I like it or not."

Logan's eyebrows fly up in obvious surprise, but he nods his head. "Sure, if you want to."

"So, do I just bend over the bed or something?" Nate asks as he flushes bright pink.

Logan chuckles and shakes his head. "No, you really don't. If you want to try receiving anal at some point, we need to work up to it. You'll need to do anal training. Ask Lexi."

Both men turn to look at me, and I nod. "Yeah, it's true. Dante and I used tiny butt plugs at first. Even then, the first couple of times we tried, I couldn't do it."

"So, if you want to try fucking me, we can do that. It's up to you. I won't be offended if you don't want to."

Logan kisses Nate softly and tenderly when he finishes speaking. My love for them is almost as intense and overwhelming as my arousal right now. Nate pulls Logan's top off over his head, and Logan watches him wordlessly as Nate trails his hand down Logan's torso to the waistband of his jeans. I'm reminded of the day we started this with Logan when we were playing strip poker, and I made a similar move.

Nate initiates their kiss this time as he unbuttons Logan's jeans. He unzips them and ends their kiss as he drops to his knees and pulls both Logan's jeans and briefs to the floor. Nate wraps his lips around Logan's cock, and my pussy clenches tightly while I watch them. Logan steps out of his clothes and kicks them aside as he puts his hand on Nate's head. He closes his eyes and throws his head back as he enjoys Nate's blow job.

After about a minute, he opens his eyes and looks at me. "Why don't you join him, Alexandra?"

I kneel next to Nate, and I lick and suck Logan's balls why Nate continues on his shaft. Nate removes his mouth and kisses me before using his hand to angle Logan's cock toward me. I take him in my mouth and worship his cock while Nate takes my previous role with Logan's balls. Nate occasionally trails his tongue up Logan's shaft as I pull my head back, and Logan groans in ecstasy.

Eventually, he warns us, "If you don't stop, I'm going to blow down Alexandra's throat instead of in her pussy while Nate fucks me."

I'm ecstatic at the idea of being fucked by Logan while Nate fucks him, and I pull my mouth off Logan's cock immediately. Nate, however, trails his tongue up Logan's shaft a final time, and Logan shudders when he does. Nate wraps his lips around Logan's head and whatever he does makes Logan gasp.

"Fuck, that's good, Nate."

"Want me to stop?" Nate asks while he pants for breath and looks up at Logan.

"Not really, if I'm being honest, but yes. I want to fuck Lexi tonight, but don't think that I don't want to blow my load down your throat tomorrow."

Nate gets up off his knees and kisses Logan before he turns to me and kisses me as well. Nate reaches between my legs and fingers my drenched pussy.

"Do you have any lube in this room, Nate?" Logan asks.

"Shit. No. I think Dante has some in his room, though. I don't normally fuck Lexi's ass, and she's so fucking wet that I don't need it to fuck her pussy." He removes his fingers from me and lifts them up for us all to see, and my juices glisten in the light. "See?"

"Indeed, I do." Logan takes Nate's fingers in his mouth and sucks them for about twenty seconds before he stops and murmurs, "Tasty." He turns to me and says, "Alexandra. Go retrieve the lube from Dante. I'm sure he'd rather see you naked than either Nate or me."

"What about Ash?" I ask and bite my lip as I realize that the lube is currently being held in the room opposite our friend's.

"I guess you'd better be quiet and don't question me," Logan says and shakes his head.

Without warning, he bends me over the bed and smacks my ass hard. I gasp, and it turns into a moan almost at once. He does it four more times, and I'm dying from the intense need for him to fuck me.

When my punishment is over, he stands me up and says, "We could practically just use Lexi's pussy juice for lube, Nate."

"She is pretty wet," he agrees before he drops to his knees and swipes his tongue through my wet slit.

"But I'd still like her to go get the lube for me. Go quickly, Alexandra. In five minutes, I'm going to call Ash and tell him to watch the hallway if you're not back here by then."

I inhale sharply, and I want to argue that it wouldn't be fair to Ash for him to do that. I also know that all of my men are big on consent, so there's no way they'd involve Ash in our sex games without getting his consent first. But I also know that Logan wouldn't hesitate to punish me if I fail in my task, either. I desperately need to come, so I don't want to risk that.

As I enter the dark hallway, I'm on edge, and my pussy aches at the thought of being caught. As much as I don't think of Ash sexually, there's something arousing about the idea of him catching me like this. Moonlight is streaming in through the windows, so I have enough light to make it to the room Dante is sleeping in. I glance at the door to Ash's room, but it remains safely closed as I enter Dante's. I make my way over to the bedside table next to Dante's side of the bed and slide open the bottom drawer.

"What are you doing?" Dante's voice is soft and husky from next to me.

"We need lube so that Nate can fuck Logan," I tell him.

"Really?" Dante asks, the surprise evident in his tone.

"Yes," I tell him, and I bite my lip as I think about what the two men could be doing in the room without me right now.

I grab the lube, and just as I slide the drawer closed, Dante's hand wraps around my arm. He pulls me down so that he can kiss me and reach between my legs to rub my pussy.

"You seem very excited by this idea, Angel."

"I really am, but I have to go back now, or Logan will punish me. I'm on the clock."

"Well, that would be a shame, wouldn't it?" Dante takes my free hand and places it on his cock. "I guess I'm just going to have to sort myself out."

I laugh and kiss him quickly before I say, "Yes, you will. Logan threatened to wake Ash and tell him to watch the hallway if I'm not back in time."

There's silence for a few seconds before Dante says, "Did he, really? Well, you'd better go quickly and close the door quietly on your way out. I'll just be here thinking about you."

"I'm sure you could join us if you want to," I offer.

Dante chuckles, "It's fine, Angel. Go now, though. Or I'll fuck you, and Logan will call Ash. Then where would we be?"

"Very embarrassed, I'm sure." I kiss him again and exit the room.

I can barely breathe as I walk back up the hallway to Nate's room. My heart pounds in my chest, and I keep expecting to hear Ash, but there's no sound in the hallway, and I make it back to the room safely.

"Cutting it fine, aren't we? You only had a bit over a minute before I called Ash," Logan says with a raised eyebrow.

"Dante woke up while I was getting the lube."

"I see. Give me the bottle, then come and lie on your back at the edge of the bed," he instructs.

I do as I'm told and watch as Logan turns to hand the lube to Nate. I bite my lip and watch these beautiful men discuss what's about to happen.

"It's basically the same as anal with a woman—lots of lube. Use a condom if you're planning to do anything like ass to mouth or don't want a big cleanup job. I'm pretty well-versed in taking a cock to my ass, so you don't need to be gentle with me. Go as hard as you want to, but it's okay if you do want to be gentle, as well. If you're uncomfortable and want to stop, I won't be offended."

"I can't believe I'm going to fuck a guy," Nate says as he stares at Logan.

"You don't have to do it. You really don't."

Nate kisses him, and when he speaks, it's in such a low, husky tone that I can barely hear it over my own panting breaths. "I want to do it, Logan."

They kiss again, then Logan bends over me, and he easily slides his cock into my aching pussy. He holds himself deep inside me, and I peer around him to watch as Nate drips lube onto his ass. He positions himself behind Logan, and I lick my lips as he slowly enters Logan inch by inch. I know how big Nate is, and he has fucked my ass before, but Logan doesn't so much as flinch.

"Fuck, you feel good. Is that okay?" Nate asks with a groan of satisfaction when he's finally all the way inside him.

"Yes," Logan says.

Nate puts his hands on Logan's hips and begins thrusting in and out of him. My pussy clenches tightly around Logan's cock as I watch Nate fuck him, but he doesn't fuck me immediately. He moans and squeezes his eyes shut tight for a few seconds before he opens them and stares at me with a lust-filled expression on his face, and he kisses me.

I love him so much, and I can feel the movement of his body as Nate fucks him. Even though Logan isn't actively fucking me, with each thrust, his cock jerks inside me, and when he finally moves in sync with Nate, I'm lost in ecstasy. The sheer connection of being fucked by Logan while Nate fucks him overwhelms me with love and lust. I can barely believe that I'm this lucky.

Logan reaches between us to rub my clit while he fucks me, and by the time Nate comes in his ass, I've reached climax multiple times. Nate pulls out of Logan, and Logan seems to take this as his cue to get his own orgasm. He grips my hips with both hands and fucks me roughly until he comes buried deep inside me.

We all head to the shower together, and there's a lot of kisses and touches between the three of us while we clean off. Logan dries me while Nate dries himself, and then Logan dries himself as well. We get back into bed, and I lie in between the two men, with the scent of sex filling the room. I'm sleepy and at peace here with them, grateful to not just have them both but to have been involved in a momentous occasion like tonight.

"Thank you for including me," I tell them.

"I wouldn't have had it any other way, Lexi. I love you," Nate says and kisses me.

"Me, either. I love you, too, Lexi," Logan says before he kisses me as well.

"I love you both," I say with a smile.

There's silence in the room for a few seconds before Nate says, "Logan?"

"Yeah?" he answers.

"I love you, too."

There's a sound of movement, and I feel Logan reach over me before he says, "I love you, Nate."

The two men kiss for a minute before Logan settles back next to me again. I don't think I've ever been happier.

Sneak Peek for Wicked Betrayal

*I*t takes us a while to get downstairs the morning after my birthday party. Nate, Logan, and I have sex after we wake up. We clean up and make ourselves presentable before we go downstairs, though, since we have a guest in the house. When we enter the kitchen, we find Ash sitting with Dante at the kitchen bench as they drink coffee together.

"There you guys are. We were about to give up and have our breakfast," Dante says with a laugh.

"Sorry. We were…busy," Nate says with a grin at him.

"I bet you were." Ash smirks back at him. "Especially if the noises I heard last night were anything to go by."

Heat rushes to my cheeks. "Shit. You heard us?"

"Yes. I woke up when you left Dante's room and couldn't help overhearing the obvious threesome you were having," Ash chuckles. "God, I'm glad Cassie wasn't here last night. I'd never have heard the fucking end of it."

"You didn't see anything when I left Dante's room, did you?" I ask quickly as I stare at him.

"No. I didn't leave my bed. Did I miss a show?" He winks at me, and the heat in my cheeks gets hotter.

"No. Just checking."

"She says that as if Lexi being naked isn't an amazing show," Nate laughs.

Ash laughs, too. "I'm sure it is. What a shame I missed it, Lexi."

I can barely speak, I'm so embarrassed, and Ash moves over to give me a hug.

"I'm just teasing you. It's all good. I was safe and sound in my bed just *listening* to you guys have sex."

"You say that as if it makes it any better," I groan.

"I don't know why you're embarrassed. It was Logan and Nate that I heard the most. If it wasn't for the fact I heard you walk up the hallway, I might have thought they were just fucking each other."

He laughs again, as though that's completely out of the realm of possibility. I look at Logan and Nate, but neither of them offers up the information, and I don't feel that it's my place to out them. Even Dante doesn't know exactly what happened last night. Hell, I'm pretty sure they're in a relationship of their own now.

"Okay then, I'll make us all bacon and eggs for breakfast," Logan says, and we thank him.

I kiss Dante good morning before I sit between Nate and Ash on a stool at the breakfast bench. We've been sitting and talking while Logan cooks our breakfast when my phone lights up in front of me.

There's a single text message displayed on the screen, and it's from Cassie.

We need to talk.

I blink at the screen for a few seconds before I turn to look at Ash and say, "Well, that can't be good."

Acknowledgments

This book wouldn't be what it is if it weren't for the people that supported me along the way.

Mum – Dirty, filthy Cruise Control. I remember when I first told you about this book, you said you didn't think you'd read it. Your curiosity got the better of you, and I should've known that it would. I'm glad you like my books, but all the same...skip!

Beate – Sorry I didn't change enough things. I just get so much amusement out of Heather pointing out to Lexi all the things I didn't change! Thanks for everything you do because I couldn't get this done without your help!

Julia – Only two more books to go, and I'll be writing April's book! The countdown is on. Thanks for being awesome and giving me feedback on unusual sex scenes. Don't let your daughter watch my TikToks.

Béné – I'm so grateful you found my books and love them so much. Thanks for the feedback you're always willing to give...along with Eiffel Tower pics!

Vera – Hey, smut sister! Thanks for being the amazing person who came up with the unit of measurement Smut-By-Volume. While this book may only have a 64.58% SBV, I just know that this unit of measurement will come in handy in the future as I strive for higher and higher values. Maybe I'll write an entire manuscript that just consists of the word 'cock.'

Daena – Thank you for always being supportive. Thank you for introducing me to reverse harem when you realised that's what I was inadvertently writing with my dirty smutfic. Most importantly, thank you for being you.

Ally – I'm glad your kinky ass is always around to give me your thoughts on my dirty scenes. Your feedback is invaluable and very much appreciated.

Kit – Thanks for offering up your expert rigging skills and advice to make sure Logan is the best Dom he can be.

Maddy – I'm sorry I blackmailed you into reading this so you could have an advance copy of *Sebastian's Baby*. I'm glad you liked the extra chapters, though, and your feedback absolutely made the book better. Thank you for being the inspiration behind Ash's birthday gift for Dante.

Tina and Arya – Thank you both for engaging with me and giving me the inspiration for Nate's birthday gift for Dante. I loved the idea of a piece of rock history in the form of a very expensive signed vinyl album.

Michelle – OMFG, I'm so freaking glad that you loved this book! I'm absolutely ecstatic that you'll be narrating the audiobook, so I couldn't possibly not thank you in advance here for what I'm sure will be an amazing, vibrator-wearing-out-worthy performance from you!

All my advance readers – Thank you so, so, so much to all of my wonderful advance readers. I love that you're willing to read my work and give me your honest thoughts on it. I love the messages I get to discuss the books and how many of you are willing to spread the love by sharing my teasers and stuff. Team Cruise Control rocks!

Mark and Lorna Reid – I'm so grateful to you both for everything you do to make my books far more amazing than I could ever manage.

Damien – You're the best husband I could ask for. As always, thank you for being there for the boys and me. I couldn't do any of this without you.

My readers – If you're reading this, thank you for being here on this author journey with me. I hope you're not offended that I defiled my characters, but I also love what Wicked Stallion has become, and I hope you do, too.

Who would've thought last March that it would come to this? A filthy, smutty version of the characters you know and love. What this book lacks in plot, it makes up for in the sheer audacity I have to write this and then set it in the Cruise Control world. ;)

They really are their own people now, though, especially since their relationship dynamics are so different from Cruise Control's. I look forward to sharing the rest of the trilogy with you, and hopefully, you'll come to love Wicked Stallion as much as you loved Cruise Control.

About the Author

Siân Ceinwen lives in Western Australia with her husband and two sons. She grew up with a love of telling or writing stories for her friends to read and enjoy.

Wicked Opportunity is the first book of the trilogy about the members of Wicked Stallion.

If you enjoyed this, please share it with your friends, and please write a review on Amazon or Goodreads.

It would really be appreciated, as this helps more people to discover the book. Reviews assist with the algorithms used by these platforms to display books, so every little bit helps indie authors to get noticed.

You can also join Siân on Facebook or Twitter for all the latest news on the Something Wicked series of novels.